Shallow Lives...
Shallow Seas

By Michael J. Rowbottom

Copyright.

Shallow Lives... Shallow Seas

Copyright. © Michael John Rowbottom

Published: April 30, 2014.

Publisher: MicroAdventures Books

The right of Michael John Rowbottom to be identified as author of this Work has been asserted by him in accordance with sections 77 and 78 of the Copyright, Designs and Patents Act 1988. All rights reserved. No part of this publication may be reproduced, stored in retrieval system, copied in any form or by any means, electronic, mechanical, photocopying, recording or otherwise transmitted without written permission from the publisher. You must not circulate this book in any format.

Shallow Lives... Shallow Seas is entirely a work of fiction; any resemblance or similarity of names is coincidental. The names Khafira and Maraka apply to fictional states and have been created to confusion with any real politically and territorially defined states.

August 2003
Assignment

She was one of those angelic Indian girls the hotels used to ship in from Mumbai before the Russians took it all over. She was gorgeous; dark, long shiny black hair, piercing eyes with brows which intensified them even more. She was in a disco; short little skirt, flashing eyes, fast music. His for the taking and he wanted her. It was always this one. He'd seen her once in one of the hotel nightclubs and was besotted. He'd had her that time then tried to find her again a few days later. She'd disappeared. Nobody knew where she'd gone; at least nobody said they knew where she'd gone. He'd had his ideas but it was best not to get involved. Just let her come back to him in dreams like this one. He started to move in on her.

Then the phone rang and he woke up dry mouthed, feeling like that corner of the pigsty they use to shit in. He'd dozed off in a chair, the BBC World service was quietly talking from a shortwave set in a corner of his room. He was back in the real world where Moscow whores had cornered the market and sweet little Indian girls were hard to come by. The phone rang insistently. Why did they always call at this time of night? He checked his watch to see what time it actually was: one in the morning! He picked up the telephone and barked "Will Hartson." It wasn't a welcome call.

"Foreign Desk, Will. Sharpe speaking."

"What do you want? It's one in the morning you know."

"Sorry it's still only ten here." He didn't sound sorry. Hartson heard a slur in the voice. The sort of slur he would have had himself at ten at night on a late shift touring the old Fleet Street pubs. That was a long time ago. There was no Fleet Street any more.

"What do you wa...," The dry throat cut him off.

"Goo' night yoursel', Will."

"Don't mock, Sharpe. You try living in this heat."

Why did he say that, it was an open goal for Sharpe!

"You've done well enough for the last few years. Perhaps you want to come home now?" straight into the back of the net. No he bloody didn't. He liked it here in Khafira. He'd settled back comfortably after the hell that had been Iraq. He'd earned his place here. He had his Toyota Landcruiser, a sailing dinghy, his own pool with the apartment block, the occasional woman, Russian usually, but sometimes Palestinian or Indian if he was lucky; no need for Randalls bloody news agency to know any of that, nor how they were paid for with their expenses account. His dream intruded briefly but he managed to put her out of his mind quickly "I'm a journalist, I want to be where the story is," he half lied. You had to appear keen even if you couldn't give a toss. They'd never know any different in London. Idiot desk jockeys!

"Which bar was the story in tonight, Will?" Smartarsed git: it had been the Marine Bay but he was damned if he'd let Sharpe lead this joust any more. "What do you want Sharpe?"

"Westminster tip, opposition MP, dodgy arms dealing possibly." Hartson struggled to take it in.

"What am I supposed to do about it?"

"What you're paid to do, in between those desert picnics of yours, check it out!"

He didn't hide his irritation. "Arms deals where?"

"Back in the northern Gulf, probably Iraq. It might be Saddam's residue still trying to fight back. More fun and games for everyone."

"It's not a playground, Sharpe! Unless you grew up somewhere strange."

Bonus, he'd got one back, deuce! He searched out a pen and paper. They were never by the telephone when he needed them. He tried to stall: "There are a lot of arms deals going down right now. End user certificates all say different things…"

"When did you ever expect one to tell the truth?"

Easy for a deskman to be cynical.

Sharpe burbled on.

"Arms dealers don't care who they sell to as long as the dollar stays the same colour."

"Christ, what's that for me to go on?

"Why don't you ask your chum the defence minister? Try the Majlis tomorrow morning."

Hartson went quiet, how did he know about the Majlis? That was secret. He'd spent months working his way in there. No other Western correspondent had got near – no other Western correspondent cared, mind. "What's the Majlis?" he bluffed.

"Will, we've both had a few tonight but don't be stupid. I'm the deputy foreign editor. I know how things work."

Arrogant tosspot.

"Couldn't you have called me in the morning?"

"You're on duty 24 hours a day. Of course you'd only be on a ten hour shift if you came home."

He just held back the curse he so wanted to direct at Sharpe. "All right. I'll try it."

But there was more.

"Come on Will, we haven't seen a decent story out of you for three weeks. Pretty features about camel racing or tourism don't justify keeping you and the office out there."

"What are you saying?"

"You've got the most volatile region in the hemisphere. You know the sheikhs, you've got the Royal Navy on special patrol down there. If you can't get something out of that perhaps you ought to go back to Bagdad – or to a weekly paper and relearn the basics."

How DARE he say that! He fumed: "What's your point?"

"Stop sitting on your arse waiting for it to come to you. You should know it never does. Go out and FIND something."

"See you, Sharpe."

"One more thing. The tip came from through the Lobby at Westminster from an opposition MP."

"You said, I know."

"Maybe you don't know there's a bye–election coming up in the West Country… home of our biggest arms manufacturer?"

Was he supposed to *know* that? "I know," he lied.

"So whatever comes out of it might not be all that it seems,"

"I don't need lessons in dealing with lies, Sharpe!"

He slammed the phone down and the curse finally came out: "Bastard!"

Pleasure Centre

She was tired, sore, and a little drunk. Visiting businessmen were a pain, but money was money. She glanced across at Hannah, naked, on the other side of the room. They looked like they'd just finished with her. Hannah smiled back and winked. It would soon be over, then they could fall into their beds.

Jose kept herself going by thinking of each individual dirham this idiot man was paying her. He puffed and grunted, and then shuddered. Jose gasped to make him feel he'd got his money's worth. Then she lay back, sighed with fake satisfaction and hoped he'd get the hint.

She'd had all three of them now. So had Hannah. That was enough. She pulled herself from under him, walked to her room and put on a dressing gown. Hannah did the same. She threw some clothes at the smug looking figures still lying nude in their apartment living room. They always looked so ridiculous like that: fat, flaccid, sweaty. She despised them all.

Still, thank goodness there were some men who wanted their services. They had survived the Russian invasion and kept going. Two Arab women who could still make money. But, then, they never took tourists or low life. They were a class act. And they had powerful friends. The clients were gone within ten minutes, out into the night, back to their hotels, or their homes. She didn't care, she had provided the services, they had paid the cash. She counted it and gave Hannah her share. Next? Straight into the shower, quickly as possible, wash them away, down the drain, into the Gulf.

"Sure you won't join me tomorrow Jose?" said Hannah, laughing.

"Certain. He's all yours, he asked for you and you can keep him. He's a pig."

"I know, but you think they are all pigs."

"That is because they are. Did you see the ugly things lying on the floor tonight? Who would want them?"

"Goodnight, Jose."

"Goodnight, Hannah."

She looked at the mess in the apartment: scattered wine bottles, a sock, food strewn on the carpet and furniture. Nothing serious, Maria could clear it up later in the morning. She turned on the shower and dowsed herself for ten minutes. She washed it all away, nothing was left, no smell, nothing of them.

May 2003
Crisis Meeting

They were at the point when even good coffee tasted bad. Too tired to think, too tired even to sleep. But they kept talking.

"We've missed something," said one, a commanding figure with a well-cut suit to cover his bulk. Silence. They didn't need telling. They *had* to find them. Another drained his cup, took a breath, and said what he knew no one wanted to hear, not even him: "What if they're not there at all? What if he got them away before we even went in?"

More silence. The room smelled stale, they'd been in there a long time. No one smoked but the long hours and coffee had beaten back the personal grooming products. "Not an option," said the well-cut suit. "They are THERE, the fact that we haven't found them only means we haven't looked in the right places yet."

His hand waved extravagantly over a scatter of maps of Iraq and Syria, satellite pictures and intelligence reports. His inquisitor's gaze followed. "Yeah, I know the line, but do we have to swallow it?" His military uniform was loosened in deference to the hour and conditions.

"Yes, we have to swallow it."

"Shit! We've had 3,000 experts looking for these ...", he hesitated over the next word and looked at the women present; too bad, "...*fucking* weapons for a month. We've had control of the country for as long. They've got Tariq Aziz and Huda Ammash surrendering in Baghdad – Mrs Anthrax herself – and still nothing. No nuclear bombs, no chemical warheads, no biological cultures. Just one squeaky clean mobile lab that *might* have been used for making Anthrax but which has been scrubbed clean with bleach"

He was telling them what they already knew.

"We haven't had enough time."

They knew that as well, but they went through it anyway.

"How much time do we need to find something that isn't there?"

"We'll find them. They're there – we haven't looked at the mountains properly yet. They could be hidden in the caves."

One of the suits did not mask his annoyance: "It's not Afghanistan for fuck's sake, they don't live in caves in Iraq. They have big sophisticated cities."

"Ok, that's enough. Do you want to tell the president what you just told me!"

"Of course I don't, nor do you. Anyway, he doesn't know any of this even exists, so don't go threatening me with him. It won't work."

"No, he doesn't know who we are, but someone does, that's why we're here; we'll have to talk to them sometime soon! You know the message: find the weapons because they're there! If you don't find them then it's because of your incompetence, not because they're not there."

Silence again; fifteen seconds passed.

The well-cut suit breathed in deeply and said, "We're going to need help." The uniform with overladen epaulettes stared at him hard. The suit responded with an unwavering gaze which said steel door and lowered his voice, "I'm saying we need help. Right now I don't care where it comes from. They want results, we have to provide those results, or they find someone else who can."

The uniform dropped his eyes, but he hadn't been summoned to this airless stinking room to exercise his moral conscience, he wasn't even supposed to have one. He knew what was meant: fuck the constitution it didn't apply in the Middle East.

"OK, get the help!"

August 2003
Khafira Seas

The lieutenant wiped his forehead, the sweat returned instantly. It was dark. He was on deck in as little as possible while staying within the Navy's loose operational dress regulations. He wiped his brow again. It still didn't work. He struggled to keep his face neutral but it kept twisting. He was trained to take on hand-to-hand combat, he was a skipper, he could deal with just about anything, but he was struggling with this! He was horrified.

He looked over the side again, peering into the warm water lit by the ship's arc light. A shape the size of a human being was a few metres below the surface, approaching fast. It was an eerie sight: a dark centre surrounded by a green glow, then darkness again. The winch was winding powerfully. It didn't have any hard work to do, just a few metres to the sea bottom. The load wasn't heavy. It could have been a dolphin, or a shark, even a manta ray.

But it wasn't. He stopped himself from reeling back as it broke the surface then quickly checked to see if anyone had seen his reaction. The rest of his crew were too busy doing the same. The lieutenant wanted to look but he knew he couldn't. It was a body all right: brown where any skin still remained, probably young, oriental... and misshapen at the bottom, where a concrete weight in the shape of a bucket encased the feet.

"Not a natural death," breathed the lieutenant. "No, I shouldn't think so," a nearby chief petty officer replied, quietly.

This was the 21st century for God's sake: not the Middle Ages. Have we come no further than this, he thought to himself! The crew was watching him now. Keep on top of it, Sam. Stay in control. He forced himself to work. He picked up a communications handset and spoke to the divers.

"Captain to Hennessy. We've got the first..." He was about to say 'safely' but realised how absurd it was. He ended the sentence, "...bring up the others!"

There was a clipped "Right!" It was hard to make out through the intercom crackle. The lieutenant put down the handset.

"What now?" asked the chief.

"We contact shore HQ. I doubt that we'll be thanked."

"Not a welcome find for anyone," said the chief, breezily, as if he'd discovered a piece of grit in his Muesli.

Sam Jackson wasn't one for introspection. He was bright and capable but would probably finish his naval career where he was now, a valued lieutenant, maybe Lieutenant commander, but no more. He would flourish somewhere else, away from the Royal Navy. But even he saw how absurd this pantomime was; pretending to each other that it was all part of the job. Convincing each other that there was no difference between this grotesque find and painting the ship. He grimaced but offered no reply before moving off to the foredeck of his Hunt-class plastic and glass-hulled minesweeper to look at the first of the four discoveries.

Why couldn't they have been mines, or torpedoes, or unexploded depth charges, or anything but this? He wished he hadn't found them; but he had and there was no avoiding it. He had to investigate everything the ship's sonar search turned up, he couldn't pick and choose what he found – supposing they *had* been mines!

Damn the whole bloody mess!

He looked over the starboard towards Khafira in the distance. The lights of the city defiantly blazed out the darkness of its night, but the bubble of that permanent day was dwarfed by the black infinity beyond.

May
Alaska

They called him the Barracuda. He had another name but no one had used it since his second week in the Navy when he'd bitten the left earlobe off a petty officer who was trying to have sex with him. The man had to be put ashore for treatment. He didn't like the name his parents had given him. He didn't like his parents come to that. Come to think of it he didn't like anything.

Except action. He loved – he adored – that. It was the only thing he did adore. Everything else he hated, savaged or tolerated. He knew lots of people but had no friends. Even his closest associates were wary around him.

Barracuda didn't care about that or anything else. He was called Barracuda because he would do anything, eat anything; shoot, gnaw, strangle, fuck or sell anything. He never asked for permission. The people who used him knew what they were getting when they signed up – not that there was ever any paperwork. Barracuda did his deals by a nod and a word. He didn't shake hands, which came as a relief to most of the people he dealt with. And he dealt with some bad people.

Barracuda owed his loyalty to only himself. He was the one they called when there was only the dirtiest of work to be done. His team stuck by him because he paid them well, always got them out, and because they were scared shitless of him. When they came into his fold they gave him their souls. There was no promise that they'd get them back at the end of term and they rarely did.

When they were on his team they lived in their master's image, so they were called The Barracudas. Barracuda One had other names for the individuals but as a unit, as a team, as a band of licensed renegade raiders, they were The Barracudas.

He spent two weeks in the brig for the earbiting incident. He never apologized for it and his life was made hell for the next two months after. But he got respect. And after that his other qualities began to impress his navy masters. His complete lack of a conscience was the main factor in swinging his transfer to a special services unit so low on the radar that it was virtually tunnelling under the seabed.

As long as he was fed and given a regular diet of women and money, and most of all, action, he did what they asked. He'd learned that there were other people in the world like him at that time. They didn't match his bred-in-the-bone malevolence, but they didn't care what was done to finish a job, or start it, or wreck it.

Happy wasn't a word Barracuda used, or really understood, nor was he comfortable. But insofar as either could ever to apply to him then they did in those years tunnelling in the shit for that special services unit. It had taken him to Nicaragua, Honduras, El Salvador, Iran and Korea. As he'd travelled he'd learned about those around him, the ones he would take with him when he went freelance.

He'd worked alongside British SAS and SBS, US Navy Seals and Delta Force, and even the Russian Spetznatz. He'd picked up contacts everywhere he went. When he went solo they gradually fell in with him.

He was smart, too. He'd done nothing at school, except raise hell and get banned early. But the big wide world suited him. He learned languages and ways of behaving. He could see a mannerism or a social set-up and he could imitate it almost instantly. He could convince anyone that he was a civilised man of erudition and education. They never saw the volcanic rage under the suave covers – until it was too late. And then it was usually way too late.

Now he was rich with homes in California, Alaska, Ireland, Sri Lanka, and Australia. He had two ocean-going yachts moored in the West Indies and the Mediterranean, and could get to anywhere he chose. He was the king of his castle. But he was nothing without action. The women, the money, the life was nothing compared to strapping on an M16 and a belt of grenades.

So when the call came to help "find the weapons", he was ready for it.

Only a very few people knew his special number. He changed it every three months and told those he thought should know. That included The Barracudas and no more than ten important contacts. Ten people he did business with for a lot of money.

The phone was ringing as he lay back in his favourite chair at his home in Alaska. The number chased him wherever he was. He didn't plan to be long in Alaska, just a few days. But it had turned into a few weeks. He'd gone for the break up, when the ice and snow fall away and spring comes. It meant he could see the last of the snow in decent light and temperatures hovering around the freezing mark during the day. The locals called it a heat wave. There were times when his savagery simply left him in that white wilderness. He could look out over the miles and miles of endless snow blanket and feel that he could start walking in it and never stop. He couldn't be without his rage for long, it was his only true companion. But sometimes it was good to let it rest, to keep it fresh and alive. Alaska did that for him.

The snow was mostly gone now and his attention had been diverted by watching Fox News Network, CNN, BBC World Service, so much so that he'd forgotten to leave. He'd stared as the Third Armoured Division ploughed on through the desert towards Baghdad and the Brits went into Basra. He ached to be there, mixing it, doing the dirty work that he knew the special forces were up to in the western desert. That was exactly where he'd been twelve years before, tracking down Saddam's Scud missile launchers and stopping them from being fired at Israel.

He'd been at his most alive then, his most savage, he had a licence to do what the fuck he wanted because his team wasn't accountable to anyone. Get the Scuds, that was the only order. No one cared how they did it, no one wanted to know. They just didn't want them raining in on Israel and stirring up the Palestinians any more than they were already. This time he hadn't been invited and that made him angry.

He picked up the phone on the fourth ring. He didn't say a word but waited for the caller to announce himself – it could only be a him, he knew few women professionally and only dealt with them on the second level.

"Barracuda!"

The voice was neither timid nor overconfident. He recognised the man immediately and knew then that he would be required to do work which would be paid for by the US Government whether they knew about it or not. He guessed they wouldn't.

"Yes," he replied.

The conversation lasted 15 minutes, the requirements were perfectly clear although never voiced. The money was adequate for him and the Barracudas and the specialist recruits they'd need to bring in to manufacture the evidence. He put the phone down and quickly went back over his mental calculations to make sure that the germ and chemical warfare experts would be properly paid.

Then, satisfied, he eased back into the chair for a few more restful moments before the action started. It was dirty, deceitful, unanswerable and meant to be untraceable if they did it right. The international reputation of the United States rested on this, there had to be chemical weapons so there would be.

The man from the Operations and Special Projects agency told him so. They were even lower on the radar than he used to be in his special forces days so the code was absolutely clear: locate those weapons and bring them to the attention of the searching teams. More importantly, do it quickly.

He drew a breath before reaching for the phone to book a flight from Fairbanks to Florida. He guessed that a call to the Shark would have to be made as well. The Shark was the biggest barracuda in the pond except for the man himself. He was a semi-detached member of the team but would play a role when asked. They'd met 12 years before and had been united, not in friendship, but by a sense of danger and outrageousness that few others in the world could equal.

But before he did all that he could enjoy the thought that he had finally been invited into this fucking war. He wasn't going to leave it without making a big impression.

August
Waking

The diplomat was having a bad dream. He was on a train going in slow motion through the Somerset countryside, past Glastonbury Tor, around the Tor, up the hill, into the Tor...and there in the blinding darkness of the stone tower appeared a light, it took the shape of his mother. She was as stone faced as the tower. She looked at him, he stared at her, she looked away without recognition. Now, they are back in the carriage, this time flying at the speed of light, with Nanny undoing his trousers. He cries out, and the train screams into a tunnel. No one hears.

Then he hears the warning signal from the old steam train as it blasts out two loud sounds. Then another two, and another two, and another two. The blasts change into the sound of a telephone sounding and the diplomat jumps in his bed. He waits a couple of seconds before answering the telephone. For those two waking seconds Tom Scott Garrett struggles to break free from the terror of his dream. Quickly the guillotine comes down and cuts it off before it can take root.

"Tom Scott Garrett."

"Sorry to wake you, Tom, something's come up at the port." It was the First Secretary. "The Naval Attaché is already on his way."

"I'll get down there straight away." There was a hint of a smile in his voice; saying nothing, happy to oblige, there to serve, grateful to be out of the dream.

"Thank you, Tom."

He drove to the port, cleared the Khafira security, then the naval guard, and two marines standing on board the Royal Navy's biggest ship in that part of the region, a frigate.

He lined up alongside a Royal Navy commander, the defence attaché at the embassy. They faced another man with a stern bearing sitting behind a small desk, Commodore David Jenkins.

Scott Garrett started the conversation, "Serious by the looks of it, Commodore?" Jenkins looked straight back, "We don't know, Mr Scott Garrett." He beckoned him over to a chart and showed the position of the minesweeper and their discovery. "It's on the edge of international waters and frankly we wish we hadn't found them at all, but now we have we can't ignore them."

"Of course not," said the diplomat.

"The question is, do we hand them over to the local police, or do we hold on to them ourselves?"

Scott Garret knew what he would rather do.

"Commodore, just for the sake of argument, how would you feel if you, as it were, *unfound* the bodies?"

There was a silence while he waited for a response. He heard the naval attaché, shuffling his feet. Jenkins stared at him for a full five seconds. Then, he growled, "What would that achieve, Mr Scott Garrett?"

"Let's be realistic Commodore, these boys belong to no-one, by the looks of it they were being used as playthings. They're dead now, there's nothing to be done for them, I doubt they would ever be identified. Frankly it could be rather embarrassing to Her Majesty's Government for one of our naval patrols to have come across them."

The commander physically twitched but Jenkins response was explosive: "Mr Scott Garrett I am well aware of the way the diplomatic service operates. I, too, have spent time as a military attaché, but right now I thank God I am a naval man!"

He looked across at the commander who lowered his gaze to the deck. He turned back to the diplomat. "Thank you, Mr Scott Garrett, you have helped me to make up my mind. Good night."

The commodore may have finished with him but Scott Garrett hadn't done yet. "The important thing is to keep it out of the press, Commodore, especially now."

Jenkins made no attempt to hide his contempt: "Do you think I am going to phone up the international press corps and tell them, Mr Scott Garrett?"

"Of course not, Commodore. I am sure you will be completely discreet. You understand the current sensitivities well. Your men may be less tuned in."

"I'll deal with my men, you take care of the reporters. There aren't that many to keep an eye on surely."

"One is enough to spread an epidemic."

"God forbid we have an epidemic of truth."

"It's just as harmful."

"Thank you, Mr Scott Garrett."

Scott Garrett turned, the smile stayed in place as he walked from the cabin, off the frigate and across the port. Commander Wilkinson walked a few steps behind.

"Sad business, Phil," he said. The commander nodded as the diplomat added, "I'd better get along now. I need to do a couple of things."

"At this time of night?"

"No time like the present."

He charged on ahead, got into his car and drove quickly out of the port and on to the open road to his apartment. If he acted fast he could prevent the discovery blowing up into an incident. Of all the times to happen, this couldn't be worse.

He raced into his villa, got an address book from his desk and dialled a number. It rang several times before being answered. When it was the atmosphere was none too pleasant.

"Who is calling at this hour?" The reply was heavily accented but in perfect English.

"Sorry to wake you, it's Tom Scott Garrett from the British Embassy. There's something I thought you might want to know."

Khafira Seas

Lieutenant Sam Jackson kept moving as he directed operations. The more he kept busy the less he had to think about it. The bodies were ugly and discoloured where the sea creatures hadn't feasted on the flesh. They'd been in the water a long time.

Another wave of sweat flowed down the skipper's forehead. Jackson hadn't noticed the heat for a while. They might have been Filipinos once, even the most cursory examination showed they had died badly. Jackson forced himself to look at the bite indentations, cuts, and mutilations. He dragged his eyes away and pushed down an urge to vomit.

"Take her due north another three kilometres and hold her," he said to the man at the wheel.

"Why?" asked a sub lieutenant.

"I'm keeping our options open. The commodore can take his own decision when he gets here."

The corpses, now covered with ship's blankets, remained on the foredeck, alone. The crew stayed aft to avoid them. Time passed slowly. Eventually, at four in the morning, the commodore's launch came alongside and Jackson snapped at his crew: "Commodore on board!"

"All right, Sam, stand everyone down," said Jenkins to the lieutenant, "This isn't a state visit. Let's have a look at them." A man in a Lieutenant's uniform and wearing the insignia of a naval doctor trailed in his wake.

"This way Lieutenant. We'll have to do something about them quickly, they'll start rotting to nothing in this heat." The doctor followed his commodore. Two ratings uncovered the corpses, another three held powerful torches to balance the shadows from the arc light on the foredeck. The commodore spoke after a few silent seconds, "Poor bastards. What did they do to deserve this?" He turned to the doctor: "Take a look, Johnson. They're ours whether we like it or not, so give me an idea of what happened!"

Jackson held back another gag but the Naval doctor wasn't put off by the sight before him. He felt around the putrid flesh and bones and gave each lost soul an examination, noting the injuries and what appeared to be bites. It was hard to tell because the sea had washed away much of the evidence. If the cuts had bled they would never know.

"I really need to get them ashore, sir. Anyway I'm no pathologist, I'm a surgeon."

"I'm aware of what you are. You know full well once we get them ashore they're out of our hands, we can't possibly hold them and we have no post mortem facilities. You'll have to do what you can now!"

"Yes, sir." The medic returned to his task.

Jackson heard one of his crew retching over the side. The doctor made notes as he examined. Jackson asked what he was doing.

"Trying to please the old man. I can't be sure but some of them show signs of old bruising as well as new."

"Wonderful."

The commodore barked an order which carried in the stillness of the sea.

"Let's get a move on, Lieutenant, we don't have all night. I want these bodies loaded on to my launch!"

He turned to Jackson. "It's sensitive as hell, Sam. Tell everyone not a word must get out! The embassy's terrified of the press getting hold of it. There's a lot happening at the moment."

"Yes, sir," acknowledged the Lieutenant, mechanically.

Jenkins had seen death in nearly every form. He'd been in Basra in the south of Iraq when the first of the mass graves was opened up. He'd witnessed the crushed bones and mutilations. He'd seen executions as an undercover operator in his younger days in West Africa. He knew the world could be an evil place. Now, try as he might, he could not divorce himself from the four corpses being manhandled on to his launch. He'd believed that his presence, a commodore in the Royal Navy, the Royal Navy itself in fact, should be enough to have stopped this mad excess in the region: fifty years ago maybe, not any more. He felt useless as he followed the bodies on to the launch and gave the order to cast off.

They were twenty minutes into their return journey and a kilometre inside territorial waters when one of the crew saw a light approaching at speed. As it drew closer it appeared to scan them. Jenkins could just make out the silhouette of a police boat against the lights from Khafira. A powerful craft designed to outrun unwelcome smugglers.

This was going to be difficult, here was a Commodore, a staff rank in the Royal Navy, ferrying back four corpses to the mainland. Just for a moment he wished he had untied the frigate and brought it, they wouldn't dare board that.

The boat approached, the light became stronger.

A petty officer flashed a powerful lantern. It blazed on to the patrol boat to reveal ten men in uniform and one wearing a dishdash, the flowing Arab robe of the summer. They all held automatic rifles, half of them trained on the launch. They pulled alongside.

"Commodore, this is a surprise," said the man in the dishdash in perfect English. "Is this a routine journey or something special?"

He recognised the port police chief. "Colonel Hassan, good morning. It's just routine. We have something to bring back from one of our minesweepers."

"It's a shame you did not let us know, we could have assisted you. You normally tell us of your movements, Commodore."

"We are coming to see you directly. We have an unfortunate cargo on board."

The light trained down on to the deck of the craft and revealed the four blanket covered bodies.

"This looks very unfortunate Commodore. Let me now take charge of what is, after all, our responsibility."

"Of course, Colonel." It was unusual, why not let his launch continue to bring them ashore. But he knew they would have to be handed over sooner or later. It had become sooner. He arranged for the transfer of the corpses to the police patrol boat.

"We should talk about this later in the day, Commodore, when we have had the chance to rest. Ma'as Sala'ama."

"Goodnight, Colonel."

Commodore Jenkins watched the patrol boat head into the distance with its navigation lights standing clear against the dark sky. It was a few minutes before he realised the boat was heading into the centre of the Gulf, not to shore. A world-weary look came over his face. He ordered the crew to carry on. He wondered how the Colonel had so quickly come to learn of their mission. Only the minesweeper crew and the radio room personnel had known.

And the Embassy man.

The moon faded from sight, the sea darkened, hardly disturbed by the hot breeze.

Finding the story

Hartson cradled his coffee as he looked out of the window on to the Gulf. Khafira bustled under his nose as he sipped. This was not the day to go out and FIND a bloody story. Didn't they know how things worked out here? You wait, let everyone know you're there, then they'll come to you. That was the way to play the Gulf. There was no point trying to talk directly to them; they never answered a direct inquiry. It was close to an insult to ask.

No he hadn't turned out much in recent weeks. Hardly surprising, it was August for God's sake. Nothing happens in August in the whole Northern Hemisphere, still less in the Gulf. What did they honestly expect him to do: go down to the souk, stop every dhow sailor and ask if they had a story! He could think of some arsey news editors who would have demanded it in his early career. But now he was a senior foreign correspondent, he didn't have to take that crap any more.

He took another sip. He hated deskmen questioning his worth in London while he took the flak out here...all right, so there hadn't been much flak recently but he shouldn't have to justify himself. He'd been sent here because of his track record. They knew what he could do. He had a hundred gongs from all over the Globe. Memos by the ton. And he'd done it without ever having to be a hero – let others do that, it was a fool's game and not for him.

But you're still only as good as your last story. And what was that? A fluffy feature about camel breeding. He wasn't certain that anyone had even bothered to carry it – perhaps some rag in Australia, they liked that sort of thing.

Face it, Will, you need a big hit if you're going to stay here. He took another sip and with it went his truculence. Instead he started to worry; he needed this job. Right, get off your arse and FIND something, like the man said! He drained the coffee and picked up his keys.

The Majlis

The Majlis wasn't busy, just some out of town Bedouins looking to get a Range Rover for their village. He held back and waited for the local petitions to be dealt with. They were all granted, the ruling family was generous. Shame about the dark side but that's what riches do to people. More riches than he could ever dream of. Hartson had been assiduous in building up his presence at the Majlis and he had become known. Anyone could go: local, ex-pat, anyone. But even after eighteen months he didn't feel comfortable there. He spoke pigeon-Arabic to them, they smiled and returned his greetings, then spoke embarrassingly fluent English. He wished he could blend in to the easygoing atmosphere that was the Majlis. But, no matter what the welcome, he wasn't a Muslim or an Arab. He was a guest, albeit the only western one he had ever seen there.

"Mr Will Hartson, Kif el halik," asked a familiar voice, enquiring after his health.

"Il hamdu Li la." Fine, God willing, said Hartson with a practiced accent that had fooled some telephone callers, if only for a moment. But that was how he did it, not wearing a tin helmet, by using words and staying out of the way of bullets.

"It is good to see you at the Majlis."

"I am pleased to be here, Your Highness Sheikh Issa bin Mahmood al Nadir." He didn't let the formality drop, nor the smile. "How is your father?"

"He is well, Mr Will." Hartson smiled pleasantly and went along with it. Sheikh

Mahmood was close to death but nobody was supposed to say so. Sometimes when he was really drunk he'd been tempted to blow the whole story: four brothers tearing lumps off each other to line up for the succession. But he would be on the next plane out the minute it hit the wires - if he was lucky, he'd heard of some who simply never turned up again. Hartson chose to drive his Khafira career with due care and attention.

"I am pleased to hear it, Your Highness."

"Is there is something I can do for you, Mr Will?"

He wasn't expecting anything like the truth, but he would be bold anyway.

"Do you know of an arms build up in the north, Your Highness?"

"Where did you hear that, Mr Will?"

"Sources in London."

"Can you be more specific?"

Even now, after three years in Khafira, he was intimidated. The man's grasp of English was un-unnervingly good. It may have been force-fed by oil money, but that in itself was scary. Rich people were different. Rich meant powerful. Lots of power. He didn't like to submit to power, but he found it hard to stand up straight in the face of it. He tilted his head deferentially.

"I'm afraid I can't, Your Highness. I think you know how politics work in London, you have spent time there."

The sheikh smiled. "Indeed I have. I am looking forward to returning there next week after my duties here. Sheikh Khalifa can suffer the heat in my place."

He smiled back. Bloody August. Can't get a thing done. Everyone important just scarpers until the heat dies down in October. Hartson was distracted by the thought and had to wrench himself back when he heard the sheikh's next words.

The smile stayed constant and real on the Sheikh's face. "Yes, Mr Will, there is concern about an increase in weapons there."

What did he just say? The Khafira Defence Minister telling him military secrets? He couldn't have heard properly.

"Where does your information come from, Your Highness?"

"Same as yours, Mr Will, London."

"How much do you know?"

"I know that certain arms destined for some parts of the world have found themselves where they should not be."

"Like what?"
"Mostly missiles, no aircraft."
"You know a lot."
"I am the Minister of Defence. I hope I do." Still the smile...
"Can you be more specific?" Silence.
"Are you worried?"
"Of course."
What had he got here?
"Will you be building up your own forces?"
"They are already very strong, Mr Will." No they weren't. A trained army would cut straight through them without looking sideways.
"Are you content to leave Khafira next week if this threat is there?"
"I can be reached at any time in England, Mr Will. This won't blow up for a while yet. Besides I have a horse running at Newbury on Wednesday."
Hartson chanced his arm. "Thank you for your frankness, Your Highness?"
"I believe I can trust you, Mr Will. I have always told you that what I say, man to man, is unattributable. You will honour that agreement this time?"
"Of course. But why?"
"Khafira can be a mysterious place, full of contradictions. Perhaps you will learn. One contradiction might be that if there are weapons in the north, or *were*, they might never have been intended for use – or even been capable of it..." The sheikh smiled, waved his hand, turned away. The interview was over.
"Shokharan Sheikh Issa." He thanked him.
"Ma'as Sala'ama Mr Will." Goodbye.
  He was shown the exit by another smiling Arab. He got into his Landcruiser, started it, put it in gear and drove away. The sheikh had never been so forthcoming, if that's what it could be called. Why start now? Unless he was trying to send a signal to Washington. But he could do that easily enough through his own diplomats. He was looking for something else which Randalls could do. Stop farting around, Will. Write it first, then think about the next move later.
  The desert beckoned. He wanted time to think and there was nowhere better than the red dunes inland. He called into a supermarket, picked up some bottles of water and soft drink, thought about some beers but knew he couldn't risk being caught driving with them, put it all into the cool box in the

rear of the Landcruiser, and headed out of town.

The new motorway was crowded, but when wasn't it these days! He pressed on the accelerator and sped up to 120 kilometres an hour. Adrenaline took him over. He passed truck after truck carrying pipes, concrete, steel girders and the like. They were building like mad, so quickly it was as if they feared that if they stopped everything would just come crashing down, like a shark has to keep moving to live.

Nobody spoke about it openly but the oil was running dry. He knew though. He spoke to the geologists and engineers. They told him they were pumping 80 per cent water and 20 per cent oil these days. And it was getting lower. That meant a smaller share of the cake for everyone.

He overtook a long truck carrying concrete blocks. The outskirts of the city brought a clearer view. He could see the dunes in the distance. He put his foot down harder on the accelerator, took the Landcruiser to 160 KPH in deliberate defiance of the speed limits. If the police pulled him over he would say he was a friend of Sheikh Issa. That would scare them off.

Pleasure Centre

Her head crashed against the wall of the apartment, she felt a kind of ringing. She tried to focus on her attacker but before her vision could re-establish he was on her again, harder this time. Her head snapped to the side as she took a right hand slap full on the cheek. It snapped back the other way when she caught the return from the other hand.

She had only asked an innocent question, he loved to play his games she knew, but this was too much today. She yelled, louder than she meant, but he had to pull back: "Stop, you are hurting!"

He came at her harder, a frenzy of fierce, uncompromising blows. He had never been this violent before. Why, it was an innocent question, a silly little favour for Maria, the maid. That was all she had asked. Had he seen her sons? If her face was marked she would not be able to work for a while. He must know that. She regained some sight and tried to look into his eyes but could see only fury. His flailing arms struck again, to the mouth. Strange, it was beginning to hurt less. She saw him mistily through a slowly closing eyelid. He was still raining blows on her. His companions were joining in. The eye closed further. She knew them all at least by sight. She didn't expect to see the third in her apartment. He would never want to be seen going in. She had never had him in the flesh before, quite an honour really.

 This was going to cost them a lot of money. If they wanted this sort of fun they must expect to pay. How much should she add to the bill? It didn't hurt at all now, she could see nothing either. She was dimly aware that her flimsy clothes were being ripped off. One of them had entered, she tried to guess which one; she thought she could tell from previous experience. It was another of the games they had played when she had been blindfold: guess who. Strange, they normally played it from behind.

 Ah, that was why, one of the others had come in as well. Shouldn't she be feeling some discomfort? There was nothing at all, she just knew they were inside her. She squirmed a protest. Then here was a crashing blow to her forehead.

 Then there was nothing.

Discovery

 The sun was throwing its last red rays over the apartment block as Jose walked in, smiling. It had been nice to have a day off. No afternoon entertaining, let Hannah take it for once. Colonel Hassan had been introduced to them by other reliable clients so they had taken him in to the fold, not that they had much choice. But if she *had* the choice, and she did today, she was happy not to party with him. She could not afford to have a conscience but it could be pricked occasionally. She knew where Hassan came from and the people he'd worked for before coming to Khafira.

 Hassan had been a middle ranking police officer in Syria. At least that was the story he told when he had arrived a year ago. It was corroborated by others she knew, so she would accept it. Now he was in charge of the Port Police. That didn't mean she had to like him.

 She looked forward to a quiet evening. They would have a bottle of wine, watch a video - an ordinary one for a change. She smiled at the prospect but let it fall immediately as she caught sight of the janitor returning the gesture. No chance. Who does he think he is? She scowled and gazed straight ahead as she marched past him, not even letting a glimpse of her tanned legs appear through her cotton wraparound. Not for him.

 The sun dipped behind the western sands and was lost for the day. Darkness was instant; the lights around the pool came on and guided her path to the other door. There were still some people around the poolside not willing to go in yet. Maybe someone was planning a barbecue tonight. That would be fun. She delayed a while by the pool, checking out the ones who worked out, and those who had enough money not to bother. They were the ones she was interested in. It was always a good idea to have a wide client base. She didn't expect to find much, the truly rich didn't live here, they lived in the beach villas. But there might just be someone with money and an obsession. She could satisfy one in exchange for the other.

Nothing caught her eye. She made her way to the lift. She was so relaxed she didn't mind waiting the extra two minutes it took to come down. It was in use but who cared. Finally its doors opened and she saw a man looking straight out at her. He could have been a possible client - slightly flabby but not fat, in his late thirties, routinely dressed. He greeted her, "Good evening," and she nodded in reply but didn't return his smile as he excused himself past her. He had the vague look of someone she had probably seen around before in the last few months but had dismissed because of his clothes. Anyway he was European, English by the sound of his voice. Worth showing a bit of leg to, though, just to tease.

She pulled the wraparound away from her thigh while looking in another direction. Make it seem like the heat was too much, like he wasn't there, he didn't count; so insignificant that she wasn't concerned about making an overt sexual gesture in front of him. Then she let it drop and flicked her gaze back at him to catch the stare.

He ignored her. How dare he! Who was this nobody to ignore her! Didn't he know who she was? Probably gay! She pressed the Number 3 for her floor and thought of the bottle of wine and the night in. She put the key in the lock and entered.

It was quieter than she was expecting; no television, radio, or music. Hannah must be taking a nap. I don't blame her after that lot, she thought. She called out: "I'm back." There was no reply. She flicked the light switch by the door and moved towards the kitchen. Her gaze was always straight, never wavering, focused; part of who she was. Anyone engaging Jose did so on her terms, in her field of vision; her rules! But the corner of her eye caught something strange on the floor. She moved her eyes to it. And then she froze, but only for a moment. A scream welled up from deep down in her body, up through her stomach, her chest, her throat... and that was where it stopped. She wanted to let it out, to vent the horror, but something else kicked in to stop her. Even in the full throes of terror she knew that to scream could make things a lot worse for her. Hannah's well cared-for, long black hair was fanned out on the floor, like a blood-matted peacock's tail. A brown eye stared at the ceiling, straight into the light. It was wide and dilated. The other was covered by more strands of hair. Neither would ever see again.

 She knew his temper, he was the only one who could have done it, the fat ugly bastard. Bastard! BASTARD! The words screamed through her head but her mouth did not move. The air-conditioning was working hard to keep up with the early evening heat. Jose stood rigid, every muscle stiff, her heart raging. Nothing moved within the apartment. It was too hot even for insects. Some sunlight had probably leaked through earlier, that would explain why the blood had already turned colour. Now only the electric light dangling from the centre of the room provided the illumination. It shone on the beige coloured carpet which covered every room in the apartment.

 She knew Hannah had died horribly. She sat frozen on a small chair by her friend. She was overwhelmed, strands of thought flew in and out of her mind but she couldn't grasp any to string them together. Then clarity pierced through the clouds and she knew she had to leave. She leapt from the chair and ran from the apartment. For some reason she switched off the light, as if the darkness would swallow it up, make it unreal. She could walk in a little later and find Hannah lounging on the sofa with a glass of wine in her hand.

 She only half closed the door, she didn't notice. She ran down the corridor, couldn't wait for the elevator, down the stairs and out of the building.

 She had to find Michel.

May
Groundwork

Barracuda never failed to deliver on a contract so this would happen no matter what the cost. He had to move quickly, he had to find something within seven days, or the deal was void. It couldn't be in the Gulf itself or in a neighbouring state, it had to be in Iraq, before the confusion died away. If the damned Iraqis had at least used some of the weapons he might have an idea of where to locate and dump his own pieces of chicanery. But they never did.

He made a few notes: it could be nerve gas – Sarin maybe – or a nuclear weapon, or Anthrax. The hardest would be a nuclear bomb. He could get hold of one but not in the time and he doubted the budget. Anyway, even his masters might pail at that.

Mustard: possible, not easy to handle but less dangerous to him and the other Barracudas so long as they were careful. He'd seen blistering agents at work, he'd watched men and women burning up inside from them. It boiled the skin, the eyes and the lungs and gave a dreadful, sordid, painful death. Still these weapons weren't meant to be used, they just had to look as if they were.

The G-series nerve agents: Sarin, Cyclosarin and Tabun; a very quick, death within seconds of getting on to the skin or into the lungs, too charitable and not to his taste. It would only take one mistake in the handling and someone could be dead. He didn't want that, he had his reputation to preserve. He didn't care who lived or died but he always got them out, so they always came back to work for him.

VX nerve agent: even worse than the previous and it hung around. It was used for long-term contamination. His paymasters wouldn't thank him for that.

Ricin: an ugly substance leading to multiple organ failure in a couple of days. A bad death again, and much too risky.

And then there was Anthrax. He couldn't take the risk. He made notes on his pad as he went through them. Most of the intelligence on this stuff was around before Gulf War One, it had been deployed against the Iranians and the Kurds and was well documented.

No, it would be Mustard!

The whole point about this war was to find weapons which hadn't been destroyed and had substances they knew existed from the 1980s. So, that's what they would find...or what he had to leave for someone else to find.

Now, the missiles: rockets or artillery shells? He only had enough time for one type. It would be rockets, fifty or so rusty old Russian 122 millimetre rockets adapted for use by Saddam's Laboratory monkeys. He knew where he could get those.

He wrote Moscow on his pad. Getting them out of Eastern Europe would be challenging, but he'd done it before. Bringing the mustard agent and 122s together was a logistical headache but he was already thinking of a way round that; it would be done at sea.

He'd put off the biggest problem until the end: how to get them into Iraq! Maybe through the north, he still knew people there from his special forces time. The Kurds would remember him. The trouble was that he couldn't guarantee a passage through Turkey. Worse still he had to get the weapons there in the first place and that would involve a long trek. Too risky. It would be more sensible to go through the south. It was still bandit country around there and he'd be able to bluff most of it. And it would be easier to place the mustard in the rockets at sea in The Gulf.

He made more notes on his pad: call the Shark, Maraka Airport, military trucks, jeep. That was just the start. He looked again at the first note, the Shark. His brow furrowed. The Shark was a dangerous man among dangerous men. He was rich beyond dependence on Barracuda, and he was impulsive. On the other hand he was the handiest man to have in that part of the world and he needed all the help he could get. He just hoped that the Shark would not be too unpredictable. His excesses had brought him close to the brink in the past.

As he looked at his lengthening list he saw the size of the task. "Shit!" he muttered, it would be tight and everything would have to go strictly according to plan. He would be working a long way from home and relying on people spread around the world to make it happen. If it went wrong it would be all over for him. He would have to rely upon what he always had: bribery and fear. It had never failed before. Now, where to dump these newly minted weapons? He'd leave them in uneven amounts – ten here, seven there, he could check the most likely areas on the UN website. Hans Blix had been kind enough to deliver a long list of unaccounted for materials a few days before the war started, so now, he just might find what he was looking for – in part. Or would he leave them all in one pile – more of a smoking rocket launcher than a gun. One thing was for sure, he didn't have time to replicate the whole of Saddam's dirty weapons programme, and he didn't have to. They needed only a few. Then, whoever it was who wanted this to happen could claim that the rest had been hidden so well it may take years to find them. By the time the years had passed who was going to care?

He concentrated on the practicalities of filling the warheads. Some would have to leak with the mustard – enough to make the searchers look twice. They'd be labelled as conventional explosives in Arabic. The Americans would be easy to convince because they wanted to be. If the UN got invited back in they might not be fooled so easily. So it had to be right. He knew it would make no sense to label them for what they were, Saddam and his henchmen had gone out of their way to avoid that, so he must do the same.

He tapped the notepad with his pen. It was meant to be a smoking gun so it had to look like one. Rocket cylinders with obvious US or European design would not work. Saddam usually converted Russian cases so that's what he'd do. There were plenty of officials in the downtrodden Russian military looking to increase their income whichever way they could. The Soviets had battered their patriotism so much that they didn't care what became of the stuff. If they didn't get it, the Mafia would. What was the difference!

He made notes of all of it on his pad of paper, writing telephone numbers and names by them at the same time. It read like a round the world journey: Dubai, Moscow, Sri Lanka, Hong Kong, London, Moscow, Khafira.

He fired up his computer and went to the UN website. He scrolled through the vast directories, occasionally smiling. What use was the stupid organisation! Every time they were really needed they just folded. He got what he wanted, bookmarked the site, then reached for his phone. He would need Merlin The Sorcerer. It was the only educated nickname he used for any of the Barracudas but the man deserved it. There was little he didn't know about making dirty weapons. That had been a big plus in The Shark's column, bringing Merlin into the fold.

The phone rang twice before Merlin answered. He simply said, "hello", neutrally.

"Merlin," said Barracuda.

"Barracuda", said Merlin.

It had started.

August
Leisure time

Hartson stared beyond his computer screen, through the neon and sodium lit foreground of his tenth storey apartment, beyond the shoreline, into dark infinity. Two minutes before he'd looked out and it was still light.

He couldn't concentrate. The air-conditioning was fine, he still hadn't taken a drink that day, it was just the hour. It made him think in an abstract way. Darkness never meant calm in Khafira. Something would be happening out there beyond his window. He didn't know what, but it was happening.

He'd been putting off the call until he could do it no longer. He wasn't scared of anyone at the embassy, far from it. But he knew what a brick wall was, he'd run up against too many of them in the past. Tom Scott Garrett was a brick wall but he was the only contact worthy of the name he had at the embassy. He was on speaking terms with everyone, including the ambassador, but the higher up the ladder the less helpful they were.

Tom was usually able to give him a steer so long as it couldn't be traced back to him or the embassy. And provided, strictly provided, it had nothing to do with British interests. Then he was an open door if you had the right password.

He stopped dithering and picked up the phone. It rang twice and was answered. He knew Scott Garrett was sitting at his desk in the embassy, often was at this time of night. He didn't have a life outside of the embassy, as far as Hartson knew.

"Scott Garrett."

"Tom, it's Will Hartson."

"Will, how are you?

They went through their pleasantries. Finally: "Weapons, Tom, getting into the Gulf via all sorts of places."

"Where does this come from?"

"Leaky old Westminster."

"Might I ask whom?"

"Opposition MP, can't say any more." Nor could he, he didn't know himself. For all he knew – and his time in the Parliamentary Lobby only lent credence to this idea - the MP had been drunk and flying some fantasy.

"You need to be more specific. Where are these weapons going?"

"The north, just where they can do the most damage."

"I haven't heard a word, Will, nothing." Bang, the sound of hitting a brick wall rang around his brain.

"Not even a careless whisper in an embassy corridor?"

"Nothing."

Tom was normally garrulous, said buggerall, but rarely stopped saying it.

"Sorry, Will, Can't help. Good night."

He'd got precisely four fifths of fuck all. An uncertain Westminster opposition MP who just as easily be trying to stir up discomfort for the British Government, and the Khafira Defence Minister telling him everything and nothing and he couldn't quote him anyway. They're just going to say I made it up, he thought. It would be full of "sources close to the ruling family say..." and "unknown quantities of weapons destined for other continents." It was nothing, how could he go with it? He couldn't.

There was only one solution in times like this, forget about it, go and have a drink. He picked up the phone, dialled a number and heard it ringing in the middlingly luxurious apartment which had been home for Paul Winter for the last six months. Hartson had played tennis with him a few times, he was a good player. Winter was a strange man in the Gulf, he really shouldn't have left the Home Counties. But his bank had insisted and he didn't want to impair his career prospects by refusing.

The phone was answered: "Paul, it's Will."

"Hi."

"Fancy a drink by the Lagoon?"

"Sure, what's the occasion."

"Nothing special." How could a banker understand what he did? He picked up his keys and went out.

Diplomacy

Tom Scott Garrett spoke quietly but with assurance from behind his embassy desk. His brown hair was well groomed and his lightweight suit pressed to perfection. He was a throwback, an old style colonial servant, a relic really. Commander Phil Wilkinson eyed him with admiration. Scott Garrett was holding forth on the importance of keeping the "dreaded" press away from them. It was all new to Wilkinson, he knew about missiles, helicopters, marine deployments, crew management, most things to do with running a ship and how to organise his men. Now Tom brought the reporters into the equation – and they were nothing short of dog mess in this career diplomat's eyes.

"I'm not concerned about the local press, we know they won't print a word. It's the foreign agencies we have to worry about", said Scott Garrett.

"I thought you had them covered", said the commander.

"Always best to be safe."

"But it's all blowing over isn't it?"

"Come on, Phil, it was your jolly jack tars who found the things. If it had been anyone else it wouldn't matter at all. We have a special relationship here and we can't afford to let this get in the way. If the bodies had been British nationals it might be different."

The naval commander kept the bluff good humour which had stood him in good stead in some of the trickiest ports in the world. But he didn't like his highly trained, highly competent sailors being called jolly jack tars.

"Let's talk to the First Secretary," said Tom, changing the subject.

The First Secretary's office featured a series of hunting prints and the desk sported a gleaming silver horseshoe which was either ornament or paperweight. If Wesley Didben did not have a public school background, and come from a landed family, then he carried off the act with extraordinary skill.

The First Secretary, had all the trappings of a diplomat, the languages, the blandness, the commitment and the deviousness. But unlike many he was prepared to show his tastes, hence the passion for horses. He had never seen an industrial area, did not know what a factory floor looked like. Again, unlike most others, he did not pretend that he did.

He would soon be made an ambassador or governor general but nowhere important. Dibden thought the whole episode of the bodies was a confounded nuisance. Why couldn't the Navy keep its nose out of other people's business? He didn't choose to put it that way, of course.

"I think a tactical pull-out from this is the best course of action. Their police have the bodies. It's up to them how they deal with it."

"Can we enquire how their investigation is progressing?" asked Phil Wilkinson.

"I think not, Phil. We should leave them to it now. I hope we can count on you to keep your men in line."

They were the commodore's men...and women, not his. But, that aside, it could only have one interpretation. "You mean gag them?"

"I mean maintain a discreet silence."

"These are sailors, I doubt it very much."

The First Secretary fiddled with his horseshoe. "How about keeping them at sea for a few weeks until it blows over?"

"That's a matter for the commodore. I am the naval attaché, not the officer commanding."

"I'll ask the ambassador to have a word."

"An ambassador cannot tell a commodore what to do, he is under orders from the Admiralty." The commander's tone was friendly, as if offering advice. Was there a flash of undiplomatic anger on Dibden's face. Or was it an illusion? "You're right, of course, Phil, but a *foreign secretary* can tell an admiral what to do." The commander nodded his acceptance and said no more. Dibden looked across to Scott Garrett and exchanged a knowing glance. Round One to the career diplomats.

The Navy

The embassy car drew up outside the gate to the port and Wilkinson showed his identification. He chose naval rather than diplomatic, he drove straight to the frigate. A marine guard saluted him as he walked aboard.

The commodore was in his cabin, he listened without interruption until Wilkinson finished. Finally, he said: "I'm damned if I'll keep one of my ships at sea for a whole month. It's bad enough here without the men getting a chance to have a bit of fun. It's too late anyway, I've brought them in for a break."

"Very good, sir," said Wilkinson as he wondered how he would convey this to the embassy.

"It's tough serving two masters, isn't it?" said Jenkins, with a softer voice.

"It's not easy, sir. The embassy is nervous about our role in this. At the very least you might like to consider ordering an information shutdown."

"That's easy, Commander. Making it work is another matter."

"Yes, sir."

The commodore smiled. "Tea, Phil?"

"Thank you, sir." He relaxed as the commodore poured a cup and handed it to him.

"Any sign of the bodies and the police launch yet, sir."

"Yes and no. I had a man watching the marina from the moment we got back ashore. The launch returned two hours afterwards. They didn't have the bodies on board."

"They could have unloaded further along the shore for better access, I suppose."

"I suppose they could, Phil. What do you think?"

May
Kaliningrad

He was a lieutenant colonel in the Russian Army, he had three small stars on each epaulette and a bottle of vodka in his briefcase. He was drunk, he was nearly always drunk but no one questioned it. Stuck out at Kaliningrad on the Baltic Sea in May there was nothing else to do except get drunk. The local German population hated him and his colleagues, because they wanted Kaliningrad to become Koenigsburg again. But it never would while the colonising Russians held onto the naval bases there. Neighbouring Poland and Lithuania held him and his kind in utter contempt because it wasn't fourteen years since they'd been under the Soviet yoke and they didn't forgive easily.

He was ill paid and ill thought of even by his fellow Russians. The once mighty Russian military was reduced to an underclass as the money went elsewhere. He looked out of his functional office onto the airfield where a lone Bear bomber stood. It hadn't taken off for months. They had a crew but no fuel. Anyway, who were they going to bomb now! He knew, even though his uniform was olive green instead of blue or yellow, that the Russians weren't going to fight anyone in the near future. The one good thing he'd managed to salvage from his collapsed career was that he'd avoided Chechnya. It was ten in the morning, the new bottle of vodka was a quarter empty. There would have been more but his second in command, a major, had taken a couple of hits from it when they came on duty together. It would not have been because the Lt Colonel poured generous measures for himself, no, he knew how to control his drinking, he reassured himself daily.

What he needed, more than anything, was to get out of this shithole to a place where there were palm trees and women. Where he could walk out on a veranda with a glass of something exotic. Anything but vodka. He'd drunk nothing but vodka since he was fourteen years old. He was sick of it. But he needed to be drunk.

That's why, when the man with the Moscow accent had called on him a couple of years ago, he'd listened. Would he mind doing the occasional job for an international "Peace" organisation, all for the greater good of humanity! As far as the lieutenant colonel was concerned it could be for the greater good of whatever it wanted to be as long as it brought in dollars. And it had. Not enough to get him out of Kaliningrad, but enough to keep him on line. It was easy information like who was visiting, what was the state of the weaponry and planes, how well-staffed they were, all information he had access to and could pass on. Five hundred dollars a time kept him going very nicely. Why should he care?

So when he heard the Moscow accent again on the end of his home telephone earlier that day offering fifty thousand dollars as a starter he'd been very pleased indeed. He hadn't said so in those terms, he couldn't. But it was the Lieutenant colonel's ticket out.

They would have to meet, of course. The deal could not be done over the telephone. Old habits lasted in the Russian Military and his phone would certainly be monitored if not permanently bugged. But they had their coded way of arranging things so the man with the Moscow accent would fly out to Kaliningrad in his private jet to confirm the details and the money. He would arrive at the civil airfield a few miles away at Bhrakovo in the late morning. The lieutenant colonel would be there to meet him. He rubbed his hands at the thought of it and reached for the vodka again. Today would be a good day.

August
The Souk

Neon lights blazed overwhelming brilliance from the new buildings, blotting out the starlight. The waters of the sea lake they called The Lagoon were a rippling kaleidoscopic bed. Wherever Hartson went in Khafira it was the same: excess. Everything was bigger, more comfortable, more colourful than anywhere else in the world. He sat nursing a Pepsi, killing a few minutes. He sat back in his plastic chair. He wished it was an ice cold glass of lager in his hand with condensation on the outside. That way it could almost be Naples or Nice.

He'd fantasised about calling in at the off-licence, showing his booze licence and getting a few cans of Grolsch to take to the Creek. But he knew better. The police would certainly arrest him, confiscate the beer, and probably drink it. No, he'd wait until he got to the bar. Anyway, he'd hit the booze licence hard this month, he had little of the ration left.

He soaked up the chaos around him. He loved it by the Creek after dark. If all the entrepreneurs and conmen in the world go to Hell then this would be the result; a mawling, shouting assault on the senses; hotter and much older than Hong Kong and which hadn't lost its connection to the past. The teeming ferryboats crossed the short journey from one bank to the other as they had done for centuries, long before the expensive limousines came. And they'd be there after they'd gone.

The Lagoon made sense. It was old. The wizened characters on the quayside looked like they were rooted in the place. They and their predecessors had smelled the same seawater, sweated from every pore and babbled good-naturedly to anyone who passed, for maybe a thousand years. The Lagoon was the Orient. It didn't attempt to be western.

The water was calm, only broken by the occasional dhow and the ferryboats. He'd taken one himself that evening, just for a break from the motorway. A five-minute journey, in the dark, with the breeze and the splashing water giving some small relief from the heat. The sun went down, but never the heat, not in August. He had ten minutes to kill. He watched idly as another ferry drew up and started a melee as one group tried to get off, and another met them head on trying to get on. Why were there never any fights? Nobody seemed to mind. There was a splash, he saw a man being pulled out of the water in a soaking Khameez. Someone must have bumped into someone else.

Everyone smiled. The ferries were only small wooden craft, it was easy to jump on and off them, or fall.

His eyes were pulled away from the rough and tumble to a striking looking woman. She was probably an Arab, pretty, youngish, wearing western clothes and walking off the front of the ferry with a fixed look which opposed all the joy around her. She stared straight ahead, her forehead furrowed, her head tilted back. Hartson, interested, looked a little closer and just for a second her brown eyes flashed in front of him as she passed. They were narrowed to pinholes in spite of the night. She looked through him as she quickened her step into a half run. No one runs in this heat. She passed the concrete apron of the cafe, ignored the road and went straight into the souk.

The crowd melted before her, then closed up behind. He stared after her. The red, green and purple lights splashed on her back as the noise from her clacking heels was lost in the clamour of the souk.

There was little doubt what she was: dressed tantalisingly, pretty; she was one of the few Arab whores to remain after the Russians came. But she looked far too classy to be walking the streets. He shrugged his shoulders, drained his now warm Pepsi, and made his own way into the maelstrom.

Her heels beat a loud uneven rhythm on the sidewalk. Why hadn't she stopped to change her shoes? She was drawing attention to herself. She was sure the noise could be heard above the clamour of the souk at night. Shouting here, shouting there, and every call made her cast her eyes in fear. Her hands gripped a bag tightly, her knuckles showed up white against the rest of her Mediterranean skin. She started to run again, but not fast. She still wore her thin black cotton wraparound which ended beneath her knees. She sometimes wore it for work when clients were looking for quick results. Route one. That was not very often. But working was the last thing on her mind.

Any time in the evening he had said, it didn't matter, he would always be there. Was this the street? She slowed to a walk, perspiration ran from every pore in her body. She was soaked, so was the wraparound. But she didn't care what she looked like, she must find Michel.

A bar

Hartson was halfway through his first lager. Now he tried to imagine he was back by the Lagoon with it. But it didn't work. The bar was air-conditioned, the drink was even colder. It wasn't the same without the balminess and noise. Just for a moment he tried to place himself outside his village pub in Warwickshire on a summer's evening. English drinking laws seemed virtually non-existent compared to this madhouse. It nearly worked, but just as the image started to take hold he let go of it. He knew better than to delude himself. He was a few minutes early. He drank quickly, always had.

"Hello, Will." The voice was cultured…and familiar.

"Diana, what brings you to a dive like this?"

"Embassy night out, we've been on a dhow trip into the Gulf."

"Any cooler out there?"

She smiled without commitment. "Wet as a dishrag, dry as a bone."

Humid without any booze, nice combination! He took another sip in defiance.

"Do you want to join us?" she added, in the sort of voice that made it clear he should not.

"No thanks, Diana. I'm waiting for a friend."

"Another time perhaps?"

If only she meant it. "I'm very busy at the moment, but it would be nice."

"Anything interesting?"

"You probably know more than me."

She leaned closer to him, her voice lowered to a sexy hum. "If it's anything to do with those bodies, forget it. It's just a rumour, you know what this place is like. There's nothing in it, Will."

Bodies? He'd been around too long to give away his ignorance just yet.

"Thanks Diana, I'll bear it in mind."

"Seriously, Will, don't waste your time, it's a load of nonsense." She smiled a conspiratorial smile. He responded in kind. There was just a hint of a come-on but Will knew better than to believe it. She was unachievable, an invisible purdah wall surrounded her and all the other embassy women. Diplomats were to be left to themselves: no permanent friends, no permanent enemies, just permanent interests. Hartson wasn't one of those. If you wanted anything from them you had to give much more in return.

She walked away. He looked at her receding form and wondered what she'd be like in bed, still pushing the Foreign Office line? He took another draught of the freezing beer as he rolled her full name around in his head, tantalisingly:

Diana Ffrench Parsons. Fine shape, intelligent face, Cambridge education, privileged in a way he never had been. Anyway, he consoled himself, if you do get into bed with these people make sure you don't get fucked. Not easy with the Diplomatic Corps. She sat down among a group of smart looking people. He recognised Tom Scott Garrett and nodded a greeting. Scott Garrett smiled back then turned to Diana Ffrench Parsons.
"Well, Diana?"
"I think he bit."
"Yes, I should think so. Fairly susceptible these journalists."
"You're sure, Tom?"
"Of course, look at him now. An easy life on expense accounts."
"We should be so lucky"
Diana Ffrench Parsons took a sip from her drink and smiled.

The Banker

Paul Winter didn't like to be late, and he didn't like to be rude. Now he found he had to be one to avoid being the other. The insufferable heat wasn't helping. A stroll around the souk before going to the bar had put him in the clutches of a watch peddler, and he didn't have the strength of will to walk away.
"No really, I'm not interested, I already have a watch."
"It very cheap, make very good present for wife." A bit of a snigger there, "Or girlfriend."
The pedlar had him by the arm now and Winter wanted to pull away. He cast around to find a way out, anything would do. The peddler tugged his arm again and thrust the watch, a fake Rolex he guessed, under his nose again. "Three hundred dirham's, very cheap."
Cheaper than the six hundred the peddler had started with but he didn't want the watch, he wanted to get away. He decided he'd had enough, he yanked his arm from the peddler's grasp. Bad mistake.
"You don't want to be my friend! How dare you!" The man was becoming agitated. "I have this valuable watch for you and you insult me."
Winter felt even more uncomfortable. Then he saw her. Nothing had changed. She was hot and flustered. A harshness overruled the prettiness of her features. She was the woman from his apartment block, the one he'd seen

going into the elevator that same evening the elevator. And she was running. In this heat! She slowed down, then sped up, then stopped. She obviously didn't know where she was. The souk was a warren of blind alleys, main streets, and turnings. It took his full concentration at the best of times, and anyone running in this heat couldn't be thinking straight.

He passed through her field of vision unnoticed, she was too preoccupied. And she had barely noticed him at the apartment block. She continued her frantic search; It had to be here. In the name of our Lord Jesus Christ where? Why have I never bothered to come here until now, she chided herself. We have been here for two years and only now do I come to find him, when I am in trouble.

She had eliminated most of the guilt from her life as she steadily contradicted every religious priority she had learned as a girl. She felt a twinge now as she tried to find her old friend, if that's what he still was. She looked across the road to make sure she wasn't being pursued. It took a moment to register, but this time she noticed him. Her heart jumped, she recognised him, knew the face, the nobody in the lift, he was tailing her. He'd followed her all the way from the apartments.

A bar

The embassy party dispersed and sidled past Hartson towards the exit. Tom Scott Garrett beamed a conspiratorial smile. For what? Diana did the same. She was dressed loosely and casually for a hot humid night in the Gulf. But he could still make out her form as it bossa-nova'd through the comfortable cotton covers – or was that just his ungallant imagination. Whatever, she was fine either way.

He was about to give up on Paul Winter. He had fallen into conversation with a visiting car dealer who was looking for a woman. Hartson, feeling mischievous, had advised him to try any of the women at the tables. It was that sort of place. Anyway, the man from the motor industry turned out not to have the courage either so they had resigned themselves to talk about cars and what kind of people bought them.

He watched Diana Ffrench Parsons disappear through the exit with never a backward glance to him as his new companion wittered on. The two fs had always been a mystery to him but he'd never asked her about their origin.

Probably some medieval Norman family. He finished his third drink in one swill. The car dealer got bored and moved on to another bar, still looking for a woman. Time was running out for him.

The souk

Winter stood on a corner and never let his gaze slip from the receding form in the black wraparound skirt. She had seen him, looked him straight in the eye, but there had been no smile of recognition, just fear as she froze momentarily and then ran, her heels beating an uneven rhythm on the road..

He was concentrating so much on her he forgot about the peddler. It was only when he felt something in his back pocket that he remembered. He turned round fast, just in time to see the peddler running off with a twenty-dirham note. He'd forgotten it was there. The whole bloody place was conspiring against him tonight. He wrote off the twenty and looked again for the terrified woman. Gone!

She had no idea where she was, nothing stayed in a straight line for more than a few metres. Please, please, please! Help me get out of here she whispered in English while massaging a crucifix she gripped in her left hand. What real faith she ever had went a long time ago, the first time she had laid down and taken the money. Her god hadn't looked after her then, she'd been left on her own to lie with the fat sweaty businessman as he used her in ways she didn't know existed. That night she discovered she could rely on no-one, only herself. But still she had kept the crucifix.

So, now she would rent her body to anyone for anything; but not her soul, that was hers and not even her old god could have it any more. Yet still kept the crucifix against all reason. It wasn't a real faith, not to her. More of a talisman, it could easily have been a rabbit's foot. She never wore it around her neck for fear of offending her Muslim clientele.

She said "please" again. Superstition replaced her will. But why should a god she didn't believe in listen to her? She had sinned enough for four lifetimes, and she still had some way to go in the present one. Or perhaps not, it could be over very shortly.

She looked behind again; he wasn't following her. She took in her surroundings: the rusting air-conditioning units poking from every wall and pushing warm humid air into the already fetid atmosphere. The dampness was sticking the wraparound against her body, outlining it like a detailed statue. She ran her hands down her sides, every curve and mound was defined. Perspiration ran down her back and legs.

She was in a tiny alley off a side street. There was a door half open. She knocked and called out in English: "Hello."

Her hand clutched the crucifix so tight it made deep indents into her palm. She heard a voice. "Jose!"

She was uncertain; she heard it again. "Jose?"

It was her name.

"Jose, qu'est ce que tu as."

It was French, He was speaking French to her. Not Arabic, not English, but French. She turned to see the figure of Michel standing two feet from her in the doorway. The crucifix dug harder into her palm, she pulled it to her mouth and kissed it. "Merci bien," she whispered, then, "What will I do, Michel, What will I do! Hannah is dead."

Michel's English was slow. He spoke just enough to get by as a waiter at the Cafe de Bruxelles on the other side of the Lagoon. No one talked to him beyond ordering coffee and Lebanese sweetmeats so he didn't need much. Did she say Hannah was dead? Morte?

"Why is she dead?"

The sobbing distorted her speech. "I do not know, but I will be next, I have to be."

"Do not be silly, Jose, why should you die? Why should Hannah die?"

"It is true, I swear it will happen to me."

He passed a calming hand over her brow. Her breathing became more even. She had a nerve coming here after all this time, and then only with a problem. But that was her nature. He could soothe her, help her, be her friend and it would cost her nothing. He waited quietly, patiently while she sobbed away the fear, then she would tell him, just like she always did back in Beirut.

Hartson's patience was gone. Where was Winter? Ten more minutes and he would leave. He prided himself on being as alert drunk as he was sober, possibly more so. He liked to think that he could take in everything going on in his environment. He wasn't drunk yet. On the way, yes, but not drunk. His ears were working well enough. Certainly well enough to pick up the conversation at the next table.

He turned to see two youngish men in casual wear but whose haircuts and accents betrayed them as British armed services, therefore the Royal Navy or Royal Marines. Their hair was cut neat and they had a groomed look about them which belied their manner.

Bodies! Did he hear that? The second time in the space of 20 minutes. He strained to hear without giving away what he was doing. Concrete? What was this about? All thoughts of Paul Winter deserted him, his nose was almost twitching with the sniff of a story. He picked up his drink, swung his chair round to their table and brazenly interrupted. "Evening lads, welcome to Khafira. Let me buy you a drink to celebrate."

They were out on to the street. Jose was unwilling, but Michel insisted.

"I don't want to be seen in the open," she said, holding his arm tightly. She cast her eyes over his shoulder as if it gave her some protection. "Where are we going?"

"To the Lagoon."

"Why?"

"It will be easier there."

He spoke faster as he guided her down the street.

"But I want to stay with you, I will be safe there."

"You cannot stay with me!"

"Why? You are my only hope, I cannot go back, I have nowhere else. Why are you letting me down now?"

Michel whirled around on her. "I have always been your friend, have you always been..." he struggled for the word in English, "...mine?"

"Of course I have always been your friend."

"Then why do you wait until this time to visit me in the souk. Why do you hardly say anything to me when I see you in the Cafe de Bruxelles with your friends?" His English became more fluent as his anger mounted.

He looked for a reaction but she had become too hard to be hurt.

"I could not speak to you Michel: you know what I do, you know the people I mix with. You are a waiter, what would they think of that?"

"And what are you?" he asked, angrily. "Something better?" He didn't need an answer.

She let go of his arm and stopped him on the side of the road. The orange and pink light from a cheap ten and twenty dirham store lit their faces in garish shades, the heat hung over everything like a smothering fug.

"Michel, do not do this to me. When they find Hannah they will look for me. I must stay with you."

"It is not possible. You will not be safe."

"Of course I will, who will know I am there?"

Michel heaved a deep sigh. "Jose some of your clients could be my clients."

She looked away, looked at the street, looked back at Michel. That had been her insurance policy; a man she could count on without having to fuck him; a contract with her as the sole beneficiary. Now he threw their joint whoredom back in her face. She looked away, down the street, through the lights.

She gasped. He was there again, the man from the apartments.

"Michel, I think that man is following me." They watched him walk along the crowded sidewalk. He didn't look happy.

"Quick, in here now!" ordered Michel.

"Jose remained rooted to the spot."

"Now woman. Venez, come on!"

Michel dragged her into a doorway out of sight from the sidewalk.

"Does he have a weapon Jose?" said Michel.

"How do I know. I haven't seen him up close."

"He doesn't look dangerous."

"Who does Michel?" She gave him a meaningful look. Everyone, everything was menacing to her at the moment.

"I know he is looking for me. He keeps appearing. He is a police informant."

"Don't you know most of them?"

"They don't tell me everything." They'd tell her nothing from now on, even if she lived. They mustn't get her.

Michel reached into a pocket. Jose saw him pull something out. Before she could stop him he rushed from the hiding place and confronted the stranger on the sidewalk.

She knew what he was doing, it had saved them more than once in Beirut. But not here, they could be dead and buried twenty metres under a dune by tomorrow if he did it here. She rushed out to stop him and saw the man close up for the first time. She looked at him full in the face. There was no malice or even purpose there. She made to grab Michel by the arm and lead him away, but her rescuer was ahead of her. He had pulled out a 15-centimetre blade from his sock and held it to Paul Winter's throat.

Michel's knuckles were white as they gripped its handle.

They'd been drinking, tongues were loosened and Hartson had the adrenaline rush reporters get when they stumble into a story. It was a quickening of the pulse and a kind of thump in the chest as he made the connections. He pushed his new found friends while trying not to seem keen.

"Did you actually see the bodies, then?"

"Only for a few moments after they were brought up," said one.

"God, it must have been hideous. How on earth does that happen?"

"God knows," said the sailor. "We didn't get a chance to look at them for long."

"Not that we wanted to," said another. "They came up on the winch and the skipper had them in body bags straight away." The man blew a deep breath. "Can't say I blame him. I didn't want to see it." They nodded and went quiet as they returned to their beers. They looked as if they'd been at it for a while. Good!

"But how can you be sure they were so beaten up?"

One put down his beer firmly and said, forcefully: "Because we saw enough of them. All Right! Too fucking much!"

He pulled back, "Sorry, I was only asking. We never hear about that sort of thing out here. There's supposed to be no crime in this part of the world, that's what they're always telling us. It comes as a shock."

The first one replied, "Did you ever find any part of the world that didn't have crime?"

Of course he didn't. "No, I suppose not. Makes you think, though. I mean are any of us safe."

"Weird question to ask around here," said one of them.

True! Why were they there in the first place, after all? He wanted to ask what had become of the bodies, but he knew that would be a question too far. He took another pull from his lager. The table went quiet for a few seconds. Hartson made his excuses and left a quarter-filled glass. He needed to stand this up with someone more substantial than a couple of drunk sailors in a Khafira bar.

The hot exhaust from an air-conditioning unit blasted into Paul Winter's face but he didn't notice. He was facing a man with a knife. Until this moment, staring at the glinting blade, he had always felt secure in Khafira. But what did he know, he was safe in his white stockade on the other side of the Lagoon! He heard a scared but aggressive voice. "What do you want?"
"Nothing." His knees shook as he said it. He breathed in deeply and tried to ignore the blade. There was a space around them, they were being left alone by the rest of the souk. Nobody was going to help him. The man spoke. "Why do you follow us?"
What was he talking about? "I'm not following you."
The cold-eyed woman spoke. "I know you. I have seen you before."
The banker tried to control his voice but it shook and wavered as he spoke: "I live in your apartment block, I...I have seen you at the swimming pool. I saw you earlier, in the elevator..." Her voice fell away. The knife pressed harder.
"You know who I am. You know who Hannah is."
"All right, I saw you in the elevator, yes, and I've seen you around the apartments, but I have no idea who you are. And who is Hannah?"
"Don't pretend you don't know. What do you do at the apartment block?"
"I...I live there, what else would I do?"
The blade's tip pierced his thin shirt and made a sharp prick on his chest. It felt oddly warm, he had always thought steel was cold. The mystery woman - deadly woman - spoke: "Michel, it is bad already, do not do anything to make it worse. If he is following us, killing him will bring everyone chasing."
Killing him? What for? The knife pressed harder again, Winter was stung painfully, his assailant looked around apprehensively. A rush of bile came into his mouth.
The man spoke. "How do you know she is in trouble?"
"I didn't." The phrase was so short there was no time for any quiver in the voice.
"Are...are you?"
But their faces had changed, the ferocity was gone, alarm took its place. Something was different, a third colour glinted from the blade. It was pink,

orange and red now. The man's eyes widened. He followed their gaze and saw a police car fifty metres away moving in their direction. Thank God, he thought, I'm saved. He didn't notice the stinging leaving his chest. When he turned they had gone. He felt where the knife had been; no skin break, no blood. He tried to flag down the police car but it drove past as his arm stayed inert. He was too shaken even to move it. He felt stupid: scared little Englishman all alone in the big bad souk!

When Winter finally arrived at the bar to meet Hartson, his fear had turned to fury. But the reporter had no time for his story. "Come on, Paul, we're going to the International."
"Why?"
"I'll tell you in the cab."
It took twenty minutes to get to the International Hotel. Winter was put out that Hartson didn't care about his ordeal, he hadn't listened to a word of it. "All right why are we going to the International?" he said, petulantly.
"Because that's where the officers hang out. You are about to find out what it is to be at the beginning of an international exclusive."
"What exclusive?"
"I'm not certain myself yet."

The lieutenant

Lieutenant Jackson was getting drunk tonight, no doubt about it; he'd been looking forward to it, he'd earned it, and he was going to make sure it would be a night to remember – or nor, depending on how good a job he made of it. He picked a venue where there was little chance of being seen by his crew – not even the officers. That meant an expensive cocktail bar on the top storey of a big hotel.
He hailed a cab at the port gate and directed it to the International. It had two bars; one for middle salary drinkers, and one for high-income sippers. He had very little gear with him, just enough to demonstrate to the reception that he was a serious contender for a room. He threw his perfunctory bag on to the bed and made straight for the cheaper bar. If he was really lucky one of the Filipina barmaids would be looking for some extra cash. They could round off the night by raiding the minibar in his room and falling on to the bed. It wasn't

heaven but it was the most fun he was likely to have this night.

His first beer went down in less than a minute, so did the second, and with them came an easing. A smile broke over his face for the first time since he'd got the notification about the bodies.

Two men, Brits by their manner, walked in and stood at the bar. They exchanged greetings. The serving girl was gorgeous, but they didn't seem to care, they were more interested in him. No chance, they may not care about the girl, but he did.

"I haven't seen you here before," said the one next to him.

Oh for fuck's sake, he thought, I'm not for you. But he was an officer in the Royal Navy so he was polite. "I only get time to drop in every now and then."

"You're out on the rigs then?"

"No, I'm with the Royal Navy."

"Ha, welcome aboard. I'm Will, this is Paul."

Jackson hated this. It was getting in the way of the optics and the girl serving them; they were his mission tonight, not friendship, and not good-naturedly fending off a gay approach. But somehow the empty glasses piled up on the bar. It was a busy night, the girl hadn't had time to clear them. The edgy one, Paul, told an amusing tale about being held up in the souk, but he seemed excitable and not the sort of person he would want to spend long with. Will was companionable enough. He'd seen a bit. What's more he looked like he could hold his drink, which was more than the nervy one could. It was all good fun, but he hadn't had a shot at the girl yet and he was getting impatient.

"What do you do here?" he asked because he felt he had no choice and actually did not care a toss.

"A bit of this and that; seeing what we can pick up. It's like everyone else really." said Will, the good drinker.

"Here you are, Sam, you're a salty sailor, you'll know about this…"

Salty sailor!

"…did you hear about the four Filipinos pulled off the seabed?"

Jackson tensed, the alcohol loosened its grip. "How do you know about that?"

"Word gets around fast in this town," said Hartson, smiling. "It's all around the bars tonight. I'll give it until the weekend before the whole place has heard it."

"No idea what you're talking about," lied the lieutenant, badly. Too late he realised he'd admitted knowing something. That was that then, he would never make commander.

Hartson pressed him: "Really, I thought you would have done. My mistake."

"Why me?"

"I figured if anyone could clear it up it would be an officer – we heard it from some ratings at another bar."

"So what's the problem Sam? What's it got to do with you?"

So much for an information blackout. It was all over the town, and they hadn't been pulled out of the water more than a day. The commodore wouldn't like it. The embassy would hate it.

"All right. It's supposed to be a secret, but if it's already out there's nothing I can do about it, you might as well get it right."

He took another mouthful of beer. "It was last night."

"Bloody hell! News travels fast," said Winter, unevenly, "How do you know so much about it?"

"It was my ship."

Hartson couldn't believe his luck. "You found them. How?"

"I skipper a minesweeper, we were in the shallows and the sonar dug them up."

"What happened to them, Sam?" asked Hartson, probably too quickly but he was on a roll.

Jackson responded irritatedy, something he would later regret: "Concrete, on the feet, beaten, eaten, bloody awful if you must know the details – and why do you want to know?

"Jesus, what are these people like!" said Hartson, sidestepping the officer's suspicion. Winter said nothing.

"Why are you so interested?"

"Wouldn't anyone be?"

Some newcomers arrived. Jackson recognised two of his petty officers immediately.

"Hello, skipper," said one quietly. "Everything all right?" Then they caught sight of his two companions. "Are we following you around?" The banker, already pale, looked furtive. Hartson, stiffened. Jackson now saw the source of the leak, but no way at all of stopping it.

"You found out about the bodies from these men, didn't you?" he said directly to Paul, the more vulnerable looking of the two. He said nothing at all and looked like he was going to be sick.

"Yes we did, Sam. I'm sorry but it's my job," said Hartson.

"Whose job can it possibly be to peddle gossip about some poor souls who've been lifted from the water?"

The answer became horribly clear as Hartson reached into his shirt pocket and pulled out his press ID card." Jackson's blood went cold, no amount of August heat could do anything about it. Now there would be hell to pay. "Bastards!" he breathed and walked towards the exit. As he passed his two crewmen he said in a low but angry voice, "Keep your mouths shut about those bodies. You know your orders. What do you think you're doing?"

"I don't understand, sir," said one.

"Just shut up, round up the rest of the crew and get them back aboard. That's a captain's order! I'll see you in the morning."

"Yes, sir."

He stormed out of the bar.

Two hours later the commodore was sitting at his desk, Jackson had changed back into uniform and was sitting in front of him with the beginnings of a hangover. That was nothing compared to what was about to come..

"You're a bloody fool, Lieutenant Jackson." Said Jenkins.

"Yes, sir."

"You knew my orders?"

"Yes, sir."

"And still you disobeyed them?"

"Yes, sir."

"How did you get fooled into telling them?"

"They let me think it was already out," said Jackson.

"You still knew your orders. I have no doubt it leaked from one of the men but you are an officer, you can't go jumping the gun. You're supposed to take command and provide an example."

"I'm sorry, sir, I thought if they were going to know about it they ought to get it right."

"It wasn't your decision to take. There are higher authorities than you or me at work here."

"Yes, sir." The commodore paused for a few moments and then leaned back in his chair. "Consider yourself bollucked. It won't go on your record, and I'll say no more about it...this time. Let's just hope your name doesn't appear on a Randalls computer screen in Downing Street in the next few hours."

"Downing Street, sir?"

"The Prime Minister's press office has an up to date operation, you know." The commodore smiled, Jackson squirmed. Downing Street for god's sake. "But you've got to watch yourself, Sam. You have a tendency to want to do it on your own."

"So, why did you take those bodies on to your launch?"

The commodore fought back a flash of irritation.

"Fat lot of good it did them, they probably got thrown straight back in. Do me a favour, Sam. Don't find them again."

"I'll just call them cannonballs, sir."

"What's that?"

"Just a joke, sir. When we were searching one of the men said all we ever found was defunct hardware from previous wars. I called them cannonballs."

The commodore didn't smile.

"It seemed funny at the time. Perhaps not now."

"Perhaps not, Lieutenant."

"No, sir."

May
Kaliningrad

The Russian officer had never heard of the Barracudas and never would. All he knew about was the man facing him now, the man with the Moscow accent. The man looked the lieutenant colonel in the eye and repeated what he'd said.

"I want fifty 122 millimetre rockets with empty heads by midnight tonight."

The officer wanted to take another shot of vodka. But he sensed that the man with the Moscow accent would not approve. He was part of the new Russia, a world he didn't understand.

He said, "Impossible. I don't even know if we have any at the base."

His companion sneered as he said, "That conflicts with the information you gave me twelve months ago. You said there was a stock of two hundred 122-millimetre rockets. That did not change in your more recent updates."

So he remembered. Now it would come back to haunt him. Not such a good day after all. Too big a risk.

"You ask too much. I will be found out and court-martialled."

The Moscow man didn't hesitate and his gaze never left the officer's eyes.

"You will be anyway, my friend."

The significance of those words smashed through the vodka.

"You would betray me?"

"I am sure there is no need for that. I would prefer to pay you a fortune to get this job done and let you retire to wherever you want to."

"But how can I do this? There are too many people who would learn. The rockets are heavy and would have to be transported."

"Does it matter who knows? You are a senior officer, you can order what you want. By the time anyone questions it you will be thousands of miles away. They will never find you – and do they really care about a few dozen old rocket cases?"

"But how can it be done? We have rules and procedures."

The Moscow man gave him a look which said everything it needed to about the rules and procedures of the Russian Military. Then he shifted his gaze sideways and talked into thin air. "You will arrange for the rockets to be loaded on to trucks and brought here to the civil airport. They will be loaded on to a cargo plane which I will provide."

"Where is that plane going, Moscow?"

The man ignored the question and continued, "You can then get into your vehicle and drive across the border. Make sure that you bring your passport, you will not want to be here tomorrow morning."

The lieutenant colonel paused. Yes, he could order his men to load the trucks and take them out. They could even put them on to the cargo plane at the civil airport. Fifty wooden crates wouldn't cause that much of a stir, especially if he put a hundred dollars into the customs official's hand. He could convince his second in command, the major, that it was not worth sending a transport aircraft out to take away the rockets. They were deactivated anyway so they could go on a normal cargo flight with a consignment of other materials. It was a poor excuse and wouldn't stand any close examination. But by the time that came around he'd be gone, out through Poland and on a flight to the Far East, to Thailand, to enjoy the women and the warmth.

"I will need money for bribes," he said.

If the man from Moscow felt any contempt, it did not show on his face.

"Of course, let us add another $30,000 in expenses," he said as he reached into his jacket pocket and pulled out a large envelope. "Here is $10,000," he said. "That should see you through tonight and the next few days. The rest will be in this numbered bank account in Switzerland."

He handed the lieutenant colonel a piece of paper but the officer was transfixed with his eyes widened in disbelief. He had never seen such a vast amount of money, just being carried around in the man's jacket pocket. He grabbed at it. The man from Moscow let him as if he were a beggar snatching at small change.

"You will find the rest of the money in the account in three days time – when I am certain that the rockets have been delivered."

The thought of getting on a plane in Warsaw and heading for Phuket was overwhelming. And all for the sake of a few rusty disarmed rockets. Yes, he would do this tonight and say goodbye to this icebox of a place forever.

August
The apartment
A continuous dribble of sweat ran off the banker's nose. He smeared his hand across his face. Then he stumbled and fell to the pavement. Hartson went to offer him a hand up but he stopped in the middle of the action. Winter was shouting at him. "You've got me drunk Hartson, you bastard. Fucking bastard." He withdrew his hand, cast his gaze around the hotel entrance, saw a small group of people staring at them, and took a step back.

"Not too loud," he muttered. "Let's get you into a cab and home, shall we?"
"Bloody bastard, I'm pissed as an Arab."

Hartson looked around again, nervously. Bloody idiot, couldn't take a drink. "Shut up, Paul. For Christ's sake, remember where you are." He offered his hand again and managed to get the drunk back on his feet, although he couldn't guarantee he'd stay there for long. He let go and was thinking of leaving him to his own devices but something stopped him. He'd invited the man out for a drink after all.

It always surprised him when he found otherwise capable men unable to take a few drinks. He knew Paul Winter was a hotshot banker who knew the angles and probably where some of the bodies were buried, although maybe not literally. But he was clueless with social skills. He never held on to a woman for more than a couple of weeks - although that wasn't so surprising. The women had their own agenda in Khafira.

He couldn't waste any more time. "Get in!" He grabbed Winter's arms and dragged him into a taxi, waiting by the side of the hotel. "Are we going on somewhere else? I can't get any more drunk you bastard." Winter started laughing. Hartson got in beside him and ordered the cab to take them to the Al Kifaf Apartments. Within seconds of the cab moving off Winter fell silent. Hartson sighed with relief, thank god for that at least. The cab took ten minutes, time for Hartson to concentrate on what he needed to do. He'd fallen on two stories in one day. That will up the average back in London, he thought. Take that, Sharpe, Bastard!

He'd found his bloody story all right. The trouble was he still wasn't sure he knew what it was, or even if he wanted it. The cab drew up at the apartments. He grabbed the banker by the arm and shook him. Winter stirred and looked out of the cab window.

"Come on, I've got things to do."
Winter appeared to take no notice of what Hartson had said.
"I'm going to sort her out, you know... and him!"
"Who?"
"Those bastards from the souk, I'm going to get them. I'm going to get them now." Someone ought to take him aside and tell him to stick to one and a half pints in the future. He was going to get into trouble soon. It was just a harmless incident in the souk. He needed to get used to the middle east, it wasn't bloody Camberley.
"Don't be stupid, Paul. Go in, go to bed, sleep it off! You've drunk too much."
Winter slammed the car door and lurched along the sidewalk to the entrance to the apartments. Hartson watched him from the taxi, shrugged his shoulders and told the driver to go on. Thank god, he'd lost him at last. Serves me right for showing off, he thought. He should never have dragged Winter along. It was late but he could get something done. He had to tell the desk in London.

"Don't you worry about me you bastard," muttered Winter as he fumbled his key into the lock and staggered inside. He was going to sort them out all right. He was no coward; who did they think they were?
He would knock on her door and have it out with her, and if the man with the knife was there then he would sort him out as well. He'd had five pints of lager; nothing could touch him now. He pressed the elevator button for the third floor and missed it completely. "Where are you, bastard?" he muttered to himself before finally hitting the right one. The elevator took him up and the gravitational pull set him off balance again.
"Bastard," he breathed again after knocking against the side wall of the elevator. The door opened in front of him, he took a deep breath and tried to walk out as purposefully as possible.
Now where? If in doubt ask a policeman. No policemen here, so he would have to do the next best thing: ask the neighbours. He measured his steps carefully down one corridor and knocked on a door. He knew there was someone in because he could hear their television. The door creaked open, a suspicious face appeared. "Good evening, can I help?"
"I'm looking for someone's flat?" The middle aged greying woman winced as he breathed on her. "I know it's on this floor, she's in her early thirties, very

pretty, wears a black wraparound skirt." It took him four breaths to get it all out. The woman had stepped back into her apartment and was trying to close the door. She said: "Are you sure you want her flat?"
"Quite sure thank you."
"Suit yourself. It's down there, number 311."
Her nose wrinkled further, the door closed firmly. She didn't much like him he guessed.
He strode the twenty steps to Number 311. There was no sound from within the apartment as he knocked loudly on the door. He knocked even harder. He shouted. "Hello, is anyone there?" He tried the door handle, not expecting it to yield but it did, the door opened inwards. He pushed his head through into the darkened room and called again, loudly, fuelled by the drink and his outrage. "Hello, it's the man you threatened to slice into salami in the souk." Nothing. Funny smell though, and so warm. No air-conditioning; why not? He was sweating, he wiped it away and thought it might be pure alcohol by now. That was funny, he chuckled, then laughed. Ha ha. Gradually shapes took form in the room, furniture, a TV, a chair...
... a grey mound in the middle of the floor.
He stepped in and the smell became overpowering, like meat going off in a busted freezer. An all-pervasive smell which got into his nostrils, his mouth, his lungs. He stepped in further and yelled again. "Come out! I want to speak to you."
The stench made him retch. His right foot brushed the side of the form. It was soft, still. He reached back for the light and snapped it on. Then he looked down again. He gagged, the beer started to rise in his gorge and he dashed for where he thought the bathroom was.

Down the corridor, the woman heard the noise. She had turned off her television. She had been in Khafira a long time, she knew not to interfere. But she knew the girls. They had always been polite. She was under no illusion about them, she knew what they did. But today had been too strange - and now this.
She was used to drunken men coming down the corridor; sometimes she wished they'd come to her apartment instead. But this was all wrong, especially after the noises she had heard in the afternoon. She was quite used

to the sounds that came from that apartment, but they always emanated pleasure, laughter. She knew what the girls did. No, something was wrong. She would call the police; not say who she was, of course, try to stay out of it as much as possible. She reached for her telephone directory, looked up the number and dialled it.
"Hello."
"Hello, please come to the Al Kifaf Apartments, number 311. Something is wrong."
"Losematik."
A non-English speaker, saying excuse me. She knew that much.
"English, please. Afroan."
The longer she was on the phone the more nervous she became. The same voice said the same thing. She panicked. "Al Kifaf, NOW!" and slammed down the telephone.

His tongue was dry and his heart was thumping hard. He was drenched in sweat. He wiped his brow, stuck his head under the sink tap, swilled his fouled mouth with desalinated water. He'd never seen a dead human being and his first had to be like this. He stepped out of the bathroom unwillingly, he tried to move his feet but they would only go at half the speed he attempted. Even that wasn't enough to prevent him getting there. Nothing called him back, let him off the hook. He had to look. He breathed deep again and looked down. She was so pale, the lips garishly red against the rest of her face. There were marks on her cheeks and he could see the beginnings of bruising on her thighs. There was a gash just below the bottom lid of her right eye. It had bled only a little and what blood did come out was now a black powder on her pale skin.
He could take no more and looked away. How long since he had walked in? three minutes perhaps. He glanced towards the door and saw it was still open. What should he do: call the police? No, call his boss at the bank? Absolutely not! Call Will Hartson, he knew about everything, he would know what to do. He picked up the telephone sitting on a piece of mahogany furniture. He dialled Hartson's number just as the first stirrings of a call to prayer pierced the night air. It was followed by more as mosques all over the city joined in the grand chorus. A shock went through him as the smell hit again.

The calls to prayer jarred against the telephone ringing in Hartson's apartment. If it was bloody London again he had an answer for them. He'd FOUND his story, he was writing it now. See how you like this, Sharpe. Not only do I chase down your lead, I dig up my own nasty little exclusive. Bollucks to you, mate. He snatched up the phone and said, triumphantly, "Will Hartson." The reply was shaky, he had trouble identifying the voice to begin with. It was English, but it wasn't coming from London.

"It's Paul. Please come round here right away." The words gushed out drunkenly. "It's all gone terribly wrong, terribly bloody wrong."

Hartson knew of twelve year-old kids who could take their drink better than this. "Paul, just go to bed and sleep it off, there's a good man." He wasn't prepared for the scream which came back down the line: "Someone's FUCKING DEAD, Hartson you bastard. Come over here now, you've got to come."

"Calm down. So you got held up in the souk. It happens, you're not hurt."

"Will you listen? I may be drunk but I'm not joking; I'm sitting next to a foul, stinking, naked body right now. It's not funny, Fuck you."

"Stop pissing around, Paul, you know I've got work to do."

"Look, I came up to their apartment."

"Whose apartment?" said Hartson testily.

"The one who threatened me in the souk." He sounded exasperated. Bloody nerve, if anyone should be exasperated it was Hartson.

"...and I found this corpse. It's here now."

"Who is it?" he asked, wearily.

"I don't know her name, she used to hang around the pool with the other one, every now and again."

A shadow of doubt crept in. Winter was too drunk to have invented it all.

"What shall I do, Will?"

"Does anyone else know you're there?"

A pause at the other end. "Yes, one of the neighbours, I asked her for directions."

"OK, get out, anyway. Go to your own apartment straight away!"

"What about the police?"

He waited a moment before answering.

"They'll find out soon enough. It'll do you no good to be involved."

There was another short pause. Come on, Paul, get a grip.
"And why is that?" The voice was deeper, accented, completely calm. He tingled. Someone else was there.
"Who is that?"
"This is Colonel Ali Abdul Hamid of the police." Hartson went cold. He couldn't bring his tongue under control to say anything. Of all the people, the hardest cop in Khafira; and the best. "And you are Mr Will Hartson of Randalls International News Agency I believe. Perhaps you would join us here at the Al Kifaf Apartments, Mr Will, if it is not too much trouble."
He regained enough composure to say, "I'll come now."
"I will send a car for you, Mr Will."
"Very considerate of you, Hamid." He put down the phone. No, Hamid, it would be no trouble at all. He couldn't quite stop his hand from shaking.

"Thank you for coming at such short notice, Mr Hartson." The words were gracious but not their intent. Hartson stared at the two uniformed policemen who had brought him. Then he looked back at Col Ali Abdul Hamid. Anything to avoid the mound on the floor.
"My pleasure, Colonel," he croaked, "I'm always happy to help if I can."
The mound was covered by a sheet but it didn't mask the stench. He wanted to vomit but he held on. He'd seen dead bodies in his time, been right up close, even closer than this. But usually he was able to get away from them quickly. Not here.
"Imagine my surprise to find you on the other end of the line with Mr...er...Mr Winter here," said Hamid with a full grasp of irony. Imagine his own surprise to be speaking to the most pervasive intelligence cop in the Gulf! "Yes, Mr Winter had been drinking with me earlier."
"You are good friends then?"
"We see each other quite often."
"Ah yes of course; international correspondents don't have friends do they, just contacts!" Not always true but close. Anyway, he wasn't going to argue.
"Like policemen, Colonel."
Hamid chuckled. Hartson looked down at the mound, there was nothing funny here. It was a macabre place to carry out an interview. Hamid paced the small room smiling, skirting around the body, rubbing his chin, jingling the keys in his

trousers. The smile lulled Hartson into a false sense of security and he smiled back. He was taken unawares, Hamid was faster than a snake. He whirled round. Hartson thought he was going for him, but he was aiming for Winter. He stared the banker straight in the face from ten centimetres away. His voice was all fury. "I do not understand why you came here, Mr Winter. Do you not have a female companion in Khafira?"

Hartson knew the best thing was to keep quiet. But Winter was no more than an innocent drunk; a pain in the arse, but harmless. The banker's reply was so English: polite, anxious to help. He said, shakily: "Not at the moment, why do you ask?"

"You must know what this place is!" Winter looked quizzically at the policeman and Hartson realised the poor innocent Home Counties hotshot hadn't seen it yet. Think, Paul: two beautiful women from the same apartment, lounging by the pool during the day. What does that add up to?

"It is a brothel, Mr Winter, a very high class brothel," said Hamid wearily. Winter replied, quietly, with no strength in his voice: "No I did not know, Colonel." He had gone white despite the Gulf tan. "I came here because I wanted to sort someone out.

"What does this mean, 'Sort someone out?'"

"It means I wanted to know something. Someone from this apartment accosted me in the souk earlier this evening." The hysteria was gone, but not the innocence, thought Hartson. Shut up, Paul!

"Clearly not this poor woman." The colonel gestured towards the blanket, "Would you explain why you were here, Mr Winter!" Not a detail changed from the account Hartson had already heard. He wished he'd paid more attention earlier. What was this: National Corpse Day!

"Mr Winter, this has been a bad day for you I think," said the colonel, softer this time.

"You can say that again, Colonel," said Winter, too soon. Don't get cocky, thought Hartson.

"I am sorry to tell you it is not over yet. I think there is much that you know that you are not telling me." Hamid's tone maintained its new softness. It made the words even more menacing. The banker looked to Hartson, helplessly. What could he do? He looked at the pale little banker and knew then that he was incapable of initiative. If anything was to be done then he would have to do it.

"Colonel, what has this to do with either of us? All Mr Winter did was find a body." Hamid turned on him and stared him straight in the eye, as if he had no right to be in the same room. "Because, Mr Will Hartson, he had a confrontation in the souk and then he is found with a dead body in this apartment. What am I supposed to think?" The softness had gone. Hamid's face was twisted with anger. He moved his gaze to the body, his voice calmed, the tone became regretful. "She was Hannah Bada. She has been here for five years." He looked up again. "She was supposed to be very good, Mr Will."

Hartson smiled despite himself. "How do you know that?" The colonel smiled back, the anger suddenly gone, and gave a meaningful look which could have been reminiscence. "That's why she was here, with her friend."

"You mean they were imported as prostitutes?"

"Certainly."

Hartson gave Hamid a knowing look. Hamid returned it. Just for a minute he thought they were two men of the world communicating together, and they might be able to find a way through. Then Winter's voice broke in.

"But prostitution is illegal."

"Of course it is," said the colonel, hardening up again.

"Then why did you allow it?"

Shut up, you fuckwit, for god's sake, thought Hartson!

The colonel sighed: "There are some things which I am obliged not to know about, Mr Winter." Hartson stared at Winter, willing him to stop. It didn't work.

"Then why have the law in the first place?"

The colonel sighed again. "Because it keeps the religious people happy."

"And the prostitutes keep everyone else happy?" added Hartson.

"The ones who can afford them," added the colonel as he made a glance over his shoulder towards the uniformed men who might not have the same understanding of his sophisticated attitude.

Hartson tried to retake the initiative. "Will you find her killer, or will that be quietly not known about as well, Colonel?" The colonel was weary rather than angry this time. "Mr Will, I advise you to forget about this yourself, if you want to stay in Khafira."

"Is that a threat, Colonel?"

"Obviously. Now you may return to your apartment." The smile disappeared. "You are now involved in this, Mr Will Hartson, understand that straight away. I came here and found Mr Winter calling you on the telephone. It is not over and I advise you not to publish a single word of this."

"Don't be ridiculous, Hamid. You know full well neither of us are connected with this."

"The evidence says something else."

"Let's hope we can rely upon something more scientific to take the inquiry forward."

"Do not joke with me!" He stepped over the body to stare Hartson straight in the eye again, his voice lowered to a growl. "This is not funny." Then he turned his back and spoke some words in Arabic to one of the uniformed officers. He in turn moved towards the two Europeans. "All right, I'm going," said Hartson. He looked at Winter who said nothing. He couldn't resist one last shot as he moved towards the door. "You'd care pretty badly if she'd been a Russian." The colonel said nothing, but his stare was enough to tell him to say no more.

Refuge

She hated taxis, this kind anyway. It was the only one they could find. Being in the back of an Oldsmobile or a Mercedes was different. But not this heap of Ford junk. "So I am being driven to Anwar in a straw wagon. How can you do this Michel?"

"Does it matter, Jose, you are at least going to Anwar's place. The transport was all I could find." She scowled at him. She didn't want to go to Anwar's place. He was a snivelling, grovelling waiter at the Cafe De Paris. She didn't mix with men like him, still less stay with them. "I can't even remember what he looks like. This is stupid, Michel." She didn't expect what followed. He was angry.

He spat: "You see only the faces with money, Jose. You have changed since you came here. I do not even know why I am helping you. You have showed no concern for me since we came, you could not even remember where I lived." Her scowl stayed fixed. "Michel, it is not the time for this." She lowered her voice to almost a whisper. "Hannah is dead and all you can do is complain that I have not maintained my friendship with you." How dare he speak like this. "What about all the times I helped you when we were in Beirut. I brought you and your family bread to eat when there was none, I helped you to find work when there was none." Michel averted his eyes.

"We should always be friends, Michel. I may not have seen you but I have never forgotten. You have never been to see me, either."

"How could I come to see you? I never know if you will be with some rich man, entertaining him in your beautiful apartment."

"It is not a beautiful apartment, it is just comfortable."

"You have seen where I live, you know your rooms are beautiful compared to that."

That wasn't her fault. What did he want her to do about it? "Michel, am I always to carry you? Do not blame me because you have a bad room and a bad job. What more can I do for you?"

"You could lend me some of the precious money you make from your rich men."

"What about the money you make from your rich men!" she spat back. It was *HER* money, she debased herself enough to get it. Why should he have any? He turned to face her. "They are not rich men. They are only men. I must make money the best way I can." Too bad, Michel, just too bad. "Just like me." She turned to the front and stared into the driver's mirror. He was looking at her. Her scowl turned to a snarl. The driver hastily moved his eyes back to the road. She looked out of the rear window as the taxi rolled over the bridge at the far end of the Lagoon. She could see the expanse of water lit up by the moon. The sheen of money shone off the surface: tall lit buildings, hotels, offices, banks. She looked the other side: emptiness, darkness, endless wilderness. They rolled on over the bridge into twentieth century Khafira: modern architecture inhabited by medieval people. She was contemptuous of them all.

May
Kaliningrad

It was nine in the evening and broad daylight in Kaliningrad. He would have preferred the cover of darkness but it made no real difference in the end. He poured the last of a vodka bottle into his glass and tipped it down his throat in one swallow. There would be no drink left for his friend the major but he would leave something else to make up for it. After all, he had ten thousand dollars in his pocket and another two hundred thousand waiting for him tomorrow morning, in Poland.

He looked outside where a party of ten men including a sergeant and a corporal had gathered waiting for him. He walked out of the office and spoke to the sergeant. "I have orders to move fifty 122 rockets from the store to the civil airport at Bhrakovo. They must be ready for loading by eleven this evening so you have one hour to load them and one hour to carry them to the destination. Is that clear?"

The sergeant was an old army man. He knew an order when he heard it. He did not question it. The army worked in stranger ways than this so he would do as his colonel ordered. Why they could not go out on a military transport like normal he did not know, it was not his business. He would have a moan about that with the other sergeants over the vodka later.

The officer walked back to his office and looked around. He would never come here again. He would be free and rich and warm. He would miss the comradeship and his friend, the major, Sergei, would be a loss, they had known each other since their posting in Afghanistan and had drawn even closer in the two years since he'd been sent to this god-forsaken outpost. Sergei was fifteen years younger but they had shared much vodka and stories during their friendship. It was a shame that he could not be here now, but he would understand, they had talked about getting out often enough. He took some paper from his desk and wrote a brief note to his friend.

"My dear Sergei," he wrote, "I am sorry to leave you in these circumstances. By the time you read this I shall be thousands of miles away and nowhere near Russia. I have finally managed to find a way out. I enclose a little something which may help you to do the same." He found a brown envelope and put the letter inside, together with five one thousand dollar notes. He closed the flap and wrote Sergei on the front. He left it on the major's desk two feet away from his. Then he left the office for the last time to make sure the precious wooden crates containing the 122 millimetre rockets were being properly loaded.

Ninety minutes later two laden army lorries drove onto the apron at Bhrakovo airport. The men jumped out in front of a DC8 transport plane with its side doors wide open. The civilian loadmaster indicated them to put the crates onto wooden pallets so that the airport staff could forklift them into the cargo bay. The operation took twenty five minutes. The loadmaster produced a piece of paper and indicated the lieutenant colonel to sign it. It was in western letters and he struggled to make it out.

"Where is it going," he asked the man.

The loadmaster was young with brown hair and an unkempt appearance. His shirt hung from his trousers despite wearing some kind of uniform with a ring on the sleeve. He gave no indication of understanding the Russian. The faithful sergeant was standing nearby and came in to help. He spoke English to the loadmaster, a language the Lieutenant colonel recognised but did not understand.

"Why must this form be signed? " asked the NCO.

The loadmaster responded sullenly and not at all grateful to be addressed in his own language. "For the airport customs," he said. Looking away. The sergeant translated to the officer.

"But you already know what is in these boxes," he replied through the sergeant.

"I cannot leave this place without a signature saying that these are engine parts." He spoke to the sergeant but looked straight at the lieutenant colonel.

The sergeant said in Russian to his officer, "But they are rockets, we have loaded them ourselves."

The officer stared at the sergeant, a look that said that he was the officer and if he said they were engine parts, then that's what they were. An NCO does not think, does not question and certainly does not contradict.

August
Hideout

She was not welcome, Anwar made it crystal clear. Why did Michel think he was such a good friend? Now she was in his hands and that made him dangerous. He knew some of her story, enough for him to guess if anything else emerged. She was safe for a few hours, no more. Sometime she had to go back to the apartment to collect her belongings. What would happen if the body had been discovered? Would they be waiting for her? She shivered, she knew too much, she knew who Hannah was seeing that afternoon. He paid good money but he demanded so much. They had never liked him, but they had no choice but to entertain him and his friends – if such a man had friends.
Anwar walked in, frowning.
"You do not want me here do you, Anwar?"
"No! You should go home. What is so terrible that you must stay here?"
They had told him it was an immigration problem which Michel was trying to sort out. Her visa had run out. She dared not risk staying at the apartment because being a prostitute was against the law. It was a flimsy excuse. She doubted if Anwar believed them but she couldn't tell him more. A careless word at the cafe would be enough; there were few in the Gulf who were not prepared to tell tales on others. She had learned to keep her mouth closed.
She looked at her watch: nine o clock and already the day had become unbearably hot. Anwar's air-conditioning was not working and he could not afford to have it repaired. She fiddled with her crucifix impatiently. Michel must return soon or he would be late for work at the cafe.
"Why do you resent me, Anwar?"
"You have money and still you come to me or to Michel. We do not have money like you. We must work on our feet, not on our backs." Lying hypocrite, he took in extra cash the same way as Michel. There was no pleasing him so why should she bother. He was a Lebanese like them but he did not think the same way. The door opened and Michel appeared, looking worried. "You cannot return to your apartment. Jose." He looked at Anwar. "Not yet. I cannot get the visa clearance until the end of the week." Anwar's eyes rose to the ceiling as he gasped exasperatedly: "She must stay here until then, why?"
"Please, Anwar, you know what can happen in Khafira."
Anwar got up and walked towards the door saying, "Michel, we must go to

work. Hurry." He left the room, sulkily. Michel quickly moved to her side and spoke softly but urgently. "They must know what has happened; there are three Police cars by the apartment block and everyone is being told to show their identity card as they go in. You have a choice Jose: you go there and show yourself, or you get out of Khafira."

Her head dropped. They will have searched the apartment, they would know who she was and they would have her passport. They were going to find her.

The Banker

Millions of dollars were passing under Paul Winter's eyes but he spared hardly a glance to see where they were going, or why. His mind was somewhere else. His office looked down on to the bustling daytime waters of the Lagoon. He watched the dhows moving in and out of their berths. A clerk brought a sheaf of currency deal papers. He initialled them without thinking. Dirham' to dollars, about half a million; not enough to send the Middle East banking system into turmoil. Not that he'd have been able to stop it today. Should he go to the embassy, get some protection for himself? He followed with his eyes another dhow and knew how out of his depth he was. This was not what he came out for: dead prostitutes, police threats! No, this was life in the raw and he didn't like it at all. He dialled a number he had been told by the bank to keep with him permanently.

"British Embassy, good morning."

The bar was busy, full of expats. Winter usually used it on Thursdays as Khafira closed down for the weekend. He had never been there on a Monday and he eyed his watch worriedly as he nursed a mineral water. He was carrying a copy of the International Guardian, to mark him out from the rest of the bar.

"Sorry to keep you waiting, I assume you are Mr Winter?" He nodded at the man in the white tropical suit and tie. "How do you do. I'm Tom Scott Garrett." He rose slightly from his chair and offered his hand. "So, you're in a bit of trouble?" Oh, more than a bit of trouble, honestly! He started speaking, the words rattled out: "I've found a dead body and I've been ordered to keep my mouth shut."

Scott Garrett recoiled mentally but concealed it. "I see. I wonder why are you telling me?"

"Because you're from the British Embassy. I can count on you, I hope." The diplomat smiled and replied: "Of course. Tell me all about it!" Winter's mineral water went down quickly as he told his tale. Scott Garrett listened, asking the occasional question. Finally he spoke: "What was the police colonel's name?"
"Colonel Ali Abdul Hamid." Scott Garrett was quiet for a few moments.
"Is that a problem?"
"He is a very important man in Khafira."
"What do you mean?"
"He has the ear of Sheikh Issa."
And the tongues and souls of a few others, though the diplomat.
Winter shivered. His eyes went up to the smiling picture of Sheikh Mahmood Bin Issa Al Nadir suspended above the entrance to the bar.
"You mean he's dangerous?"
Tom nodded, gravely. "That scarcely does him justice."
"What should I do?" Winter pushed away the remains of his water and grabbed a passing waiter. "Large Scotch!" He'd come for reassurance, he'd got the opposite.
Scott Garrett said, "Normally I advise people to keep their heads down in these circumstances...and stay in touch regularly. If you do as you are told, Paul, nothing will happen. If you had been here a little longer you would have known that."
Winter's heart sank. "You mean I shouldn't have bothered you!" Scott Garrett hesitated just long enough before saying, "Not at all, Paul. We're here to help after all. We Brits have to stick together. By the way, let's just be sure: you say you knew neither of these women, not the one in the souk nor the one in the apartment?"
"Absolutely not," said Winter, indignantly, " I'd seen them of course, but I'd never spoken to them."
"Good, good... it makes it so much more difficult if there has been some kind of involvement."
Scott Garrett looked at his watch.
"So, what happens now? I go and hide for a few days?"
"You go back to work and try to forget about it. I shall make discreet inquiries."
"How will you do that?"

Scott Garrett smiled as he rose from the table and patted Winter on the shoulder.

The diplomat
Scott Garrett had an affable exterior manner, but he did not hide his contempt for others from himself: idiot expat greenhorn! He could do without this nonsense. He had more important things to do than worry about a stupid banker and a dead whore. He returned to the embassy and made straight for the First Secretary's office.
Dibden didn't waste time. "What have you told him?"
"To keep quiet."
"It happens quite a lot out here, I understand."
"I'm afraid I don't have access to the statistics."
"Of course not, and anyway I believe they read zero in each column." The First Secretary picked up his horseshoe and weighed it in his left hand.
"Do you know anything about this place at the apartment block Tom?"
"I know of it. I was offered to sample its pleasures a few months ago after a party." The horseshoe became still in Dibden's hand.
"I refused, of course."
"Of course, Tom, best to keep it sheathed while on duty." He replaced the horseshoe.

The night fell. He knew when it was best to keep his mouth shut. Keep it sheathed eh! Up to a point, but a man can only take so much. Of course he wasn't interested in the apartment girls when they were offered; they would have been too compromising, too dangerous, especially as a present from a rich local businessman.
His interest in women had always been academic. They only featured strongly in his life when he was asleep, and he rarely remembered them. He had been obliged, over the years, to perform the act with various women and he had done it competently enough. But his heart was never in it. He couldn't trust them. He couldn't trust anyone. He'd learned to take his pleasures without need for love.
He didn't use the four-wheel drive tonight. It had diplomatic plates and he didn't want to cause any sort of stir on the other side of the Lagoon. He would

take a cab to the West shore and catch a ferry. It was only a short walk on the other side.

It was so much easier this way; no questions, no name, just a commercial transaction and it would all be over in half an hour. No need for commitment. Everything has a function, no need for it to have a purpose as well? Leave that sort of thing to the philosophers. He walked out into the hot night to find his functional pleasures.

The souk screamed out in lights and noise. He walked on, soaking it up and sweating it out again. He'd made little effort to disguise himself. He had been out there for two years and had failed to get even a light tan. He always wore a pale suit. He did not enjoy being outside even in the warm winter and took no part in the sport ethic of Khafira.

He looked like any European tourist pretending not to be intimidated. His thin lips were set in a straight line ready to curl up into a smile. His short brown hair shouted that this was someone who did not really belong in this melee. He traced a path to the alley just away from the main commercial area. It was one of many secret corners he used in the souk for his satisfaction. The lights were dimmer there, he had to adjust his sight before descending the last few feet. He knocked on the door.

Two hours later: back at his villa, a cool shower, make his skin tingle, wash off the souk and everything to do with it. Then a drink, listen to the BBC World Service News, and bed. He was relaxed for the first time in days. The whisky tasted good. He held a tumbler three fingers full in his right hand while he turned on the shortwave radio set with his left. It was on the hour. "This is the BBC World Service. The time is 2100 Greenwich Mean Time." He listened and sipped the whisky as the news continued and mostly washed over him…until….

"And finally there are news agency reports of bodies being discovered by Royal Navy patrols in the Southern Gulf area." He jumped involuntarily in his seat. The whisky spilled on to his shirt. How did they find out? "Randalls News Agency says naval sources have confirmed four bodies have been found. The British Ministry of Defence refuses to comment…" The glass tumbled to the floor, the remains of the whisky splashed over the polished tile surface. Will Hartson, damn you to hell! "Our Middle East correspondent says the Ministry's refusal to speak raises several questions…" Oh, for god's sake, why would there be questions! They were four Filipinos, who cares, what have they got to do with anything? The bulletin finished, He sat down, the radio carried on with a taped programme by a disc jockey from the 1960s. How the hell were they supposed to keep a lid on it now!

May
Deception

Another shot of vodka would be helpful now, the Lt. Col. thought. Just one to get him through these tricky few minutes. "I will sign it," he said, not even looking at the form being thrust at him. "I do not want to have to take them all the way back tonight. It will be a bureaucratic mistake in Moscow."

"Can I see the order, Colonel," said the sergeant. Perhaps we can clear up the confusion."

"It is back in the office, I am afraid. Let us not waste any more time."

He took the form from the loadmaster and signed it. The loadmaster muttered something which the sergeant chose not to translate, maybe he didn't understand the accent, it was not American or British. Then the loadmaster beckoned a man over in a loose fitting shirt and carrying a clipboard. The colonel knew him to be the customs chief at the airport and a man even more susceptible to bribery than himself.

He looked at the cargo manifest handed over by the loadmaster and then said to the lieutenant colonel, "Why are you sending engine parts from here when they could go from your own airfield."

"They are too small a load to send a transport plane. I have been instructed to send them through here. They are going to Moscow so they should not concern you."

"That would be true if the DC8 flight plan had been filed for Moscow, but it has not. It says they are going to Maraka in the Persian Gulf. So it is very much my business."

"Are you trying to thwart the operations of the Military, *Customs official*?" said the lieutenant colonel, contemptuously. It achieved the opposite of what he intended. The customs man stared him straight in the eye and said, "Take them off the plane! I am not allowing them to leave here until I am satisfied."

Son of a goat! The plan was falling apart because of one irritating bureaucrat. The army officer abandoned his contempt, allowed a smile to creep across his face, and approached the customs man.

"This is silly. I am sure the flight plan has accidentally missed off Moscow. You can never tell with these cargo planes where they have been or where they are going. For all we know this one has only just landed from Frankfurt. When it finishes in Maraka it will probably end up in Belgrade. They have no idea where they are going or where they have been most of the time.

The customs man did not react. The officer took his elbow and steered him to the other side of the undercarriage, away from the eyes of the sergeant and the loadmaster. He pulled a five hundred dollar bill from his pocket and put it into the man's hand.

"Will this make you satisfied?" he asked. The man took the bill and said, "It makes me curious, it might satisfy me, it will not necessarily make me silent."

Deeper and deeper into the shit. He pulled another five hundred and said, "You can get enough vodka to keep you quiet forever." The man took the bill and paused for a few seconds before saying, "All right. You know what you are doing, it is none of my business, but don't think you can get away with it all the time. You are playing a dangerous game with military hardware. I will say the crates are going to Moscow and stamp the paper." He pulled out a small stamp and pad from his pocket and did as he said he would. The officer breathed in suddenly. He didn't realise he'd failed to take a breath for nearly a minute. He grabbed the form and didn't wait to see the customs man walk back to his building. He went straight to the loadmaster and handed it to him.

The sergeant was still there. He said, "Is everything in order, Colonel?"

"Yes, of course. Now, you have finished here. Take your men and return to the base. I will see you tomorrow." The sergeant acknowledged the order and left to martial his men into the trucks. The loadmaster nodded one final time as he supervised the closing of the DC8's side doors. He disappeared behind them. Behind him the officer could hear the army trucks driving off. Beside him the four old Macdonald Douglas engines of the DC8 were winding up ready to leave. He moved back to his jeep two hundred metres away. He would stay until the plane took off. After that his new life would begin and whatever was planned for those rockets and that flight plan would be someone else's business.

The DC8 taxied from the apron to the head of the runway. It was the only flight leaving that night. He watched it start its run then lift off halfway down the runway and climb into the night sky. Its navigation lights continued to blink long after the plane's outline had merged with the darkness. Then the runway lights were turned off, together with nearly every other light at the airport. There was still light in the sky, that would help get him down to the Polish border. He pressed his top pocket to make sure his passport was still there, then reached into a corner of the jeep and pulled out an unopened bottle of Stolichnaya Vodka, the stuff only the highest ranking officers drank. He untwisted the cap, put the neck to his mouth and took a long pull. As far as he was concerned this was the last bottle of vodka he would ever drink. It would be gin, whisky and brandy from now on. He started the jeep and drove it in an erratic weaving pattern out of the airport into his new life.

August
Café society

Hartson knew she was out of his league, so did Diana Ffrench Parsons if he really stopped to think about it. But where does that kind of attitude get anyone? So, no harm in trying, eh! And where else but the posy faux French Belle Époque of the Cafe de Bruxelles? He enjoyed going there as much as anyone, especially on Randalls' expenses. His natural grazing ground was a grubby cafe in the souk with cockroaches to add flavour. But not when trying to impress Diana Ffrench Parsons, the Ice Queen Of The Desert. She would have been much too choosy and you don't get anywhere in life unless you put in a bit of effort. He was prepared to put a lot of effort into this diplomat.

They sat on elegant bentwood chairs which might have been imported from Montmartre, but almost certainly came from Mumbai. Every now and again his mind drifted while his gaze stayed on her. Was she really sitting at the table with him, talking to him, making out she was interested? He was mind-pinching himself to make sure it was real. Yes, she was really there, at the same table as him. A fluky shot: a chance call to the embassy. Would she care to meet for a little chat? Yes, that would be fine.

He'd scored a date with the frosted confection…the icing on the cake.

"Do you normally meet your friends here?" she asked.

"Only when I want something."

Her face betrayed nothing: "How can I help?"

"Thanks for that steer about the bodies."

Her eyebrows were straight, her gaze was constant, she was skewering him. He looked away and made a show of eating his Baclavi. He cast his eyes around the room and met them coming back in two directions from the mirrored walls, no one could hide, but no one ever wanted to at the Cafe de Bruxelles. The women, mostly white, sat in small groups eyeing the men. They drank tea or freshly ground coffee and ate tiny sandwiches with slivers of filling. Some, more daring, had ordered from a range of colourful Lebanese sweetmeats. There were a couple of higher-class Russian hookers looking elegant in a corner sipping tea, waiting. The men, mostly Arab, sat in small groups talking to each other, or alone reading a newspaper, making the occasional call on their mobile phones, eyeing the women. One of the women behind him muttered conspiratorially to her companion. "He had me three weeks ago."

Who had her?
"You lucky thing. How did you get away with it?"
"Adam had to go to Kuwait for a couple of days."
They both giggled, quietly. A drip of honey fell on to his plate, he smiled at Diana who was listening as well.
"What was he like?"
"As you'd expect, he liked things a little...," she paused leaving them hanging, "different."
"How different?" came the cautious but eager response.
"Enough to make it worth my while." There was a chinking sound, like jewellery being shown off. He couldn't resist any longer. He glanced in a mirror to see one of the women, blonde, probably in her late 30s, well cared for, displaying a gold ladies Rolex watch with diamond time marks on each hour. She caught his gaze and then looked away indifferently.
Her companion looked on jealously, "What do you have to do to get that."
"Whatever he asks dear," she said ruefully while rubbing the Rolex.
Diana broke the spell. "My steer, Will?" He pushed the women out of his head.
"Bodies, Diana."
"Ah?"
"Yes, four mutilated Filipino boys found by our Navy boys...and girls and which you told me to ignore." The words did not come out of his mouth that easily, he had never been much good at pretending to be macho and careless, but that was what a foreign correspondent was supposed to be so he went along with it. The drinking and womanising he seemed to take to very easily, though.
He continued, "You presumably read the wires...talk to your colleagues...watch the news channels, listen to the World Service?"
"Yes, I do," she said evenly
"So what happened to those bodies?"
"Why do you care about four little Filipinos?"
A gorgeous smell of percolating coffee filled his nose.
"Unworthy of you, Diana."
The gaze turned to a smile. "I'm a Foreign Office diplomat, Will, you're expectations should never be too high." She lowered her eyes. It wasn't much but it was the first thing she had ever shared with him. A tiny wave of triumph washed through him.

"Where are the bodies, Diana?"

"I'm sorry, Will, I don't know." The smile was still there, she might even be telling the truth.

"Tom Scott Garrett was handling that one, not me, it's above my pay grade. I've kept out of it."

The triumph drained; Scott Garrett, different game, old school Foreign Office. He had sent her over to him in the bar in the first place, now he saw it.

"Would you like me to find out some more?" she added.

Beware of diplomats bearing gifts.

"Of course. But why would you do that when you've already tried to set me off on the wrong trail? What's the deal?"

She locked her gaze onto him again, then, not as evenly as before and with a slight intake of breath she said softly: "How about continued good relations with a respected member of the British media."

Continued! When did they start? But that wasn't what she was saying, was it!

"Why?"

"What harm can it do? They weren't Brits."

"They were found by one of our ships."

"Accident of fate. It's out of our hands. As far as I know, the Navy handed the whole thing over to the Khafira Port Police."

Hassan? Now there was a man he definitely did not want to mess with. Even brave reporters would think more than twice about confronting him. He continued, but even quieter: "Just a steer on what happened to them after that."

She paused, then said: "I'll see what I can do, Will." Then another pause and a slight intake of breath before, "Perhaps we can meet up later this evening?" It was so casually said, as if he was the ambassador or one of the sheikhs; he knew Diana liked the sheikhs. Could this be what "continued good relations means?"

"Excellent, here again?" he responded just a little too keenly.

She regained her evenness. "Why don't you come round to my place? We can have a drink by the pool."

Her place!

"Nice idea." Some miracle of willpower controlled the shake in his voice.

The moment was broken by a loud chuckle and he looked up. He recognised who it belonged to and knew enough to cover his irritation.

"Good morning, Samir Latif."

"Mr Hartson, Miss Ffrench Parsons." She smiled back at him. The women behind had stopped talking. They looked straight at the large man who had slipped in to a chair a couple of tables away. The one with the husband in Kuwait massaged the Rolex on her wrist. So it was him. Poor Adam in Kuwait could never compete, not with Samir Latif, anyway.

May
Maraka

It was early morning, the Sun not yet above the horizon but spilling enough light to see clearly. Barracuda watched the chartered DC8 coming in. His powerful field glasses picked it out eight miles from the airfield. It was on the limit of its safe range but he could not run the risk of it landing en route to refuel, who knew what prying customs might find! So it had flown directly from Kaliningrad, that was the condition of the hire and the charter company knew better than to ask questions of Barracuda. He stood on the apron at Maraka and followed the plane as it brought his precious cargo closer and closer. His team of unloaders stood by a few hundred metres from the runway.

Maraka was an accommodating airport. It was smaller than the international hub in neighbouring Khafira and with fewer facilities and inquisitive eyes. The main airlines rarely stopped there, the smaller ones and charters used it because it was cheaper and less showy. Maraka had to have an airport, because Khafira had an airport and whatever their deadly rivals had, they must have as well – no matter that they couldn't afford it. Maraka had no oil so made money the way it had done for centuries: as a freeport, a smuggling centre for those less concerned about diplomatic terms. Dhows from India, Iran, Pakistan and North Africa still moored up in the calm inlet laden with unaccounted-for cargo. But these days so did aircraft at the airport, especially from Third World Cargo operations looking to make their money whichever way they could.

So, when Barracuda asked for a quiet place to unload his aircraft away from the main terminal and the customs office the most senior airport official made no secret of the terms. There would be a "facility fee" to make an area available and to "streamline" customs "formalities". Customs in Maraka dealt only in bribes. There were no rules, anything could come in, but the man with his clipboard had to be paid, otherwise it stayed on the plane. That was the way it had always worked in Maraka, and most of the small "import/export" states on the coast in that part of the Gulf.

Barracuda was relying on this Swiss banker-like discretion. He had even been offered his own storage space if he wanted it – for an arrangement fee. He thanked them for their courtesy, but he knew where this cargo was going.

He kept his eyes on the DC8. It was closer and lower now, and the sun was above the horizon so the navigation lights were no longer visible. Five more minutes and it would be down and parked in his temporary private corner of Maraka Airport. His desert trucks would take them from there to the lagoon where a dhow was moored.

Right now the trucks were a dirty white colour and the Barracudas were being extra careful with them because it wouldn't take much to expose the military desert camouflage paint underneath, it was a thin white paint which would wash off with a hose. They had Maraka number plates which would be switched to military when the time called for it. But for now Barracuda was content to allow the authorities to believe that they were smuggling gold, or whatever they chose to think. He didn't care, he wasn't planning on being around long enough to answer any questions.

He got into his newly purchased Landcruiser and drove the kilometre to the unloading point. It was a tough car, built to take the worst ravages of the desert in any temperature. It needed to be for what lay ahead in the next few days. He had changed the plates within seconds of driving it from the lot.

The DC8 touched down as he reached his destination. He parked, kept the engine running for the air-conditioning and watched the jet taxi towards him and the Barracudas. It drew up alongside, the engines cut and the front port door opened to reveal a dishevelled young man with his shirt tail hanging out of the back of his trousers. Barracuda glowered at the slovenliness of the man, but he had no control over him. The unloading steps from the airport approached the door, while Barracuda's own forklift team drove to the back. The scruffy crewman disappeared back into the plane. The steps were operated from a Nissan pick up with what looked like four teenaged Filipino boys inside. They got out, unhooked the steps, and manipulated them inexpertly up to the door. Barracuda opened the car door and emerged into the heat. The scruffy crewman appeared again.

"You want these fucking crates," he said matter-of-factly, the swearword falling out of his mouth like water from a tap. Barracuda scowled and nodded. He could play much harder than this little man. "You know there are fifty of them. It took ten Russian soldiers to put them on in Kaliningrad!" said the young man.

Barracuda blinked in the harshening sun. Everyone had heard it: the flight crew, the Filipino boys – Barracuda cast around to see if there was anyone else but there was no one. He wanted to shoot the foul-mouthed vermin there on the spot but he knew that would be too much even for the flexible Maraka authorities. If the Filipino boys had heard any of it then they'd know a dangerous amount, even if they didn't know what it meant. Barracuda made a quick decision. "These boys will help," he said pointing to them. "Want some extra dollars, boys?" he called out to them, cheerily. All four smiled back – two of them were wearing fetching gold crucifixes he noticed. Of course they wanted the money, look at them, thought Barracuda with contempt, dressed in their cheap jeans and T-shirts from the counterfeit stores. Of course they wanted the money.

Three of the Barracudas unloading party looked at him but said nothing. Barracuda himself kept smiling and pointed to his nose. Whatever he was planning it would be settled later.

August
Summit meeting

It was early, the Sheikh was working at his desk. Colonel Ali Abdul Hamid walked straight into the vast chamber – room barely described it. Only Hamid could do this, any other servant of the state would have to bow, beg permission and wait a long time. They traded the traditional greetings, then:
"You are busy today, Your Highness?"
"I am busy every day, Ali Abdul Hamid. I am the Defence Minister, there is much that I must worry about."
"Of course, Your Highness."
"What do you have to tell me, Ali Abdul Hamid?"
Hamid braced himself: "There have been complications, Your Highness."
"What complications?" The sheikh's smile disappeared.
"The whore's body was found by a European."
The colonel waited during a long pause. It wasn't his place to break the silence. Sheikh Issa toyed with a silver horse he always kept by his desk; a model of a classic winner ten years before.
"Is he an important European?"
"Not in himself, no, but his friend is Mr Will Hartson of Randalls News Agency and while Mr Hartson is also not important, what he does is!"
Sheikh Issa grimaced. "That does make things harder."
How did you let this happen, in other words!
"What have you done?"
"I have warned them both that they must not say anything to anyone or they will suffer."
"Mr Hartson is not so easily dissuaded. Do you think they paid any attention?"
"I believe they did, Your Highness."
"Good. I would not like to lose Hartson, he is a useful man to have here." The sheikh looked down at his papers.
"Have you seen the BBC World Service, Colonel?"
"I regret I have not had the time Your Highness."
"There is a story about bodies being found by Royal Navy patrols." The sheikh looked up again. "In our waters, Hamid." Hamid bowed his head. "The story is attributed to Randalls News Agency. Make sure it stays out of our own newspapers. I do not want anything getting in the way, at the moment."

"Yes, Your Highness."
"I imagine Colonel Hassan will have known, of course?"
Hamid smiled. "Of course."
"I do not like Khafira's dirty laundry being washed so openly, Hamid. Did you know of these bodies?"
"I did not, Your Highness, I have been busy with the whore and its…complications…I hardly need say more."
"True, Hamid, that is an important enquiry, but somehow Hartson has stumbled upon two embarrassing stories in less than 24 hours – and I thought we had him under control. I do not want Khafira to look like the murder capital of The Gulf, Hamid. I have enough to worry about with the other issue. Bring Hartson back into line, Hamid, but do not harm him…seriously. I need him for my purposes, not his."
"Yes, Your Highness."

Distraction

It was eleven o'clock and the temperature was 105 degrees Fahrenheit in Winter's apartment. He had a headache and he shook. He splashed water on his face from the cold tap. It was warm, the kettle switched itself off, he made coffee, then he called the bank: slight infection, nothing serious, must have picked it up in the last couple of days, back soon, so sorry. He picked up the morning paper and leafed through it, but took in nothing. He looked casually at the motor ads and then sharpened his focus. Why shouldn't he get a desert car, a four-wheel drive! He'd wanted one ever since he got here but the bank had given him a Toyota saloon and he thought that was that. No, he had enough money, he could get one, maybe even a Range Rover. Wouldn't that be great, take his mind off things? He drained his coffee and scoured the ads hungrily; what were the chances?

May
Maraka

Barracuda watched the forklift trucks lifting the wooden crates on to his waiting trucks: so far, so good – if good was an appropriate word under the circumstances. The next step would be trickier, refilling the warheads. He hadn't opened them yet but he knew that the 122mm rockets were packed with conventional high explosives, a fuse and a detonator to spread it around. He had told his Russian contact to keep the propellant – no matter how old - that was all part of the deal. What was more, he couldn't leave rockets lying around with chemical agent in the nose and nothing in the cylinder to send it. That would be shoddy, not even the Iraqis would do it. It had to be completely convincing.

He jumped aboard one of the trucks and told one of the barracudas to keep the Filipino boys away for a few minutes while he opened it. He wrenched it with his bare hands and looked down into the space. He gave a short satisfied sigh as he saw what he wanted to see: a three-metre long cylinder, 12 centimetres in diameter with four short fins at the back and a pointed warhead at the front. These could never be fired in anger, they were too decrepit, but they were exactly what he wanted – and what they wanted. He tried to lift one out and he could tell immediately from the weight that the propellant was still in it. That was all to the good. He laid it down gently, far more than anything else he'd ever laid down, even a dying comrade, then replaced the wooden cover to the crate and smashed it into place with his fist. It stayed. He allowed a smile to play across his mouth. He could deliver them to Merlin as they'd expected. Now he had to move quickly. He marched back to the truck and watched the Filipino boys fumbling with the crates on a forklift. Christ they were young. They had no idea what they were dealing with. Still, they wouldn't be alive for too much longer so it would never bother them. It certainly wouldn't bother Barracuda.

It took forty minutes to load the trucks: sixteen in one and seventeen each in the other two. Barracuda called the Filipino boys over and pulled out a wad of hundred dollar bills. "Here," he said, "Have a hundred each and thanks for your time boys." The Filipinos stared at the green notes in his hand, too shocked to grab them. He didn't hand them over but continued, "I'll double it if you help me unload them at the other end."

The Filipinos looked at each other in disbelief. This was half a year's wages in a morning. One of the two wearing the crucifixes said, in perfect but heavily accented English, "Will it take long? My brother and I are expected home in Khafira when we finish this shift."

"A couple of hours," said Barracuda. You'll be home before your mother even knows you went. Don't worry, I'll talk to the airport, they'll let you go."

"What about our work here?" asked another one with a gold crucifix.

"You'll get eight hundred dollars between you, how long will it take to make that kind of money working at this … airport!" said Barracuda, just reigning in his temper; they'd find out about that soon enough anyway, but not here.

They didn't answer. Barracuda couldn't afford to wait but he couldn't deal with them right here within the airport perimeter. Maraka may have an anything-goes attitude but they would draw the line at rubbing out airport staff in broad daylight.

"OK, I need the help," he said, "I'll make it three hundred dollars for each of you." He waved the bills in front of their noses to emphasise that he meant it. That did it, all four nodded and Barracuda told them to jump up on one of the trucks. He turned away and muttered to himself, "Needless complication." He'd happily rip apart the loadmaster jerk who'd forced him into it. Now he'd have to nursemaid the little runts until he got out to sea and the rendezvous point. He turned to look at the DC8 but the jerk had gone and the doors were closed. He made a note of the plane's serial number because he was a vengeful man, then brought himself back to the moment in hand. Time to get these piles of rusting scrap to Merlin. The chemist would replace the warheads on Barracuda's new floating laboratory. He wiped a small bead of perspiration from his forehead. It was nine in the morning and the sun was starting to hurt.

August
Café disaster
Paul Winter was furious, he raged at the wheel of the vehicle he had bought only 30 minutes earlier. How could he have been so stupid? He smashed his not especially resilient fist into the steering wheel hard and winced with the pain at the same time as the horn made him jump. Winter was not a man of the world and this day was underlining it.

He shook his hand to get rid of the stinging pain. But at least the car was still going. It was steaming, backfiring and wheezing like a 100-year old man close to expiry, but it was going. Why had he fallen for the chat? Why couldn't he have waited, taken his time, saved his money? But no, he had to go for the first thing he saw, didn't he! Too bad, anyway, he was close to his destination and there was one pleasure he was going to have, one he'd been planning on since the day he arrived in Khafira and saw the smart cars at the Café De Bruxelles. That was where he was going and just for once he would be one of those posers in their fancy vehicles. Afterwards he would see about getting his money back – although that was unlikely in this camel-trading mad house. Then the engine became lumpier than ever and the air-conditioning stopped.

There was a line of gleaming four-wheeled drives outside the café, carefully coiffed and exhaustively cleaned by Filipino workmen who had to beg taxi rides to get to work each day. The shiny European-style cafe exterior shone expensively at him as he drew up. Then it happened!

Inside the café Anwar was working hard. He cursed under his breath in Arabic because the work was piling up and Michel was nowhere to be seen. And now Samir Latif had walked in: great, his main investor. The last thing he needed was for Samir Latif to see a poorly run operation, it would be the end of it. And what would happen to Anwar then? He was just a poor Lebanese on the run. He wiped his brow and went to clear a table.

"Can I get you anything else?" he asked a group of women.

One responded suggestively: "Not at the moment, thank you Anwar my sweet; not here anyway." The others looked at her in fake shock and smiled conspiratorially before looking back to catch his reaction. The best thing to do with these women was to pretend he was embarrassed, even interested in their advances. He needed their custom and he would do whatever it took to keep it.

Then the atmosphere changed. There was no warning, the cafe froze, Anwar dropped to the floor sending a tray crashing. Not here, of all places? Some of them were Beirut veterans, others witnesses of war in the region, the rest lazy expats. But they all seemed to know the sound of gunfire when they heard it and they heard it right outside the cafe. Hartson looked out of the front window, trying to see a gunman, or evidence of a round being discharged. He didn't exactly find a smoking gun, more a haze of fog centred around a beaten up and aged Range Rover. Gun? No! Backfire, yes! Then he started to laugh, Samir Latif joined in, so did Anwar, then the whole cafe. There was nothing outside except the once-white Range Rover with steam gushing from its front and smoke from the back. It was suffering from automobile ague, thought Hartson, AA, the sort of pun subeditors would love. He turned to share the joke with Diana. She was smiling too, in fact smiling enough to show her near-perfect teeth. He turned back and his smile faded. Paul Winter, of all people, was slamming the door of the offending car, now walking up to the cafe entrance, now coming in. Oh no, was he looking for him? Not here, for God's sake. He wanted a rest from the irritating man. More to the point he was with Diana Ffrench Parsons and he didn't want anyone diverting him, or her, from his purpose.

Winter knew that a backfiring four-wheeled drive in this company was as acceptable as a camel fart in one of their shopping mall boutiques. He had yet to hear that happen, but he'd been told and he didn't want to know. But it had happened, he was there, it was his car and everyone knew it. What he really wanted to do was hail a cab and get the hell out of there to anywhere else. But they'd seen him and there was every chance that someone in there would recognise him – he was a banker after all, and Khafira made high priests of the people who looked after their money. He had no choice, he took a breath, raised his chin, stared straight ahead and opened the door to the café. If he had looked down he might have avoided it but he didn't and immediately tripped over a small step. His humiliation was almost complete.

Hartson looked on from behind a newspaper as he tried not to be seen. His companion looked at him quizzically. He knew the banker had walked in to the Cafe enough times to know the layout of the place, and he knew he was having a hard time – He'd found a rotting corpse, after all, and then been threatened by the police so that was enough for anyone's year let alone an hour of one night. He was obviously having a bad time. But Hartson was damned if he was going to be the nursemaid. He looked back at Diana from behind his newspaper; she, to her credit, had not moved a facial muscle. Of course he should expect nothing less from a professional diplomat.

Anwar approached the banker, his high tenor voice clear as a bell above the hushed whispers of the cafe. "Can I show you to a table, sir?" he said without a hint of irony as he helped Winter to his feet. "Thank you very much," replied Winter, stiffly, as the café proprietor gently closed the door and put him close to Samir Latif. Winter had never said a word to Hartson about his clients; he'd never even named them. But it was obvious to the reporter that Samir Latif was an important man in the banker's life. Everyone deferred in some way to the rich thickset man sitting in the café, but he obviously had power over the banker. Oh yes, Winter's eyes were everywhere, he almost bowed to Latif, they exchanged a handshake which was perfunctory from Latif and grovelling from Winter, It was actually quite unpleasant to watch someone debase himself so much in front of so many people. Oh yes, Latif was high on Winter's priority list.

"What would you like, sir?" said Anwar.

"Tea." replied Winter, stiffly. The cafe stayed almost completely silent. Only the sound of Hissing steam and clinking crockery threatened to break the spell. Hartson was mesmerised. Anwar delivered a tray of tea paraphernalia: hot water, cup spoon, sugars and a selection of teabags.

"You might find it easier to carry your own teabags in your Range Rover, Mr Winter."

Now Samir Latif was speaking to him.

"I beg your pardon?"

"That way you can just stop every time you feel thirsty put one in a cup under your radiator." Not hilarious, not really funny, but enough to provoke an outburst of giggling from the women's table, and guffaws from some of the men. Hartson stayed straight-faced. He knew Samir Latif could be cruel. He looked again at Diana: was that a smile, a full open-faced smile?

"You seem to have an enviable supply of steam, enough to rival the cafe.

Have you considered going in to business? Perhaps as a travelling catering service." Now, that was quite funny, thought Hartson.

There were more guffaws and giggles, his face creased, his cheek muscles ached through trying to keep them straight. Winter wasn't seeing the joke, though. "I am sorry you find it so amusing, Mr Latif. It hasn't been any fun for me."

Winter heard himself say the words and wondered what he was doing talking to one of his biggest account holders like that?

"I understand, Mr Winter, you have had a trying morning. But you must learn not to take life so seriously. Join in the joke, everyone else is enjoying it." As he spoke he spread his arm in a generous gesture through the whole cafe. "You must learn to relax. Look at our dear Sheikh here; do you ever see him without a smile on his face?" Samir Latif's hand pointed directly to the obligatory picture of Sheikh Mahmood Bin Issa Al Nadir. The hush redescended. Hartson knew how close Latif was to the ruling family; everyone in the café knew. Winter would now be wise to shut up.

"You are right of course, Mr Latif," said the banker. Hartson relaxed and glanced at Diana. She had brought her smile under control and stared straight ahead; the women behind had gone quiet, they seemed disappointed, thought Hartson.

The drama had made the reporter forget to keep his newspaper at eye-level and just as he remembered and brought it back up, Winter spotted him. It was too late to do anything about it so Hartson raised his hand in a reluctant greeting. "Hello, Paul." He was going to say, "Everything all right?" but realised how silly it would sound. Winter simply nodded back at him and looked away to Samir Latif – a banker may be a high priest but a rich client in this magesterium gets into financial heaven very easily.

He asked, politely, trying to restore his dignity: "I hope your new jet is performing better than my new car, Mr Samir Latif. I know it cost considerably more." Hartson smiled at the confirmation of his guess. So Samir was a client. Samir Latif replied: "I have enjoyed some very enjoyable trips in it in the last few months, Mr Winter. Thank you for arranging so much of the paperwork. I have no idea why they wanted it paid for in Japanese Yen but the world currency markets are as treacherous as the local tides, I suppose."

"It's always safest to go for the hardest currency you have."

"You must join me for a trip, soon?"

Hartson couldn't resist, even though he knew it was folly. "What happened to the previous one, Samir Latif, did the ash trays fill up??

Diana's face was impassive but he saw her pupils narrow. He'd gone too far, she was compromised, a diplomat could not be seen to endorse that kind of remark. No, bad idea, Will, bad idea!

Samir Latif's smile faded, but not completely: "It was time for a change, Mr Hartson, and we must keep the wheels of industry moving, must we not? Every jet and yacht bought and sold means someone somewhere is being employed." His smile returned to full beam again looking down to his newspaper. The philanthropy of the man, thought Hartson, but at least he had a sense of irony.

The cafe calmed and began to return to normal. He turned back to face Diana. "How to turn disaster into a triumph," he said.

Neither of them noticed a man in French waiter's uniform walk in. He was mouthing something in Arabic to the man behind the counter. Hartson's limited command of the language told him it was an apology. But the reply was lost in a flurry of action. This time Winter, who he thought had managed to get a grip on himself, launched himself across his table and threw himself at the newcomer. Hartson's smile froze on his face. What the hell was he doing now? The Rolex woman looked up in fresh anticipation. "He is entertaining, isn't he!" she said to her friend. The banker was upon the newcomer before he had time to react. He pinned him by the arms and was holding on hard. Hartson wished he'd never met the idiot. He glanced at Diana who was transfixed. He looked again at the newcomer who was obviously a waiter here. There was obviously panic in his face, which was hardly surprising. Winter was now grimacing and calling to the other waiter to fetch the police. His victim was gradually getting control and had pushed the banker's arms back. Hartson scanned the room and took in the scene. It is the curse of the reporter, no matter how lazy or evasive, that they will see what other people don't, their eyes roam further, they take in more and they make connections. So Hartson looked at Samir Latif; was that a smile on his face?

"Hurry up, help me," yelled Winter.

By now Anwar was there, straining to release the captive. "Sir this is one of our staff, Michel, he is harmless." he yelled in his high voice.

Then another voice, deep with authority and a hint of menace: "Come now, Mr Winter. Let us calm down. Where is your sense of humour?" said Samir Latif. The whole café seemed to shrink at the sound of it. But Winter was unstoppable. "This man nearly killed me in the souk two nights ago." he said to no one in particular. He paused to gather breath. "Next thing I know there's a dead girl in my apartment block, and...and I think he or his girlfriend did it."
Hartson was horrified. Shut up Paul! Shut up! What did Colonel Hamid say? Don't say a word to anyone! Idiot! Who would have thought a banker like him could forget how to be confidential. How did he behave during a currency crisis?

Samir Latif's voice went even deeper, every one of the women at the nearby table stared at him unblinkingly. Power, thought Hartson, here was an open display of it. Samir Latif filled the room without shouting or booming: "Surely not, we have seen no reports in the newspaper of this," he said, holding up his copy of the Khafira News.

Hartson spoke lowly to Diana: "I'd better do something. I'll see you later, perhaps?" She smiled back at him and said quietly, "Look after him, Will."

He moved swiftly to Winter's side. "Come on, Paul, let him go! This will do no good." Winter did nothing for five seconds as he stared at Hartson, then released his grip and slowly got up. Michel shrugged him away and looked towards Anwar. Winter scowled and said furiously: "It was him, Will, in the souk, with the knife. It was bloody him!" Hartson had forgotten the incident mid the crisis which followed. "Quieten down," he growled, "you're on the fast track to getting thrown out of Khafira as well as the cafe. And me with you. Just stop for a moment." Then he whispered: "Samir Latif may look like he's smiling, but he won't like this, he's not European, he's an Arab in an Arab country and you're breaking his rules."

Winter looked across at Samir Latif whose face bore a politician's smile – all mouth and no eyes. He knew little of Khafira, he had allowed himself to think it was a wilder version of the Home Counties. Maybe it wasn't after all. And if he had to lose a bank client then please could it be anyone other than Samir Latif. Then he saw the waiter, the man in the souk, and was about to roar out about the injustice of it all when he realised how useless it would be. He let Hartson lead him, step by step, towards the door. As they reached it, he gathered himself and turned back.

"Please forgive me, Mr Samir Latif, I have had a bad morning. Thank you again for your invitation, it's best that I leave now."

Samir Latif nodded and smiled with his mouth, Michel looked anxiously in his direction before moving on to engage his colleague. Hartson just wanted to get him out. He almost dragged him through the door in the end.

May
Kaliningrad

It was a brisk morning in Kaliningrad as the Major made his way to his office. It was early but he wanted to get there before the lieutenant colonel so that he could at least have part of the day when he wasn't being subjected to the whingeing moans of an old time military drunk hopelessly out of his depth in the new Russia. The major liked a drink, but he didn't like taking vodka with the old fool first thing in the morning, although he'd had to. Otherwise his time in Kaliningrad would have been intolerable. He faked it, pretending to knock it all back in one, but managing to conceal the large part which remained unconsumed. The colonel was always too drunk to notice.

So, the major spent his time making sure his commanding officer was happy while he got on with trying to run the army unit. It wasn't easy but he looked forward to finishing his time there soon and going back to Moscow or St Petersburg where his career could continue its upward course.

He drove up to the gate and stopped to allow the barrier to rise. No one came out to lift it. He tooted his horn impatiently, then again when nothing happened. Finally after over a minute, a dishevelled looking corporal emerged looking alarmed.

"Have you been sleeping on duty?" asked the major, angrily.

"Yes sir, sorry sir," the man responded. "I was working late last night as well."

"I know of no work to be done last night, Corporal. Don't try to fool me!"

"I'm sorry sir, it's true. I was with the sergeant and the colonel at Bhrakovo Airport."

What was the man talking about? There were no orders when he left the previous night. The colonel had bade him farewell and said that was all for the day. He wanted to ask the corporal what the work was but he knew he could not do that, he was supposed to know everything. "Of course, corporal," he said. "Smarten yourself up and stay alert for the rest of your duty."

"Yes sir," said the corporal as he raised the barrier. The major drove straight to the office. He opened the door, put down his briefcase and looked at his desk. There was a note in an envelope addressed to him. He snatched it up and ripped it open. There were ten five hundred dollar bills in it and a small, scribbled letter. He read it and then looked up at the dollar bills again.

What had the stupid fool done? He raised the sergeant on the phone and asked him to confirm what he had been doing at Bhrakovo Airport. "The colonel ordered us to carry fifty 122mm rockets to be transported to Moscow," he said. The major slammed down the phone: fifty useless antique rockets, a five thousand dollar bribe and a mystery transport from a civilian airport. It stank and it had happened on his watch. He had tolerated the colonel but certainly owed him no loyalty. Until now he had felt only pity and occasional disgust, now he was furious. He had to alert Moscow immediately.

Did the rockets really did go to another Russian military destination? Somehow he doubted it. He was about to dial the number when the telephone rang. It was the civil police. A lieutenant colonel had been found dead in a military jeep in a ditch a kilometre from the Polish border. He had four thousand dollars on him, a passport and a near empty bottle of Stolichnaya Vodka. It seemed that he lost control of the jeep.

The major put down the phone and looked again at the ten five hundred dollar bills on the desk. The stupid old drunk had finally done for himself, but not without leaving a legacy for him. He picked up eight of the bills and put them in his shirt pocket, the other two he left with the note. He wondered how many the civil police had pocketed when they found the treacherous bastard. Then he called the army police, followed by Moscow and waited for the storm to start. Missing rockets, bribes and a dead deserting colonel: a big deal, too big for him to hide, or even want to.

It didn't take long. Fifteen minutes after he finished his last call two army police corporals had stationed themselves outside his office. He was asked, politely, not to leave unless it was with one or the other of them, and certainly not to use his telephone. He was escorted to the toilet at one stage where he carefully hid the $4,000 in the cistern – he knew enough to realise that the dollar bills were made of linen, not paper, so would not disintegrate. Ninety minutes after that an army police captain stood at the door to his office. The major ushered her in and pointedly did not offer vodka.

"So the colonel took fifty 122mm rockets, left you a note with a thousand dollars, and loaded them on to a civilian cargo flight bound for Moscow?" she said.

"That's it," said the major.

"I'm surprised you didn't just put the money in your pocket. Who would ever know?"

"I suspect that you would know, captain. The letter made it clear I was receiving something, it wasn't going to be a bottle of vodka."

"No," said the captain, eyeing him. "Is that all he left for you?"

"That was all," said the major, evenly.

"Your honesty is admirable, major. A thousand dollars can buy a great deal in Russia."

"I will admit that it was a temptation."

She looked down at the two five hundred bills on the major's desk and said, "Let me remove any further problem for you. I will take charge of the money."

"Of course," said the major. "You don't mind signing a receipt for it?"

The captain stared at him for a few seconds, long enough for the major to know what she was thinking, then she said, "Yes. It goes without saying."

It so often did, thought the major. Nevertheless his back was covered, he had four thousand dollars for no good reason, and his career remained untarnished. None of this could be laid at his door.

"What happens next?" he asked.

"Intelligence officers are coming out from Moscow, we have put the sergeant and the other nine men under orders not to move or talk to anyone except me and my staff." She fixed him with a gaze which in other circumstances might have been attractive, but on this occasion made him want to curl up into a corner and hide. "The same goes for you, Major. Nothing to anyone. We have a dead lieutenant colonel and fifty rockets which have disappeared from what should be an impregnable arsenal. I have had little time to make any inquiries but one thing has become clear: there was no order from anyone in Moscow to remove these weapons. We have investigators at Bhrakovo right now checking on the flight to see if it did go to Moscow. There is a flight plan, but you know what that is worth, and no evidence yet to substantiate that a cargo plane arrived in Moscow from that airfreight company. From what I am told the customs list shows a cargo flight going there but Polish Air Traffic Control says something else."

"What does it say?"

"Maraka."

"Maraka in the Gulf, a vodka spit from Iraq!"

She did not respond to that but said, "What was in the 122mm rockets, major?"

"Nothing worth having as far as I can tell. We didn't even have a launcher for them. They were made in the 1970s and were just being kept here because no one could think of anything else to do with them. They're useless as weapons. We never took off the warheads but the fuses and detonators will have corroded to dust. The tubes are so old the propellant should have leaked into the chambers years ago. They'll never be fired."

"All the more astonishing that the colonel would want to take them to a civilian airport and send them to the hottest, tensest, most dangerous place on the planet, then?"

She was correct in every detail. The major was stymied. He could not think of a logical theory to pull together the absurdity of what was happening. The colonel had obviously been bribed to provide a few dozen scrapped rockets, but for what possible purpose!

He looked at the captain and smiled for the first time that morning. It was ridiculous, after all.

"Maybe vodka will help us understand it," he said.

"Major, this is so strange that I think it may be the only thing which will help us make sense of it."

She took the proffered glass and allowed him to pour a generous measure of some unidentifiable clear liquid from a bottle. She was more used to Stolichnaya but she would humour him. He was obviously innocent, in more ways than one, she thought as she looked at the five hundred dollar bills again. They clinked glasses and drank.

August
Pursuit

The stricken Range Rover was no longer steaming. That was the only positive thing to have happened in the last 15 minutes, thought Hartson.

"You can't get away with that, Paul. They'll pack you up and put you on the very next plane."

"What was I supposed to do? Smile and say nothing? You saw that woman's body, just like I did." There was no getting away from that which made him even more exasperated. "Just remember where you are, will you: you're not in England, things work differently out here. You wanted to come. What did you think you'd find? Bexley Heath in the sunshine? It doesn't work like that. It's a hard, ruthless place. How do you think they hold on to their money?"

"I know how they keep their money. I do it for them, remember, I'm a banker." Hartson didn't know where to start or stop with Winter. He was a clown in so many ways, yet sophisticated in others. He continued with his lecture anyway: "Then you know normal rules don't apply. Stop pretending they do. Stop being so bloody English, there's no place for it out here." Winter fell silent and looked moodily at the Range Rover.

Hartson said, crisply: "Come on, get in! There's a place just up the road that specialises in heaps like this. Who did you buy it from, anyway?" Winter said nothing but reached sulkily for a business card above the steering wheel, then he threw it back. "It doesn't matter."

"You didn't think of asking someone who knows about these things first?" Winter stayed silent. "Car traders in England are dodgy enough, Paul. Do you think they're more honourable out here?" Winter reversed into the road and drove off with the engine roaring – it never purred. Temper, temper, thought Hartson. He glanced at the temperature gauge, it was in the red.

The cafe quietened, but behind a screen in the tiny staff area Michel and Anwar spoke earnestly in French. "Elle doit partir toute de suite, Michel." Michel replied that she could not leave straight away, she had nowhere else to go. "Tant pis, je n'ai plus d'espace. Appel-lui maintenant et lui dire de s'en aller." Too bad, she must get out. Call her now and tell her!

Michel gambled that the conversation in French could be vaguely heard but not understood by the cafe. His protestations came to nothing, Anwar had never been happy with her there, and now he knew about the death in the apartment he wanted nothing to do with it. Michel reached for the telephone and dialled Anwar's number.

Exit strategy

She was calmer but the frown remained. And now she was calculating. Hannah was dead. She knew the killer. She dared not even think his name for fear it would lead his cohorts of crooked policemen to her. He would never pay for this, he was too powerful. That was the way of things in Khafira. Justice was bought like everything else. Just like her. Justice for Hannah was out of reach. Anyway, why try? She was dead. Now was the time to count her takings, get the money and get out.

She had done well for 32 with no qualifications - except the obvious. Their clients were generous, and she had banked it all, unlike Hannah. Hannah was soft: good at sex, not business, she blew it on parties, cocaine and clothes.

But Jose had piled up ninety thousand US dollars. Her money was in a dollar account at the Middle Eastern Bank ready to shift anywhere in the world. It was safer there, she believed, away from prying eyes. She'd worked hard for it, and not always on her terms. There were things she'd done which she could never have told her mother – even if she was still alive. But anything was better than going back to the wreckage of her life in the Levant. Anything!

Ninety thousand US dollars was enough to get her out of Khafira, to make a start somewhere else, and not as an expensive prostitute. It was not too late to go to university to study law, the way she'd always wanted. There was a way out of it all if she could get through the next few days. But she had to get the money from the bank before leaving, and how the hell would she do that? Police were always at the bank, police were always at the airport, police were always at the Lagoon. They would be looking for her. She knew what had happened to Hannah – she was damned certain she knew. They couldn't afford for it to get out.

The phone rang. She shivered. She knew better than to pick up the receiver so she listened as the answering machine responded. She sat, heart pounding while the short message played out. Then she heard Michel.

"Prend l'appareil, Jose, c'est moi, Michel." Why must she pick up the phone?

"Depeche-toi! C'est tres important." He was speaking French, that meant he didn't want anyone close by to understand. She reached for the receiver. "Why are you calling?"

"Il faut en partir immediatement, Anwar connait l'histoire des immeubles." Anwar had found out about Hannah and the apartment?

"Did you say something?"

"Non, l'Anglais est venu au cafe. Il m'a vu." What Englishman? Then recognition, she had only met one in the last two weeks: *that* Englishman, the one in the souk. She froze in fear, where could she go now? No matter what she did or where she went Khafira had a way of finding out.

"Where do I go? I have only two hundred dirhams."

"Je viendrai a toi. Reste la. Peut etre nous pouvons aller chez moi." Your place! Wonderful, how relaxing, just what she needed right now, sharing a floor with cockroaches.

Michel walked out of the cafe without a glance to anyone, except Samir Latif who was busy with his phone anyway. Samir Latif finished his call and spoke to Anwar. "I hope Michel is all right, he is a good employee you know. I have always taken an interest in him." Anwar knew of his partner's interest in Michel, it was one which made him jealous sometimes but that was the way of the world. Anwar had the business-partner, Michel had the man, sometimes here the partner was more important, unless you were poor, and Michel rarely had money.

"It is just something we must clear up between ourselves. Michel has imposed a female guest upon me and my Lebanese hospitality has just run out." Latif looked serious for a moment then smiled, "You are a cafe proprietor Anwar, your hospitality must stay constant." They laughed together. "But of course, you Lebanese must stick together!" Samir Latif's smile receded and he returned to his newspaper and making telephone calls. Anwar looked on, uncomfortable with his dirty dishes, envious of his sponsor calling up millions while drinking coffee.

Winter had waited fifteen minutes but it felt more like three hours in his heightened state. Hartson twitched impatiently a few metres away. A man with black grease on his face and dirty overalls brought his head up from under the hood of the Range Rover, and told him the bad news. He needed a new hosepipe for the radiator...Oh, and he needed a new radiator, this one was for Northern Europe, massive tropical tanks were what they used out here, they stopped cars overheating. When could he have it? Tomorrow. Then fix the hose in the meantime, please! Winter waited, inspected the work, then paid the bill. The mechanic warned him: "Drive slowly, and don't go in desert. Wait for radiator tomorrow."

Winter waved away the irritating man, he'd had enough advice for one day. Hartson could not be so easily dismissed. "Take me back to my office now, Paul, I've got a lot to do." He sounded bored. But he often sounded that way.

Winter pulled away and headed back towards the Cafe De Bruxelles en route to Hartson's bureau. His speed was down to fifty kilometres an hour. What he didn't want, for all the world, was for it to backfire again so close to the place. He slowed even further to nurse it past and hoped no-one would look up as he passed. He stared intently at the smart facade. He had got within fifty metres of the cafe, when he saw the knifeman walk out. This time he kept himself under control. The man looked like he was in a hurry. He slowed to 10k and saw the man hail a cab.

"What are you doing now?" asked Hartson, impatiently.

"I'm going to follow him, Will. Now just shut up, please!" He was tired of being in his shadow all the time. He stepped on the throttle and followed the cab. "For fuck's sake, Paul, what do you think you're doing? You're not bloody James Bond. Stop this madness and take me to my office!" But Winter was having a rare moment of decision. He stayed at a discreet distance as they made a slow trail towards the commercial area. Here he was in familiar territory, the bank was in the middle of it. They drove straight through and on to the Lagoon where the man got out fifty metres before the bank. There was an old residential area close by. It was run down and belonged to the time when Khafira had no oil. This was the area where the inhabitants from lower down Khafira's social order lived. There were no gleaming automobiles, the women dressed in traditional Pakistani or Indian garb, the men simply wore cloth around their waists like wraparound skirts. Wherever the money went in Khafira, it didn't find a route to this place.

"So far, so good," said Winter. He looked directly at Hartson. "Are you coming?"

"What for?" replied the reporter, crossly.

"You're a journalist, I thought you might want to know what was going on." Hartson shrugged his shoulders, in truth he wanted to knock this whole nonsense on the head and if he could do the same to Winter it would be a double victory. But he would never get any peace until it was sorted so he affirmed: "OK."

Winter parked the car by a music store – it looked rough enough to be safe here. They walked to where they'd seen the man disappear. Winter felt more determined about this than anything he could recall. He was going to find out once and for all. What more could he be afraid of? He was already a murder suspect and he was learning fast that justice here didn't mean fairness.

They waited for two minutes in the shade of an overhanging concrete balcony. There was a perfect view of the Lagoon. An old wooden dhow glided past on its way into the Gulf.

Hartson's patience was all but gone: "Are we going to be here much longer, Paul? I have a lot to do."

"I don't know how you can be so blasé. I want some answers. Please humour me."

Hartson slumped back against the wall and sighed heavily. Winter's gaze had been distracted and as he turned around he jumped. Two people were running towards them from the old town: two very familiar people. She wasn't wearing the same clothes but he'd seen her often enough at the apartments to know, she was unmistakable.

"That's her, Will, that's the woman."

The reporter pushed himself off from the wall, newly alert.

"She doesn't look very dangerous to me," he said. By now they were forty metres away. "Nor does he come to that."

"Try saying that with a knife at your throat," said Winter, tired of the reporter's casual dismissal of his fear.

"I'm quite happy as I am thank you."

Ten metres away the couple's steps faltered. Winter tensed, ready for a knife. The banker braced himself for the worst. But it didn't happen the way he feared. Instead, In broken English the man growled, "You have done enough. We are all in danger now because of you. Leave us alone!"

The woman spoke menacingly: "Why are you always following me?" She turned to Hartson. "Who are you?"

"I'm just along for the ride," said Hartson, breezily. Winter, emboldened by Hartson's presence said defiantly: "I want to know why you nearly killed me in the souk?"

Hartson was weary of the whole business. He'd tagged along with Winter because he felt some responsibility towards him – although God knows why! Now he was pissed off with this silly little Englishman act. All right, he'd stumbled across a whore and her pimp in the souk and had a knife drawn on him. Well, so bloody what! He was still alive wasn't he, he hadn't even been touched. He'd just walked into the real world for once and he didn't know what to do in it. Start bloody swimming, he thought. Then he spoke: "Paul, this is enough. You're fixated. Just leave them alone, this isn't Surbiton, or wherever it is you come from, it's life in the raw in the Middle East."

The banker didn't seem to hear anything. He just stared at the whore with the frozen mouth.

"Are you listening, Paul?"

Winter ignored again but this time said, with what he hoped would be venom, "And what about your friend in the apartment? That wasn't a pretty sight to greet me."

The trouble was that he didn't have the venom in him, no matter how hard he snarled and spat out his words, he was still Paul Winter, the affable banker from Surrey. Hartson couldn't help himself. He laughed at his companion. No one else joined in, not even the whore who now unfroze her mouth.

"Why were you in my apartment, Englishman?" she said with eyes that would teach a snake its business.

There it was. He didn't have an answer. He was lost. All she'd done was look at him accusingly and ask him a question, and the silly sod was sunk. What was he doing out here in the heat and confusion? He should be at home being miserably late on a train from Waterloo. That was the world he belonged in.

The woman's gaze was unwavering and unnerving; Hartson studied her more closely. She was pretty and hard, obviously. Could she kill? Anyone could kill. But she looked and sounded too clever for that. Anyway she was scared. Something had happened in that apartment, something big enough to interest Colonel Ali Abdul Hamid. Why should he care about a dead prostitute, even if he knew her?

The air was pierced by the loudspeakers of an adjacent mosque as it went into the overture for the call to prayer. Five seconds later another opened up, and another after that. The old walls echoed and repeated the cacophony which was a symphony of sorts – but not to their ears.

Hartson raised his voice above the noise hoping to impose himself on the situation: "Why is Colonel Hamid so interested in your dead friend? What do you know?" The woman turned her eyes on him and he felt their chill. Then they shifted again. He glanced at the man and saw his eyes had moved away as well and were now contorted with panic. He turned to see what had caused it. He saw a two-tone green Mercedes with a flashing red light on top. It was a hundred metres away and moving at a leisurely Gulf pace. Without another word the man thrust the woman's hand into Hartson's and shouted to her, "Go with him, they mean no harm, I am sorry!"

Hartson turned to ask why, but already the man was gone. The woman stared after him with her mouth agape. Then she withdrew her hand and yelled, "Get me out, now!"

There was no time for questions and certainly no use asking Winter to have an original thought. Hartson dragged them both to the Range Rover. He bundled her inside, climbed into the driver's seat and turned the key. It started first time. He mouthed a silent prayer then shouted at his new charge to get her head down. He wiped a veneer of sweat from his brow as he tried to keep calm. He engaged first gear and pulled away. Another dribble of sweat tracked down his eyes, his cheek and off the end of his chin. He was too busy to care. He looked in his rear view mirror. He was not pleased to see the police car emptying into the area from where they had just come. What the fuck was he getting into!

He could make out a familiar figure in the mirror and went cold; Colonel Hassan, the Port Police boss, even nastier than Hamid. What was he doing there at exactly that time? And the second time in the space of an hour that he had come into the reporter's life. None of the men in uniform seemed to notice the receding Range Rover, they had no need, it had only just come into Paul Winter's hands and he assumed they weren't looking for it – or were they? He drove at a sedate speed to avoid being noticed, regularly keeping his eye on the speedometer. He watched the temperature gauge, the rear view mirror, the road. The woman cowered in the well of the passenger seat, Winter was slumped in the back. If the radiator overheated again he would have to stop; he prayed to his non-existent god that the replacement radiator hose would hold. There might be police behind or in front - and what the hell was this whore doing here anyway!

"Are they following us?" she asked, in a shaky voice from beneath the dashboard. It was barely audible against the sound of the sick engine. Hartson looked down. "No, not as far as I can see." She wore a pair of cream roomy slacks and a long sleeved red cotton blouse. There was a strong smell of perfume, expensive Hartson guessed, although he was no expert. But there was no hiding the shine on her face; no amount of make-up could beat the combination of heat and fear, and the Range Rover's useless air-conditioning wasn't helping. Hartson was sweating in fountains. He had a fugitive call girl and a shaking banker in a beaten up old Range Rover, which should have been scrapped years ago. He looked in the mirror and saw Winter sweating and breathing hard.

"Why have you got it in for my friend in the back? What did he do?" he said to the hunched figure in the passenger well.

"Shut up and drive, you stupid man."

He hit the brakes hard, there was a screech of tyres on hard tarmac, just the sort of noise to draw attention. He knew he shouldn't have done it but if there was one thing he hated it was being given orders by someone he didn't know.

"I'll put you out right here in the middle of the road if you don't tell me. Who are you? What are you running from?" He looked ahead at the road. There was no reply.

All right, let's try something else, he thought.

"Why was your flatmate killed?"

"Drive, now!" she commanded, uselessly.

"For fuck's sake, drive, Will!" said Winter, from behind.

Hartson stayed still. The more he was ordered about, the less inclined he was to obey. Finally the woman said: "Very well, *I will tell you*, but get me *out of here!*"

"Please do as she says, Will," whimpered the banker, "It's dangerous stopping in the middle of the road."

"Welcome back, Paul."

He put the car into gear and pulled away.

"So what's it all about, *madam*?"

He looked down into the well again and met a gaze of pure vitriol; she didn't like him at all

"I am Jose Badradini, I live in the Al Kifaf Apartments," she said, coldly. "I am avoiding the police because my friend Hannah has been killed."

"And you had nothing to do with it?" said Hartson, in his best sceptical tone.

"Of course not."

"Then why are you hiding from the police?"

There was silence for a few seconds. Then, "I cannot tell you."

He made no effort to disguise his sarcasm. "OK, Jose Badradini, I believe you, so does my friend in the back. Don't you, Paul."

"Stop joking, Will, we've got to do something with her."

They made a strange couple in the car: her cold and spitting, him hot and fretful. She must have something about her. Hookers usually wound up washed up dead on the Khafira beach if they crossed the locals. She'd managed to survive the Russians and their pimps, and still flourish. People in high places, he guessed, that was the Khafira way. He looked in the mirror, saw the banker squirming on the back seat and decided he'd had enough for now. He doubted very much if Jose Badradini had killed her friend, certainly not the way the covered corpse had been described to him. But he had things to do today: big things. She would only complicate them. He knew he couldn't take her to his place and she certainly couldn't go back to the Al Kifaf Apartments. So Winter would have to take her somewhere else. He'd catch up later and find out what this mess was about. Right now his In Tray was stacking up: four bodies and a bit of arms trading needed his undivided attention. And then there was Diana Ffrench Parsons – maybe his In-Out Tray. Strange, yesterday he'd been searching for some action. Today he wished it would stop coming.

He found a lay-by, pulled over and stopped the car.

"What are you doing?" asked the woman.

"I'm going to catch a cab back to reality, Jose Badradini. Your friend Paul can continue driving you in this nightmare." He looked down into the well. She was scared! Only for a moment, quickly masked by a scowl, but he saw it. And with Colonel Hassan sniffing at her tail, she would have good reason. He softened. "Don't worry, no one's followed us, you're safe for the moment. Stay where you are. Paul, get out of the back and drive the car."

"Why, what are you doing?"

"I've told you. Do what I say."
He opened the door of the Range Rover and stepped out onto a tiny street, deserted in the seering sun. Paul took his place at the wheel.
"Take her to Maraka, they won't look there, not officially anyway! Put her in a hotel."
"What do I use for money?"
Stupid question.
"You're the banker, surely you can think of something sensible. How about credit cards? Just think for yourself Paul, you're going to have to. I can't keep doing it for you."
Winter said no more but got into the driver's seat, put the car in gear and drove away. He didn't even say farewell.
The chief Gulf correspondent for Randalls International News Agency stood in the ferocious sun watching the car drive off and hoping a cab would come quickly. This was a bloody good yarn, but he could never tell it. Hamid or Hassan would have him thrown out the same day – or possibly worse. And who would care: a Lebanese prostitute murdered by who knows whom, a Brit falsely in the frame? It wouldn't make more than an inch on an inside page. So he abandoned them to their fate while he got on with the job of Diana Ffrench Parsons. Sod it, he couldn't hold the man's hand forever!
A cab miraculously appeared in the still-deserted street. He got in and drank in the cool, air-conditioned air gratefully.

May
Maraka

Three dusty white trucks drew alongside a beaten-up dhow in the Maraka Lagoon. A customs man was standing by it but only to keep others away. Barracuda had paid him well. He would not look, he would not even ask, he would simply stand there and stamp the form when told he could. The dhow was used to bring in rosewood furniture from Mumbai. It was a sturdy craft capable of carrying heavy loads. The wooden crates with their ageing rockets would be nothing for them. Barracuda ordered his men to unload the wooden crates from the trucks. Then he told the four Filipino boys to get into the hold to stack them. Once he'd got the boys off the quayside, they were his, he could keep them. They would be a present for The Shark, he could leave them on the yacht for a special treat and his ally could do what he wanted with them. Who would ever miss four Filipino boys in the Gulf for god's sake! Maybe their mother, but who was going to care about her?

It took over ninety minutes to load everything. As the final crates went on board Barracuda jumped up and went into the hold. "Thanks boys," he said. "You've been a real help. I just need you for a couple more hours then you can go home and be rich for the rest of the year." One of the boys wearing a crucifix said, "Isn't this the end of the job, sir?"

"Not quite."

Another tried to push past Barracuda saying, "I cannot stay any longer. I must return to my home." Barracuda stayed motionless, didn't even need to raise a hand. The boy just slid off him and back into the hold. Three more Barracudas joined him and the boys became sullenly quiet. They stared at the floor as the door to the hold was sealed. Barracuda indicated to four of the team on the dockside to go. They got into the trucks and his pickup and drove away. He would meet them later a hundred miles down the coast in the dead of night. The remaining two Barracudas stayed on the dhow. He went up to the wheelhouse and told the captain to move out. The man understood very little English but enough to obey a simple command. The dhow took half an hour to clear the lagoon. The captain spoke in Arabic constantly to the harbour controller on his radio. Barracuda knew he couldn't hope to imitate that but he could study the workings of the craft as the skilled helmsman took her out through the shallows just outside the lagoon and into deeper water. The captain pointed at a dirty chart on the wheelhouse table.

"Where?" he said.

Barracuda wrote some co-ordinates on the map and quickly plotted them.

"No problem," said the skipper. "Three hours. You pay then!"

"Sure," said Barracuda, smiling as he continued to watch the way the boat was handled. If there was one thing he'd learned about in his long years adventuring it was how to work seagoing vessels. He'd even taken lessons on a Chinese junk for the hell of it. This wouldn't be a great deal different when it came to it. He cast his eyes over the decks to check the crew numbers: five at most, and the boys in the hold. They would be easy, he could get rid of them after the crates were transferred to The Shark. He hoped to hell the man wasn't making a circus out of it, it would be just like him and this was not the time.

The captain smiled as he ploughed on deeper into the Gulf.

Barracuda smiled back.

August
Conscience

Phil Wilkinson was a naval man through to his toenails. He knew it wasn't a clever idea to rock the boat, but he had also been brought up to know the difference between right and wrong. He lived in a changing world, what was wrong yesterday was sometimes right today. But he was certain some things stayed wrong forever, murder being one of them. He emerged from Tom Scott-Garrett's office at the embassy with the diplomat's words still jangling dissonantly in his ears: "Nothing more to look at, Phil, they got cut up in a water skiing accident." Tragedy but not ours to worry about!"

There was something in Scott-Garrett's manner that told him that his objections – injuries, concrete weights, distance from the shore – would not be welcomed. The diplomats had decided that something was more important than the fate of these poor souls. But what water skiing game puts concrete blocks on the feet!

The commander had a conscience which would not easily be silenced by the pragmatism of diplomatic necessity. Right now, he wanted to be in command of his own ship, setting his own course and leaving the devils at the Foreign Office to work their black magic somewhere else. He knew this was a job he had to do if he hoped to make to Rear Admiral – and he wanted that – but not at the cost of his soul.

He left the embassy without a word to anyone and headed for the port, still furious. He was not wearing uniform but followed the rules. The commodore greeted him with a knowing smile. He reported everything he had heard at the embassy meeting.

"Bit of a bugger isn't it, Phil!"

"Yes sir."

"Are you sure you should have broken your chain of command to tell me? You're serving two masters – or riding two horses, or playing both sides...pick any one!"

"I'm a navy man sir. This cover-up stuff doesn't suit me. Don't think I'm not aware of what we have to do but I always thought we stood for something. The fact is those poor lads were murdered, not chopped up by a speedboat propeller."

"Phil, I don't like it either – and I saw the bodies - but you'd better learn to swim with the sharks. Remember, their world isn't the same as ours...and we're in their world." Wilkinson fell silent. "Go and have a drink, Phil, I'll see what I can do to keep Sam Jackson quiet for the time being."

Unwanted company

Paul Winter knew how to have a good time, just ask his chums at the rugby club back in Surrey! He was the first to put on the women's clothes at the annual dinner, the first to jump fully clothed into the swimming pool, and the first to lead the singing with whatever dubious lyrics came into his head. He was bright, not very deep, and thoroughly accustomed to his South East England way of life of late trains, dinner parties and extended stag weekends with his associates. He liked women, had fun with them, sometimes even relationships, but knew very little about them. If he had more depth he might have realised that his normal behaviour only tested the outer limits of his morality. Because that's what he was, deep down, where his thoughts would probably never reach, a moral man! He believed in loyalty and following the code, he just didn't know why. His world was defined by figures and graphs, rules and regulations, being told what to do, being in the tribe. Now he faced a dilemma. He could do one of two things: throw her out right here on the main road near the hotel strip, or drive her straight to a police station. One was self-preservation, the other might be the right thing to do, or it might not.

He was a law-abiding man, of course he was. He broke the occasional rule like driving after drinking more than he should, and speeding of course. The odd traffic cone in his younger days had wound up in the rugby club rogues trophy cabinet – but that was expected. All the same, he thought, he had a duty to society, to help the police. He also believed that if someone was innocent of a crime then the evidence would prove that soon enough. He believed the system worked, that police and courts got it right and were a force for good. That comfort allowed him to get on with his banking job and do the things middle class people are supposed to do. Why shouldn't the same rules apply in Khafira? So he couldn't see why the fierce, terrified woman cowering in the seat well next to him wanted to run when she could sort it out very easily by telling her story to the police. He would tell her, do the honourable thing, but that's where they should go. He pointed the Range Rover towards the central zone.

"Where are you taking me?" she demanded, ridiculously, still from the passenger seat well.

He replied in a high-pitched squeak which fought against the growl of the engine. The police should sort this out, it had nothing to do with him and hadn't that colonel warned him! "Straight to the police. I don't know if it was you who killed your friend, or someone else. But I'm sure you know something about it. I've done nothing. I don't want you in my car any longer."

She screamed: "You can't do that."

"Why, are you going to kill me as well?" He surprised himself with his defiance.

"I haven't killed anyone," she responded coldly, the anger gone as quickly as it flared.

"So who killed your friend?"

"Not me, I just found her there. She was already dead."

Winter glanced down. She looked preposterous but that could not hide her cold ferocity. He turned back to look at the road, he couldn't concentrate if he looked at her. "Good story, why not tell it to the police? I had the pleasure of finding your friend."

"So did I. I can thank you for the police trailing me can I?"

"Nothing to do with me," he countered with false defiance, "Anyway, if you have nothing to hide you have nothing to fear."

The woman sank down further into the seat well and looked down. He could see her sighing but he couldn't hear it, the engine noise smothered the sound. He checked his gauge again, the motor was still growling. The heat was rising inside, though. He was getting damper. His light cotton shirt wasn't enough to contain it. He looked down again, she was sodden with sweat, defeated. So, she may be the boss in the bedroom, but she wasn't here. He was in command now. She looked up again, newly energised, a fire lit up the eyes in her glistening face.

"If you surrender me to the police I will be dead and disposed of within forty eight hours."

"You know they don't have the death penalty here."

"You do not seriously suppose I will go in front of a court do you!"

"Yes, why ever not?"

She shouted back, angrily: "Because I know too much. Because there is no law here, just whatever the sheikhs will allow."

"That's not true. I know how tough the laws are, and how fair. Women have equal rights in Khafira; they work alongside me. I should know."

"Only if their families allow it. My God you must be British. You still think there is a rule of law."

What did that mean? A Toyota Landcruiser pulled up alongside and its driver gazed in and smiled. The girl bunched up even tighter in the well. He pretended to watch the workmen on the roundabout planting flowers, cutting grass, digging holes, checking water supplies. They drove on, the Landcruiser spurted ahead, Winter put his foot down to catch it, then realised what he was doing and eased back. He looked down into the well again.

"Surely you can prove you're innocent. You can't have anything to fear."

"I have everything to fear. I know who really did it, I know who she was seeing that afternoon, I saw him come in and have a drink. I cannot be allowed to live."

"You're exaggerating."

"You stupid Englishman, you just don't see do you. They make the law whatever they want to here. There are no electors, no one is accountable."

She was well versed, but what did he know about prostitutes?

He listened, his foot eased on the throttle. He thought again about going to the police.

"Then why bother to have a law at all?"

"Window dressing. It keeps western governments happy if they appear to have a caring face. They may be oil rich but they still have to deal with the rest of the world."

"You're making it up to get me to help you."

She went quiet again and raised her head above the level of the side window. The time was twelve thirty, the temperature in the Range Rover was almost unbearable. They passed some workmen by the roadside digging foundations for a new building.

"There you are Mr Englishman. Look at them."

"So what!"

"You know that there is a temperature above which outside workers are not allowed to work?" No he didn't know that. "It is forty seven degrees. If it gets any higher they must stop because it is said to be too dangerous."

"What's your point?"
"What does the temperature gauge say on your wreck of a car?"
It read 52 degrees. Must be a mistake. There was a digital clock a hundred metres further down the road, it gave alternate time of day and temperature readings. "Well you can see clearly enough," said Winter, "It's forty six point five. I still don't see what you're getting at."
"Look again at your car thermometer you stupid man."
"It must be wrong. The whole car is screwed up."
"It is 52 degrees, Englishman, believe me!"
"But I heard the weather forecast, it said forty six."
"From the government's own meteorological office."
"And this device here?" he said indicating the clock outside.
"Altered not to read beyond forty six and a half." He was dumbfounded. "Can you not see that they have no concerns about the health of these workers, they just want them to do the work. They are Filipinos and Baluchis, why would these men care about them?"
"All right, what does any of this have to do with the dead woman in your apartment."
"Nothing, I am just showing you how they will happily break their own laws if it suits them. The law is whatever they say it is."
Doubt started crept in. "If you didn't kill her who did?"
She breathed in deeply, and muttered almost inaudibly above the engine, "Are you sure you want to know?"
"I'm being accused of it, you're bloody right I want to know."
"You don't believe anything else I say, why should you believe me now?"
He wanted to shout at her. He was boiling over. It had been a crap two days. Crap! Crap! Now she was playing games with him. "Just fucking...." the command died in his throat as he routinely checked his rear view mirror and saw what he had least wanted to see, a flashing red police light.

Bedroom diplomacy

"Dry or medium," asked Diana Ffrench-Parsons. She moved around her comfortable apartment with a silky ease. What was happening here! Why him, why now?
And there was warmth in her voice.

"Dry, thanks."

He watched her move in her compact sexy way. She was a middle-ranking diplomat and qualified for a place in a decent walled compound: a few palm trees, verandas and gardens. Hartson relaxed into his cane chair and accepted the drink, ice cool, from Diana's lingering hand. Yes, it was *lingering*. She was dressed informally. Her long brown hair was loose, she wore light baggy trousers and a thin cotton top. Her breasts weren't a prominent feature but he could detect clearly that she wasn't wearing a bra.

She sat down beside him, smiled and took a sip. So did he.

"I give up, Diana, I have to ask: why are you entertaining me here? I'm the enemy?"

She smiled, conspiratorially: "It's always a good idea to know your enemy, Will. Anyway, we're all Brits together, aren't we?" The last phrase was ironic, he got that. She cast her eyes down; submissively, he wondered? "I just thought if we got to know each other better we could help each other out now and again."

What now: play this out as two artificial conversations, or confront her directly? He opted for provocation: "You mean you'd give me embassy secrets?" Not that he believed that for a moment. She smiled at the same time as pulling back a few inches. "Hardly. I'm too junior to know many."

"And what would I give you?"

"You're well positioned at the Majlis. Sheikh Issa knows you, even likes you. He may tell you more than we can find out ourselves." Now that was a surprise. If anyone was well positioned with Sheikh Issa it was Diana, he thought. What could he get to know that she couldn't? How could he put it delicately?

"I thought your connections were at least as good as mine, Diana."

A rueful smile played across her eyes. "I'm a woman, Will. It's true that my access is quite good." He smiled back. "But you've been out here long enough to know how a woman fares in this Arab world." Good enough.

"So what exactly do I get in return?" he said.

"Reliable information."

"Like what?"

She sipped her wine, gazed out to the pool and beyond. It was darkening quickly. "Like those bodies."

"Yes."

"Rich men's playthings, flung overboard when the bastards had finished with them."

He sipped his drink for a few moments. "How do you know?"

"We know they were beaten up and they had concrete attached to their feet; you got that right. You may not know that the port police virtually hijacked them on their way back to shore on the commodore's tender. They weren't meant to be seen again…and they weren't."

"Interesting. But how do you make the link with the rich men's pleasures?

"Big pressure from the sheikhs to shut it down. That only ever means it's them or their friends."

"Can I quote you?" It was a joke, she didn't take it that way. Her cool went. "Don't you dare! This is strictly off the record. I'd be sent home. And if you print that the same will happen to you, Will." So there was the catch.

"You trust me not to use it then?"

"Common sense tells me you daren't." She was right. If they were rich they were friends of at least one sheikh.

"So why tell me?"

"I believe in being well-informed, so do you. That's how we do our jobs. If you file a story you want it to be right – and so do we…although we might not like the story being filed in the first place, of course. Will, I believe these are called back-channels, informal but frank exchanges between people who should not normally mix."

"So you've been put up to this? You're slumming it."

"Actually, no, but there are those who think lying to you is the right way to go and I went along with it. But look what happened, you got the story anyway so we look silly and your trust in us has gone. I think it's counterproductive and will backfire on us."

"So you will give me what you know?"

"As much as I can without endangering diplomatic interest."

"Just one more thing…which rich men are you talking about…"

Without pausing for breath, she said: "Have you had enough wine? Can we go to bed now?" Now that's the way to throw a man right of balance, thought Hartson. Why him? Will Hartson from Warwick University, a drinking adventurer with a distaste for physical risk and a reporter. With her, double first from Cambridge, diplomatic high-flyer, ambassador-material? Wasn't this a classic diversion?

"Sure," he responded, hoping the tremor within was not betrayed by is voice. Her intelligent eyes widened in a smile unmistakable in its intent. No irony, no teasing, it was really going to happen; he was about to conquer Miss North Pole, the unscaled peak! Or was she conquering him? She put her glass on a table and took his hand. "I hope you don't mind this Will, It seems a good way of coming to an understanding." So this is what it's like to be used, he thought. Not so bad, really!

"Why me, Diana? I thought you went for the high flyers."

"I go for whomever I want, Will." He smiled at the grammatical correctness Her finger pressed against his lips, to be replaced immediately by her mouth. If icebergs melted that quickly the world would be under water in a matter of minutes. Distraction therapy again, Will. Get on with it!

"And you want me?" he asked her, directly still not believing.

"Yes."

She kissed him again, her arms were around his shoulders. He'd never been especially impressed with his physique, it was all right but he was no Adonis, hundreds of pints, bottles and glasses had sculpted him another way. She didn't seem to mind. He returned her caresses, first her back, then her hips. Then he cupped a small breast through her cotton blouse, the nipple was hard, he started to breathe heavily. God this was good. The blouse came off and dropped to the floor in a tidy heap, what else would it be, this was the prim and neat Diana Ffrench Parsons. His hands felt the full warmth of her. She pushed them aside but only to force her own through his thin cotton shirt and on to his chest. He was now as hard as oak. Her hand drifted down and felt the erection straining at his trousers.

If there was one thing Diana had learned about men it was that if you had them by the balls their hearts and minds were bound to follow. Now she had Will, and he was about to have her. It was an entirely satisfactory relationship. Sheikhs were fine, and ambassadors at a pinch. She was drawn to the power and the exoticness. But that was the catch, it had to be on their terms. She rarely came from those encounters feeling satisfied. There could be surprising tenderness, but not a great deal of care. And most of the time she would accept that.

But she'd always been attracted by the other side of the tracks, and that was Will: redbrick university, clever, not governed by her rules, everything she would want to be if she could run a parallel life. A rogue, even a bit of a coward, but that didn't matter, she wasn't going to marry him. She encouraged his hand on to her. He reached down the front of her briefs, and found the spot. He massaged it gently, she felt herself moistening. She loved it like this, it was ever so slightly forbidden. She was letting him into her castle.

He explored her moistness, she felt his hardness against her, holding back. Good. She led him on to the bed, her briefs and baggy slacks were placed on top of the cotton blouse. She looked at the neat pile before pushing his head down gently to her lap. She hoped he would get the hint. He did. She lay back and let him massage her with his tongue. This was good, better than for a very long time. It was on her terms. She didn't get this with the sheikh, he didn't care to explore her. Often enough she'd be turned on by the power, anyway. But it wasn't her power.

She started to move with the rhythm of his tongue. She reached a short climax, but didn't make too much of it. She knew there'd be more tonight. She'd been eyeing him for a while. They shared something: he was prepared to lie and cheat to get what he wanted, and so was she. But the pull came from the contrast, his disregard for rules. He jumped right across them if they got in the way. His mind was effervescent and lateral. She admired that. It was so different to the propriety of the Diplomatic Service.

She shuddered, let out a gasp, her legs jerked up and sideways. That was good. He continued working at her coalface but she reached down and lifted his head, she wanted him inside her. He was so good at taking hints. Maybe they'd do this again. He pulled himself up and began to wipe his mouth but she stopped him with her hand. She wanted to taste her juices on his lips as he entered her. How wicked. How wonderful.

It was worth a few embassy tidbits, provided he kept his word as well.

May
Open Seas

The dhow was four hours out of Maraka, the coastline of the emirate and its neighbour, Khafira, was now just a hint on the horizon. They were in the middle of the Gulf and their destination was ahead, gleaming in the afternoon sun. It must have been stifling below deck in the hold but that wasn't his concern. The Filipino boys would soon be somewhere else. The captain pointed ahead and said, "There?" Barracuda nodded. He'd spent the time watching the captain and now had a good notion of how the vessel worked. He checked the diesel tanks and they were half full, they used no more than an eighth of their supply despite ploughing out at full speed. So, there was more than enough to get them back and into the hideaway he'd marked out earlier where the trucks would be waiting. Now came the hard part: transferring the rockets at sea from the decks of a dhow to the hold of a yacht. It was a calm day which was good, but there were fifty of them and they couldn't afford for any to go overboard. They'd be found by minesweeping sonars and then where would they be! They came alongside the large vessel and tied on. The captain cut the motor and let his dhow be secured to the yacht. Barracuda beckoned him down to the hold.

"You help us unload," he said.

"Money," said the captain.

"When we have finished," said Barracuda.

Barracuda saw the Shark standing at the rail of his boat looking down on them with a big grin. Merlin was standing by his side, expressionless. Merlin's face never had an expression, he was incapable of feeling, thought Barracuda, not even blind rage. Never mind, he did his job and he served his purpose. He wondered what the chemist ever got out of all the money he and the Shark put his way, though. He didn't appear to care about men or women, didn't drink and had no interest in sports or gambling. The only life he had was making bad things to do harm somewhere.

"Barracuda, my friend, you are here. Come aboard and bring your cargo! I will have the port doors opened," said The Shark, expansively, as he always was. Barracuda looked down to his left where, already, two custom built hydraulic sea doors were opening in the hull. That at least would mean they could pass the missiles from the deck straight into the bowels of the ship.

He wasted no time on pleasantries but set his men, the crew, and the Filipinos, to transferring the crates. It took an hour. The sea doors closed again. The Shark appeared again on the top deck, with two buckets of something foul smelling in his hands. "Now, My friend, this has been completed, perhaps we can enjoy ourselves with a little shark fishing before you return with your crew."

"Good idea," said Barracuda. The captain of the dhow looked at him suspiciously but Barracuda held up a wad of five hundred dollar notes and a smile spread right across the man's face."

"OK," he said, "We will wait."

Yes, you will, thought Barracuda as the Shark chucked the two buckets of chum bait into the water. Sharks from 30 kilometres away would pick it up and would come, it would take only a short while before they got there, maybe 25 minutes. The captain clutched his new fortune and grinned at his crew. They all grinned back. The Shark spoke to them in Arabic, "Come aboard my friends, may God be with you, enjoy my hospitality for a short while!"

"Shokharan," said the skipper as he and his crew moved towards the ladder.

They never got that far. The other barracudas and their leader caught all six before they had a chance to turn their backs. They were rendered unconscious by heavy blows to the back of the neck. Barracuda retrieved the bundle of five hundred dollar notes from the captain and left it to his associates to tie up the crew. None of them moved, they might not even come round before it was time to throw them overboard, he thought. Too bad, they had enough to do without waiting for that little pleasure. "Good work," called The Shark, "They will be with us very soon. But you appear to have left some untouched," he added, pointing to the Filipino boys. Barracuda smiled and said, "They're a present for you, Shark. I know about your Arab hospitality, enjoy them at your leisure."

"You are more than generous, Barracuda. Let us get you all aboard and relaxed. As you see, Merlin is here, and so are his special requirements." Barracuda had expected nothing less. Merlin magicked up his ingredients wherever he was. Barracuda knew enough about Mustard agent to guess that they wouldn't have been too hard to find. Hydrogen, carbon, chlorine and sulphur. Merlin had told him the name and he'd remembered it: Bis(2-chloroethyl)disulfide. He was fucked if he knew how the bag of chemicals

would turn into the sadistic blistering agent, but that wasn't his department.
 He indicated to the other Barracudas to throw the still breathing bodies of the dhow crew overboard. It took them two minutes. Not one of his men hesitated. Barracuda looked out in the bright haze to see what had arrived. Already the sharp outline of a dorsal fin had broken the surface two hundred metres away. He turned his back and climbed the ladder. The others could bring up the Filipino boys. It was a shame that he hadn't tied ribbons around them for the Shark.
 Never mind, it's the thought that counts.

August
Chase

The police siren pierced her senses. She could see the red flashing light reflecting from the rear view mirror on to the Englishman's eyes. The image strobed straight into her, sending her heart racing. She tightened even more into a ball under the dashboard and wished it would all go away. How could she hide now? She would be dead within twenty-four hours. Bastard, Michel, why did he have to desert her? He had always been a coward. And to leave her in the charge of this stupid Englishman. She fought down a scream.

The Range Rover slowed. The Englishman spoke, shakily she thought; that would not help. "They're chasing us, I haven't a hope of outrunning them in this." His eyes moved to the instrument panel. She couldn't see what he was checking. "How many of them are there?" she asked, the sounds coming from high in her throat. "I can't tell. I can only see one." The Range Rover stopped, so did the siren. She could not see what was happening, she could only read the reactions on his face.

"One of them is getting out of the car," he said. "He's reaching to his side." Pause, "He's coming to the car."

"Aren't there any more?" There should be more than one. "They're probably covering us from hidden positions." Did this man want to scare her into a coma? She shrivelled even tighter into her ball.

"He's here."

She wanted to cover up her ears with her hands and pretend none of it was happening. She heard the sound of an electric motor in the door. The window wound down partially. She bit her thigh hard. Winter wound down his window so that it was half open. Now was his chance to be rid of her, to hand her over. But he didn't take that chance. He was beginning to learn about the way it worked here. Instead he took another chance, an uncharacteristic risk, a leap into danger...and it was frightening. "Good evening," he said, in apologetic English.

"Alikum a sala'am." The policeman smiled. "Your licence please."

Winter reached into a pocket and pulled out a plastic card with his photograph. He presented it through the window and waited, hoping the officer hadn't seen his hand shaking. He prayed it was in order, he had never bothered to decipher its mysterious Arabic symbols.

An age passed, another policeman was walking around the vehicle inspecting it. He kept his eyes strictly level away from the foot well. Finally the licence was handed back. "Be careful how you drive, Mr Winter. There is a speed limit even in Khafira."
"Thank you, I will be more careful."
He started the engine, waited for a few seconds while the police car pulled away, then he did the same. "I wasn't speeding," he said. There was a sneer in her reply: "It's not why they stopped you. They're searching, but not for you. My god we came within centimetres of me being found…" She wasn't going to thank him then. "Where to now?" he muttered trying to control himself. There was no reply. He looked down. She had unfolded from her ball and was slumped against the door. For a moment he thought she'd fainted.
"Anywhere that is not a police station." She said eventually.

May
Mustard

"This will take days," said Merlin. "I can't prepare enough agent to fill fifty rockets in five minutes. We'll have to dismantle the heads and reassemble them as well." Barracuda held a bottle of cold water, misty with condensation, in his left hand. His right was on Merlin's shoulder. He knew that if that's what the chemist said, it was what he meant. Merlin never bluffed and he'd made his own calculations based on the same criteria. Once he'd seen the condition of the 122-milimetre rockets he knew it would take a while. They clearly hadn't been serviced in years. Each warhead would have to be carefully opened and its detonator disarmed before they could start to empty them – assuming that everything hadn't crumbled to an unstable mess inside.

"I know, Merlin," he said. "They were the best we could come up with in the time. They had to be untraceable and look like the real thing. And we had to have them yesterday. If our paymasters had anything to do with it they'd already have been found seven days ago." Merlin grunted then said, with no irony at all, "Have you ever considered attempting the possible for a change. Life might be easier?" Barracuda smiled. No, he hadn't. He didn't want a simple life. He wanted it filled with impossibility and hardness.

"Do what you have to do, Merlin. I figured we'd have to leave some on board for you to finish while we go in with the first batch. Give me 30 to get started with. We'll pick up the other twenty in a few days."

"Sure," said Merlin. "I'll get the cleanest looking rockets first."

Barracuda left him in the bowels of the ships working his evil arts. Merlin was only part of the preparation. They would need to paint over the Russian symbols with a series of fake Arabic serial numbers. No one could expect to decipher them, or even would want to. It was what was in the nose cones that mattered.

He waited while Merlin separated the warheads from the rest of the casings, the Shark looked on. "Why not repaint the whole rocket each time?" he asked. "They've got to look as if they've been around for a while. We'll brush off any rust on the outside. They really don't look all that bad until you examine them up close. Anyway, we don't have time. Barracuda felt himself beginning to erupt and, for once, held himself in check. He didn't expect his plans to be questioned or doubted. This was why the Shark could sometimes be a loose canon. He was too independent and well connected to owe his life and living to Barracuda, but he was too valuable not to have around.

Barracuda breathed in deeply and walked away to where Merlin was decoupling the warheads. "They came off easier than I hoped," said Merlin. Well, there was something to be thankful for. Maybe they'd been changed in recent years. The job of dismantling still had to be done but at least something was going right.

"No time to stop between tasks, Merlin. Get one of those things open and let's see what we have inside."

"Patience, this will take time, we're not dealing with Blue Tack here."

August
On the beach

Hartson stepped lightly along the gravel path from Diana Ffrench Parsons' villa to his Landcruiser. He could wait for weeks for something to happen and now it came in threes. He took a deep breath and smiled. Maybe he should have stayed the night, or was that going too far on a first date! He'd sleep well tonight, anyway. He was in no hurry. Why not drive down to the beach. He looked at his watch, one in the morning. He was still completely awake, alive, feeling as vital as a man does when he's just pulled off the impossible. He wanted to see the Gulf in the moonlight, smell the damp air, look at the stars. To stand on the white sand and indulge himself to his heart's content. Life wasn't so bad tonight. Christ, this was a good posting, the women and the booze were on constant tap.

The roads were empty of traffic, Khafira was an early waking place. He didn't even bother to indicate as he pulled off the beach road and on to the sand, there was nothing behind or in front. The Landcruiser strained as its wheels bit into the soft surface. He stopped, turned off the engine and got out.

It was almost completely silent, save for the murmur of a vehicle going about its business somewhere else in the city. The Moon wasn't high, but it still cast a brilliant light, though not so much that he couldn't clearly make out several stars away from its whitening glare. He looked at them. The memory of her lips imposed itself on Orion, the hunter. Her eyes shaped themselves over the Plough as he scanned the night sky. Her scent filled his mind's nostrils. Her taste was still in his mouth. The cynicism of the years had taught him that if you want something so badly that you ache for it, then you will never get it. You're not supposed to, you shouldn't be aching. He couldn't remember aching for Diana, not much anyway. He'd lusted after the impossible, but that was very different. She was a dream, a gorgeous, wonderful dream. And he'd just had her. His chest surged, he burst out laughing, adrenaline took over and possessed him for a few moments. There was nothing and no one to worry about on the beach. He took great draughts of air and guffawed as loudly as a man does when that rarest of things happens: a dream comes true.

The fit lasted a minute, he finally quietened to a chuckle; then he heard it. It was the unmistakable sound of another four-wheeled drive jeep on the sand. Someone else celebrating a triumph, perhaps. Unlikely! He stared in the direction of the noise. He could make out a shape, Toyota Landcruiser probably. No lights. Why not? The moonlight was enough to guide his eyes, it was probably the same for the other driver. The vehicle was approaching but at no great speed. He looked at the stars again, he tried to find a shape that would fit her face. He couldn't call it Diana because there already was one. He'd have to call it Ffrench Parsons. He strained to find some even faintly outlined points of light that would do the job. Come on, there are millions of stars in the Milky Way, there must be a few I can use. I only need ten. They wouldn't form for him. The Moon blasted everything but the brightest out of the sky.

The sound of the Landcruiser pushed everything else aside as it got closer. It was fifty metres away, now, and heading straight for him. What on earth did it want at this time of night? He tried to see if he could recognise police markings on the car, but he could see none. They often patrolled the beach hoping to find expat women skinny dipping. He'd been there one night the previous year when they had. What fun for everyone; the girls didn't care, the police only wanted to look. They drove away in the end with a warning. "You must keep clothes on if you are on beach. Please remember next time." That was the Gulf for you.

The vehicle was right by him now, the engine idling. He could make out the outline of the driver and a passenger, and was that someone in the back? He didn't feel threatened, he never felt threatened in Khafira – except by Hamid, but that was a different kind of threat. Crime didn't exist, wasn't the Ministry of Information forever ramming it down his throat! Then the lights sprung to life, straight in his face, full beam, blinding him. What the hell...!

He heard a door open against the noise of the idling engine, then another, and a third. A figure in a white dishdash blocked off the light from one of the beams. He wore a Kuffiah on his head with a black cord as a headband. Hartson had never seen him before.

"Good Morning, Mr Will Hartson."

They knew his name? "Good morning, can I help?"

"I believe there are many ways in which you can help, Mr Will. Will you give me the keys to your vehicle please and then come with me!"

"Why?"

The man in the dishdash didn't answer, he looked instead to another silhouetted figure two metres away. The man, dressed similarly, moved forward, grabbed his arm and shoved it hard up his back. He let out a cry.

"Be quiet please, Mr Will. The keys please."

He gasped out his reply. "They're in the car, in the ignition."

The interlocutor glanced to a third man hidden somewhere around the Landcruiser and said something in Arabic. A few seconds later a reply came. There was another Arabic command, his arm was released.

"Now if you will come with me, Mr Will."

"I want to know why. Who are you?" Again there was no reply but another Arabic command. The man who'd held his arm had moved around to the front. His arm exploded in a punch to the solar plexus. He felt the gutting hideous pain that went with it for the first time in years. He slumped forward, gasping for breath, soaked in agony. He finally managed to get out some words, "You know I... am a friend of... Sheikh Issa... You know what... he will do to you."

"Mr Will, I do not want to keep hurting you. Please stop making threats. I am especially aware of your relationship with his highness Sheikh Issa. He pays my salary."

"What do you mean?"

"Work it out for yourself, Mr Will, you will have a lot of time on the journey."

What journey? He nearly asked but saw his assailant moving closer. He didn't want to risk another assault, God knows what it would be this time.

"Now come with me, Mr Will. My associate will drive your car back to your apartment block garage. I am sure that will make you feel much easier."

"Yes, thank you. What do I call you?" Another order in Arabic. Oh no. He didn't see where the blow came from, but he felt it right enough, and the one that followed. Two crashing swipes to the chin. His head stung, he was sure his brain had been dislodged. He was temporarily stunned. A few seconds later he was manhandled into the back of the anonymous vehicle. The stubborn streak in him that made him a good reporter, when he didn't stop to think about it, started to well up with another question but he'd learned his lesson. "You will know more at the end of the journey, Mr Will. I advise you to rest, conserve your energy. You will need it." Unexpectedly he offered a bottle of water; Hartson took it, he was dry. He'd been sweating so hard there was no fluid left in him.

The moon was now high in the sky; they'd been driving for ninety minutes according to his watch. The lights of the city were a long way behind them, the only illumination came from the Moon. The dunes, much bigger out in the desert, loomed out of the darkness like a moonscape with expansive shadows hiding who knew what.

He had said nothing since he had been bundled into the car; nothing had been said to him. He was flanked by the man who had spoken to him, and the man who had hit him. All three were on the rear seat of the Landcruiser. It was still surprisingly roomy. He finished his bottle of water, another was not offered. He was still thirsty. At least he'd been able to see where they were going, he hadn't been blindfolded as they left the city. They were on the main road to the oasis town Al Durwar across the desert in Maraka. The time was 2:30, the roads were empty, the car was silent, not even a radio played to keep his captors amused. None of them smiled, not even the driver in front.

The one he assumed was the chief spoke in Arabic again, he thought he heard the word Yasser, left. They were turning left. The vehicle did exactly that, as he thought it. No signals, the driver simply spun the wheel and the vehicle was instantly driving on desert sand at right angles to the road. The engine laboured as the tyres wrestled with the sand. The driver shifted down two gears. The engine picked up again. A deep sense of foreboding came over him. It would be quite possible to be killed and buried in these dunes and never found until his bleached bones turned up in five years time after a sandstorm. By then he could be anything, even Filipino, and no one would ever care; least of all Sheikh Issa. He had upset someone badly, by the feel of it. Too much digging about the arms story? No, the sheikh wanted that to get out. The boys in concrete? Possibly, but why would he care? that wasn't Sheikh Issa's style.

His head fell forward as the Landcruiser bounced along the uneven desert surface. Had he screwed the sheikh's woman? Please don't let it be that. He decided to risk another beating. "What have I done?"

"We are nearly at the end of our journey, Mr Will. You will know shortly."

"You could at least tell me..."

His interlocutor looked in the direction of the guard on the other flank and formed his mouth into a shape which Hartson sensed was going to be Arabic. He raised his hands defensively. "All Right! All right! I'll wait."

The Arabic words never came, the man turned his face to the front again. The Landcruiser drove on relentlessly. They had been off the road for half an hour skirting around dunes, occasionally climbing one. They knew the territory.

The man barked another Arabic command; the vehicle slowed, then stopped. There were dunes on all sides, the moon was beginning to wane, the shadows lengthening. Hartson looked up and saw the silver tops of the sand mountains, and felt scared. They overwhelmed him and he was scared enough anyway.

"Get out please, Mr Will."

The man had opened the rear door and was standing outside. Hartson was about to obey when he was pushed roughly from behind by his assailant of a few hours before. He tumbled on to the silver moonlit sand, landing hard. The air was drier in the desert, and much cooler. The smells of the Gulf didn't spread this far. They were obviously a long way inland.

"Mr Will, you have published details of an incident recently which did not happen."

"What incident? He wished he'd held his tongue. He looked anxiously at the attacker behind him but there was no movement." The man continued in English. "Accounts of the discovery of some bodies in the sea. This simply did not happen, Mr Will and your publication of these lies has made already delicate relationships very precarious for Sheikh Mahmood and his sons."

"Of course it happened, it's common knowledge that it happened."

"Not any more, Mr Will. That knowledge has been changed, do you understand? Now, it did not happen."

The picture was becoming clearer all the time.

"Another thing which did not happen was the discovery of a body in the Al Kifaf Apartment Block, Mr Will."

He'd never said that it did, not publicly. He knew that one was sensitive, but he had done nothing about it - except help rescue the tart from the souk when Hamid came looking for her. Stupid move, Will.

"But I saw it," he said, resignedly.

"You were mistaken. Obviously, having got it wrong, you will not pursue it any further."

"Obviously not. What are you going to do to me?"

"This is a warning, Mr Will. You are not welcome in Khafira if you publish false information."

"You brought me all the way out here to tell me that?" They weren't planning to kill him then.

"Certainly."

"And now you're taking me all the way back. Why didn't you just knock on my door and tell me there?"

"I don't think the message would have been made quite so effectively, Mr Will."

"So I have learned the lesson."

"Not quite, Mr Will, the lesson is not over." He issued another order in Arabic, not another beating please! He tensed, put his hands up to his face in anticipation. Nothing happened. The trio moved away, returned to the Landcruiser. With mounting horror he saw the doors closing. His persecutor wound down a window as the engine restarted. "Colonel Ali Abdul Hamid sends his regards and hopes you will contact him soon. When you return to Khafira."

They were leaving him in the middle of the desert, with nothing. It was three in the morning, the dunes seemed to close in on him already.

"You can't do this. I have nothing with me to survive."

"Do not worry, Mr Will. The sun will be up in another three hours, you will see quite well then. It is a long walk back to the road, but if you start early you can be there before it gets too hot."

"Goodbye, Mr Will. I should try to sleep for a while. You have had a busy night what with one thing and another."

The Landcruiser moved off, he could hear it for ten minutes after it left. He tried to pinpoint where they were, was it a straight line? Were they coming back for him after all? It was just a scare, they'd pick him up and take him home. But as he heard the sound recede further into the night he knew this was for real. He had been in some tight spots in the world, but never on his own. Now he was terrifyingly alone. The Moon was even further down in the sky. The high dunes loomed over him. He shivered with fear and cold. Bastards!

Maraka

The Range Rover was parked in Maraka outside an anonymous hotel. It was a forty-minute drive from Khafira but far enough from the police, at least for the time being. Winter had managed to nurse the heaving pile of groaning, rusting engineering across the state border but he knew enough about modern policing to know it wasn't that safe a hideaway.

He said: "I'm worried about the car."

"Nobody is looking for it, or you. They only want me."

"I'm worried about you."

"You need not worry about me. I can take care of myself, Mr Winter."

"Oh, sure you can. That's why you're here with me right now."

"They will not look for me here. It is virtually another country. There is more rivalry than co-operation between them. It is very unlikely they will have alerted the other states."

"How can you be so sure?"

"I have entertained enough of them in the past, don't forget."

"But surely they lose out by not helping each other."

"God, you are so English. You have never heard of losing face?" He shrugged as if to say he had. "No you have not, otherwise you would know how important it is here." He said nothing, he didn't understand it. "If the police get it wrong or someone goes on the run they will not tell the other states because then they have to admit they failed?"

"Yes."

"So, we're safe."

"You are. They have probably got spies out in the other states searching right now for me." He looked around worriedly. She put her hand on his and stroked it. She would tease him now. "Do not worry, Englishman, they probably still think we are back there. They will not want to make a fuss about it in case the real story emerges."

"The real story?"

It was more a plea than enquiry and she knew she would have to get him on side and keep him for a while yet. She opened up.

"You know what I do?"

"You're a prostitute."

"You know I have entertained some of the most influential men in the state?"

"I can guess."

"I doubt it, Mr Englishman. You know I worked with Hannah in the apartments?"

"I do now."

"Hannah was a friend of mine. She came from Lebanon. She had been here for six years. She was very good at what she did." He shifted, uncomfortably. She read his eyes. "You cannot afford me, Englishman," and she dangled a gold bracelet in front of him. "A present from a client, can you match it?"

He said nothing. That was what she wanted. She withdrew her hand again and continued, "We get to learn a lot doing what we do. We know a lot about the men who come to us; what they are capable of, what they are not capable of."

"You were going to tell me who killed Hannah," he said.

She dropped her eyes. "You will not believe me."

"I can't say, but I'll listen to you."

She looked down at her drink, raised her gaze to meet him again. "No, not yet, Englishman." She resisted calling him stupid, that would only drive him further away. But she could still tantalise him.

May
Mustard

Merlin pointed to a metal canister which contained the freshly made mustard agent. He could smell it. It hinted at garlic, or onions, or something really tasty. It was anything but that of course. Merlin had made him put on a full protection suit within minutes of getting on board. He'd opened the canister and shown Barracuda the contents, a light yellow thick liquid which would have to be handled with maximum care. It could hang around for days if spilled and none of them could afford to take in any of it in the lungs.

Barracuda left him to his dark work and went up on the top deck. He looked down at the dhow moored alongside, now completely empty of cargo and crew. Then he gazed out to the port side where the crew had been dumped. It was bloodstained where the waters had not moved much in the slow breeze. It had been an hour since the sharks had first been summoned and there were several fins to be seen, but there was nothing left for them. All the evidence had been destroyed. No one in Maraka would bother to ask about them, they could have been going anywhere in the region: Bandar Abbas, Mumbai, Aden, Muscat, Karachi, Dubai, Sharjah, Abu Dhabi, Dohar. The whole point was not to tell anyone so they would never be missing, and no police would be bothered about looking for them. That was part of the risk they took.

The sharks would still grow in number as the blood scent travelled through the Gulf, but they'd go soon enough when they saw there was nothing left.

Barracuda opened his laptop, keyed in his codes, and typed out a message to the leader en route with the trucks to the rendezvous point.

"Close?" it read.

Five minutes later a reply came.

"Two hours. Good so far."

Barracuda would have liked a beer, several in fact. But he could not take the risk. He could not slacken his attention or relax at any stage in the next few days. He got a weather map up on the web and checked for anything which might get in his way in the next few days. Nothing at sea, dust storms in land. No change. He knew how to deal with that.

The Shark appeared alongside.

"Where have you put my little present, Shark?'

"They are being kept in good condition until such time as I can unwrap them. I shall look forward to it."

The Russian Section at GCHQ wasn't the hive of activity it had been fifteen years before. Everything changed in 1991 when the walls came tumbling down and the USSR split into fragments; the west looked away for a while, letting the vast country keep tearing itself to pieces. That was fine. A weak Russia was no threat. While the crime bosses ruled they'd have no economic clout and that's how everyone wanted things to stay.

It was for that reason that GCHQ on the edge of Cheltenham in the United Kingdom still kept a watch on their radio and e-mail traffic. It was a stripped down version of the desk which ran things before the change, but it was still important.

Code cracking was second nature to the executive officer on duty that afternoon. She'd done history at Oxford Brookes University and had been a member of MENSA since she was ten. She'd walked through the Foreign Office exam. She did the Times and Telegraph crosswords before coming to work most days. They represented no challenge. Nor did this e-mail intercepted from Kaliningrad to Moscow. It didn't even have a top priority code. It was a crime but what drew her attention was not the fact that the unusable 122 millimetre rockets had been taken. It was where they seemed to be going. Maraka. Very strange. What use could fifty ancient unlaunchable rockets be in a neutral state like Maraka? All the information was there: a flight plan for Maraka, an alleged destination of Moscow, a civilian cargo plane. Maybe it was some rich and bored middle eastern collector. Whoever and whatever it was they couldn't just ignore it.

She took the decoded message to the person who would want to know about it. He rubbed his head and said, "I haven't a clue but it must mean something. It can't be coincidence that they've wound up so close to Iraq, even if they can't be used."

He thanked the executive officer and looked down at his papers as an encouragement for her to leave. Once she had done so he picked up a telephone to London. Three levels later a decision was taken to let the Americans know and to alert all embassies in the middle east, especially in Khafira, next door to Maraka.

August
The souk

Tom Scott Garrett was dressed anonymously. It was mid-evening as he took his familiar route using a cab and ferry to reach the souk. He trod his familiar path and adjusted his eyes as the light dimmed in the alleyway. He rang the bell. No response. He rang it again. Still nothing. Too bad he would have to give it up for tonight, he couldn't risk anywhere else and he refused to use the phone. He pushed the door lightly to register his irritation. It gave way. No problem after all. He walked in and up the stairs. He pushed at the door he had come to know well in the last few months. It gave without challenge. He was about to call out when the words froze in his throat and he found himself gasping.

This was unfamiliar territory, he didn't know what to do. His body had gone into a rictus which he had never experienced before. His ossified face pointed down to the battered bloodied body in front of him lying supine on the bare floor. It was naked except for a pair of briefs and he could see burn marks on the chest as well as bruises just about everywhere. He had suffered before he died.

His breath burst into short rapid gasps, his heart thumped dangerously hard. What did he do now? He was powerless and his practiced smile was no use at all. Finally some words defrosted in his throat. "Michel... why?"

It may only ever have been a commercial transaction with the Lebanese pretty boy but Scott Garrett had invested himself into it anyway, inasmuch as he ever invested himself into anything. He could afford to, he believed. The women and men of the upper echelons were his tools, part of his work craft; Michel had been something else, away from all of that, still something to be kept at arm's length until he needed it, but there – like a doll to be picked up or left depending on what he was doing. It was still a kind of closeness, children grieve for their broken dolls, don't they?

Maraka

The cheap hotel window looked out on to the wide Maraka inlet. The Moon was rising. There was a broad sheen on the surface of the water. Sparse lights from the road encircling it paled; it was nothing like the fierce neon of the Lagoon a few miles away. There wasn't the money for that in Maraka.

It was peaceful. It did nothing to calm her turmoil.

They had taken a room on the edge of Maraka Town by the inlet. There were few trimmings but enough for her to be physically comfortable, at least by normal standards. She did not see it that way.

There was a television broadcasting the local TV channels. "Not even satellite," she complained. She caught Winter's look, she'd re-hooked him. Now he could tug at the line. She wasn't convinced of him; he wanted to leave her in Maraka while he returned to the apartment block in Khafira. She was scared he would not return. She told him. "I can do nothing here, I have no money, no credit cards, I dare not go to your precious bank to sort out these things. Now you want to leave me in some low life hotel in Maraka."

She'd heard the reasons before: he was under suspicion for Hannah's death; the apartments were being watched; if he didn't turn up it would look as if he had made a run for it. But it all sounded like excuses to her. He wanted to ditch her, lose her in this bare downbeat hotel room and go back to his life. What else would he want to do? If the positions had been reversed she would have left him to his fate a long time before. But she needed him.

He tried again to get through to her: "They're not looking for me at the moment. I can take the Range Rover back there without being noticed. Trust me."

Trust him?

"How do I know you won't tell the police to save your skin?"

Did she see a flash of hurt? Good. He was wriggling on her hook; she felt safer, for the time being.

"I can't get your things from the apartment, but I can sort out the bank account." There was a catch in his voice. She felt awkward. She did not like to feel awkward.

"Anyone else would have handed me over to the police straight away," she said.

"An Englishman's word is his bond," he said, cheerfully.

Not the Englishmen she'd known. "Not any more, Englishman. You're all as grasping and scared as the rest of us, now."

The television continued in the background. The hotel air-conditioning worked efficiently, everything appeared to be safe for the moment. He sighed., "Not all of us, Jose."

"You're a modern day Chevalier, Paul Winter, be careful where you put your lance." There was a silence. She was playing with him, letting out the line a little. Then she wished she had not. His forehead furrowed deeply, his colour changed to pink, his eyes started flashing. He erupted furiously.

"Look, I'm going out on a bloody limb for you, and all I'm getting is you taking the piss. Just stop, will you!" She didn't understand all the idioms but she got the anger. Time to turn contrite, she needed him, fool that he was. It was him or nothing.

"I am sorry, Englishman." Pause, she had to take a risk and gamble on him believing her. She needed him closer, dangerous but necessary. "Paul, I cannot ever be sad, I cannot love, I cannot hate. I can never make friends because I grow too close and I lose them." That should calm him.

Then she hardened. No need to get too close. "And I will not get close to you." That, at least, was true.

He looked at her, resignedly. It was working.

"You needn't bother, I don't expect it." He said as he turned away, She wasn't prepared for what followed. He whirled back round on her, his face filled with anger, frightening. "You fucking whore. Who the hell do you think you are?" What a fine English gentleman he was. She smiled ironically, he moved to the door. "I'll see you tomorrow."

Before he could reach it she moved to intercept him and breathed into his ear as she held his arm. "Paul, stop!" She put her hand to his face and looked him straight in the eye, then spoke softly: "Thank you for everything you are doing. You are all I have." She kissed him lightly on the lips – a desperate manoeuvre and she hated doing it, but whatever it took, she thought!

He stared at her, don't stare, Englishman, I have done too much already. Don't STARE!

Finally he left without saying another word. She watched the door close then clapped her hands against her head. What had she done now?

It was late by the time Winter reached the apartment block in Khafira. If he had been more worldly he might have anticipated what awaited him there. But he wasn't. There was a green Mercedes police car outside the entrance. His breathing quickened and he tried not to look at them as he passed. They watched him. One of them was speaking into a radio. It had to be about him, who else? He parked in the underground garage and walked out around the side. By now his heart was pumping so hard that he was panting. As he emerged from around the side there was another Mercedes, this time black. He didn't understand how car rankings worked in Khafira but he was able to take a stab: black meant high-up. His step faltered when he saw who was getting out of it. His legs lost their strength, he nearly tripped. Was it noticed? He fought hard to control them, trying to hide his facial expression at the same time.

"Good evening, Mr Winter. You are very late home," said Colonel Ali Abdul Hamid.

"It's only one in the morning, I am sure there are people out later than me," he virtually gasped as his heart almost exploded into his mouth. He noticed, irrelevantly, that the colonel was wearing a pristine white dishdash.

"Very likely, Mr Winter, but how many of them have found a dead body in the last few days?" Winter had no trouble keeping the grim look on his face. He started to move into the building. Hamid's firm hand prevented him.

Where have you been, Mr Winter?"

"Drinking with friends."

"Mr Winter, I am a Muslim and so I am not supposed to be familiar with alcohol. But experience tells me you have not touched any today. There is no smell about you."

"They were drinking wine, I was drinking orange juice. We were at a barbecue." The lies were coming thick and fast and each new one compounded the previous.

"I would have thought a man who has experienced what you have experienced in recent days would want to take a drink, Mr Winter. Why are you staying sober?" He struggled for an answer and hoped the delay of a half second did not register with this persistent policeman. "I was driving, it's dangerous to mix the two things."

"Very commendable," said Hamid, smiling. He appeared to move away, but stopped halfway down the steps and turned. "Who were these friends?" Winter faltered, who were they indeed? He tried to think of someone, it didn't matter who. Of course. "My companion from the other evening, Will Hartson. He lives in the Hilton Apartments."

"Yes I know where Mr Hartson lives. Are you absolutely sure you were with him."

"Certainly, why?"

"I was led to believe Mr Hartson was otherwise engaged tonight. Perhaps I was wrong. Goodnight, Mr Winter. I suggest you have a drink before you go to bed." He turned away again and this time got into the front passenger seat of the black Mercedes. Winter continued into the apartment building trying to control his shaking hands as they fiddled with the key. Once in the elevator he slumped against the side and pressed the button for his floor. Christ, they not only knew where Will lived, they knew what he was supposed to be doing tonight. He got into the apartment and went straight to the fridge for a can of beer, opened it, took a long draught, and carried it to the telephone. He checked the answering machine: nothing from Will. Why not! He should have phoned. He'd lumbered him with the woman after all. He started to dial the number.

He was three digits into it when he put the handset down. Industrial espionage: telephones, bugs. He'd done the course back in the UK. He would bet his month's salary that the phone was bugged. And he was a banker, not a gambler. He took another swig of beer and tried to think it through. He couldn't go to the police. He could always try the embassy, but that Scott Garrett man had made it clear he'd already wasted enough of his time. There was one thing which kept coming back to him no matter how much he batted it away: he could go round to Will's place. He was getting tired of the humiliation Will heaped on him. But what choice did he have?

He went back down to the Range Rover, past the police car and into the car park. As he drove out past the police again he saw one of them speaking into his radio. He didn't expect to be challenged. He wasn't.

The traffic was light, hardly anything at all. He drove at speed, made a noisy gear change at the brightly lit multi-coloured roundabout by Hartson's apartment, looked at the big raised garden in front of him regulating the traffic. All the flowers of the Orient kept alive in the impossible heat by an endless, pointless, supply of desalinated water.

He didn't think he was followed.

She gazed idly at the television, trying to involve herself but failing. She switched from the English speaking programmes to the Arabic; they were even worse. Everything was so censored it took all the drama and purpose out of it – often even the sense. Anything relating to bare flesh was out as was drinking alcohol; all out. She smiled despite herself. She knew the people who made these rules, the same people she entertained in her apartment with drink and sex.

She turned off the cheap TV set and walked across to the window one more time. She made sure the light was turned off, then gazed out on to the moonlit scene before her. She distracted herself with the reflection of the Moon in the inlet in front of the hotel. Maraka had a port, but this inlet was the foundation of its old existence. Here was where the pearl divers and smuggling boats had moored up. Not any more, it was surrounded by a road, four hotels and some restaurants. She was seized with a desire to walk out of the hotel, along the promenade encircling the inlet, maybe drop in on one of the restaurants. But it was too late and too dangerous. And the real reason she had gone to the window was to make sure, for the tenth time that evening, that she was still safe and undetected.

The Englishman had gone, she doubted if he would return despite his best intentions. Once he was back in Khafira he would see the folly of helping her. He would take a strong drink and forget her. She thought she knew enough about him to know he would not tell the police where she was, but she could expect no more. Why should she? She didn't deserve it: he owed her nothing, the opposite in fact. She was on her own. For God's sake she had kissed him on the lips, she never kissed on the lips. She shuddered at the thought and her own vulnerability, she had let herself do it.

She sat down on the bed again unable to sleep. Her thoughts drifted to Michel, to Hannah, poor Hannah. Why her? She had been a good woman, whore or not. She had cared about people. Not like herself who was just there for the money. Hannah never saw the customers as just commodities, she saw them as people wanting to be loved or tended to in some way. Yes, she took the money, good money, but she cared for them. Poor foolish Hannah. She cared about everyone, even the Pakistani runners from the restaurant across the road from the apartment. How many times had the two of them ordered a meal from there when the evening was free? And Hannah always asked after them, how were they and their families? Always remembering when something was wrong and giving a little extra tip.

And the maid, Maria, always a word for her. Always listening to her problems and worries about her boys, the difficulties of bringing up Filipino teenagers in a rich place like Khafira, hadn't they run off or something! And now Hannah was dead and she, Jose, hard woman, businesswoman, was alive. She had always known there was no justice in the world. She had just seen it confirmed once more.

Michel's face came to her. The bitterness welled up. Michel had betrayed her, he had thrown her on to this Englishman and run away. He had not even tried to get her away after leaving Anwar's place. As soon as he saw the police he panicked. If it had not been for the Englishman she could be buried somewhere out in the dunes even now, hundreds of kilometres away from the city, in another sheikhdom. For God's sake the Englishman had nearly taken her to the police anyway, it was only her quick thinking which had stopped him. It was all because of Michel. And after all the help she had given him: giving extra bread rations, hiding him from the militias, smuggling him out of the war zone into Khafira, using her influential clients to make sure he got a visa. Then when trouble came he literally threw her into someone else's arms and ran.

Bastard, Michel! Bastard!

Answer, you sod! Winter pressed the button against Hartson's name on the apartment's intercom. It buzzed uselessly. Come on, this is important! Everything is important now. Just pick up the receiver and speak into it. Nothing. Bastard, you said you'd be here. He buzzed again, and again. Still nothing. Wake up, even if you were asleep you'd have heard by now.

Ten minutes elapsed with no reply. Only one thing for it: phone him. He walked back the ten metres to the Range Rover and picked up his mobile phone. His shirt was ringing wet from being out in the humid night. He punched out the number and sent it. He heard a call tone. It rang four times. Finally, the giveaway sound of an answering machine left him in despair. "Will, this is Paul. Do you hear me? Paul. Pick up the phone please, NOW. I said, NOW!" He waited. Nothing. He ended the call. A weariness came over him, all he wanted to do was sleep. He dragged himself back to his car. He longed to be back at the apartment, in bed. There was no fugitive woman in Maraka, no dead body upstairs in the brothel, no problem at all. He hauled himself into the

Range Rover and started the engine. He drove away from the Hilton Apartments in a trance, careless of anything else. There was a fleeting satisfaction that the air-conditioning seemed to be working better in the car, probably because the heat had fallen off to thirty degrees. At one o'clock it was still mercilessly hot. His eyes were tempted to close, just for a second, just a little rest. He fought them but they persisted. They closed again and he felt the wobble of the powered-steering wheel bring him back.

Then, he was wide awake. The adrenaline pumped through his system like so many other times that day. The flashing red lights and the siren beat into his skull for the second time in a few hours. He'd been followed and now it was all up. He pulled over.

The first thing Winter noticed about the police station was how clean it was. He also noticed how dirty it became in a short space of time. It was a modern building with ornate tiling on the floors, and the occasional arabesque design on the walls and ceiling. He was waiting in the foyer with a uniformed guard. He hadn't been taken to any cells. His offence was drinking while driving – despite not having touched a drop all day. He had been waiting for an hour, time enough to see a team of Filipino cleaners make two half-hourly sweeps of the foyer. It was the early hours of the morning and the workers were being pushed to their limits. The police seemed not to care about the cleanliness of their police station. His guard regularly hawked and spat on to the polished floor. Others casually tossed cigarette ends without any intention of hitting an ashtray, and pieces of paper were strewn everywhere, until the Filipinos came around again, and everything sparkled for a few minutes.

This was a side of Khafira he had never seen, nor was ever meant to see. He saw the Filipinos being treated like inanimate objects, simply pushed or kicked out of the way. That contempt was not extended to him however. He was treated with respect and courtesy from the moment of the arrest. His two uniformed officers had politely told him it was against the law to drink and drive in Khafira, had taken him from his car and put him in the police station. They hadn't gone so far as to offer a cup of tea, but it could have been a lot worse.

But then it got a lot worse. "Hello again, Mr Winter." A chill went through him. The figure of Colonel Ali Abdul Hamid appeared, apparently from nowhere.

The uniformed guard stood up. So did Winter. Hamid walked around the long foyer pacing slowly, getting the measure of his man then whirled around suddenly. "You are behaving erratically, Mr Winter. You should explain yourself."

"I was just driving from a friend's place. I left something there."

"That was careless, Mr Winter, what exactly was it that you left?"

He was stymied; what *had* he left?

"Nothing important, just a...a...a pager. I normally wear it on my belt."

"But not at all important?"

"No, not really."

"So you could have left it until tomorrow morning, rather than go round to Mr Will Hartson's apartment unannounced?"

"Well, no, you see... I... er... I still need it."

"So I see. You are wearing it now."

"Exactly, the bank must be able to contact me at any time."

"Indeed. In fact I was sure I saw you wearing it a little while ago. Was I mistaken."

"...I...I suppose you must have been."

Hamid said nothing for thirty seconds as he continued to pace around. Then, "Let us not play any more! You have not been with Mr Will Hartson this evening. This I can state without any contradiction; he has been busy elsewhere."

"Ho...How do you know?"

"It is my job to know. What are you doing, Mr Winter? Until tonight I was prepared to leave you alone provided you did the same to me. Have I intimidated you so much that you are inventing stories. What are you doing?"

He had no answer. Hamid drew out a cigarette from a packet of Marlboro and lit it with an expensive looking gold lighter. He drew in deep while never taking his eyes from his interlocutor. "I am especially concerned that someone like Mr Hartson, Chief Randalls Correspondent for the Gulf, should not make your unfortunate discovery public." Winter said nothing and waited for a direct question. "I must ensure that the news does not even leak into a tiny part of Khafira, let alone the rest of the world. Do I make myself clear, Mr Winter?"

He croaked out a response. "I understand perfectly. I have said nothing." The lying made him feel uncomfortable. "I hope you do, Mr Winter, Khafira can be very unforgiving." While he spoke he flicked ash on to the floor despite an ashtray's presence only half a metre from his arm. The Filipinos were around again and one of them expertly swept the ash into a dustpan. Hamid kicked out as if it were a troublesome dog causing the man to spill his pan all over the floor. Immediately two uniformed officers descended on him shouting in Arabic and striking him around the back of the head. The man quickly swept up the spillings and withdrew trying to avoid a rain of blows to his back.

Winter was astonished. Hamid said nothing, he looked as if he had not even noticed what had happened. "You must be careful what you do, Mr Winter, I am forced to watch you carefully." Winter had a sudden dread of being followed back to Maraka the following day and being found out. He dismissed it and asked, "Am I really a suspect for this killing, Colonel?"

"Yes, Mr Winter." He fixed him. "Don't get me wrong, I do not believe for a moment that you had anything to do with it, but that does not mean you will not be blamed." The whore's lecture on the rule of law sprang into his mind. "Just be careful Mr Winter, do nothing, say nothing, and you will come to no harm...probably." They had him. Whichever way he turned, whatever he did, they had him.

"Now go home. Go and retrieve your car and get some sleep."

"What about the drinking and driving?"

"We try to be understanding here, Mr Winter, but proceed carefully." He turned on his heel to walk out. Winter watched him all the way down the long foyer and out of the exit. His guard grabbed him by the sleeve, yanked him up, and pointed to the exit.

"Go!" he said, firmly. He walked out the same way expecting to find a police car waiting for him outside. There was none. Then he realised what they had done. He would have to walk back the five kilometres to his car, there would be no ride. It was three thirty in the morning, the temperature was 31 degrees, the humidity at 100% he guessed from the sweat already running from him. Damn them!

The Desert

The Sun was over the horizon and already burning. Hartson had a tan like all the expats, but that was no protection against the savage intensity of the desert in August. The coldness of the night was long gone, the glare bit into his eyes from every angle. It reflected off the sand, it came straight down from the sky. He had no water, he was in a mess. His watch told him it was ten past six in the morning. He tried to navigate by the sun. He knew it would always be south of him, and at this time, south east east.

His head throbbed, the exhilaration of the previous night was a harsh memory. Dehydration from drinking wine with Diana and the other exertions had depleted him beyond normal tolerance. But what was normal tolerance in the middle of the hottest desert in the world? He was thirsty, not achingly so, but it was still early. The heat would rise, the sweat would pour, he could be dead within a few hours unless he found the bloody road. They said due west. He'd been dragging his ill-equipped feet through the red sand for probably an hour and a half. He'd judged direction by the faint signs of light he'd seen on the horizon. He'd heard nothing: no car, no lorry, no engine, no aeroplane. He was in the middle of the true meaning of wilderness. He wasn't cut out for this sort of nonsense, leave that to the heroes who liked covering wars, civil unrest and disasters; they got off on it, he did not! He'd only gone in to Iraq because he was told to and to refuse would have been professional suicide. "Time you got out a bit more," said his news editor, "Of course, someone else can always go if you think you're not up to it!" Or, you'll be coming back to London and working nightshifts until we've decided to let you go! Not much of a choice but he'd managed to dodge the bullets and still file some stories, courtesy of a friendly army press officer – actually, she'd been very friendly. Somehow he'd fallen on his feet again – or, in this case, his back – she was an army captain, after all, she expected to be on top.

None of that was going to get him up the mountainous dune before him, rippling with sand waves. He looked at it forlornly, he'd already climbed two, reached the top and seen nothing but more dunes before him. Even if there was a road he would never know it, how could he? The sand would soak up every sound long before it could reach him.

It was hopeless, bloody hopeless. He cursed everything to do with Khafira, the Middle East, the sheikhs, the Brits, the world, Randalls. He hated them all and it got him not a step further up the dune. He needed a miracle. The sun had risen by another few degrees, the temperature was climbing, the heat was on his back, the shade was on the other side of the dune. If he could get up this mound in half an hour he'd still benefit from the relative cool on the other side. He'd have to be quick. He strode out purposefully, tried to put the headache, the thirst, the weariness, behind him. It lasted for thirty seconds, he wasn't a fit man, only average, runs and press-ups were for others, when he talked of parallel bars it meant two lines of optics side by side.

The sand sapped him rapidly, every metre stride he took up the dune got him just a few centimetres further forward. He stopped, but that was even worse. Getting somewhere, however slowly, was better than standing still. He had to carry on, had to get up that dune so he could get down the other side. He would have to force himself and pray, yes pray, to his non-existent god, that something would turn up on the other side.

It took him an hour, he weakened with every step, the sun got higher, the time was well past nine. The effort had made him sweat, just as he'd feared. He was in the middle of a daylight nightmare. He gasped for air, a searing breath of it went in and out of his lungs and he felt no better.

When I said I'd have to find a new dream this wasn't what I had in mind, he thought. Stay alert! Be chirpy, like in those wartime desert films! They always had a sense of humour. Cheerful cockneys calling each other Chalky and smiling as the sun fried them and Germans shot what was left.

He tried to smile but it turned to a grimace before properly forming. This wasn't Pinewood. Only another few metres. But by now, the sun was so high that the shade would be useless on the other side. The sound of his breathing, his heartbeat, his thinking, drove out all else. He heard nothing, he saw only the crest of the dune a few metres above him. One more heave, his aching dry body forced him to the top. He collapsed in a breathless semi-conscious heap and stared up at the blazing sky, careless of whether the sun burned a hole through his head. There was nothing left. He had to rest, perhaps to sleep, to be out of this torture, into an unreal world where there was no sun, no sand, just sex and sea. The image started to take him over, as he surrendered to his exhaustion: he didn't feel the burning sun on his neck, he was in the shade of a large parasol with a half litre glass of fresh lime juice and soda cooled by half a dozen ice cubes; he leaned over casually and took a pull from the straw.

It was the cue for a thousand horns to sound throughout the bar. Where did they come from? Bloody noise. Shut up! Fuck off! Then there were only a few, then even fewer, enough to count, only two, or three. The limejuice disappeared taking the parasol with it. He jerked awake. One horn was still there, he was certain of it. Loud enough to be a kilometre away, perhaps, even in the empty desert where sound travels forever.

He was near the road, he must be. He heard it again, with the unmistakable sound of a big diesel engine. No, two. He shouted, "Help", but it came out as nothing more than a wheeze. He tried to get up but nothing would move. He tried again, this time a leg came up and it was enough to tire him.

Another supreme fucking effort, terrific! Just when he thought life was as good as it could be. He reached within himself to find reserves. He knew they were there, he'd needed strength in the past, just not very often. He'd make it, it wouldn't be comfortable, it would be easier to lie on top of the burning dune and simply braise himself to death in his own sweat. But the line of least resistance wasn't always the best solution. He gathered up his willpower and forced himself on to his knees. It became easier after that. Another push put him on his feet, shaky, but standing.

The sun was at his back, he could see clearly the gap in the dunes forming a valley. Two hundred metres down the slope he could make out the tarmac of the road. There was a huge truck, probably from the construction industry, disappearing into the heat-hazed distance. The road was empty for the time being, it wouldn't stay that way, not at this time of the morning. He looked at his watch, five past eight. He started to make his way slowly down the slope using what remained of his strength to hold his body rigid. He was scared that if he didn't it would melt into an amorphous puddle in the sand. And all the while he thought of Sheikh Issa, and Diana, and Hamid, fucking Hamid!

Open Seas

Sam Jackson didn't know if it was a good or a bad thing to be exiled to the middle of the Gulf for the next two weeks. He was beginning to learn there were more sharks on land than in the sea so maybe he and his crew were safer out there. But he resented it nonetheless, because the Navy didn't trust him enough to keep his mouth shut. Who made those decisions anyway?

The minesweeper moved slowly out of the harbour on her way to begin her task: yet another broad sweep of the Gulf from the Qatar tip to the Umm Al Qasr harbour. The harbour gave on to the open seas, still shallow in that part of the region. It was busy.

"Careful through these powerboats Helmsman, we don't want a bad start!"

"No, sir," replied the man who had introduced cannonballs unwittingly into the ship's lexicon.

Jackson scanned the open sea and alighted on an imposing vessel lying at anchor two kilometres out from shore. He focused his binoculars and read the ship's name "Sands Of Al Khaleej." He repeated the name then asked on the bridge, "Anybody heard of it?"

"Yes, sir," replied the helmsman, "It's a yacht. It belongs to one of the big men on shore. I think his name's Lafitte, something like that."

"How do you know so much helmsman?"

"I just keep my ears open, sir. There's not much else to do on shore except get drunk and you can't keep doing that forever." Jackson begged to differ but thought better of it.

"The navy could use an intelligence network like yours, that's for certain."

He let his eyes feast on the craft for a while, in the way that all seamen will admire another boat. It was pristine, he could see dark skinned labourers or cleaners working on the decks. They must be part of the permanent crew.

The day passed quickly. It took three hours to get to the start point of the survey where he ordered work to start straight away. They were beyond territorial waters and north of Khafira. The sea was calm and warm. There was no cooling effect to be got from the Gulf waters. In the shallows it took on the same temperature as the air making it even hotter on board the plastic and glass minesweeper.

He described his plan for the next few days to a sub-lieutenant. They would cover a grid pattern of two square kilometres and then move to the next until they came within sight of the Straits. They would have to stay out of Iranian waters so the pattern would be curtailed in that area, but all the more acutely observed. They would then sail back to their current position and work the same system towards Qatar.

The day passed, nothing showed up on the scan, nothing showed up at all in fact. It was a boring, repetitive job which dragged and Jackson prepared to hand over the bridge to the officer of the watch. "Knock me up if anything happens," he said, as he headed for his cabin.

The darkness of the Gulf descended, the stars stood out brilliantly in the night sky. The light from the shore was too distant to obliterate them and the moon hadn't risen yet. The view was rare enough for nearly all the crew to stop amid their tasks. The sky was a mass of grey, not black. Bright stars mixed with thousands of not so bright stars, to create what looked like a celestial cloud, the Milky Way.

The call came at just after nine o'clock. Jackson was sweltering in his cabin with his shirt off, poring over a chart. There was a knock on the door, he called out "Wait!" while he donned a fresh shirt. He could not be seen without one no matter what the circumstances, he was the captain, an officer in The Royal Navy. He opened the cabin door to see a young seaman.

"You're wanted, sir. They've found something."

"Thank you," he said, crisply, and made his way to the bridge. The ship had slowed down and was almost stopped. There was an air of tension on the bridge.

The sub-lieutenant said: "I think you'll want to see this, skipper." He pointed to the most recent series of soundings and two blobs, spaced by half a kilometre, were plainly visible.

"Nothing marked on the charts?" asked Jackson. The other officer shook his head. "We'd better take a look at them." He stayed on deck waiting for the first signs of contact from the diving team. It came after twenty minutes. "Four bells." They'd found the first blob. The lead diver's incredulous voice came through loud and clear on the intercom, "You're not going to believe this, skipper. It's one of our friends from the other night, concrete and all."

Jackson hung his head and then brought it back up again with a snap; he was the captain, he had to act like it, but right bow he wished he wasn't.

A desert road

The truck driver had two words of English: "No" and "Problem." He scattered them liberally through his conversation as they headed along the road back to Khafira. It was a limited exchange for all that. Will Hartson spoke no Baluchi nor Urdu; the driver, a dark skinned, merry looking man with a permanent cigarette in his mouth, spoke no English and only a few more words of Arabic. He didn't even know the word for water but understood exactly what Hartson meant when he pointed desperately at the bottle on the truck passenger seat only seconds after stopping.

He had stood on the now roasting tarmac in the shade of the cab and drained the bottle while the driver looked down curiously. He seemed to be trying to ask what had happened but even their combined Arabic couldn't get round it. It took a final act of willpower to raise his body into the cab but the water helped and he made it. It wasn't air-conditioned but it was covered, he'd taken in water, in a while he would feel better.

They rolled along the smooth road in silence for an hour. Hartson relaxed knowing the physical challenge was over. He looked up at the smoking Baluchi, still cheerful as he made his way along the road mechanically. He'd stopped for him, given him water and shelter, been a human being despite no common language. People could be good in extremes. Maybe life wasn't so bad. He smiled at his saviour. But four Filipinos and a sliced up whore balanced the score.

He looked away again and his mind drifted to unwanted territory; Hamid, what is his game? Did they mean to kill him? They could have done that easily enough without going through this pantomime. Or did they want him to suffer? They could have dumped him anywhere and never have to answer for it. Instead, they'd left him within reach of the road.

The truck rolled on until they approached the outskirts of Khafira. The tree lined road into the city past the airport already warned of a civilisation. He could see the skyscrapers of the city clearly rising above the now flat desert. It was freakishly hot and humid. The Baluchi driver was dripping, his singlet wet through. Another of his serial cigarettes was balanced on his lip. He looked around, smiled and pointed straight ahead: "No problem."

"No problem." He parroted back and summoned a smile.

Hartson's head and arms were now red and burning angrily but he tried to ignore it as they travelled on through the thickening traffic to Khafira Central. The contrast between open road and the desert and the Khafira congestion was striking, they waded on through the traffic lights and construction wagons until Hartson could see the port ahead. He could walk from there. He shouted at the driver, "There, there!" The driver stopped by the roadside and Hartson climbed down from the cab. He called out thank you in Arabic, "Shokaran."

"No problem." The truck moved on to the port, Hartson moved at a right angle into the street which would take him to his apartment. He should rest and sleep, have something to eat, but right now they were secondary concerns.

"Good morning, Diana. Was it a nice evening?"

"Very good thank you, Tom." Diana Ffrench Parsons smiled sweetly, but not knowingly, as they entered the embassy compound together. Yes, it had been very nice, thank you.

She knew her power, she saw the reactions from men when she smiled or made a clever comment, or laughed at their jokes. It was fun, but in the end there was a professional outcome. Dangling the strings of a sheikh, a senior diplomat, a junior minister, or a news agency correspondent gave her access, and power. But doing it with Will Hartson had given her satisfaction. The sex had been surprisingly good, thank you, Will, not exactly an Alpha male, but sometimes it was nice to have a break from them. And the lesser specimens had the compensation of being more considerate. But it wasn't that which made her smile as she walked into the embassy this morning.

She checked herself in the mirror, the merest hint of makeup, hair done up so that she wouldn't be tempted to flick it. Diana had learned her technique early. She learned at school that she was attractive and wouldn't have to try too hard - a relatively severe institution in Sussex. She loved to tease the male staff, not overtly, but cleverly. She looked serene, never licked her lips, never batted her eyelids, never played with her hair, rarely crossed or recrossed her legs. She was cool, demure, magnetic without ever having to betray any interest in her male quarry. That's what kept them dangling. And now Diana had Will Hartson in her puppet chest.

She had direct access to the main movers in Khafira and in the embassy. It was power beyond the normal reach of such a junior diplomat. But then Diana wasn't planning to be a junior for too much longer. Even so, despite the ease with which she could dial up any one of the powerful men in her address book, she was still a woman and diplomacy remained a man's game, in this Arab land at least. She could do nothing at the Majlis, never enjoy that peculiar male bonding she had tried so hard to understand. But she could look in from the outside, if Will Hartson gave her the telescope.

She sat down in the small office which she'd occupied for the last eighteen months. It wasn't claustrophobic, but it was limited. She'd made little attempt to change it. There were no patriotic pictures on the wall, no mementoes of Britain, just a generic print and a couple of pot plants. She had never thought it worth disguising.

The telephone rang.

"Diana Ffrench Parsons, good morning."

"Hello, Diana, perhaps you're surprised to hear from me."

Will Hartson? A little keen don't you think, Will! Don't be boring about this, there's a good boy. She kept a coolness in her voice. "Hello, Will, I hope you slept well."

"Very funny, Diana." There was a pause. He didn't sound ardent, was he making some sort of point? She was damned if she would break the silence. He finally broke it for her. "Why did you set me up, Diana?"

"What?"

"As if you didn't know. You'll be pleased, or completely unconcerned, to know that I did not sleep at all last night, not from reliving the passion of our coupling, either."

"What are you talking about, Will?"

"I spent the night in the dunes of the Empty Quarter, a hundred kilometres away. On my own after being beaten up and dumped by thugs answering to your friends the sheikhs."

"My God! And you think I had something to do with it. How could you think that, I mean why?"

"Perhaps they didn't like me sleeping with you – and they knew, believe me!"

A coldness came over her, numbing her tongue, disabling her voice. Had she made one of the sheikhs jealous? She hadn't counted on that, it didn't fit into her scheme of things. She used sex for access, she assumed everyone else did the same.

"Are you all right? Where are you now?"

"Back at my apartment. Thanks only to a kind Baluchi truck driver."

"I'm so sorry to hear this, Will, but you must know it has nothing to do with me."

"You're ambitious, Diana. I'm just a reporter, nobody likes reporters, they get up too many noses. Diplomats like us least of all."

"I know you're upset but that's not fair."

There was a pause, the tension was tangible. Diana broke the mood this time. "I'd better meet you."

"Do what you like, call me later, when I've had some sleep." The line went dead. She was left holding the phone.

The souk

Scott Garrett was at pains to present his life as bland. A cheery non-committal smile was usually enough to ensure he was passed by without remark and without comment. That was the way to fit into any group. His minor public school had instilled it into him at an early age. It had been reinforced at Oxford, not one of the fashionable colleges either. A good second class degree before they introduced upper and lower divisions marked him out as bright without being desperately scholarly, then his old school was enough to swing his entry into the Diplomatic Service. And his waking life lived up to his cultivated image. Mr. Bland of Her Majesty's Foreign and Commonwealth Office. A man with no opinions but information about everything. A man who eschewed politics but elevated discussion on the weather to Aristotelian heights. A man who was well versed in Bishop Berkeley and Sartre, and could recite the premises of both and many others, but as for which he preferred? Not his field old boy. Only at sporting events had he been known to show an interest for any party: the varsity clashes on the Thames, at Twickenham, the Parks, and then only in the right company, and none too loudly.

When little Tom Scott Garrett had been taken to his first prep school by his nanny he had turned his back on an emotional existence and never tried to regain one. He had gone through the years of bullying, buggering, meanness and stupidity which every public schoolboy had to endure and inflict, with the same unrevealing, disconnecting smile. He had been bred for the diplomatic service like Ceaucescu's orphans were made for the Securitate.

But the night was different. The night brought dreams which he could not control with his smile. There was no manipulating this other life, it controlled him. He rarely remembered his dreams. Sometimes he would awaken with a vague sense of disquiet but he could not pin it down. Sometimes he was convinced he did not dream at all. He had no idea what any of it meant, he had never consulted Freud or Jung on the matter although he knew of their work. He believed the world of dreams was another existence which had no relevance to him.

But he had bad dreams most of the time. The only dreams he ever remembered were bad dreams: dreams about women inflicting pain on him, men hurting him, being tossed around by a gang of soldiers before being thrown to a savage wolf pack. One dream hadn't left him alone the last couple of nights. It wouldn't leave him alone during the day either. This one was different: Michel in a strangled heap on the floor, dead. He didn't normally dwell on that sort of thing; it was a volatile region, you never knew who you were dealing with. No, consign it to memory, best thing, got to get on with life. Nice chap Michel, shame he hadn't got to know more about him.

Still a dull sensation nudged at him, something wasn't right, He felt out of sorts with himself. He looked at his diary and decided that work was the best way. There was the usual run-of-the-mill day to come starting with the little lie he needed to drop in the ear of the Randalls chap, Hartson. Get that over with first. He lifted the receiver and dialled the first digit when a vision of Michel's battered face appeared just behind his eyes. His finger paused on the phone pad. Perhaps he should have called the police. His finger shook unexpectedly. No, not a good idea, he couldn't guarantee their co-operation. Abdul Hamid was a useful fellow, knew the score, but this was too risky. He couldn't rely on him to keep it quiet. Even if he could there'd be a debt, and that sort of thing has a way of appearing at a time in one's career when it's least wanted. Questions would be asked back in London. It only needed a rumour that he'd been cavorting with a male prostitute in a seedy Arab souk and one or two might want to know if the man's judgement was all it might be. He had done all he could to lay a false trail. He had told Michel he worked with a motor dealership, he didn't need to know any more. Michel had never known his name, he had simply said "Mr. Smith." Terribly English. Terribly Tom Scott Garrett.

That alone couldn't possibly trace him. He hadn't minded being called "Mr. Smeeth" by the Lebanese rent boy when they were engaged in their couplings. It was part of the game, kept it formal, no emotion. He could pretend to himself that he didn't care about for the lovely young man he'd found at the Café de Bruxelles.

His finger returned to the phone pad and he started again, a different number this time. The phone rang once.

"Will Hartson."

"Tom Scott Garrett, how are you?"

"What can I do for you, Tom?" asked a weary sounding voice. Probably been drinking again. These reporters knew how to bend the rules.

"Will, I just thought you might like your card marked on the business with the minesweeper and those, er, unfortunate boys."

"It would make my day."

"It seems it was a speedboat accident."

"Really?" said the reporter.

"Seems they were taking a dip during a work break at the southern port and got cut up by one of the young locals with a powerboat."

"Extraordinary."

"Isn't it! Poor chap never even knew he'd done it, apparently."

"Very good of you, Tom. How did you come by this?"

Scott Garrett didn't falter. "Contact with the police. He says the post mortem showed up deep cuts from a propellor blade. Nasty business. They checked among the powerboat owners, there aren't that many, and one said he'd hit something a few days before."

"So it's all sorted?"

"Innocent accident by the sounds of it."

"That would account for the bruises I suppose," continued Will.

"Absolutely," said Scott Garrett confidently.

"On all four of them?"

"That seems to be what happened."

"Funny, I'm sure you're right but even a twin-engined powerboat would have trouble hitting four swimmers."

"Seems strange but this chap has never let me down, Will."

"It doesn't account for the concrete of course," said the reporter matter-of-factly. Was he buying this, or not! Damn, this was the line they were feeding! Everyone at the embassy bought it, why not this jumped up scribbler!

"Never happened, complete fabrication. Who ever told you that must have been watching too many New York gangster movies." He heard a laugh, he chuckled too.

"Very kind of you to let me know. Any idea where the bodies are?"

He had to think for a moment. "I should imagine they've gone back to their families, Will, you'd better ask the authorities." There was another chuckle. "I think we both know where that will lead, Tom. There's no chance you could pass this contact of yours on to me is there." He reciprocated the chuckle. "None at all I'm afraid, Will. Would you do the same for me?" They laughed together. "Must have a drink sometime," said Scott Garrett as he concluded the call.

The handset stayed in his hand as a vision of Michel's hideously mashed face appeared. A beaten, scored face; bruised on the cheek, sliced under the eye, burned with cigarettes on the lips and eyelids.

Michel hadn't been run over by a speedboat, either.

Hartson replaced the receiver. Propellor my arse, he thought! It wasn't even worth a call to the police. It would take a very bad speedboat driver, and admittedly there were plenty of those around, working blindfold to do the damage to the Filipinos that he'd heard from Lieutenant Sam Jackson. Sailors' talk was it? We'll see. He winced as he reached up to get a file, his notes from the naval encounter at the international. His arms had gone seeringly red, the back of his neck scorched him, he wanted to go to bed and sleep for ever. Then Tom Scott Garrett calls with an improbable story about a speedboating accident. Why did they want him to shut up? He was so tired, so pained the answer wouldn't come. He knew it was there, he had all the clues, he just couldn't piece them together. He threw his pen on to his desk in frustration and cried out at the same time as the roasted skin rubbed on his arm.

Why was he being warned off, it was a local matter? The big wide world was unlikely to care if four Filipinos had been killed by a speedboat or not, so Randalls wouldn't normally care either. But the trouble was that Hartson had come up the hard way to get where he was. No easy university route followed by a cushy postgraduate course and then on to a national newspaper. He started at sixteen on a weekly rag in the midlands, making the tea, calling in on the ambulance and fire stations every morning. And most importantly the police. He had spent years following stories in Warwickshire. He'd been threatened, abused and frightened. He knew how things worked. He'd also learned how to avoid getting hurt...and everything about this was screaming to him to stay away from it, he could end up in the foundations for the next big hotel here.

But he also knew when people were trying to fool him and he didn't like that because his contrary streak riled up. His eyes had stayed open through his years in the Midlands and the evening paper in London. The short stint with BBC radio had done little to change things, and his two-year tour as a lobby hack at Westminster had convinced him that honorable people rarely go into politics. He had seen more honorable, less duplicitous crooks being sent down in Crown Court than the denizens of the Houses of Parliament. He had been astonished to find there was virtually nothing they would not do, no lie they would not tell, in order to serve their own ends. Hartson was in Khafira to cover the politics, the economics, the shifting sands of the Middle East, and he had managed to do that so far by not shifting too far from a bar stool or his office chair and just occasionally The Majlis. But he still had a nose for a good old-fashioned story, and he hadn't lost his sense of injustice in this wild landscape. He was being steered away by the embassy, and frightened off by the Khafira police. Why?

Just one more call. He picked up the phone again, dialled a direct line at the embassy.

"All right Diana let's meet this evening after I've had some sleep."

"I'm sorry, Will. I have plans this evening."

"Don't worry, Diana, I won't be trying to jump into your bed for a long time, if ever," which was true, the thought of his burned body rubbing up against someone else's filled him with dread at the moment. "Neutral ground, Cafe De Bruxelles, six o clock!"

There was a pause. "All right, it can't be long, Will."

"Just be there...please!" He replaced the receiver without waiting for a reply. And hoped his attempts at being masterful would work. Then he saw his answering machine winking at him. He hadn't bothered to check when he came in. He played it back: bloody Paul Winter, not him please! What the hell had he wanted? Why so urgent, why so bloody needy? I want sleep, he thought, I can't talk to you now. Later! He stopped the call after three seconds and made his way, painfully, to bed.

May
Open Seas

Merlin might have been smiling, thought Barracuda, he could never tell. He had every right, he'd delivered exactly what he said he would. He'd presented him with thirty 122 millimetre rockets complete with reconstructed warheads containing detonators and mustard agent. Barracuda had no way of knowing how Merlin was celebrating, was that a smirk? Or, was he counting the ways he could spend his money? The Shark knew him better, he had brought him into the set-up, maybe. One day, he would try to find out; but he did not care really, it did not impact on his life.

Barracuda looked down at the hold of the dhow where the rockets had been stored, this time without their Filipino companions. So far so bad, he thought. Barracuda was the new master of the dhow and was taking his time to get used to the controls of the vessel, but he knew where he was going. The other Barracudas were lazing on deck as the surprisingly fast craft ploughed on to the coast north of Khafira. He scanned the horizon every now and again but their way was clear. It wasn't a normal shipping route. The Shark had given him the rendezvous point, an old smugglers' inlet hardly used these days – unless the bribes hadn't worked and the odd chancer wanted to try his luck there. That was where the trucks should be waiting. He didn't expect any trouble from the local port police, The Shark assured him he'd squared everything with them. The senior officer was a confederate who would take personal charge of sea traffic in that part of their waters. He would be left alone.

That's why he was so damned useful. The Shark had the entire region in thrall to him one way or another: a port police colonel here, a sheikh there, a general over there. The Shark dealt with everyone and still he wanted to play the international adventurer with Barracuda. Never mind, the job had been done and the 30 rockets in the hold were in the condition they needed to be. He looked to his port side and instantly went into combat alert mode. A powerful launch was approaching from three kilometres. He trained his binoculars on it. There were maybe five on board, all wearing green uniforms. They were still too far away to make out what kind of men they were but whatever they were this dhow, fast as it was, couldn't outrun them. He knew enough about it to get them to the RV point, but he knew nothing of the local tides. Worse, the launch was coming for the dhow from a right angle from Khafira. They'd be intercepted. Who was on to them?

He went through his choices and cursed The Shark for sending him down the wrong alley. He could blow them away – what would it take to wipe out a handful of Khafira port cops for Christ's sake? Fuck all. But they were connected to the shore by radio and he couldn't afford for questions to be asked. On the other hand much bigger questions would be asked when those cops got on board. Much bigger questions!

"Stand ready," he called to the crew. "We have visitors on the port side. They needed no more instructions, each picked up his favoured weapon and walked to the port rail. The launch got closer, Barracuda could see the crew more clearly. They had weapons, M16s by the look of them, but they weren't at the ready, they lay by their sides. A machine gun, mounted in the bow, was unmanned. One man was clearly more senior, Barracuda could make out an elaborate gold brading on his epaulettes. What the fuck was this about! His men stood with their weapons concealed under the rail. They waited. The launch drew closer, much closer. Still the green uniforms looked relaxed, their weapons untouched at their sides. It was a powerful launch and was going to cut them off easily. But it didn't. Instead the boat picked up speed and passed fifty metres in front of them. The man with the epaulettes appeared to smile and made a brief gesture with his hand. The launch carried on a parallel course with the coast and left them behind. Then the dhow's radio crackled in to life with a heavily accented but perfect English.

"We are just ensuring that the coast remains clear for you."

Barracuda knew that no one else had heard it except, possibly, The Shark, because it was their own reserved frequency. This must be the Shark's port police colonel. Barracuda's relaxed but he was angry. This was a service he could do without. There were five guys on that fucking launch. That was five more people who knew that the dhow was heading for where it was. He didn't like it but there was nothing he could do about it. He grabbed the radio mike and called out, "Thanks for the attention. Let us know if you see anything we don't."

"You won't," replied the accent, "Except maybe the occasional shark. I am sure you know how to deal with those."

If only, thought Barracuda.

August
Bank transfer

Winter startled awake. He flailed his eyes around the room: nothing! He heard the noise of a construction gang outside and eased back on his pillow. It was late in the morning. He raised himself up again, got up and pulled aside the curtains. There was a loud group shouting in Urdu above the noise of their power tools. As he moved away from the window he became aware of the stiffness in his legs and tenderness in his feet.

He was close to fainting when he finished the five kilometre trek back to the Range Rover. The temperature had stayed at a constant thirty degrees, the humidity at 100 per cent. By the time he'd got to bed it was five in the morning. He'd fallen on top of his bed and went straight to sleep. Now it was morning, a new day. It was all in the past and the darkness of night; reality was here with him now, it had been a dream.

Then he put his foot down on the floor, winced and knew it wasn't a dream. He was still thirsty. He took a bottle of water from the fridge and gulped it straight down. He took in the familiar scene around the kitchen. It was his. He was home, on his own. But reality wasn't the comfort of this kitchen, it was a woman in a hotel room in Maraka. He breathed in deeply, and moved to the phone. He paused just as he was about to punch in the code for Maraka. The phone tap, the surveillance, the journey to see Will Hartson, the police! The handset was still in his hand, he replaced it. No phones! He would try to call Hartson again. He dialled the number. It rang three times, a weary voice answered. "Will Hartson."

"Thank God! Where have you been, Will?"

"For fuck's sake get off the line and leave me alone, Paul. I want sleep."

"What's the matter with you? I've had a bad night you know."

"You poor little soldier, so have I, now fuck off. I'll call you later."

"We have to talk, Will, soon."

"I'll call you later. Now FUCK off." The line went dead.

His feet stung, he set about getting himself right; plasters, embrocation, more water, a breakfast of Muesli and skimmed milk. He hardly tasted it. The phone rang. He reached for it nervously. "Paul Winter, good morning." He relaxed as he heard the voice at the other end. It was Samir Latif's personal assistant; was he available for an excursion on Mr. Latif's yacht in two days time? He had to accept, Latif was a major bank customer, he had no choice. Another complication. Still, at least Samir Latif had remembered his offer. That was the kind of person he should be mixing with, not a refugee prostitute. How tacky! In fact, why didn't he stop now, turn it all over to Colonel Hamid and go back to his ordinary life? Why not wash his hands of the thing, it's not as if he'd asked to be involved? It had nothing to do with him, he'd just been an innocent bystander as she roped him in. It would be so easy just to walk away, so tempting. He thought about it, wrestled with the ramifications, his obligations as a citizen, his future. It should have been a simple choice and he knew of few people in his short life in Khafira who would have spent more than three seconds on making a decision. But he'd given her his word, and that had to mean something, at least to him, even in this age and in this place. Who said words don't cost anything? He of all people was supposed to know what things cost.

Then the idea hit him – to his surprise, ideas weren't his forte, they were the province of other people. He just looked after peoples' money. But that was the point: he was a banker, and just for once it might be useful beyond the precincts of the bank. He had the knowledge, all he needed was the nerve. All right so he knew almost nothing of this overheated country. But he could plan an escape route through his own bureaucracy. He knew his way around everything: the branch network, customs rules, shipping routes and currency tricks, because that's what he did every day, it was his job. That's how he'd wash his hands of her. He smiled for the first time in days.

Fuck you too, Will Hartson! I can go where you can't.

Maraka was quieter than its larger, richer neighbour. There was less traffic, fewer people and not much noise. It had virtually no oil so it retained more of the flavour of the old Gulf. Her hotel was not international class, it didn't have good service, but that was the least of her worries. It was midday, she had dozed through the night but never truly slept. She had been alone, but she always slept alone. Customers were for sex. Sleeping was her private luxury, no one had the right to impinge on it, and no one ever did. It was implicit in every contract. It hardly needed spelling out, every one of her customers had a wife and family to return to. She rarely, but sometimes, had to explain the rules to some lonely man who wanted warmth as well as sex. Warmth was not what she sold, it would cost too much.

Noon, and still he had not called. What was he doing! She switched on the television and idled away the next half an hour watching the English and Arabic channels. Now that was a good idea: television. She could become a TV presenter somewhere else in the region. Not the Gulf; maybe in Egypt, or even Morocco, she had perfect French after all. She looked at the Arab channel and watched the smiling woman with the big mouth and loud jewellery. She looked gorgeous, untainted and clean. The realisation crept in that the game was over, or her part in it. There would be no more customers, no more money, no more running away from whatever she was most scared of. She could break out and go to Morocco but so what? She still had to confront what had terrified her all her life. If she had not loved her mother quite so much and if she hadn't died when she was ten then commitment would have been easier. Now she was past thirty, on the run, maybe close to death somewhere.

She had never loved anyone after her mother. The thought took her unawares. She shivered, got up from the chair and paced around the room. It nagged at her. The beautiful Arab woman was introducing a film, from Egypt, from the 1950s. The woman smiled, her teeth nearly blanked out the screen with their whiteness. Jose did not need the wall of a TV screen to make everyone adore her, not like the woman strobing her white teeth. She hit the remote control angrily and looked at her watch.

Phone you English bastard!

Winter walked into the cavernous, newly-built bank, nodded at the armed guard and went up to his office. One of his personal staff asked how he was and why he had come in, but he bluffed it easily enough. He'd left something in the desk he said, too important not to have with him. He excused himself and went straight to his office, closed the door and fired up his computer to access Jose Badradini's file. It took only a few seconds to flash up on the screen. He studied it and straight away he saw something was wrong. The file had already been pulled from the computer earlier that day. Files were never pulled except for annual review. Hers wasn't due for another eight months. He examined it nervously. What the…! Good god, they'd reached their tentacles inside his own bank; as sacrosanct as any church, but they'd damned well done it anyway. They had frozen her account; every transaction no matter what the currency. They were after her all right and they had known exactly where she banked. And now he that had pulled the same file they might be after him too. He checked his own details. They were unaltered. He kept virtually nothing in Khafira anyway. He was paid from London and sent it straight to an account in Jersey.

He set to work. His profile was powerful enough to override nearly every authority in the bank. The word "nearly" mattered here but he would be able to deflect any tracking programme on the account so they wouldn't find out what he was up to – not for a while, at least. He overrode them to leave a false trail, created a new file, reduced her balance to make it seem as if she had never had much in the account. He made out transfer documents for most of it to go to a bank in Mumbai. She could withdraw it there. He guessed she'd need expenses in Maraka to get out so he sent a few thousand dollars to a bank there. If only Will Hartson was around, he would know how the next part of the plan would go. Winter knew nothing about bribes or illegal exits, Hartson would. But somehow they would buy her an illegal passage out at the Maraka port. He knew how lax their rules were; she would be able to get out.

The phone rang by her bedside and she rushed to answer it. It was the first contact she had had since the Englishman left the night before.
"I'm in Khafira and just about to leave. I can't use the phones in the apartment, they're bugged I think. I'm calling from a public phone."
"It has taken until now for you to call me. I do not believe you are coming at all?" Who used public phones these days, anyway? Were there any?
"Of course I'm coming. I have to be careful of not being followed."
"Can't you even do that right?" There was a pause.
"I don't know."
"Hurry up, Paul Winter." She hung up.
Sixty-five minutes later there was a knock at her door, she opened it cautiously. It was him. She said nothing but looked beyond him for the half expected policeman. There was no one. Her relief came out in a flurry of anger. "Where have you been? I have been worried. I thought you had run out on me."

"I'll tell you later. First we have to get to the port." She started to interrupt but he continued: "Just pack your bag, clean your teeth and shut up. We're going there now." She went quiet. She had pushed him too far. She said no more and did as he asked. But she would not be ordered about, she would have her revenge on this silly Englishman for this act of humiliation – subjugation, even! She went into the bathroom but left the door open enough for him to see her reflection in the mirror. She let the bathrobe slip to the floor and stood fully naked in front of the mirror. She fondled her breasts teasingly, tossed her hair, smoothed her hands down her thigh. Then she looked straight into the mirror and caught his longing. Don't order me about, Englishman!

"Hurry up!" he said, turning away his eyes.

She chuckled quietly as she saw his gaze creep back to her reflection. She stepped into a pair of briefs and slowly massaged them up her thighs until they were in place on her hips, then she passed her hand over her pudenda. So that worked where shouting at him did not. Whatever it took. He would pay for humiliating her. She could sense his desire pulsing through the cheap hotel room. He would have bitten through a steel door to get to her if he thought he had a chance. That was enough, she smiled in the mirror for him to see then pushed the bathroom door shut as she slipped a t-shirt over her exposed breasts. His view was cut off.

The cafe

Diana's smile died as she walked into the Cafe de Bruxelles and caught Hartson's cold gaze. He'd slept fitfully. He felt as bad as when he'd got into bed, just after shouting at Paul Winter. She had some explaining to do.

"What would you like Diana?" He breathed metaphorical ice on to her with the enquiry. Was she flustered? Was he the one puppet who had managed to cut his strings? If she only knew.

"A mint tea please." The voice was inviting, unconcerned. Surely she must at least be curious. "You look terrible, Paul. Was it that bad?"

"Yes, Diana, it was." His exposed skin radiated a raw sting which the perfunctory sleep had done little to calm. He burned badly. She put a hand on his cheek. That was unexpected. How far are you taking this game, Diana?

"Is that a bruise?" Yes, Diana, it's blue, and red, and a bit yellow now. But he only nodded. "You poor thing." So now she was a nurse. "Don't bother, Diana, I

already know about your bedside manner, if you can remember that far back."
She withdrew the hand. There was a hesitation while it hovered around his cheek. Was she going to slap him? Perhaps he deserved it. No he bloody did not. The hand went down to the table. He called a waiter, ordered mint tea, then looked her straight in the eye. "I was picked up within twenty minutes of leaving your place, Diana. Sheikh Issa's men working to Colonel Ali Abdul Hamid." Her face betrayed nothing, her eyes hardly flickered. "I was beaten up, dragged into a Landcruiser, and dumped in the middle of the dunes." He stopped to take a sip of his coffee. She watched him for a few moments before saying: "What does this have to do with me?"

"No, really, apart from a few cuts and bruises, and nearly dying, I'm absolutely fine. Don't be so concerned."

"For god's sake, Will stop behaving like a teenager. I'm very sorry you got hurt but I don't see that I have any connection."

"What about our mutual friend Sheikh Issa? You have had connections with him haven't you?"

"This is stupid jealousy isn't it! It's none of your business who I meet or what I do."

"Don't you get it? I was tailed from your place, they knew where I'd been."
She fell back on diplomatic obfuscation: "Coincidence!"

"Of course, why didn't I see that! So your association with Issa has nothing to do with it?"

"My association with anyone has nothing to do with you." There was a hint of anger, was he getting to her? The mint tea arrived; she looked away and concentrated on the spoon, stirring slowly. "If you must know, I haven't seen Issa for three months, not alone anyway. And before you say it again, he's unlikely to be remotely concerned about you or anyone else. It was up to him to call and he didn't."

Poor Diana.

"I'm sorry, I didn't realise you cared."

She caught him straight in the eye, "I don't." She looked as if she meant it.
A waiter cruised the tables clearing cups and ashtrays. The cafe was getting ready to close, the clientele would be moving on to the cocktail bars and restaurants soon. Diana studied the blue swelling on his cheek, and the angry redness on his arms and face. Could she really be responsible for that? She

shifted uncomfortably; no, she couldn't believe she was. So what if he was followed from her place, that didn't pin it on her. But it nagged at her.

"Your pal Tom Scott Garrett called this morning. He said that story about the Filipinos was a total misunderstanding. They were cut up by a speedboat. Total accident, the rest: sailors' embellishments."

That was news to her.

He continued: "So the embassy doesn't want me near it, either. You're absolutely sure you weren't part of the set up? I know how snugly dear Tom nestles in with the local security men."

She was affronted, how dare he! Diana used sex for her own purposes, no one else's. The idea of taking him to bed to set him up labelled her a whore. She wasn't. She leaned in with emphasis: "What I told you last night stands. I don't know what Tom's playing at, no one's told me. I saw the early circulars, it was no speedboat accident. There was even a navy doctor around somewhere."

His bruised face came alive, the man had a persistent energy, she admired him for that. But she remained guarded against his unpredictability.

"Did you see it?"

"What?"

"The doctor's report."

"No, the Navy kept it to themselves. We weren't even supposed to know he was around. The Navy has a tradition of believing it flies the flag for Her Majesty no matter what. Ambassadors can go rot."

"Amen to that."

She let out a chuckle. "Will, please know that I didn't set you up. I wanted you, I knew nothing about any kidnap."

"Give me something else, Diana, preferably something which doesn't get me dumped in the desert again, or end up with concrete weights on my feet at the bottom of the Gulf."

She owed him nothing, nothing at all, he had no right to think he did. Damn it, it was her career for god's sake! She looked at his face again, all red and angry. It was kind of cute in the rough way that journalists can be, an appeal soaked in drink and resentment. All right, maybe she did owe him something, but she didn't know why.

"Lobby terms?"

"I'll keep a secret, it's my job."

"Junior minister's coming here in a few days time."
"Who?"
"Fielding."
Fielding! The man came in and out of his life like a visiting parasite: university, Lobby and now here.
"Ah. What for?"
"Obvious isn't it! It's secret, no fanfares, or official welcomes, the Foreign Office wants it kept strictly private. No one outside the embassy's supposed to know."
He said nothing, waiting for more.
"I can't give you more, Will, you know that."
He still said nothing.
"Oh for goodness sake: he's here to smooth through an arms deal. That's why everything is being kept hush-hush and they don't want any old hack spoiling the party by turning up bodies in the Gulf."
"But Issa's in Berkshire at the moment, wouldn't it be easier to see him there?"
"You know Issa, he likes to play hard to get."
"I'll take your word for it."
She pulled back very slightly.
"Enough, Will: Fielding's talking to people of…" she made a quotes sign with her fingers, "influence."
He looked at her quizzically.
God, Will, do I have to spell it out loud? He's seeing Samir Latif!"
"Now I get it."
"We're quits."
"You'd threaten your career for this?"
"…I…I didn't hear it from the embassy, it's above my pay grade. And I trust you to keep me out of it." As she ended the sentence she looked at a picture of Sheikh Issa positioned close to his father, Mahmood.
"I think Issa's playing a much longer game, he thinks a long way ahead."
Ah, thought Hartson, now that's reliable intelligence.
A waiter made a show of looking at his watch and hovering over them. They were the last in the cafe. Hartson's cold front thawed. "All right Diana, you're absolved. We'd better go."

She hesitated. She didn't immediately get up.

"Can I fix you something to eat at my place Will?"

This woman was impossible to predict, as mercurial as a flash flood. She had a talent for throwing him off balance. He hadn't expected that. And yes, he was sorely tempted, too sorely. The back of his neck was still burning, he thought his shirt was going to burst into flames; his arms were still raw pink. "Very kind but I need some rest Diana. Thanks for last night, it was wonderful," he flashed his radiating pink arm at her, "But I can't take the afterglow." She laughed out loud then checked herself quickly. It was the first time he'd seen her do it and she hadn't been quick enough to stop him seeing the relief leaking from her.

But Hartson needed to see a navy doctor before anyone else.

May
Rockets

By the time the dhow reached the deserted inlet Barracuda had mastered the controls. The vessel didn't have a deep draft but it was enough to cause trouble if she ran into shallows; the police launch was acting as a pilot craft and guided them through. He looked with his binoculars to the shore where he could make out his three trucks and his pickup, all now stripped of the thin white coat of paint he'd had put on for the Maraka-unload and now covered in US Armed Forces desert camouflage. He would have struggled against the sandy shore if he hadn't known what to look for, so that had gone well. And so had the rendezvous. There wasn't another soul in sight or on the horizon. The Shark had been as good as his word. The police launch turned back into the Gulf and disappeared.

The Shark had assured him that tying up the dhow in the inlet would be easy, thousands had done it over the centuries, so why should anything change now? All the same he used the laptop to send an email ashore. "How's the draft? Can we unload safely?" Two minutes later a reply came: "Fine at low tide, old stone jetty. High tide a problem. Rises six feet."

Shit, just perfect. It had all gone too well. He could tell from the progress the dhow was making that they were running in with the tide. Well, at least he'd have deeper water to moor in. He shut down the laptop and concentrated on bringing the dhow into the inlet. She was a surprisingly responsive craft with a huge rudder. It took him a few turns before he learned not to overcompensate. The dhow made a zigzag pattern in the water as she made a stuttering approach to the narrow inlet. As he got close he straightened the wheel and hoped nothing would get snagged. Once through he saw the stone jetty. At high tide it was a foot above the water line, which meant the rockets would have to be lowered down. They weren't that heavy but it was a clumsy operation and he didn't like the extra uncertainty it brought. Still, he had no time to wait for the tide to go out. That would be another six hours and he wanted to be inside Iraq by then, one way or another.

There was an unfortunate bumping sound as the hull touched the stone jetty. Barracuda winced. He was enough of a seaman to care about getting it right. Not so much to let it ruin his day, though. The Barracudas stood by to tie up against long steel stakes they'd driven into the hard sand. Barracuda stood at the starboard rail of the dhow and called out, "Stop sunbathing you shitheads. I want them off in forty minutes."

The Barracudas got to work. It was as difficult as the boss had feared. The rockets, still in their crates, were carried first from the sweaty hold on to the deck, then passed down again. At over 150 pounds each time it was hard and delicate work but it had to be done quickly.

Then, half way through when fifteen crates had been safely unloaded and put into the waiting trucks, what Barracuda feared would happen, did. One of the men, maybe too confidently, let a crate slide off the starboard rail before anyone was ready to take it. It smashed on to the stone jetty with a splintering crash and Barracuda heard a loud metallic chink at the same time. It didn't ring out cleanly like a bell, it had a fractured sound about it. His rage, no longer having to be hidden, surfaced quicker than a great white chasing a surfer. He didn't say a word but his face was almost bursting in its purple redness. He grabbed the offending man by the arms and hit him hard in the stomach. He picked him up and was about to throw him over when another Barracuda stepped in and stopped him. The rage wouldn't go away though. He roared down to the jetty, "Open what remains of that fucking crate and see what's happened!" Two men walked towards in gingerly but Barracuda could already smell on the light sea breeze that the warhead had been compromised – or that Merlin had been in such a hurry that he hadn't resealed it properly.

Gradually his rage subsided, but not before the two men had opened the splintered crate and it was too late to stop them from putting their hands in. They didn't say anything to begin with but slowly it began to dawn on them that the gooey mess they were feeling wasn't right. Barracuda recovered himself and yelled to them, "Get in the water, fast, everyone else move away. Throw a tarpaulin over it, don't let it spread. If it gets on your skin you'll be out of action for weeks. Move!"

They moved. They did all he said. The two men jumped into the sea suddenly yelling as the pain hit them and started scoring into their skin, taking off the upper layers. At least the salt water would help to cauterise the wounds, thought Barracuda. But what use would the men be to him now? At least it hadn't vaporised, they'd all be breathing fire right now if it had. He couldn't allow it to stay on the jetty for long, even covered by a tarpaulin. He jumped down from the dhow and walked up to the leaking rocket. There was nothing for it. He couldn't quarantine it so he picked it up, wrapped in the tarpaulin, all 155 pounds, and took it to the jetty front where he dropped it into the water. It would sink to the bottom and be a problem for a few fish maybe, but not for him any more. It was the price he had to pay for being hasty – and the rockets couldn't be too secure, whoever was to find them needed to stumble upon the mustard agent quickly.

 He turned back to his men and said, "Get on with it. We still have fifteen more to do and I don't have time to play doctors and nurses." They knew better than to question him. They did not live in a world of compassion; if they did they would not be on that jetty. He let the two injured men rest for a short while before asking, "Can you still hold a gun?" Both replied, probably thinking of payday, that they could and would. "Right," said Barracuda, "If you can fire a gun you can handle the rest of these crates. Get going." The men nodded and concealed their pain as they carried on with their task. Cruelty was part of their life. They wouldn't have known any other way.

August
Maraka

Winter's eyes drifted to her when he thought she wasn't looking. But that was rare, her gaze never seemed to leave him, it devoured him in a contemptuous stare as if everything in her life was his fault. The sooner she was gone the sooner he would be able to get back to normal. Someone else in his position might see it as an adventure, but that wasn't a word Winter used often. They were in the hotel room in Maraka It was late afternoon. The air-conditioning wasn't as efficient as they would have liked.

"Have you any idea what a hole this is?" she said.

"It's perfectly all right. It's quiet for one thing."

"Exactly!"

God, she was infuriating. "Do you have to countermand everything I do?"

"You do so many stupid things."

That was enough! Time she learned just how much he was doing for her. "You're absolutely right there. The stupidest has been trying to help you. Maybe I'll just leave you here and return to Khafira to get on with my life. You can do whatever you feel like – why not take a walk along the inlet? How well off are you for money? No? Still you can sort that out, can't you! You don't need anything from me."

"All right, you've said enough. It's not as if my life is great right now."

She sat silent for a few minutes. It was all over. She could never come back, not even as a respectable lady. This was the best she could hope for: skulking out of the country to India, probably, with no papers. So much for being a TV presenter! Even the Englishman was tired of her. She took out her now grubby handkerchief and used it to wipe away some mysterious sweat from her eyes. And in that moment, she realised what she had to do: she was pushing him away and right now he was the only thing she had. She put the handkerchief away, softened her voice and tried not to choke on her words. "I am sorry." She got up from the bed and moved towards him, her arms by her side, lips pouted, eyes somehow configured into a sort of smile. "You are trying to help me, I know. You have no reason to." She raised a hand to his cheek, he started to withdraw but stopped. "Thank you," she said and then reached down her hand to his, drew it up gently and placed it on a breast.

Whatever it took.

Anger

The minesweeper was quiet. Her engines put out their normal pulse, but there was a silence about her. No one shouted, or joked, or grimaced, or sang, they went about their tasks, wordlessly.

Jackson, though, was seething. He knew he would do no good by bringing up the latest discovery. It was meant to lie at the bottom of the sea, and so they would, but he felt no better about it. He'd known for days that the Filipino corpses had never made it to Khafira, but he was still surprised. He was harbouring a hope that the port police had dealt with it in a proper manner. But instead they had spat in the face of the Royal Navy and the British Government. He'd been proud to serve both, now he wondered if either really counted for anything. In which case what did he, an officer in the Royal Navy, amount to?

The position was marked, the body left. Nobody made cracks about cannonballs any more, the crew had seen the bodies when they were first pulled out. There was nothing to laugh about. Jackson sent a ship to shore communication for the commodore and waited for an answer. He knew now the body was in international waters it was out of anyone's jurisdiction. He wanted to scream but his officer's epaulettes weighed heavy on his shoulders and he contented himself with a deep sigh. He was building up a lot for the next time he went ashore. What was the point of being in a crack military unit if this was the result? Maybe that journalist had stuffed his Navy career, but what kind of a career was it anyway? Sod it! If we turn a blind eye we condone it, he thought. We sanction everything that they do, and they still shit on us. There was obviously some deep diplomatic game going on but it stank. He shouldn't be working to cover it up, nor should the Royal Navy. He had a mind to stop in mid-survey, bring up the sad, wrecked corpse and take it back to the mainland. Let them try and stop his minesweeper with a police tender. It was just a daydream, he was in command. An international incident would be stupid. He scanned the horizon for a distraction.

A rating yelled out to him: "Message coming through sir." He waited a few seconds before reading out loud the response from the Commodore. "Do nothing. Continue your task. Body out of national jurisdiction. Leave it there!"

So there he was: impotent and useless. This mutilated, eviscerated corpse had once been a young man and he belonged somewhere, he'd been loved by someone, now they were to leave him to disintegrate at the bottom of the sea. Someone had cared enough to give them what they believed would be God's protection but a fat lot of good those gold crucifixes had been. And they were still on the bodies when they were retrieved. Whoever saw the last moments was rich enough not to care about gold or crucifixes.

He hardened his face, squared his shoulders, and looked out to sea again. But for all his officer's rings and badges of command he felt lower than a mercenary corporal selling his services to some be-medalled South American gangster.

Medic
If Hartson had been trying to get hold of a Navy doctor in the UK he would have been forced to scale a military fence, or bluff his way through the security gates and avoid being checked on every corner of the base. That wasn't his style, too much work and anyway, he'd be found out before he got near anything. But Brits abroad tend to find each other, like most expat groups, no matter if they're in the armed services or something else. The strangest alliances formed of diplomats, engineers, bankers, chancers and anyone who happened to be passing through. So finding the right Navy doctor hadn't been so hard for Will Hartson. The odd question here, a free drink there, an unguarded conversation with a rating or two. No need to give away what he was. Now he was sitting beside the doctor who was out of uniform and drinking alone. Hartson made a casual comment about the icy beer and the air-conditioning and pretended to shiver.

"Might as well be at the North Pole eating icicles for breakfast," he joked.

"Too right," came a moderated northern accent and the easy familiarity that an encounter with a stranger can sometimes bring. I've come close to doing that," he added, and Hartson knew he was in.

"How come?"

"Part of the training. I'm an officer in the Royal Navy."

"How do you do, I'm Will Hartson. I work in communications." It wasn't strictly a lie. "You must be with the new flotilla?"

"Yes and no, I'm a Royal Navy doctor. Anthony Johnson, Lieutenant." They shook hands. Hartson thought it absurd that both hands should be freezing through holding the beer.

"I can't think there's much work for you out here."

"More than you'd think. There're five hundred officers and men stationed here at the moment. They still break bones, have fights, suffer hernias and piles, get social diseases."

"Did you need to join the Navy for that?"

"Believe me, whatever the Navy has to offer it beats what I was doing. If I'd stayed on in the National Health Service I would have had to quit by now. Joining up seemed like a good idea." He'd already knocked back a couple by the look of him.

"Do you find the forces and being a doctor compatible, I mean do you have to do the same things as the other officers?"

"I wear the uniform and make the same noises as an officer. After that I wield the occasional scalpel for an appendix op, I never go near a bayonet or a gun."

"How do they feel about that?"

"Oh it's fine, we've been around on ships for centuries. They know what we're there for and they're grateful for it."

"Don't you have to learn the drills and all that sort of thing?"

"I did a month at Dartmouth when I entered. It was daft, all the Navy doctors, lawyers and nurses had to do the course but it was painfully obvious that none of us took it seriously. It drove the drill instructors mad. Mine was a sergeant in the Royal Marines. He got red in the face every time I put a foot in the wrong place or shouldered arms at the wrong time. But he still had to call me sir. He'd seen action in the Falklands and Northern Ireland and was one of the toughest men I had ever met, but he still had to call me sir because I was an instant officer."

Hartson didn't care about the intricacies of naval etiquette, but he was happy to pretend that he did. "And I promise you I'm not very brave," continued the doctor. Hartson bought two more ice-cold pints and they bantered some more about the temperature. "I didn't anticipate having to treat frostbite out here," he joked.

Hartson laughed. "You Navy doctors must have a more exciting time than fixing up a chief petty officer's piles." They both grimaced.

"You get the occasional interesting one. I mean treating divers for the bends, that sort of thing." Lt Anthony Johnson had still not been joined by any of his Navy colleagues and Hartson assumed he did not fit in with the way of things on board ship. He was a qualified doctor with seven years education at a university and more in the National Health Service; that made a different kind of officer.

He pressed on: "So it really is that run of the mill?" Johnson took a sip from his pint.

"Not always, I got one a few days ago which actually made me sick. Believe me I've seen most of the things that can happen to a human body, there's not much that can throw me." Hartson nodded. "It's not the actual mess that's done to the corpse…," that's the idea doctor, tell me all about it! "Corpse? Don't you treat the living?"

"Normally yes, but I had to be an instant coronary pathologist for the brass that time. One of our ships found some bodies dumped in shallow water a few kilometres out. I was called in to check them over."

"Good God!" Hartson simulated surprise with a practiced air.

"They'd been abused, and I would say tortured." It was almost as if he had become practiced at saying it. The words came matter-of-factly out of the surgeon's mouth, but that was the Navy training because he went on to say: "It's the intent that gets to me. The mutilations I can deal with – they happen all the time in road accidents and bomb explosions. But these weren't caused by that kind of thing, they'd been inflicted by some kind of torture."

Hartson looked on, silently; the drink was oiling the doctor's voice and the words were tumbling out. "There were cigarette burns on their mouths, and bruises on every part of them that was left. They'd been beaten badly." He paused for a moment. Don't stop now Dr Johnson, not when we're so close.

"It still makes me sick to think of it now."

"Who would have done such a thing?" gasped Hartson, convincingly.

"I don't know but they looked like they made full use of them first.

"What do you mean?"

"I'm no pathologist but I'm sure they were raped."

That's my boy, keep it coming. Fuck you Scott Garrett. Thank you Diana. Speedboat accident indeed!

"It seems impossible. You're sure it wasn't an accident...like a stray speedboat or something?"

Anthony Johnson looked at him as if he was a moron. "Couldn't have been anything like it, they were too far out to sea. Anyway concrete had been attached to the legs. They were sunk like fishing weights. And they weren't dead when they were thrown in, there was water in the lungs…well, what was left of them after the marine life had feasted on them!"

Hartson recoiled, despite himself, the reality of it soaked into his cynicism.

"It must have been for some weird pleasure because they weren't robbed."

"How can you tell?"

"Two of them had quite valuable looking gold crucifixes around their necks. The boys were only about fourteen or fifteen the lot of them. They must have been given by family or something like that."

"Doesn't sound as if they did them much good." Hartson wasn't acting any more.

They drank their beer quietly for a while.

Déjà Vu

Sam Jackson dreaded the next time a call came to say something new had been scanned. He knew it would be another of the boys, but he couldn't ignore it just in case it wasn't. The call came anyway. He checked his uniform and went about the task as efficiently as possible.

"You're sure nothing's marked here?"

"Nothing at all, sir."

"OK let's take a look at it."

The divers went down. Ten minutes later the signal came back up the line, "Four bells."

"What have you got?" barked Jackson.

"It's another one, sir."

"You're sure? It couldn't be a dhow sailor lost overboard?"

"The concrete is as hard as it ever was, sir." He lifted his head and breathed in deeply. The line crackled again, "There's a gold crucifix on this one as well." No doubt about it then. "All right, come up, leave him down there. We'll mark it on the chart." The crew looked at him uncertainly. He knew he had to give them some sort of lead, but he was damned if he knew what it should be. He gave an order to carry on with the survey once the divers came back aboard. He warned them to stay alert. "Next time it might be a real threat. We can't be complacent."

He went back to his cabin to think.

Diplomat's dilemma

The telephone rang on Tom Scott Garret's desk making him jump out of a trance. "Good afternoon, Mr. Scott Garrett, This is Colonel Ali Abdul Hamid speaking."

"Hello, Colonel Hamid, how nice to hear from you again. How can I help?"

"I wonder if you have needed to speak to one of your countrymen, a Mr. Paul Winter, in recent days?"

He breathed out slowly. "Doesn't ring a bell immediately, Colonel. There are quite a few British people out here, of course. I might have met him at a function somewhere."

"It's nothing urgent, Mr. Scott Garrett. I just thought you should know the picture." He listened as the colonel explained the story he already knew about the dead woman.

"Of course, I can rely upon your discretion in these matters, Mr. Scott Garrett?"

"Of course, Colonel, anything to keep our two countries holding hands happily."

"There is one further complication. If Mr. Winter should contact you I am anxious to talk to him about another incident. He was seen manhandling a waiter at a cafe yesterday. Actually he accused this man of trying to kill him."

"He does get in the wars doesn't he!"

"It appears to be so. The same man was found dead in his room yesterday evening."

Unfamiliar noises started to go off in Tom's head. "You think he did it?"

"I doubt it very much, Mr. Scott Garrett. Incidentally the man was found in an area of the Souk with which you are very familiar, I think." His heart beat harder. He had been so careful not to be seen, to disguise his movements.

"If Mr. Winter happens to call you and mention a Michel Habibi perhaps you will let me know?" The noises became louder, his heart was now pounding, the name sent a stream of perspiration running down his back. He felt ice cold at the same time. He hoped Hamid could not detect the quiver in his voice.

"I'll let you know straight away, Colonel."

"Thank you, we do not want any complications with your ministerial visit so imminent."

"Absolutely not, Colonel." He replaced the receiver and stared at the wall.

May
Into the dunes
 Barracuda ordered his men to hide their weapons as they approached a border coalition control point. He didn't want to get in a shooting match with coalition forces; that would be stupid. He didn't care who he killed, his paymasters or their enemies, but he saw no reason to risk the mission for the sake of a simple mistake – in this case their weapons being spotted as Kalashnikov automatic rifles, or AK 47s. He and his men were dressed for the desert camouflage outfit of the United States Army. He wore a uniform with the concealed insignia of a major. For the next few hours and days the Barracudas would be emissaries of the US Special forces and that was an act he could carry off well enough – but no self respecting special forces man would carry an AK 47, it just wasn't reliable, still less accurate. What it could do was spit out a venomous number of rounds in a very short space of time. Fine for a massacre, useless for the surgical operations special forces were trained to carry out. They had weapons of their own choice and most picked the M16. Few would take the Brit SA 80 – even the Brit Special Forces laughed at it. But no one would pick an AK 47. No one except the Barracudas because when they did their dirty work they needed to leave evidence that didn't implicate the coalition. There was no use dumping mustard agent rockets if he shot the place up with M16s. Who the hell would believe the rockets were genuine?
 He approached the control where he saw, with relief, a US soldier walk out to meet him. Brits might be more suspicious, they knew a hell of a lot more about security. Barracuda wound down his window and winced as the blistering air of the desert scorched his face.
 "Can I see some ID please, Sir," the soldier, a private first class, asked.
 "I'll show you my rank, son," said Barracuda with a vague Midwest accent while opening the flap on his jacket to expose the major insignia.
 "Thank you, Major, Sir," said the soldier. "Are these men with you?"
 "Yep, we're all in this together."
 "Where are you heading, sir,"
 "I can't tell you."
 "Special forces, huh!"
 "Can't tell you that either and you'd better not ask too much more, son, we

have a job to do."

"Yes sir," said the soldier as he raised the barrier.

Barracuda pressed the electric window button and let the air-conditioning wash over him. He eased back into his seat and took the jeep and his convoy forward. Great! Easier than dynamiting fish in a pond. They were in, and now they were heading into the desert. Barracuda spared not a single thought for the condition of the men whose hands had been excoriated by the mustard agent. He didn't need to. He didn't devote any thought to the faulty warhead he'd dumped into the inlet at high tide either.

He certainly didn't turn round as he left to see the dead fish floating to the top as the tide went out, taking them into the Gulf. He didn't see the traces of mustard agent being dragged out slowly to the deeper waters of the Gulf where it would come into contact with more marine life, get into its gills and destroy them.

No, Barracuda was in a hell of a hurry and if he'd sent the rocket with its agent to the bottom of that inlet it was hidden from him and everyone else as far as he was concerned.

But it wasn't.

The paint was barely dry on the rocket fuselage; it would take only a few hours to dissolve in the warm salty seawater of the inlet. And a slowly extending trail of dead marine life was leading a trail straight to it, just waiting for a passing fisherman to notice that something was wrong. It would stop soon, the mustard agent would become so diluted that it would have no effect. But before it did, the dead shark, the dead manta ray, the dead sea snake and the hundreds of dead mullet and heavens knew what other fish, would float to the surface in a steadily spreading triangle leading to an apex at the mouth of the inlet.

And there, right by the jetty, two metres beneath the surface at low tide, was the fuselage of a Russian 122 millimetre rocket leaking mustard agent. But Barracuda, who normally thought about everything, had allowed his rage to get in the way, and he hadn't considered the mess he was leaving behind, or he didn't think it important.

Who was going to care about a few dead fish, after all?

August
Give a little...

She fucked, rutted, shagged and any variation her clients could dream up. She had no nice term for it. Now this romantic nonentity thought he'd made love to her. Jesus Christ, protect me from all men, she thought, contemptuously. And he was still talking. Her main aim had been to shut him up.

"I know you've had many men. I doubt if one more makes a difference, but you did for me." Oh, the little boy was humble as well as stupid. Well, she was on safe ground here at least. Sex was one thing she could give without compromising herself. Let him have her, it would cost nothing. Survival, she thought. That's all that counts. Now she had control of him.

Winter awoke from his post-coital doze, she was already awake beside him, looking more hollow eyed than earlier in the morning. Perhaps now he might get some answers. He stroked her arm and detected a shiver of intimacy from her. She restrained the impulse to push him away and stop him touching her. Sex was one thing, but closeness was not on the menu.

Winter was emboldened, though and stroked her again, this time on the neck. Oh how she hated this: hated, hated, hated it! And still he was talking.

"I still don't know who killed Hannah. I still don't know why you're running from the police. If you know, surely all you have to do is tell them and you'll be in the clear."

He waited to see the words "stupid Englishman" form on her lips but they didn't.

She fought back her irritation and tried to keep her body relaxed. She would have to put up with these questions and this physical attention. And she would have to provide some answers. She looked away while she gathered herself. "We were popular in our apartment. The most powerful men in Khafira came there. You might even have seen them." Winter said nothing. "The top businessmen, the leading police and military officers. In fact anyone who could buy a favour with the sheikhs."

"And the sheikhs as well?"

"Never at the apartment. Sometimes Hannah or me would be invited to one of their occasions, usually as the entertainment for a visiting sheikh or leader. It was lucrative, we had a lot to thank Samir Latif for."

"What did he have to do with it?"

"He recommended us to Sheikh Issa. We were one of his man sources for VIP entertainment. Samir Latif was always generous with his money and his recommendations."

Now he knew he was in over his head. "You do move in high circles."

"We only moved, we weren't part of it, just paid help, like you and your bank. You look after their money, we looked after something else."

"What does this have to do with Hannah dying?"

Her brow creased. "We had a quiet afternoon that day, only one booking, he asked for Hannah. I could take some time off, so I did."

"And...?"

She took a deep breath, averted her eyes, spoke slowly. "It was Colonel Hassan, chief of the Port Police. He was a regular, he'd always preferred Hannah. I can't say I'm sorry about that."

"And you think it was him?"

"It WAS him. I went out just before the maid, Maria, she was late leaving. I saw him coming up in the elevator. There's no doubt, he was her last customer. She never really liked him but he paid well. There was someone else with him but I couldn't see who, he had his back turned"

"Could this Maria help?"

"I should not think so. She was late because of some mystery about her boys. She'd been to the police station or something, it all passed me by. She probably wanted to speak to Hannah about it. She often poured out her troubles to Hannah. I could never be bothered to listen."

Winter let the casual lack of concern pass, he was learning that was how it worked out here.

"Perhaps we should speak to Maria, she may know something."

"What would she know, she's just an ignorant Filipina woman."

"Let's just give her a call now."

"She is not on the phone, She lives in the Khafira slums. No one is on the phone there, we always had to send a messenger when we needed her."

"Maybe we can contact her another way."

"Why should we?"

"Apart from anything else she might have been hurt, or worse." Jose looked away. Winter couldn't read the expression on her face, if there was one. She was being awkward over something important.

"Don't you care?"

Her face whirled round on him, fury burst through the tiredness. "I want to be *out* of here. No I don't care. None of this is my doing, I can't win, you can't win, Maria can't win. THEY will win every time. All I can do is go. Now let's get on with it please."

He shrank from her. Yes, they'd get on with it but not until he'd made a phone call, though.

Research

"It's just a tip from a local source. All you have to do is find out if Fielding is coming here." Hartson was impatient, why couldn't the bloody newsdesk understand what he wanted. It was simple. "I've told you there's nothing on his diary. If he's going out to the Gulf he's keeping it very secret."

"Exactly."

"Why would he want to do that?"

"Do you read your newspapers? Have you noticed it's a volatile region?"

"Don't be sarcastic, Hartson. Are you making a point?"

"Two words: defence and contracts."

Never mind, he'd plough on anyway. He ended the call and was about to leave his workstation when the phone rang. That was quick, too quick. He picked it up, "Will Hartson, Randalls Gulf Office."

"Will, at last."

Oh shit, Paul Winter. "Where are you?"

"Is your phone safe?"

"Probably not. Try that other number I gave you; that's as safe as Randalls' security can make it! I have a satellite-bypass system."

The line went dead and moments later another receiver on the desk sounded. Hartson picked it up, wearily. Winter didn't waste time on pleasantries.

"Maria is the maid, she was in the apartment before the death. Can you speak to her?" Hartson took down the details, reluctantly. He had enough to do, this was a complication he didn't want. But as he listened his resistance ebbed away. Had those people really been in the apartment where the girl's body was found.

Finally his reluctance disappeared to be replaced by cautious enthusiasm.

May
Thinking again

Morton looked at the empty meeting room and then his watch. He tried to be stoical about his masters but sometimes his disgust would burst right through and he would have to wipe the sneer from his face before anyone saw. Had he really just heard his Defence Secretary say there was every chance that Saddam had destroyed the weapons of mass destruction before our boys went in?

Well! The sneaky bastard, thought Morton. Just when you think you know what a guy is he goes and does something that leaves them all flailing around in the sand. Goddamned Saddam Hussein had spoiled the party by doing exactly what he'd been told to do by the United Nations. Of all the lowdown tricks; just so that we wouldn't find the weapons. What an operator. And then the secretary's deputy went and said the whole thing was a bureaucratic set-up anyway, he virtually admitted they were looking for an excuse to finish off the job they started in 1991. That made Morton really angry because he'd laid out sixty million dollars on an insurance policy to make sure the damned weapons were found. That was sixty million dollars that could have gone somewhere else other than to save the administration's ass. But it seems the Secretary for Defence didn't give a shit about saving his ass or anyone else's. He must think his pants were ironclad. What was strange is that they probably were. The good old American people – at least the ones who voted for this president – didn't see a whole lot wrong in what they'd done. Shit, No! They'd gone in to Eye Rack and kicked Saddam's butt. They'd finally got pay back for 1991, and 2001 in New York. It sure as hell felt good to win something again. Hell yes!

All that would have been OK. Morton had worked with politicians of all kinds, elected or not. He knew how the world worked; he helped make it go round. The sixty million bucks wasn't really a problem for him, he could hide it in the budgets and think of some plausible excuse for losing it. It wouldn't be the first time. Fuck, if Reagan had managed to get away with Contras in Honduras, this should be nothing.

No, what had really got on Morton's tail today was that after the Defence Secretary had blurted out his shameless admission, the goddamned Brit Prime

Minister went and countered him. He'd gone out to Kuwait and then Iraq and said, right there and then, that the weapons would show eventually.

Well, excuse me Mr. fucking white-assed Brit but who have you been speaking to? Couldn't they get their stories straight before they opened their mouths in front of a camera? But he knew they couldn't, the lure of glory is so great they lose their balance. He had to wait for them to fall and then pick them up again.

Except the Brit, he could fall anywhere. He was a fucking Liberal anyway, no matter what nice things the president said about him. Now it seemed the weapons would be found but it would take months. They weren't a priority, not any more. And there was Morton only a few days before being told they were Number One on the wanted list. Go find those weapons, he was told, we don't care how! Now they didn't matter any more. Now they didn't need them Now no one much cared if they turned up at all.

That left Morton with a problem. What was he to do with his "special search team?" He couldn't just abandon them, they were vengeful men and hardly loyal. God knows what could become of the weapons they were sent to "find". Worse, suppose someone went public! They'd have to be paid no matter what. But every day they carried on with their special search was a day they might be discovered. He knew Barracuda's methods; they'd be good for a quick fix, would have fed the public mood when no one was asking questions closely. But the questions would be much tougher after the heat died down.

Morton checked his watch again and made his decision.

August
Slum

The blocks were barely maintained, the air conditioning units poking out from every apartment were rusting and not functioning, the occupants desultory and hot. Hartson made sure to lock his Landcruiser when he arrived. His heart wasn't in this but he knew he couldn't ignore it. A crowd of manual workers from the sub-continent stared at him as he walked to one of the blocks. This was the downside of Khafira, the slaves' quarters in the city-state. Free to come and go as they wished of course, the employers even paid for the flights to Mumbai, Madras Calcutta, Delhi, Lahore and Manila. But they stayed because to return home was even worse than staying in these slums.

He entered a block no different from any of the others. It could have been Ceaucescu's Bucharest. The elevator didn't work, inevitably. He found himself walking three flights of stairs. The staircases weren't air-conditioned and he wasn't fit. He was breathing hard and sweating when he got to the place he was looking for.

He knocked. Twenty seconds later it opened tentatively. He saw a small woman in a clean blue dress appearing to cower.

"Yes," she said, suspiciously.

"Are you Maria?"

"Why do you want to know?" The voice lacked confidence but was delivered in clear and correct English.

"Please can I come in and talk to you?" Maria opened the door a little more, looked down the corridor and beckoned him in. He did his reporter's trick of taking everything in while he had the chance. There were a few pieces of cheap furniture clean and well ordered. He looked at her: she was petite, poised, intelligent eyes, attractive to a certain kind of man. He saw a photograph hanging prominently on a wall close to a crucifix. It was of two young men with her, aged maybe 14 and 15.

She said: "A white Englishman coming around here causes eyes to turn. Why are you here?"

"Maria, I have come on behalf of one of the girls from the apartment where you clean."

"Are they in trouble?" The question came so quickly he stumbled for an answer.

"Yes there is trouble. How would you know?"

Her eyes hardened. "Because I work there as a maid, how else! The police have not let me near there for the last two days." She paused, fear was all over her face. "What has happened to them?"

She'd have to know sometime. He drew a deep breath. "Hannah has been killed."

"Oh dear, Jesus, no." Maria sank into a chair, "Playing those silly games with those horrible men who did not care. I tried to tell her so many times."

He cast around, feeling uncomfortable in someone else's grief. There were two doors leading off in one direction and two in another. He guessed that one area was for sleeping the other for bathing and cooking. It looked as if the two could be combined in the same space.

"Were you a friend of hers?"

"Why do you want to know?"

"I'm trying to find out why she died. You knew her well."

"The police know I work there. Sometimes I was still there when they came for appointments."

"Why are you frightened?"

"I had to become used to the police where I came from. The Philippines ten years ago was no place for an independent educated woman. "

So that was it. "Why did you come here?"

"I have a degree in social sciences and I thought I could get work in the academic field here." She gave an ironic chuckle, "In the end it was all I could do to get work as a maid in a whorehouse. But I had to feed my two boys somehow. The alternative was to do what the girls do... I mean did." She looked meaningfully at him.

She was probably in her mid-thirties but she had a look, an appeal, which was timeless. It wasn't beauty, nor even prettiness. It was an intelligence which lent her face nobility. Hartson looked into her dark eyes and felt a depth which chiselled into his own psyche.

"How did she die?"

"Badly, I'm afraid."

She looked away, held her hand up to her face and started to sob.

"I am sorry. I have lost so much and now this. I was only speaking to Hannah about my boys the last time I was there."

"What about your boys?" he asked.

"They worked at Maraka Airport – they could not get work in Khafira, they were too young. They are only fourteen and fifteen. They disappeared in May two years ago. They went to Maraka with some friends and would always be back by the evening. I had made a meal for them, but they never came. And no one at Maraka Airport would help...I think they were working illegally, you know what that place is like. I never heard from them again."

"What about the police?"

She grimaced. "No chance, what do they care about two missing Filipino kids? They just told me to fill out a report in Arabic and go away. They expected me not to know any."

"And you do?"

"I'm fluent, as in English, Spanish, and of course Pilipino."

"So what did Hannah have to do with this?"

"I had never bothered them before, it was only after I had exhausted every other possibility, even my own embassy...you can imagine how little they felt they could do! I tried first to speak to Jose – we are both Christians – but she was not interested. Then I spoke to Hannah and, you know, she would always listen, she was a really good-hearted woman. I think she will be in heaven anyway, even though she did what she did. It was only a few days ago, I wondered if she knew anyone who could help."

"Did you have anyone in mind?"

"I know who most of their regular clients are...were. She knew a lot of big people, and police officers. She had one that day..."

"Colonel Hassan of the port police?"

"How did you know?"

"Perhaps I can tell you more later."

He got up and moved a few inches to the window. He wanted to look on to open space, see the Gulf, the desert, the greenery stuck in the middle of it. He just saw another apartment block with strings of washing on every balcony.

"You were one of the last to see Hannah alive, I think. Maria. What can you tell me?"

"Nothing. I left the apartment a minute after the colonel arrived."

"He said nothing to you?"

"He ignored me completely. What do you expect? He had someone with him but he had kept his face hidden – that happened all the time. The girls had a big business and I did not dare ask who some of their clients were."

"Did he say anything to Hannah?"

"There was something about more arriving a little later. They'd decided to have a party if Hannah didn't mind."

"What did she say?"

"She was smiling but I don't think she meant it. She preferred to have Jose with her if it was busy."

"Who were the others?"

"I don't know. I had to leave at that point."

"Nothing more?"

"That is all."

He thanked her and started to move to the door. She touched his arm lightly and he paused. "Can *you* help me find my sons?" One more complication he could do without, but she was pleading and he could not just dismiss her like everyone else had.

She got up and went to the picture on the wall.

"These are my boys."

He looked again at the picture he had glimpsed earlier, but this time there was a click in his mind as things came together. They had gold crucifixes. What did the navy doctor say about gold crucifixes? They were young. They were Filipino. A rush of panic filled him s he realised that she would never see her boys again!

He fought down his feelings and hoped she hadn't seen it, but he also knew how smart she was. He could not face telling her, not now. He mumbled a meaningless phrase, "I'll see what I can do," and left, leaving her standing lonely in the doorway.

He never thought of himself as a brave man, and he wasn't, but now he realised he was a coward.

Summoned

The phone rang on Tom Scott Garrett's desk. He jumped as he did every time at the moment, for fear of Colonel Hamid being at the other end of the line. His career-blandness was struggling. He answered the call slowly and then breathed out, it was Lesley Dibden, the First Secretary: could Tom please pop along to his office? Bit of a problem from London. Hope it won't take too long. He put down the phone and walked along the corridor to his superior's office. Phil Wilkinson was there. Dibden looked up.

"Morning, Tom, hope all's well."

"Absolutely."

"Phil here has some bad news, I'm afraid." He looked at the commander who was standing stiffly.

"The minesweeper turned up the same bodies again, beyond territorial waters."

"Are we certain about it?" asked Scott Garrett.

"Same bodies, Tom, right down to the concrete. At least I hope so; God pray there weren't more of them. Whatever happened to them after we handed them over we can only guess. But they didn't get brought ashore for analysis or any police investigation. They were just taken further out and dumped again."

"Awkward." Wilkinson could no longer contain his frustration: "Speedboat accident my arse!"

"Quite, Commander," said Dibden, "although perhaps less salty vocabulary would be helpful. Moving on, we could do without this so close to the minister's visit."

"We must keep it quiet." Said Scott Garrett looking pointedly at the commander, "We can rely on your chaps, can we Phil?"

"You can for the time being, they're out on duty for the next ten days because they didn't keep quiet last time. Ironic, I suppose, they go back out and turn them up again."

"This is not my province," said Dibden, "But I imagine they'll have to be posted somewhere else as soon as they come back in. Phil, they can't stay here now. It only needs this little tidbit to get back to that interfering reptile from Randalls and there'll be hell to pay, ministerial visit or not."

"I'll speak to the Commodore," said Wilkinson.

"And I'll speak to London," said the First Secretary, "And Tom, I wonder if a word in the right ear about the Randalls fellow might help...is his visa up to date...or his passport? You get the idea?

"Absolutely," said Scott Garrett.

May
Change of plan

The room was quiet and more ordered than the previous month. They no longer sat into the late hours. The desk was clean, light came through artificial windows, the air-conditioning worked efficiently and everyone was dressed and presented impeccably.

"What a difference a few days makes," said Morton, "The picture has changed."

"How so?" asked his tormentor, Billy.

A flash of irritation, Morton's brow creased; couldn't the bastard at least let him finish his sentence! "I'm coming to it, Bill."

The others looked at him expectantly.

"You've read the briefings and if you haven't you'll have seen the newspapers and the TV news. The goddamned Jihad is back and up to its usual tricks."

He knew, they all knew, that the brief lull after the fall of Baghdad had come to an end. In front of each of them was a list of atrocities carried out by Islamic suicide bombers in Saudi Arabia, Morocco and Jerusalem. The death tolls hadn't been finalised but ran into hundreds.

"The message from our masters is that the hunt for Weapons of Mass Destruction is no longer as high priority as it was two weeks ago. The political and diplomatic focus has returned to Osama and his cohorts."

Billy interrupted again, "So we're off the hook, Morton. We can fade out of the picture and throw these shitty maps and satellite diagrams into the trash."

"Not quite," said Morton, still sitting on his irritation, "We're in a holding pattern. We have to scale down the operation and redivert the resources into the hunt for the terrorists."

"Christ, said Billy. We're so close to providing what they want."

"That's fine, Bill. The trouble is they don't want it right now. They can wait for a couple of years maybe. No one's looking there any more, the court of world opinion has switched its attention and it's no longer Uncle Sam on the stand, it's the bombers again."

Morton was in control again, but he knew there was an unanswered question hanging which none of them dare utter for fear of admitting their part in it. He wasn't going to be so stupid as to volunteer the thought so it would just have to remain hanging.

Then the man called Bill spoke again: "Does that mean we call off our special search party, Morton? They might be close to, er, *finding* something." Morton looked at him as if to say, what special search party? But it was a pointless gesture, his previous delicacy was blown to hell and this wasn't a press conference where he could brazen it out. Everyone in the room knew what he knew, even if it had never been acknowledged. He'd have to explain what would have to happen with the Barracudas and whatever they might have been "close to *finding*."

"We won't be needing their highly specialist skills any more."

Morton wasn't sorry to be reining in Barracuda. He was a dangerous man and it was always a high-risk strategy dictated by necessity. It could easily have been blown. More than anything it needed political will to back it up and that wasn't there any more. His superiors could now easily tell the rest of the world, and the queasy Brits, that they'd return to the weapons when they had the time. Meanwhile they'd keep teams on the lookout in Iraq. Who knows, they might even find something.

"Any more questions."

Another voice spoke for the first time.

"Are we back to searching the caves again, Morton?"

"We'll wait to be told," he said. "Now I have some things to do. If you'll excuse me."

They excused him. He left the room and returned to his office a few minutes away in the same building. He opened his computer keypad and typed an email message. He filled in the address knowing that Barracuda would pick it up on his satellite link, wherever he was – probably skulking around in Iraq. He didn't want to know. He just wanted him off the scene and out of the way.

He typed in a codeword to identify himself and wrote, "Abandon Search! Leave!"

August
Hotel

Winter leaned over to wake her but found an empty space. His heart stopped at the thought that she'd gone. Then he heard the shower and breathed again. He opened the bathroom door and saw her under the shower. She caught his eye, twitched and then carried on.

"We'll have to go soon."
"I know."
She dressed silently, he did the same, she gathered what few things she had and went with him to the car. He would check out of the hotel later. They drove to the bank where he'd transferred the money; he was in there a light year, she thought. Then he emerged, got in the car and handed the over. A bulky plastic wallet embossed with the bank's logo. She examined it: twenty five thousand dollars.
"Where is the other five thousand?"
"I had to leave something in the account or it would have been noticed straight away. Don't be so suspicious!"
"After everything you have seen and you can say that to me?" He had no idea, that five thousand wasn't just a pile of dollar bills, it was so many days and nights in the apartment submitting herself to the demands of sweaty, ugly businessmen; it was her valuing herself and she hated leaving any of it behind. It was *her*, the price she had put on herself and the price she had offered in return. She looked down. "What a waste! Do you know what that five thousand cost me? If I leave it there I leave a part of me."
"Is it a part that you want to keep?" He had no idea where the question came from. He hoped she didn't answer. Instead she looked him straight in the eye. He couldn't stand the gaze. She was threatening him somehow.
 He started the car, pulled out of the bank car park and headed for the Maraka port. He guessed visiting ships' crews would stay around the area drinking coffee in the cafes. He had no idea how he was going to do this, he was scared of this world of rough sailors. He parked the car and they got out. She wrapped her head in a scarf and wore sunglasses, she could pass for any middle eastern woman like that and any prying eyes would be fooled. They walked around the area looking like tourists. Finally he spotted a man in a white shirt and blue shorts in a small portside café. He guessed ship's mate or master. They took a table close to him. The officer looked them up and down and then fixed his gaze on Jose. She crossed her legs showing just enough to convert the gaze to lust. Winter shifted uncomfortably, she was good at it and he didn't like it. He started a conversation with the man who answered with a thick Clydeside accent. Winter could barely make it out, she must have found it impossible no matter how many languages she spoke. The gist was that he was

first mate on a freighter leaving for Mumbai later that day. Ideal.
"Do you ever have room for passengers?" asked Winter.
"Depends."
"Supposing someone wanted to get away from here in a hurry, is there room for that sort of thing?"
"If it's legal we can take people." His answers were to Winter's questions but his eyes never left Jose.
"What if someone needed to get out without the proper papers and exit visa, can you help?"
"Sometimes." His eyes stayed fixed on Jose. "It depends on what they're prepared to pay."
"How much money would you need?"
He carried on staring. She repositioned her dress to cover what she had earlier exposed. There was a smell of roasting chicken in the air, the lunch offering from the grimy café.
"Money's fine, but the crew likes a diversion in those long hours at sea." It didn't sound like it was the first time he'd said that.
"What do you mean?"
Jose intervened. "It's obvious what he means." But the sailor carried on: "They have to work their way across."
"Work! Doing what exactly?" Winter asked, still not understanding. The other's eyes stared at Jose without interruption. Until a few days ago she would have never done it, not in those circumstances. She had come too far to be a ship's whore and no matter what she did to earn her money she was determined that it should at least be with rich generous men, not greasy, filthy sailors in the middle of the Indian Ocean. Now she couldn't be so choosy; now she was on the run. She knew the risks, she knew the way the world of men worked. Who was to say she wouldn't end up over the side a hundred kilometres out of Mumbai? But she might meet a similar fate if she stayed here.
But just as she was about to nod her agreement Winter jumped in: "Good bye, have a pleasant trip."
"Not as pleasant as it could have been," replied the first mate, humourlessly. His gaze did not move from Jose as Winter grabbed her by the hand, silenced her protests and walked away from the café.

May
Desert encounter
It was a clear cold night in the desert and Barracuda was doing what he did best, preparing to kill. His convoy moved in the darkness to minimise detection by satellites. All the same, he kept his eyes trained on the starlit skies, looking out for the telltale light which gave them away. Even against the extraordinary firmament of the Milky Way the satellites showed up clearly. He was confident enough, there was no moon to speak of and they'd camouflaged well against the eerie silver sand that is the night desert.

Barracuda had a plan: they had stumbled on a line of Iraqi army trucks in the darkness in the middle of the Western Zone. They still had soldiers so they must have come from Tikrit. Maybe some last Saddam loyalists had made a break for it under cover of darkness. No one wore uniform, but that wasn't surprising. Baath party and army uniforms disappeared to be disowned on April 12 when Baghdad fell. Suddenly there were none and no one admitted to having worn them.

No uniforms maybe, but there was battledress and they were carrying small arms. They didn't know it but their trucks and rocket launcher had just given Barracuda his perfect solution. They would have to take them out without damaging the hardware, otherwise there would be questions like: why are the trucks burned to hell and the missile cases untouched? At least the UN would ask those questions, the Americans and the Brits may not be so choosy.

The biggest headache now was whether the men on the trucks were any use as soldiers. Saddam's Republican Guard was supposed to be an elite force, but experts at self-preservation. If they couldn't win a fight, they didn't take it on. Barracuda remembered that from his days in the Special Forces 12 years before. They'd melted away when it came to combat, they vanished out of their uniforms and into the suburbs. But it was almost certainly them who had put up resistance in Tikrit, Saddam's home town.

Now, what would these guys be up to? Heading for Syria? High-tailing it out of town before someone fingers them?

Whatever, thought Barracuda, let's get on with it! He gauged their strength: about fifty. Barracuda had twenty, two to each Iraqi truck but each of them a bad man in a fight. They'd be OK. The Iraqis couldn't have located them yet, otherwise they'd have taken up defensive positions and they hadn't. Perhaps their portable generators had drowned out the Barracudas' engine noise.

He trained his glasses on them – they were configured like an old fashioned American wagon train: six trucks, one GRAD launcher capable of firing 122mm rockets and mounted on a Ural 375 six wheel drive and a blazing fire in the middle; it was surreal. They were half a mile away and he strained to hear, he could just make it out, the sound of music, Arabic music.

He panned his glasses to another part of the camp. Shit, they were dancing. Someone was playing some kind of stringed instrument, they clapped their hands and sang.

Beautiful. They would cut through them like a butcher's knife. He felt his blood rising. He knew that circling them might give away their positions, they might still hear the sounds of the four wheeled drives as they moved about. So he called up two of his lieutenants and told them his plan.

"We're going to creep up from here and throw CS gas mortars in to the circle. Get everyone masked up. There's no wind tonight, they'll either get caught or run for it. We'll have guys on the outside ready to cut them down when they do. Just be careful of the trucks, they mustn't be damaged!" The two lieutenants nodded.

"Get going!" said Barracuda, harshly.

They slipped away. He raised his glasses again and reassured himself that he was right, that none of the Iraqis was prepared for a fight. They weren't. He led his men out to the action. This was what he came out for, fuck the missiles, they were just the price he had to pay for the orgy he was about enjoy.

They crawled to the Iraqi camp. The music carried on the still air. Nothing changed as they approached.

Barracuda stopped 100 metres South of the encampment and deployed his two lieutenants to triangulate their attack. He set up his small artillery, gauged the distance, and laid out an array of CS mortars. He held back putting on his mask until the last moment. He hated wearing it in the desert. He waited 20 minutes while the others took up their positions. Two crisp clicks on his intercom earpiece told him they were ready.

When it came it was as if everything went into slow motion. Barracuda spoke, rather than yelled, "go" in the intercom and dropped a mortar into the tube. Almost instantly he saw the sky light up from the others as they started raining in on the encampment. The bombardment lasted five minutes. The Iraqis just folded. He had expected a much tougher fight, instead he saw trained soldiers throwing their weapons out of the encampment in a desperate bid to surrender.

Fuck, he hated that. They were soldiers, they'd been trained to fight and he knew enough about this group to know that they would have had a privileged life in Iraq under Saddam. Well, they could surrender if they liked but he was still going to kill them. The one thing that passed through his mind was that they deserved it. It was the closest he would ever get to morality and he didn't spend a great deal of time with the thought. He radioed to his lieutenants to move in on his command. The camp was surrounded. The music had stopped, there was no dancing to be done now. At least while they were still alive he could get them to unload the rocket launcher. He got his Arabic translator to get them all to lie down. They did as they were told. He ordered a party of twenty to be formed to unload his trucks and to empty the launcher.

They were half an hour into the task when Barracuda heard what he had been dreading, an aircraft. It was too far away for him to tell what kind it was but it had to be either American or British and neither would be likely to miss this little set up if they came within five miles. They'd be targets for a missile attack and he could do without that tonight. At the very best their heat sensors would pick up the activity and their thermal cameras would pick up the number of warm bodies. They wouldn't tally with the number of bodies he was planning to leave here.

Fuck and damnation, they had to get out, because he always got them out. He called one of his lieutenants over.

"How far have we got?" he asked.

"The launcher's unloaded, it was carrying 122 mils, conventional and up to date."

"Get on with it!" said Barracuda, impatiently. "There's an F16 or a Tornado somewhere up there and not far away. We've got to get out. How many of ours have you unloaded?"

"Ten."

"Ten!" said Barracuda, angrily. "Fuck it, put them with the launcher, leave the rest on board our trucks."

"What about what was already in the launcher?"

"Put them in the trucks. We can't have any confusion about what's here."

"Fucking mess?" said the lieutenant.

"Fucking right. Get your AK 47 when you've finished."

The man went back to hurriedly finish his task. Barracuda watched him pick up his AK 47 and his frown eased, he smiled. He looked at the ranks of Iraqis either carrying rockets or sitting quietly being guarded by the other Barracudas. He checked his own AK 47, got out another magazine because one would never be enough – even with two weapons on the job. The lieutenant rejoined him and Barracuda couldn't help a huge grin reach across his face which turned to a snarl within a couple of seconds.

The Iraqis were looking at them in a surly manner, maybe they expected to be taken prisoner. Oh no boys, this is no Coalition patrol sticking to the Geneva Convention, this is Barracuda and his men. Bye Bye.

He pulled the trigger on his weapon and held it. The lieutenant did the same. The noise of the rapid automatic fire drowned out the screams. A modified Kalashnikov, using the favoured 7.62 millimetre ammunition, can spew out 600 rounds a minute. It's not accurate and not much use beyond 400 metres. But here it didn't need to be accurate and the targets were three metres away. Barracuda needed his second clip but now his blood was boiling so much that when he finished he waded into the pile of bloody bodies, some dead, others dying, and just swung the AK 47 into any flesh near. The lieutenant and other Barracudas stayed back. They knew this was his moment, his rage, his passion. They left him to it. If any of them didn't like it they didn't say. They knew they'd be paid and Barracuda always got them out. He could do what he liked.

Finally, he finished. He returned to the trucks, kicking aside scores of ammunition casings which clinked dully in the sand. He had surprisingly little blood on him. He could still hear a jet soaring sound, maybe it would pass them by without noticing, maybe not. He wouldn't take the chance.

"Let's get out of here," he said, calmly, the rage spent.

They got into the trucks wordlessly and headed south, away from the jet sound, as fast as the desert sand would let them. It wasn't until an hour had passed that Barracuda paused to think of anything other than running.

He still had nineteen 122 millimetre rockets loaded with mustard agent. The ten they'd left with the corpses would be a start but they needed more to make it seem more realistic. His blood had cooled since the killing rage, he was ready to look at all the angles. That's what he did so well. That's how he always got them out. He needed to leave two more mustard-rocket deposits – nine at one location, ten at the other. Still, he was ten up-to-date and functioning rockets in profit; someone would want those somewhere, a bit of back-scratching for the Shark, maybe! His thoughts were disturbed by a light flashing on his laptop warning him of an incoming message. He stopped the convoy, got out of the vehicle, walked to a point away from the sight of the others and keyed in his codes.

He read the message.

What the fuck! Couldn't they make up their minds! Pull out! Take the weapons with him! Shit! It was too late to go back to the slaughter scene to retrieve them. Dawn was appearing in the eastern desert sky and there was every chance that the Iraqi convoy had already been spotted and mapped. No, they'd have to move on and keep their cargo of unusable, unfireable rockets until they could dump them.

What a waste of fucking time!

He would still get the sixty million dollars but that didn't make him feel any better. It wasn't the point, never had been.

He called the men together and said, "Change of plan. We're going back over the border. Make sure your weapons are loaded!."

None of them said a word. They trusted Barracuda to get them out so they'd do what he said.

August
Telephone call
Hartson felt the back of his neck, it was getting better. It was another fierce morning: stupidly hot with clear skies. He was in the Randalls office. The phone rang, he picked it up lazily.

"Randalls, Will Hartson."

"It's Diana." He sat up straight.

"Hi."

"I'm calling from home, you never heard this from me..."

"Right."

"They've found those bodies again," she said.

"Which bodies?"

"Don't be obtuse." He wasn't being obtuse. His collection of bodies was mounting by the hour.

"The Navy found the boys again."

"The speedboat victims?"

She chuckled. He could hear the irony.

"Yes, with the concrete waterskis."

"Where?"

"Beyond territorial limits. It looks as if the Port Police dumped them after taking them off the Navy's hands. Nice people out here."

"Sometimes, Diana."

"What will you do?"

"I'll decide that later."

"Mum's the word please, Will."

"Guaranteed, Diana...and thank you."

"I think it's the least I could do."

"I think you're right."

"News blackout at this end, Navy too. I need say no more."

"Because Fielding's coming."

"I shouldn't be at all surprised."

"Yes, thanks. Er, we must do it all again sometime."

"Yes, we must. Ring me."

Maybe he would. He rehearsed a crack about bringing his toothbrush and sun block cream but it took him too long and it probably wouldn't have been funny anyway.

"See you, Will."

The phone went down.

Breaking free

They drove around Maraka trying to think what to do. She'd gone as far as she could with him. She should dump him now; she had the money, if she could get hold of a car, even this one, she could do it herself. She toyed herself with a plan to commandeer the Range Rover. She could get him to stop for a drink on the road. She'd feign exhaustion, smile at him sweetly and ask him if he could fetch it for her. Then she'd take the car and leave him to it. He could hardly call the police to track her down. It was simple. She smiled at the thought of being free of him, on the road, on her own. Like always.

What did she owe him, anyway! He'd already messed up one chance for her with his misplaced chivalry. She would have screwed her way across the Indian Ocean with that freighter crew, she wouldn't have liked it, but she'd have done it. She might even have been on board right now if he hadn't interfered, they might have already sailed and she would be heading towards the Straits of Hormuz and freedom – of a kind.

Then Winter broke into her treacherous thoughts. "If you're such a big friend of Samir Latif, couldn't we use that to help?"

"How? The police want to find me, everyone will disown a Lebanese prostitute for the shame of it. Not a chance, not even Samir Latif."

"But he's a generous man, you said so yourself, and I've seen it with my own eyes. And he's a man of the world; couldn't we go to him for protection?"

She didn't like to admit it but the idiot was making some sense. Samir was the most powerful man in Khafira after the sheikhs – and he was more powerful than most of them in reality. All the same, it was a big risk.

"Maybe, you can try, I suppose. You have his number?"

Yes, he did, he always needed to be on call for Samir Latif and he was a good banker. Could things be looking better?

May
Desert patrol
The coalition navigator knew something was going on. He'd been told of no activity in that quarter of the Western Desert but there was clearly something very wrong on the ground. He indicated to his pilot to make another circuit as he tapped in some coordinates to his computer. It was still dark and they could see nothing with normal vision. But their thermal cameras told them there were the still warm engines of trucks and the signature of something organic. They didn't move so they were probably dead, but they hadn't been for long. Whether they were Iraqi or coalition was unclear.

The navigator pinpointed the position and radioed them to his control which passed it straight to a special services unit fifty miles away. He could do no more except take the pictures back to the base and let the intelligence people have a look.

The special forces captain received the radio message and thanked Christ that something was happening this night. It had been dull up until that point, now it was going to liven up. It would take him and his patrol of ten men about ninety minutes to get to there so he got them straight on it.

He just wished it had been a US air force plane which had found them, not another Brit. He was getting tired of the snooty bastards always getting it right. They begged borrowed and stole their equipment all the time, there was nothing in their supplies which was anywhere near as good as the American alternative – except, maybe, the food.

But still they got things done quick and well.

Fuck them. Well, at least it would be Americans first on the scene at this party. He decided to drive himself and let his sergeant ride shotgun. He revved the jeep motor and let the tyres dig into the sand.

"Tally ho," he shouted, in mock imitation of a Brit officer he'd met somewhere.

It took two hours to get there driving through desert dunes by starlight. A greyness appeared on the Eastern horizon behind them as they arrived at the destination. The special forces captain stared for a few seconds as he let the scene sink in. The captain had seen plenty in his life as a soldier, but he'd never seen a massacre quite like this. Men had been shot up and then smashed about. They were all dead, some of them cut in half by raking automatic fire by the look of it.

But who the hell had done it?

It couldn't have been coalition forces, his unit was the only one anywhere near the area and no airstrike would have done this kind of damage. It would have done a hell of a lot more, or a lot less, but not this.

No, the weapons had been used on the ground, except maybe for some mortar fire. There wasn't any sign at all that the poor dead bastards had managed to defend themselves. They'd just been cut down and left. Still, what was an Iraqi military convoy doing out in the desert so long after they were supposed to have lost the war? Whatever it was, it could only have been bad.

So, what were they doing out on the prowl? And who the fuck had managed to find them?

"Check every square foot of this place!" he yelled to his men. They hardly needed telling. Some of them had already started to examine the bodies and the ground near the trucks.

One of them, a staff sergeant, picked up a handful of spent shells from the ground and called out to his commanding officer, "Here, Al."

"What'ya got? "

The man held up his hands and let the dozen or so brass 7.62 millimetre shells fall from his hand in a dramatic cascade.

"Fucking' AK 47, man. Who in hell can have done this?"

"It can't have been us," said the captain, "And it won't have been the Brits. They hate Kalashnikovs as much as we do."

"How about Kurds," said the NCO, more in hope than expectation.

"We'd better stop guessing, Pete. For all we know they were blown away by their own guys. Let's see what they left behind!" By now every one of the company had come forward with their own handfuls of spent shells. They tossed them into a pile in the centre of the camp. They made a sound like an out-of-control cash register.

"Something smells here, Pete. I want you to go over every inch – and check that GRAD launcher. Check the ammunition, the weapons, check every fuckin' thing you see here. I want to know what we're calling in before we do it."

He drafted three of the men to act as lookouts. The rest got on with their task. So what the fuck happened here? Kurds? No, they were too far away and they had American weapons.

Syrians, maybe, because of the ammo, but unlikely, no matter how unwelcome the Iraqis were over the border.

Coalition? Impossible.

Iraqi renegades? Crazy, but the most likely.

Then the staff sergeant called from the GRAD.

"There's empty wooden crates, and some rockets stuffed into the launcher." He called to a corporal to help unload. "They're fuckin' heavy, man," said a corporal as he took the fin end of a rocket from the rear of the launcher. "Well you're a big strong man, Mikey, you can handle a little rocket like this. It's just a little A-rab toy, wouldn't scratch you if it hit you smack in the forehead – wouldn't do damage, anyhow,"

"Fucking' funny, man," said the corporal. "You think I can't lift this bastard?" he said as he heaved out the rocket from the launcher. He went to grab the warhead end to balance with the fins but he hadn't calculated for 155 pounds of missile. He didn't get there quick enough and the warhead end fell hard against the metallic base of the launcher. "Jesus, Mikey, get a grip. We're not playing here. This is a 122 mil rocket, or didn't you notice that. It'll have a detonator in the front end and a fuck of a load of explosive."

"Shit," said the corporal.

"What's happening?" called the captain. "Have you got it under control over there, Pete?"

"We have now," said the staff sergeant, breathing in deeply.

Then he stopped breathing altogether for several seconds.

Finally he yelled, "Shit, I smell onions. Cover up all of you. Mustard agent. It's in the launchers."

The captain put his desert scarf over his face as he ducked down and reached for his Noddy protection mask.

"Smoking fucking gun, " he muttered when he'd put it on.

August
The Majlis
　The Majlis was quieter than when Hartson was there a few days ago. August was biting into the hierarchy's social life away from Khafira. Everyone important was in Europe or America and, as he rubbed his pained limbs, still burning from his desert ordeal, he wished he'd done the same; this was not fun.
　Sheikh Issa was absent, chasing the love of his life on the racecourses of France and England. He ought to know who the resident sheikh was but he hadn't been bothered to check the faxes from the Protocol Office in the last two days.
　Then his eyes fell on a man of medium height, black moustache and completely covered in his summer dishdash and Khufia. Oh shit, Sheikh Khalifa! Of course it would be him, there had to be someone and this playboy juvenile would suffice in August when he couldn't do too much damage. It wasn't that he didn't like Khalifa, but he was worried by the man's stupidity. Sheikh Khalifa had been born to the role, the second son, but he wasn't up to it. He had no grasp of politics or power, and no concept of international relations. He just liked to play with his toy Boeing 747... and its crew. Nothing wrong with that either, but sitting in authority at the Majlis was a problem.
　Hartson took a deep breath and approached the sheikh. He was greeted by a fragrant smell which he couldn't quite place. It was presumably something way out of a normal person's price range and probably even beyond a Randalls expense account. "Your Highness Sheikh Khalifa, good morning to you." A pair of dark eyes gazed out interestedly from the innocent-looking face and fixed him.
"Good morning, who are you?"
"I am Will Hartson from the Randalls News Agency Your Highness."
There was a brief pause, he watched the sheikh's face, it didn't register much. Then a smile beamed right across it.
"Of course, Mr. Will, I have heard of you. You are welcome, is there something I can help you with?"
"You are very generous Your Highness, there is something which has been troubling me in recent days."

"Please continue, Mr. Will."

He took another breath. Khalifa had no idea of what went on in Khafira, he just lived to play. Still, nothing ventured etc.. "It concerns the discovery of some corpses in the sea just off the coast."

"That is very sad, Mr. Will."

He knew nothing.

"I have heard something of this."

What!

"I am told by my advisers that these boys died as a result of an unfortunate accident."

"Is that your complete understanding, Your Highness?"

"Yes. A terrible blow for the families of course, we must do something to compensate them for their losses." Maria holding the picture of her boys came into Hartson's mind, followed by the memory of his cowardly exit in Maraka. He searched the sheikh's face for some compassion but found none; it was in his words, but nowhere else. The boys were an abstract concept, a lost stake in a casino game. Too bad, better luck next time.

"Your Highness does that mean you know who they are?"

There was a long, uncomfortable pause.

"Colonel Hassan of the Port Police has been dealing with this matter, Mr. Will, you are better advised to speak to him."

Sheikh Khalifa made a dismissive gesture with his hand; that was all he had to say on the matter.

So, Hassan had jumped on that inquiry as well. Colonel Hassan of the Port Police again. Hartson had met him only twice, it had not been a meeting of minds. Hassan hadn't been forthcoming to say the least, but no Gulf policeman ever was. He hadn't liked the man in the way that he, until the last few days, had liked Ali Abdul Hamid. Hamid seemed a reluctant bully, Hassan the opposite. Some officers can give the brush off without giving offence, Hassan seemed to revel in the insult. Hartson was researching a feature on middle eastern smuggling, probing in its way but nothing out of the ordinary. He had cornered him once at the port, and once at the central police station. He wanted to know if the police were able to control the inflow of smuggled maidservants from the subcontinent. Hassan had been brief. "These are police matters. It is none of your business. Do not ask any more questions." The second time he'd simply stared at him before pushing him out of the way. No, he didn't like Colonel Hassan; the same man, he now knew, who was at the apartment block before Hannah died. And no, he especially did not want to confront him again – without some serious back-up.

Uncomfortable coincidence? Except that two of those submerged corpses belonged to Maria the maid. He churned it all over and was going to risk breaking the protocol of not continuing to speak to the sheikh once he had finished the audience. But he delayed too long in his follow-up question, and, anyway, it was clear there was nothing more to be gained from talking to Khalifa. God he was a shallow man. These were four boys who had died in Khafira and this overprivileged fop couldn't care less. He was so incensed he was about to throw everything to the winds and run back to the disappearing sheikh but as he made his first step he felt his arm being grasped firmly. He whirled round furiously, but the protest fell silent before it had risen from his throat.

"Colonel Ali Abdul Hamid. You're never far away are you!"

Hamid was at the Majlis. He never came to the Majlis normally. But that was a mystery to be sorted out later, right now Hamid was glaring at him, anger flaring from every facial feature. He growled menacingly, only just audibly but there was no mistaking the intent: "No, Mr. Will. Now don't bother his highness Sheikh Khalifa any more. He is a busy man."

Hartson had already been pulled to the entrance. Khalifa was somewhere in the distance talking on his phone.

"What's worrying you Hamid; am I getting too close?"

"Just go home." He shoved him through the door.

"And please don't try to speak to Colonel Hassan. That I implore you."

The impact of the last remark did not strike Hartson until long after he had got back to his car, driven furiously for three kilometres and gradually regained his dignity. Then the words came back to him. "Please don't try to speak to Colonel Hassan."

Why not? Hamid had arranged for his kidnap, thwarted him, and threatened him. Now he was pleading. He was only too aware of what could happen if he ignored the plea. He rubbed the soreness on the back of his neck. No he wouldn't talk to anyone else in Khafira now. He knew all he needed to know.

Hartson punched the last few letters into the keyboard, ENDS! Now let the flak fly. It was a big risk but he knew his sources were good: a navy doctor and a diplomat. There was no doubt that the boys had been abused and left to die horribly; and there was no doubt the British embassy wanted nothing to be known about it. It went without saying that Khafira felt the same way. And then there was his old chum Fielding, coming out tomorrow. No publicity, no contact. Arms sales, equals safe jobs in a marginal constituency closing in on a bye-election. Messy! This was going to embarrass a lot of people, that was the point, speaking truth to power. Oh the nobility of it, thought Hartson as he reached for a beer.

He'd weighed up the cost and called Diana to recheck the information. He was about to make enemies of the embassy, Khafira, and the Navy. And he seriously wondered whether it was worth the price of possible banishment with all that meant: no more desert picnics, dodgy nightclubs, Indian delights no more easy life in dreamland. No more Diana! But in the end it was his job and if he couldn't do that then what was the point? He sighed, this was now a big story, much bigger than when he first got wind of it. His reward would probably be a one-way ticket back to grey London. Really!

His finger hovered over the key which would send the copy to Randalls. Then he chastised himself and pressed it; what was he worth if he was prepared to sell out his life's work for this lotus-eating land! There, it was done and there was no pulling back. He had the consolation of thinking that it would earn him a gong at Randalls and that they'd post him somewhere else nice – New Zealand would be good.

He picked up the telephone and called Diana for the second time that day to let her know what he'd done. She was frosty, but that was her default position anyway. Afterwards he sat quietly for a few moments. Something else was eating at him, more than the probable loss of his sunshine life. He still had one more thing to do; he owed it to himself, to salve his conscience, to convince himself he still had some kind of courage. In the morning he had to tell Maria, because he knew no one else would bother.

Repercussions

Dibden was holding a facsimile sent direct from London. "This was just one, there are plenty of others," said the First Secretary. "Have a look at it will you.

It's from this morning's London edition of The Guardian. Shouldn't think the international edition will get past the censors here." Scott Garrett scanned the copied article, it did not make happy reading. "Not too good, eh, Tom. Any ideas where it may have come from?"

"None at all. I fed the Randalls fellow the line about speedboats. I was sure he swallowed it."

Dibden continued, "And there does seem a lot of detail here about what happened to those boys." The First Secretary turned to Wilkinson. "Any chance that could have slipped out from your men?" The commander looked pensive, they weren't *his* men, he was a diplomat for the time being, although please don't let it be for much longer! "We put a tight lid on it after the last episode. It can't be any of the crew from the minesweeper, we sent them back out."

"Well we all know it's not likely to be the police." Everyone nodded. "Whichever way, the damage is done, and it's been done twice through the same source; bloody Randalls! London isn't happy about it, I need hardly say." Scott Garrett studied the rest of the fax then said, "The ruling family isn't going to like it at all. They'll stop the story here, but they can't do any more than that. It couldn't have happened at a worse time, today, for good sake. What does the ambassador say?"

"He thinks we should approach Sheikh Issa with an unofficial but very fulsome apology. Throw him the usual line about Britain having a free press with all its drawbacks. We'll have to get London to do it, Issa's on his racing travels."

"And the journalist, Hartson?"

"Nothing really, simply say the fellow got his information completely wrong. He's a well-known drunk who prints unsubstantiated gossip. Doesn't deserve to be in Khafira."

I'm not sure Sheikh Issa will buy that. He knows Hartson well.

"That's where you come in, Tom. I understand Khalifa is in charge in Issa's absence. Might be easier if you buttonholed him somewhere – this morning, for instance! Fielding's arriving at midday. Let's get rid of Hartson before then, eh!"

Hartson never enjoyed knocking on the doors of the bereaved, but here it had been loathsome. He was driving away from the slum blocks with their strings of washing shrivelling in the fiery sun. The image of Maria with tired eyes sinking into a chair, not moving for five minutes, defeated, was burned into his inner sight. He did not think she was even breathing at one time and his repeated enquiries about her well-being drew nothing.

It had been no better the first time he had done it twenty years before. Then his local paper news editor told him to see the wife of a man killed in a mountaineering accident. He could remember his trembling hand knocking on the door just as clearly a score of years later. It was a horrible job, but for some reason few people resented it in those days.

But not this time. No local paper out in the Gulf would touch it. And there was only one person to grieve. He had been the messenger and he had braced himself for the full assault of emotional distress; the wailing, the questioning, the periods of calm, the frenzied outbursts, the utter desolate frustration of it all; he'd steeled himself to be blamed for it, he knew he could put up a wall against that, but not against the dreadful silence which followed Maria's one exclamation, "Oh please God, No!"

She had gone to her wall and picked up the plastic framed picture hanging by the crucifix. He saw it briefly before she clasped it to her breast and sat still on the chair, motionless, dry-eyed. He'd been around too long to fight off all sense of grief for himself, some of it had to leak through. Finally he could do no more than put his hand on her shoulder, say sorry, and walk out. She had no one now, no redress from the police, no family, no friends. She hadn't moved. He felt her loneliness seep through and he hurried out. There was a coldness in the room which belied the heat and he wanted to be away from it.

He drove back to his apartment with his mind somewhere else. He didn't notice the marked police car parked outside the building as he pulled on the handbrake and walked in. He was still trying to rid himself of Maria's face as he rode the elevator. It was not until he got to within five metres of his apartment that he realised the door was open. Then Maria's face disappeared.

He stood on the threshold of his apartment watching three uniformed policemen bundling books and clothes into his suitcases. Hamid was in a corner smoking a cigarette, watching thoughtfully.

"What are you doing?"

"Mr. Will," replied Hamid quietly, "I am afraid your time in Khafira has come to an end."

"What!"

"I believe you wrote an article which has greatly displeased Sheikh Mahmood. Mr. Will, wherever you go next I hope you will learn to get your information right."

Hartson's shoulders slumped.

"What's upset you, Hamid?"

Hamid looked around the room to see what his men were doing.

"I am not upset, the Sheikh is upset. You have accused him of presiding over a group of thugs and abusers. You have no justification for this and you are leaving to prevent any further misunderstandings. I shall take you to the airport myself, there is a plane to London in four hours time."

"My information is accurate, Hamid, you know that."

Hamid again looked around, his men continued their business, unconcerned.

"It probably is, Mr. Will, it probably is, but as far as I am concerned it is not. That is what Sheikh Mahmood says, and it must therefore be right."

"That's enough pretence, Hamid. We all know about Sheikh Mahmood. Who are you using his name to cover for? Is it Issa?"

Hamid swung his gaze to his men again then spoke in a lower, more conspiratorial voice. "I am sorry, Mr. Will, I do not make these rules."

"But you do carry them out."

"Yes, for the time being, I do."

Hamid's phrases: For the time being, Please don't talk to Colonel Hassan, I IMPLORE you!

"What is your game Hamid?" he said, quietly.

Hamid's face hardened, the mouth twitched. "I am not a sporting man."

"You'll at least let me call my London office to let them know."

"Please do," said Hamid, indicating the telephone. "The line is still connected. Perhaps you will also tell them there is no point in them sending out a replacement, at least in the near future. Your organisation's activities in Khafira have been suspended." He tried to detect triumph in Hamid's voice, but he found none.

He made the call, watched closely by Hamid. He wanted to file a short story right there but he knew Hamid's thugs would have grabbed him and the phone before he could even get the dateline out. He just gave a terse message to say he would be back in London in ten hours time. He put down the receiver and turned back to Hamid.

"How can you live with yourself, Hamid? You know what happens here. You do nothing to stop it. You're supposed to be a highly trained senior policeman. What do you gain by protecting these smugglers and gangsters? They're not even your people, you're a Palestinian for the sake of Allah."

Hamid's eyes darted around the room, checking that none of his officers had understood what was being said.

"That is not a matter for discussion here. Be silent now!" Hartson watched sullenly as his remaining effects were packed up inexpertly and thrown into the corridor. That was his life being tossed about.

"Is there anything you will require on the plane, Mr. Will?" asked Hamid. Your balls, thought Hartson. Now is not the time for your Arabic pleasantry. You're throwing me out of the country, no need to be polite, arsehole. But his thoughts stayed unvoiced.

He quickly sorted out some toiletries and a laptop. The bags were taken by the uniformed officers to a waiting vehicle outside the building. He was directed towards a dark Mercedes. As they walked the few paces to the car the searing heat felt as if it would burn a hole in the back of his neck.

Hamid must have seen him wincing. "You will not miss our glorious summer weather, I suspect." He said nothing. Hamid was right, though, he certainly would not miss this furnace. He'd had a deal too much of it lately, mostly courtesy of Hamid's thugs. He hoped Heathrow would be covered in dark cloud when he got back and that he'd have to put on a sweatshirt or something similar. He hadn't done that for two years, even the Gulf midwinter was sunbathing time.

They got into the rear of the Mercedes, Hamid barked some orders in Arabic and the car moved away.

"Do you never long to go home Hamid?"

"That is an unworthy question, Mr. Will, you know I have longed to go home for many years."

"But you could do it. You're not banned from Ramallah. Or is it the power and the money you have here?" He wasn't going to pull any punches now; what the hell, he was being expelled, he was leaving in less than four hours.

"No, it is neither of those things. I have a job to do here and I will do it as well as I can. When I have finished I shall return to Ramallah and offer my experience and services. But I will return there when I am ready."

Hartson looked through the tinted window, watching the familiar landmarks go by: the flower draped roundabout with its army of tenders and confusion of hosepipes, the flat towers of the workers' slum areas, the surreal glass and concrete creations they called modern architecture.

He was saying goodbye and he wouldn't be coming back again – not legitimately and probably not ever. Damn it, Hamid knew what he had written was the truth! Now he was being thrown out of his home and cut off from his friends and colleagues; insofar as it was possible to have friends in Khafira.

"How many murders have you solved since you came here, Hamid.? He looked directly into the colonel's eye. Hamid didn't flinch.

"There has never been a murder in Khafira since I joined." Hartson simply looked at him.

"What do you know?" said the policeman, suspiciously.

"Why should I tell you? I'm going now."

"Not everything is as it seems in the Gulf, you have probably come to see that in your time here."

"So how many murders have you solved?"

"I am telling the truth when I say I have solved every one."

"And covered up everything at the same time."

"This is not London or America, no one is accountable out here, you know that. If the sheikh decides it's legal then that is the case."

"How often does Sheikh Issa intervene?" No more pretence, he was going, straight talking.

"The sheikh is a good man, Mr. Will, the same cannot be said for all of his friends." Hartson paused to take that in; Issa's friends?

"Does he intervene for them?"

"He is the ruler, he often intervenes if he believes the law is wrong or being poorly applied."

"Because he's a *good* man!"

"You need not be so cynical, I told you everything is not always as it seems."

"All right, Hamid, I'll tell you how it seems to me: you have a police force which ignores the discovery of four dead Filipino boys and then throws out the reporter who points it out." Hamid's eyes widened and he started to speak but Hartson carried on. "And you have a murdered prostitute in an apartment block for which you're trying to blame an innocent woman. And you dare to tell me you've solved every murder. You don't care who you blame as long as the sheikh and his friends keep their hands clean."

Hamid's face reddened, Hartson could see the fury rise as the eyes narrowed and the shoulders hunched; then he exploded: "I had *nothing* to do with the first, the second is still a sensitive matter." There was a pause. "Where is your friend Paul Winter?" Hartson realised his mistake too late. He ignored the question and continued his attack. "Why? Because half the gold braceletted aristocracy of Khafira had used the woman before she was killed. For God's sake, Hamid, she was even tortured in exactly the same way as those Filipino boys."

Hamid replied instantly: "How do you know? Her body was covered when you came to the apartment."

He had said too much, that remark was easily traceable to Paul Winter, he wasn't the only one who had seen the body, but almost certainly the only one likely to talk. "I have my contacts?" he said, trying to sound confident.

"Your friend Mr. Paul Winter has told you, perhaps? I advised Mr. Winter to keep quiet, clearly he did not listen."

"He's not the only person I know out here, Hamid."

Hamid looked him straight in the eye and said: "You have meddled in things you do not understand. We do not work the same way as the west here, but we do not like killers and we do not like torture. Understand that I speak for Sheikh Issa when I say this. If only you had not gone to the Majlis and seen Khalifa!"

"Why?"

"Because he is not the solution, Mr. Will Hartson."

"You mean he's the problem….?"

May
Underwater

They were from the Special Boat Squadron. They weren't supposed to be there but they knew how to avoid the Khafira patrols. Khafira wasn't part of the conflict. The SBS were welcome at the port where they disguised themselves as normal Royal Marines, but any hint of operations other than minesweeping would see them being thrown out. So the two divers went in at about 20 feet under, just in case the port police were anywhere nearby.

The major and the sergeant had the help of an underwater Rigid Inflatable Boat with a muffled motor running on compressed gas and completely enclosed which was saving their legs and lungs until they needed them. They let it take them through the clear waters of the Gulf – away from the shipping lanes and the speedboat playboys it could be quite stunning under the water. But the major and the sergeant weren't the types to spend much time appreciating beautiful scenery and wildlife. They had a job to do. They wanted to find out why that wildlife was dying. They could have left it to the Khafira Port Police but they – or their naval masters – didn't think they'd get the answer they needed. It might be nothing at all, just another oil spillage in which case it could be ignored. But in these sensitive times they had to look at everything, just in case. They were close to a theatre of war and there was dead marine life originating from a narrow inlet.

They churned on through the warm sea until the underwater RIB brought them to the entrance. The major took them to a couple of feet below the surface and put up a mini periscope. He quickly scanned the inlet and saw a dhow tied up half a kilometre further in. They continued into the inlet, noticing the dead fish on the surface at the same time.

The major pointed in the direction of the dhow and they moved towards it. The water was much murkier in the inlet and vision was restricted. They made their way towards it, slowly. They went to the bottom of the inlet with the RIB and left it there, twenty metres from the dhow. They kicked up to the hull and moved along it listening for signs of life. They could make out nothing. The major put up the periscope again and scanned 360 degrees. He could see only the dhow, a stone jetty, sand and the surface of the inlet. He indicated to his sergeant that they were going up.

They burst through the surface but both men kept their protective gear on and their air tanks operating. Whatever was killing the fish could just as easily kill them. They looked around and still saw nothing.

"Let's take another look below," said the major.

It was twenty metres from the hull of the dhow, a long cylindrical shape. The major recognised the outline of a 122 millimetre rocket. His torch made out Russian markings with some white paint marks over them which had faded. He indicated to the sergeant to bring the RIB over. When he returned they picked up the rocket between them and loaded it on to the platform, the weight was easier to handle underwater. As they did they could see something seeping from the nosecone.

"Shit," said the sergeant into his headgear microphone.

"Did you get any of it on you?"

"No," said the sergeant. "But I think we've found what we've been looking for." The major nodded. The reached into a locker on the RIB and pulled out a thick plastic sack. They didn't need to tell each other what to do. They worked quickly to cover and seal the leaking warhead.

They spent another half hour searching the inlet but all they found was dead fish, a turtle, and a manta ray. They decided to leave. They needed to get out and back to their frigate. The rocket went with them. The major would tell his commanding officer who would pass it on to whomever. He didn't need to know, his job was done.

Neither saw, on the landside of the deserted dhow, two uniformed port police, but they were sleeping in the heat of the day under the a loosely erected tarpaulin and whatever was happening in their world they never found out that the job they had been sent to do had been made redundant.

August
The airport

Scott Garrett waited in the VIP reception area of the airport with the ambassador and the First Secretary. He wasn't needed to meet Fielding, he was passing time waiting for Hamid and Hartson. Good riddance, and thanks for the tip, Hamid. The First Secretary broke into his reverie. "Tom you don't suppose this scribbler will turn nasty when he gets back, do you?"
"How do you mean?"
"Start writing pieces about embassy complicity with foreign governments, getting him turfed out, that sort of thing."
"Always a chance. But if he's doing it from there, there's less of a problem here. We don't have to justify him, London can take care of it. Anyway, where's the proof?"
"All the same it might be choppy for a while."
He had read the overnight messages. He knew the opposition party had enjoyed a field day with the possibility that the Foreign Office might be buttering up a regime using the Royal Navy as the knife spreader. The imminent visit had ceased to be a secret and the minister had endured the previous twenty four hours fending off persistent inquiries about their plans and their policy. It was going to be a bumpy ride anyway.
"You know him quite well, how about encouraging him to keep quiet."
"I haven't got anything to threaten him with."
"I'm sure we can make up something Tom."
He maintained a deferent pose.

The dark Mercedes pulled into the departure area, Hamid and Hartson got out. The air scorched them for the few seconds it took to get from the car into the air-conditioned terminal. Hartson though that would be the last time he would be seared by it, the rest of his time in Khafira would be in an air-conditioned airport, and departure gate. Strangely he realised he'd miss the heat, it made life special.
"I will have your baggage checked in, Mr. Will," said Hamid. Just at that moment Scott Garrett appeared from the VIP lounge, they watched him approach in his easy, confident, diplomat's way.

"You play chess I think, Mr. Will," said Hamid, "Understand that you are only a pawn and easily sacrificed if it means saving the king."

Scott Garrett spoke: "Sorry about this, Will, I did try to do something but they were pretty angry about the whole thing, you know."

"Convenient for you I suppose. If I'm not around who's going to give those Foreign Office chaps a hard time?"

"You don't think for a moment that they're connected, Will."

"Please, Tom! I wouldn't dream of such a thing. I'm sure you did all you could. You've been so helpful to me in the last two years, I see no reason why you should suddenly change. It's just a damned coincidence that Fielding's coming out as I'm going."

"Absolutely. Is there anything I can do for you, try to smooth your passage home?"

"That's very kind, you might see if you can get my seat made up to Club Class."

"I'll see what I can do." He walked over to the BA desk and flashed his diplomatic Identification.

"The bastard's going to do it," he breathed to Hamid.

"You never know if your paths will cross in some other part of the world. It is best not to burn bridges, Mr. Will, that goes for you too."

"I'm well aware, Hamid. I just owe him one."

"You have learned a great deal about our ways since you came out."

"Yes, Hamid. Enough to know I've hardly started. I don't know where to place you. Are you good or bad?"

"Sometimes you have to be bad to be good."

"That sounds like a fake Chinese proverb."

"There are things which you don't know, and I fear never will. But if it is any consolation to you, nor will anyone else." Hartson gave a rueful smile which he turned to shine on Scott Garrett as he approached with ticket in hand.

"No problem, Will, have a good flight, sorry it had to be like this."

"Very kind, Tom. Her Majesty's Diplomatic Service does it again. I hope I can repay the favour."

The colonel had a glint in his eye which registered his own recognition of the exchange. "I can rely upon you to stay here for two minutes while I attend to something, Mr. Will," he said, and walked off.

Scott Garrett extended his hand, Hartson took it and managed a halfhearted

grip. "Good luck, Will. Better luck next time, it does happen you know," there was a short pause. "But there is so little we can do when drugs are involved."
"Drugs?"
"We'll do the best we can to make sure it doesn't reach London of course."
"You bastard, you'd threaten me with blackmail for something I haven't done." His fury rose, his face reddened, the muscles in his arms tensed, ready to grab the diplomat by the throat and shake him so hard that the man would disintegrate in front of him. He was no strongman but Scott Garrett wasn't either and by the look of his puny legs and arms never had been, he could take him and make a bit of a mess fairly easily. Rule One, never get into a fight; Rule 1a, unless the other guy's a wimp and you won't get hurt. He moved his hand fast and Scott Garrett flinched, but just then Hamid reappeared and grabbed Hartson as if to arrest him again. "I will see you through the formalities, Mr. Will, I am obliged to ensure you leave," he said.

Unhappy crew
The minesweeper was a boiling pot; the constant operation of the diesel engines, the bathtub temperature of the water and the blowtorch sun on the plastic and glass hull saw to that. Jackson watched the horizon. The commodore was on his way out in a tender with news for the whole crew. The ship lay at anchor in the shallow area of the Gulf a few kilometres out from the shore. No work was being done, the orders to stop had come through at the same time as the news of the commodore's visit. They had turned up all four bodies by this time and marked them on the chart. There was a brief outbreak of tasteless humour; one wag had put a yellow Post-It sticky label on the chart with a cartoon of an old fashioned cannon with a human cannonball shooting from it. The circus style safety net had been substituted with a deep sea trawler's dragnet. Black humour was often the way to deal with tragedy but not in Jackson's eyes. He had ripped off the cartoon, not quite controlling his fury in the process. No one admitted to the handiwork, he hadn't expected that they would. But it didn't happen again. The Minesweeper was not a happy ship as the tender containing the commodore came into view.
Jenkins wasted no time once he'd hauled himself on board. "Sorry Sam, your time is up in the Gulf, same for everyone else on the ship. We're dispersing the whole crew, all of you, and bringing in a new one."

Jackson was astonished, "What have we done? Surely if there's a problem it's down to me, I'm the captain."

"I don't think there's anything you could have done, Sam. You just did your job a little too well. The Khafira police clearly never wanted you to find those bodies again, and neither did the embassy. You've queered their pitch, that's why you can't say anything, and why you'll have to go."

"Where am I being sent, Antarctica, on an icebreaker?"

"Gibraltar, the weather's better and it's ours. You can find what you like in the Atlantic and it won't matter...except that you're being put on land for a few months."

"Doing what, commanding the Barbary Apes!"

"Face it, Sam, it's bad luck but you're running an unhappy ship. Difficult to know what else you could have done but the fact is fresh blood would have had to have been brought in anyway."

"Where are the rest going?"

"Portsmouth, Dartmouth, everywhere we might still have an influence."

"No wonder we can't stay here, then," said Jackson bitterly. We had so much influence out here we had to evacuate a minesweeper to please the local crooked politicians. Britannia rules the waves, Bye bye. Jenkins thought about a sharp putdown but the trouble was that he agreed with his lieutenant.

"Meanwhile carry on with your work and good luck!" he said instead.

Jackson gave a weak smile and escorted him from the wardroom to the tender. The same eerie quiet which greeted him was there as he left.

Leaving

Having a Khafira police colonel at his side meant Hartson was spared the hour-long drag through immigration, he was processed in five minutes and was airside before he'd realised. Getting though was one thing, but at the expense of someone else in the queue. Normally that wouldn't bother him, but here he knew how they treated people and he felt guilty, even if he was being deported. He could see the queue from his position of comfort, every one of them a Pakistani, Indian or Filipino, Hamid ignored them all, putting him first – he was a European and whether or not he was a deportee he was still higher up the social ladder than those poor souls.

"You don't care who killed those boys do you, Hamid! They're just Filipinos to you, little better than workhorses."

"Not really, Mr. Will, they have nothing to offer us, we give them work and that is an end to it."

Hartson said nothing more, it was pointless, he knew what Hamid thought. They didn't pay the poor bastards at the bottom of the Gulf. They *did* pay Hannah, but no price can be worth death, surely!

"Now that we have some time on our hands perhaps you would like to look through Duty Free before you go," said Hamid. Hartson could think of no good reason not to so he went with him to the extravagant souk they called Duty Free.

He paid scant attention to the incoming passengers browsing through the same area before they moved on into Khafira. He could tell them by the labels on their bags. The Duty Free sales area had no restrictions on who bought from them, incoming or outgoing it was all money, there were no regulations to say otherwise.

The two men walked through the brightly lit area. Well-dressed, heavily made up Filipina women stood patiently at their sales outlets; they didn't need to hawk, custom would come to them. Hartson considered some perfume for his mother, a bag for his sister, a last piece of unnecessary electronic gadgetry for himself. He had no woman to buy for.

Except Diana! Too late for that, he would never see her again. He thought about something else and looked again at the goods and became absorbed for a long time as he walked up and down examining everything in sight.

Hamid stayed by his side saying nothing. Hartson was in the act of picking up a tiny taperecorder when his attention was wrenched away to a party of travellers in suits, rare in the Gulf. The clothing gave them away. Hartson saw a familiar face in the middle of the phalanx. They had stopped to look at the gold sales area. He spotted the British Ambassador and the First Secretary, and right alongside them was dear old Dennis Fielding, former university chum and now her Majesty's Minister of State at the MoD. They had shared many a bottle from student years to when Hartson did his stint at Westminster. Dear old Dennis, what a chance. He hastily replaced the taperecorder and paced the few metres to the group. Hamid, distracted, failed to stop him.

As he approached he could see the look of surprise on the First Secretary's face. When the ambassador turned he too registered mild alarm but swiftly covered it.

"Dennis how the devil are you?" he said, cheerfully.

A man in a light grey suit looked up from the gold counter and straight into his face.

"I'm sorry, do I know you?"

"Dennis? Don't be silly, you know bloody well who I am.'

Bastard, he'd been well briefed. He couldn't possibly have guessed they'd meet up but nothing had been left to chance; well, if that was the game there would be no holds barred.

Fielding's features were impassive: "I'm sorry, I have nothing to say to you."

Hartson could take betrayal from politicians, policemen, colleagues, even women, that was all expected; but not from friends, that was intolerable. Fielding was no casual acquaintance, he was - had been - a firm friend.

"We'll leave aside the slight on our seventeen year-old friendship, shall we, Dennis. We'll pick that up next week." The minister looked mystified. He turned to one of the embassy officials.

"Who is this?"

The First Secretary replied: "He's a journalist being expelled as we speak minister."

Careless! They should at least have pretended not to know why he was there. Hartson turned to Hamid to see if he had any reaction. His face was a blank. But he was doing nothing to dissuade him either. Right now he should be intervening, using his muscle to move him out of the way, but he wasn't. Right, Fielding, you asked for this – and sod the friendship.

"Should you be dealing with a regime which sanctions murder and conspiracy minister?" he said, loudly.

The dozen or so faces in the Duty Free area turned to see what the noise was about. The minister's group made to move away, the First Secretary looked over his shoulder and said: "The minister hasn't got time to answer ill-informed questions, Mr. Hartson."

Hamid now moved towards him menacingly. "Stop now, Mr. Will, you have insulted the state and myself." But he would not give up that easily. "If you sell these tanks and missiles can you guarantee they will be used by the local armed services, or will they be swallowed up by arms dealers?" Fielding, professional politician that he was, seemed to falter in mid-stride. His mouthy smile remained in place but the eyes narrowed. Hartson studied his former friend's face but not for long as he was whisked away by Hamid's strong arm, and another belonging to a uniformed airport policeman. They marched out of the Duty Free zone and into a neutral area.

"One more display like that and I will put you in irons for the remaining forty five minutes of your time in Khafira. Be quiet!" There was a coldness in his voice and face which made Hartson pull back. Don't forget what these people can do, he thought, and Hamid was no human rights campaigner. He settled down in a seat and committed to memory every word of the recent encounter, he would write it up on the plane. It wasn't much of a story, truth be told, he couldn't see many being bothered about a politician not answering questions about a corrupt regime, it happened all the time, how else did the world turn. But he was mad as hell over Fielding's Judas-rejection. No doubt he would apologise when he got back, that was the way of things, but too bloody bad!

Scott Garrett waited for his party to emerge, they looked none too happy when they did. The smiles were there for the hosts but they were diplomats' and politicians' smiles. "I thought we had that bloody hack under control," whispered the First Secretary, as they passed out of the airport and into their waiting limousines. The ambassador kept Fielding talking, feigning ignorance about the journalist and commenting on the weather.

"You might want to change quickly, gentlemen. I think you'll find the weather too warm even for your attire."

Fielding knew the form, he responded in kind and said nothing about Will Hartson.

"You must be feeling the difference. Let's get you to your hotel quickly and give you a chance to recover from the flight."

Scott Garrett travelled in the limousine with them to discuss their itinerary. Protocols needed to be observed now that their visit had been made so public, one was to pay a visit to the sheikh in residence. Shame it had to be Khalifa. They would pretend they had visited Mahmood for the sake of form. The original idea it appeared was to talk with intermediaries because they had the sheikhs' ears and the diplomatic niceties could be ignored in favour of straight-talking. That would be capped with a private meeting at the end. It was easier that way. But Randalls had ruined that for them. Now all manner of local policy matters would have to be dredged up to give some front to the visit. After that they could get down to the nitty-gritty with the intermediaries.

That was where Scott-Garrett's value lay, in the dirty underbelly of the detail. He had kept an eye on these people for a long time. There was little they would not do for the right amount of money. He had files on all of them.

May
Discovery

They dealt in their own reality, a different world from the powerless. They talked of the impossible, collateral damage, casualties, elections, vote winners, politics and most of all, right now, intelligence. It was five hours after the discovery of the smoking gun in the desert. Triumph was in the room: in the faces, the hand movements, the smiles, the backslapping and handshaking. Not everywhere, there were pockets of resistance, of uncertainty – but none of them would have dared say disbelief.

Morton was there but not with the usual team, they worked lower down the scale. This was a different room. Morton reported back, or not depending on what he and his associates had been up to. And today he had something to report, whether he liked it or not.

"Ladies and gentlemen," he addressed the meeting - no one of cabinet rank, Morton would never get to meet anyone as high as that, nor even touch the hem of the garment of those who only gazed upon them, "We have located chemical weapons in Iraq." There was an outbreak of noisy cheering from the Americans. The Brits and Australians restrained their joy. Fucking butt-clenchers, thought Morton. But he now had to make the best of it even though he knew the ink on his order to pull out was still drying in the Gulf heat.

Everyone in the room already knew it but the announcement needed to be made, so did the applause which followed. It was a staged meeting for the Brits, they needed these weapons more than anyone else in the room.

"Mustard agent in 122 millimetre rockets in a renegade Iraqi convoy. No room for doubt, our own special forces located them five hours ago."

He could never know if the find was real or whether it was one of Barracuda's adventures. It didn't really matter so long as the rockets looked the part and he could rely upon Barracuda to get that right, that was why he'd hired him. He didn't want to know the details, he hadn't even specified which kind of weapon was to be found so nothing could be laid at his door.

But he still had an uneasy feeling. It didn't get any easier when the Brit intelligence guy started speaking – some man drafted in from the Washington embassy. What could he know about any of it! But he still asked questions.

"This is excellent news," said the Brit, "But can we have more detail? How many, what condition the weapons are in, who was carrying them, that sort of thing?"

"I'll get to that Jonathan," said Morton. "Ten 122 rockets have been found, each with mustard agent in the nose cone. They looked old but were loaded on to a GRAD launcher."

"So, they were usable?" asked the Brit.

"Let's say yes, Jonathan. I think that's the answer you want to hear. I know damned well your government wants to hear that."

The Brit smiled uncertainly but carried on with his questions.

"I hope we've shared every area of intelligence in this war. If we haven't then what has been the point?" He shuffled some papers in front of him before he said, "So, we know, as you know, that fifty 122 millimetre rockets have gone missing from a Kaliningrad military base in the last four days. We also know they went to Maraka, one border away from the Iraqi border. They are unfireable and contained conventional explosives."

"What's your point, Jonathan?" said Morton, irritably.

"Let's keep asking the questions. If this is going to be the triumph we all want it to be then it's got to be better than the false assumptions we've made about mobile biological weapons laboratories. Not one has proved to be much more than a chemical toilet – or bathroom, as you say here."

No one laughed.

"What more do you want to know? Asked Morton, coldly.

"let's complete what else we know about events in that region in the last few days, Lou."

A silence came upon the whole room.

The Brit continued.

"We know that Royal Marines special services divers found a 122 millimetre rocket four metres below a jetty in an inlet in Khafira – just a few kilometres from the Iraqi border."

"Speak English," said an American. "What's wrong with miles!"

"We're European now," said the Brit.

"Don't we know it," said another American.

"We know that rocket had a warhead filled with Mustard agent which was leaking into the gulf. It was killing marine life so it can only just have got there. It was close to a dhow which appeared to be related to the Marie Celeste because there wasn't a soul aboard."

"My heart bleeds," said yet another American.

"We know that if there was one thing the regime was good at it was servicing its weaponry efficiently. Why would it leak? Why was it there and not over the border? The rocket had Russian markings with what looked like recently added Arabic symbols. The sea had taken most of them off."

"The chief broke in.

"Of course it'll have Russian markings, they almost certainly came from Russia."

"My concern, Lou, is that this find may not be genuine. You have to admit that it's a hell of a coincidence. How did your men find out that they were filled with Mustard?"

A shiver ran through Morton's whole body but he stayed poker faced. Couldn't the fucking genius shut up! "One of them was dropped and started leaking."

"That makes two leaking 122 mil warheads," said the Brit, evenly.

"Jonathan, I believe you have a saying that goes something like, don't look a gift horse in the mouth."

"Yes, we do, Lou. Sometimes you have to look, though, in case it turns out to be a Trojan horse."

One or two laughed, the rest stayed silent, except for one man at the far end of the table who muttered to his neighbour, "What the hell kind of horse is a Trojan?"

Lou continued, "The fact is we could use these weapons now. We're losing a man a day in Iraq and the victory shine is beginning to look just a little tarnished. Folks here are asking why their sons and daughters should still be out there dying for a cause they haven't quite got hold of any more."

"Really," said Jonathan, with an icy reserve. "You might have heard that my Government is under considerably more pressure than that. Your president is still likely to be re-elected because of the war. My Prime Minister fears exactly the opposite. We need these weapons more than you do, but we need them to be absolutely bona fide. There can't be a hint of suspicion."

"What do you think's happening here, Jonathan? You surely don't think we planted the fucking rockets!" said Lou, raising his voice.

There was a short silence. Morton eyes ducked down to his papers and a shiver ran through his whole body. Lou couldn't possibly know about Barracuda, the Brit would never know.

"Don't, please, mention even the idea of planting the weapons. I know this room is secure but the whole idea fills me with dread. If even the slightest rumour were to get out that these weapons had been deliberately left there for our discovery it would be the end of it all."

"Easy, Jonathan," said Lou," Nobody planted anything that I know of – and I guess I *would* know."

Morton knew he had to look up at this moment because not to do so would make a noise capable of bursting right out of that room. He couldn't afford that, the Brit couldn't afford it, and Lou would fry him for it. A bead of sweat broke out above his hairline. Only Morton knew about it and he hoped it wouldn't fall down on to his brow. He smiled at Lou, as if to say the idea was so ridiculous it didn't need answering.

Lou looked around the room glancing at every face. Finally he returned to the Brit and said, "Nothing's been planted, Jonathan. They may be crap weapons but they're genuine. We want to go with this."

The Brit paused for a few moments and then said in a slightly raised voice which had managed to acquire more heat in the last couple of minutes, "Please, give us more time to validate these weapons, Lou! They're almost too good to be true. Why did they come apart so easily? Why do the markings match the Russian ones? Why was one found in Khafira? It may all add up but the arithmetic isn't all that obvious to me, or my colleagues."

Lou looked around the room again and saw a Mexican wave of shrugging shoulders and nodding heads.

The Brit broke in to stress his point, "I presume you read the papers, so you know our Government has revised its position slightly. We're now looking for evidence of the programmes for weapons of mass destruction. We believe it's quite possible that Saddam destroyed the actual weapons before we went to war."

"Whatever rings your chimes, Jonathan," said Lou.

"This is no joke, Lou. If you've found proper weapons we can all throw our hats in the air and shout that it's over. But if they've been faked it's too much to risk. We don't need them that badly."

"Nor do we, Jonathan, but it sure would look good on the election posters."

"Ours too, believe me!"

Lou smiled, he could afford a few days, nothing was hanging on it.

"All right Jonathan," he said, "I'll give you four days. After that we go public."

The Brit sighed and then nodded.

Morton stayed motionless in his chair, trying to affect the impatience of his colleagues but knowing he had to work quickly. How many more of the stupid leaking Russian firecrackers had Barracuda left behind for the smartarsed Brits to throw back in their faces? What the hell was wrong with Barracuda! He expected a better job than this, even if they had virtually no time to do it.

Then Morton made a reluctant decision, one which he knew would have to succeed or would spell the end for his career and the reputation of the United States intelligence Service.

And his own life.

He would have to get rid of Barracuda and his men. He shivered as he made a mental note of his next contact in the Gulf. If this man didn't take out one of the most ruthless hitmen in the shadowy world of so-called international security, then no one would.

And it was doubtful if the man could pull it off.

But Morton no longer had a choice.

The man called himself the Shark. He'd better be able to chew everything he bit off.

August
Help

Winter found himself with the hotel room telephone in hand, talking to Tom Scott Garrett.

"I see your problem," said the diplomat, soothingly.

"Oh yes, we can call on all sorts of discreet services here."

"Thank God!"

The diplomat laughed at the other end. "Don't worry too much, Paul. It'll have to go through the ambassador, of course, but I'm sure he won't see a problem. No one need even know she's here, and if need be we can smuggle her out in a diplomatic car."

Winter let out a deep breath. Finally, someone was on his side.

"Thank you so much, Mr. Scott Garrett."

"When do you think you might get here?"

"Difficult to say, sometime between mid- to late-evening tonight."

"Marvellous! I'll be here waiting for you. Drive up to the gate and ask the man to let you through. I'll leave instructions and your name there."

Winter put the phone down after a long round of profuse thanks and smiled down at the haunted looking woman lying in the bed. "It's going to be fine. We've got the British Foreign Office on our side."

Scott Garrett put down the phone and thought for a few moments. He picked it up again and dialled a number. It rang three times before being answered.

"Tom Scott Garrett here again. I may have something to solve one of your difficulties, Colonel Hamid."

Winter's voice broke into her resentful thoughts, "We'll have to go." Another move, another drama, another crisis, more danger. She shifted her eyes to his face with an effort and barely managed to hide her contempt.

"We won't make it," she spat, "Take me back to the port, We can find another boat for Mumbai, they come and go out of there like ants to a nest." But he wasn't listening. "Why should your government be willing to give me asylum? I am Lebanese, a prostitute; not a political prisoner, not some victim."

"You're on the run from a vengeful police force, seems like perfect asylum material to me. If you're in trouble anywhere in the world you can usually rely on another Brit to help out."

Did he really believe that? Why had she not just taken the Range Rover earlier and got rid of him?

"How can you be so sure? It would be the last thing I would expect from my country."

"But your country is divided in so many different ways. Do you mix with fellow Lebanese here?"

Hannah had been Lebanese.

"No, but I never mixed with anyone here."

"It sort of proves my point. Us Brits stick together. We form friendships and associations, we create our own society, we're very close."

Your own ghettos, you mean, she thought.

"I think you mean you are all arrogant, superior and narrow minded." She regretted saying it the moment the last word left her lips. He went quiet for several minutes. She had offended him, stupid. She had to bring him back. "I am sorry, Paul, you are a good man." She studied his face for a reaction, she saw a smile, thank God for that, why did she say these things? She needed him and here she was pushing him away. She made a mental note to try harder, make the act more convincing, he seemed to have swallowed it so don't jeopardise it!

"What will you do when you have got out of this? Where will you go?" he asked.

"I have not thought that far ahead. Maybe I will go back to Beirut, maybe America, maybe even Europe."

But in truth she dared not think beyond the next few hours.

It was working out agreeably for Tom Scott Garrett and he was in a bright mood: Will Hartson was now out of the picture, he could say what he liked from London, no one would listen now; assuming he still had a job of course. And handing over this prostitute woman and offering up Winter and the woman would square things with Hamid just in case there were any further questions about Michel. He didn't like being in debt to anyone, particularly a brutish Arab police chief. He liked to be the one pulling the strings, not the other way round. If they could just see Fielding safely out of the Gulf, and with what they came for tucked into their briefcases, then everything could return to normal and he could go back to his life of selective socialising.

There was a knock at the door, Phil Wilkinson poked his head round.

"Afternoon, Tom, just thought you'd like to know the minesweeper crew's been taken care of. They'll be off as soon as their feet touch dry land in ten days time."

"Good, Phil. Any gripes?"

"No-one's happy. It's not how we would have done it but you have your eye on a bigger picture, I suppose."

"Quite! It's probably for the best. We've stirred up enough trouble around here in the last few days."

"Yes, of course."

The wheezing Range Rover growled along the road, through the brilliant starlit unpolluted night. They came over the Maraka border into Khafira. The sky turned orange obliterating the stars. His heart beat faster as he caught sight of the city skyline. The tall hotel buildings stood out in the dark instead of being dwarfed by the huge expanse of sky. They were lit in every colour, all the way up to the top storeys. He looked at Jose: she appeared calm. Just a few more minutes and she'd be safe in the arms of the embassy. There was no reason why he should be worried, especially with Tom Scott Garrett going out of his way to help. But he still couldn't quite believe it was going to be all right.

"How long until we get to the embassy?"

"About twenty minutes."

He slowed down, not even truly conscious that he was trying to spin out the time before he handed her over. He was sure that would be the case; how could they meet again? Where?

"Why have you slowed down?"

"I don't want to attract any police attention now that we have come this far."

He believed it himself. How could he ever tell this story when he finally went back to Britain? The craziness, the exoticness, the danger, the adventure! It wasn't something they would understand readily at his rugby club. And how could he describe this woman? Would he describe her at all? Or would he wake up in his apartment very shortly to find it was a dream after one too many the night before?

The lights of the city enveloped them. "I am afraid Paul, can I trust these people?"

They stopped at a red traffic light.

Of course she could, in so far as anyone could be trusted. "I think you can."

"Think! Think isn't good enough. You're not telling me what I want to hear, Paul. I must know."

He could never really relax with her. "I won't use my cellphone, we'll find a telephone and call, just to be sure. Is that all right?" She nodded. It took three minutes to find a telephone. He parked the Range Rover and went to make the call. As he heard the ringing tone he looked up at the road. A police car was travelling slowly down the street.

Damn! He shouldn't have left her. She was only ten metres away but he couldn't sprint to her. He watched it drive past the Range Rover. Was it slowing? Were they looking?

"British Embassy, good evening." He ignored the answer and continued to watch the car. Why wouldn't it go away?

"Hello caller, good evening."

His eyes never left the car as he finally responded. "Mr. Scott Garrett, please!" The seconds were like hours as he waited to be put through. He stared at the police car, frozen to an ice statue, as it passed the Range Rover. Could they see through the tinted window? Was she slumped in her seat? Had they spotted his numberplate? Did they care about it?

"Scott Garrett." He heard it, but said nothing, still watching the police car.

"Hello, Tom Scott Garrett!" The car passed by slowly, but steadily. He let out a long sigh.

"Hello, who is that please?"

"Sorry, it's Paul Winter here."

"Ah yes, Paul. Are you nearby now?"

"I'm fifteen minutes away. I just wanted to be sure everything had been cleared at your end."

"How do you mean?"

"With the ambassador."

"Oh yes, pure formality. I have to do it for form's sake but it's no problem at all. You just turn up here!"

"Thank God, I'll be there shortly." He put down the receiver and trotted back to the car, the after dark heat bringing out an instant sweat. "It's all fine. The ambassador has approved the whole thing. Don't worry any more, you'll be safe in a quarter of an hour." He leaned down and kissed her. She seemed too distracted to respond.

They made faster time than he expected. Traffic was light, they got to within a kilometre of the embassy after only eight minutes. He used the side roads to avoid being exposed. He came to a crossroads and slowed just in time to see a police car racing down the main street with its lights flashing. There was no siren but he noted that it was going in the same direction as he was about to turn. His heart beat faster again. He took a parallel side street by reversing back. In the distance he could see another flashing light, again going in their direction. Whatever was going on it was becoming dangerous for them to continue to the same destination. The police could discover them by accident.

"Just a slight delay," he said, reassuringly. He glanced down. She was hunched in a foetal ball.

"It's not going to work!"

"Of course it is, we're almost there!" He saw exhausted resignation on her face, the look of defeat; she must not give in, they were within touching distance. "I'll park up in an alleyway, hide the car, and walk down to the embassy. It'll be fine."

He did as he said, the Range Rover was well concealed in an alley with no lighting. He set off the two hundred metres to the embassy being careful to walk in the shadows. He noted another police car going the same way without its lights flashing. As he got within a hundred metres he became aware of cars positioned at discreet intervals around the entrance gate to the embassy. The streets were narrow, in the older part of the city. The old buildings concealed the embassy wall. The police cars wouldn't be visible from the road until a vehicle was almost at the gate.

What were they there for? His heart sank again. Whatever it was he and Jose could not possibly go there, not tonight.

He arrived back at the Range Rover covered in perspiration and hating his next words. "We can't go there tonight, it's surrounded by police cars. They're obviously waiting for someone."

"You poor, naive Englishman," said Jose, with a new harshness in her voice. The words lost their force half way through as she slumped back into the seat.

"Don't you see it's us they're waiting for!"
"How?"
"Why else would police cars station themselves outside at the exact time we are arriving?"

He had not wanted to see the treachery, but now he was forced to, the logic of it was seeping through his pride. Was there anyone in this fucking country who didn't want to make him look foolish! She was talking to him, he barely heard.

"It's over Paul, I can't continue. Leave me alone." The last words were delivered with a weariness which seemed to have shaken hands with death.

"Don't talk like that, Jose. I'll get you out, I promise."

Curse the bloody embassy, curse the fucking ambassador, curse the whole shitty world for being such a foul place. To betray your own countryman in his hour of need! If there was a way he could have strangled Tom Scott Garrett at that moment he would have done.

Maybe he should just hand her over, what else could he do? He hit his hands hard against the steering wheel and looked upwards for inspiration. None came.

The embassy was quiet, only a skeleton security staff remained. Scott Garrett picked up his jacket and walked to the door. It was nine thirty and time to leave. He thought he would have heard something by now but assumed everything had gone satisfactorily. He walked out into the night heat, breathed in and felt he was drowning. He smiled at the security man on the gate.

"All quiet," he called, matily.

"Certainly is, Mr. Scott Garrett."

It was only when he got to the gates of his villa that he noticed the car behind him. It had drawn up directly outside. He looked to see who it was. His heart started thumping when he saw the distinctive features of Colonel Hamid. Had he come to thank him? No, that wasn't Hamid's way. He never thanked anyone. The smile stayed fixed, a tight lid over a boiling cauldron.

"Mr. Scott Garrett, a word please."

"Of course, Colonel, won't you come in."

"Thank you no, this will take no time at all." He lit a cigarette and breathed its exhaust straight into the diplomat's face.

"I do not like having my time wasted, Mr. Scott Garrett. Be warned of this. I personally have little time for people who betray their countrymen but you have been very useful to me in the past. I need hardly tell you that your two friends did not appear at the embassy and that has made me very angry. It is unwise to make me angry, Mr. Scott Garrett. I am finding your usefulness decreasing to zero."

Wretched couple, what had kept them? His smile didn't falter. "There's obviously been a misunderstanding, Hamid. I'm sure they'll make contact again, then you can have them." Hamid's eyes, threatening even when smiling, became sinister. Scott Garrett tried to avert his gaze but he couldn't he was forced to look straight into Hamid's eyes and he shuddered. He saw only contempt there.

"You disgust me, Mr. Scott Garrett." He turned to go to his car. Two steps down the road he paused and threw a final sentence over his shoulder. "I have not forgotten Michel Habibi."

May
Retreat

Barracuda led his convoy back along the route they'd come but this time stopped 15 kilometres from the border. Going back through the checkpoint would be crazy. The way things were there might be a warning about them now; who knew what treachery had emanated from Washington? He, and his team were expendable, that was why they were paid the big money, that was the risk they sold. He rarely thought about death and didn't think of it now; he needed to eliminate any chance of being discovered so they'd sneak out through the dunes where the border was most porous, that was 20 clicks either side of the border post and the main highway. Highways were a no-go now. But they needed to get out of the Iraqi Desert before a nosey coalition aircraft found them with their sensors. That meant moving about in the daylight, in complete opposition to the way they came in. Heat sensors would be ineffective during the furnace of the daytime desert and they could camouflage if they heard any jet activity. All the same, Barracuda kept his specially designed radio tuned to the military frequency, just in case. At least they were lighter going back so they could make more speed.

Given a quarter chance he would have just dumped the remaining rockets in the dunes and left them. But that would be obvious and his paymasters would not thank him – no launcher, no evidence at all, just some tampered with rockets filled with mustard agent. And by the looks of it Washington and London did not need them to be found now.

His laptop pinged announcing an email: from Shark; "Bring everything back, I will provide interim storage!" He might have been talking about imported televisions.

He responded; "Will do. Expect shipment, next 24 hours. Please arrange secure transport." He would head back to the dhow, reload everything there and take it back out to Shark's vessel. Good, he had a plan and an escape route. Something nagged at him, though, he couldn't pin it down, but there was an element in this shifting jigsaw that was out of place. Of course he'd made the whole thing up so quickly, in the space of days and a haze of dollars, that much of it was still swirling around waiting to find somewhere to settle. But part of it wasn't ringing true: he might have expected any of it to happen, hell, he knew the risk of setting up phony weapons, they could have been pulled back at any time. Maybe, if he hadn't been busy getting him and his men out, he might have seen it.

August
London

It was damp and depressing. One look at the greyness covering Heathrow killed off any romantic notionsHartson had induced in himself during the flight. There was no denying it: Khafira was a good place to be, even in August. The plane touched down on time. He collected his bags and made the deflating journey through Immigration, Baggage Reclaim, Customs, and Exit. He shivered in the sterile atmosphere. He thought of a sun-bleached beach on Christmas Day, eating roast turkey in his swimming costume while Filipino waiters served him and the rest of his party with sprouts and cranberry sauce. Last Christmas, when he carried on the party on the beach after dark with just him and that blow-in from NBC in the enticing ice blue bikini. Absurd and wonderful. Now he had a sense of foreboding. Being kicked out was never a cause for celebration.

He was still wearing the thin shirt and flimsy cotton trousers he had on when he encountered Ali Abdul Hamid in his apartment ten hours previously. Not enough for a cool English day, even in August. He didn't expect to be met, but there was a woman carrying a small piece of cardboard with his name scrawled on it. He approached her cautiously.

"I'm Will Hartson."

"I've come to take you directly to head office," she replied efficiently, in a cut glass accent. He was so surprised he hardly had time to take her in.

"What for?"

"They want to see you urgently." She didn't smile. He studied her as she led the way out of the concrete and glass terminal to a Mercedes in the short term car park. Dark power suit, skirt slightly above the knee, slim but not skinny legs, dark brown hair in a bob, blue ear studs, no neck jewellery. She turned as if to make sure he was following; cold blue eyes, to go with the ear studs? They didn't have too many like her in Khafira, She was right out of the Diana Ffrench Parsons school of career women. This iceberg leading him to the car park announced herself as the editor's personal assistant, she didn't elaborate with a name. Those were the last words she spoke until they got to London and Hartson disliked her so much he couldn't be bothered to discover any more about her. The complimentary Champagne he'd enjoyed in Club Class wore off leaving him with a hangover – two bottles, it had been a long flight and he'd expected to get at least half a day's rest before this ceremony. Too bad!

The building was new, mostly glass, tall, a mile and a half from Fleet Street. The woman accompanied him into the external lift, up to the top floor, into the office. She announced him and left. She wasn't like the Fleet Street women he used to know: too well cut and he suspected a rigid moral system inside that cute little skull. He preferred them as they used to be, as flexible as him on the moral front.

The door closed. He hadn't been to the new headquarters since the organisation moved in two years previously. It was as alien as the Khafira souk. He was more likely to get lost here. It was a big room, old black and white pictures on the walls showing its only other occupant in younger days with various heads of state, film stars and sports celebrities. He'd lived a life had Frank Wilson.

The door slam echoed around the room.

"What do you think of her, Will?" said a man with thinning grey hair, looking directly at him.

"She looks good, sounds good," replied Hartson, uncertainly.

"She wants my job."

"Rather young isn't she, Frank?"

"Thirty four, no she isn't. She'll have it in a couple of years."

"What happens to you?"

"Retire, write the novel, clean up the garden, become a consultant."

"But you're only fifty now."

"Too old for this game, Will, it's changing faster than anyone can keep up. It's not about journalism any more, it's about profit."

"Is she any good?"

"She's good at what she does."

"Where has she worked?"

"Nowhere you or I know. She's a business person, never seen a story in her life. She covers meetings, budgets, strategy conferences." Bang went the moral rigidity idea.

Wilson got up to wander around the spacious office. He didn't seem at home in it. "History at Oxford, MBA at Henley Management College. Everything is a resource to her, including you and me."

"Why is she your PA?"

"Learning some of the ropes - she'll probably use them to hang me." They laughed. He turned, his voice hardened. "Drugs, Will." He was taken aback before he realised. "We've had a call from a weasel at the Foreign Office. He said you were dealing, that's why they threw you out. True or false?"

"What do you think?"

"True or false, Will!"

"False of course."

"I just needed to hear you say it. What are they up to?"

"I got in their way, pointed up some embarrassments. There are people being hung out to dry out there for the sake of a bloody arms deal to save a constituency here. The FO didn't exactly come to my aid when the police were throwing me out."

Wilson frowned. "I wasn't the first to hear about it, they went to the money people here first. They know how it works these days."

"And?"

"They want you out."

"What about my side of it?"

"Doesn't count, you're getting in the way. Randalls is a big organisation now, you know that. We've got all sorts of interests, those are being compromised." He paused. "You've upset quite a few people, one way or another."

"Isn't that our job? Comfort the afflicted, afflict the comfortable?" There was silence. He looked down. "It has changed, hasn't it!"

"Afraid so, Will."

"Am I being sacked?"

"I told them to fuck off; risked my pension, I should think."

"Thanks."

"So they threw you out of Khafira. We should be splashing you everywhere."

"But you're not."

"Not yet. Tell me about it?"

"Bloody good story. Foreign Office arranges to get me thrown out, then trumps a false drugs allegation."

"Can they prove anything?"

"There's nothing to prove. On the other hand the weasels have been known to invent evidence."

"Fuck them."

"There was more to it, though. I'd been treading on a few toes out there. I'd asked some unwanted questions about those bodies…"

"Which bodies?"

"The mutilated boys the Navy found."

"Oh, yes, of course."

"They didn't like that and they didn't like the story I wrote."

Wilson just nodded.

"Fuck them. But swearing doesn't make me feel any better. And it won't do any good."

"Fuck off, Hartson, I know you too well. When did you ever get purity?"

They fell silent for a few moments. Hartson was beginning to seethe. They weren't content to disrupt his life in Khafira, they wanted him sacked as well. Bastards, fucking, *fucking* bastards.

But they'd overlooked something. However matey Scott Garrett was with Hamid he hadn't tried to push this drugs line at him – or if he had, Hamid hadn't swallowed it. He may have overstayed his welcome there but they didn't pin any drugs stuff on him, that was just the FO, and clumsily at that. Who did they think they were dealing with! Did they lose all reason operating in that fairyland?

"One thing…The police didn't hit me with the drugs stuff, that was just the embassy. Sounds like they wanted to scare us off at this end."

"And …"

"They're strange people: hospitable and hostile, devious and open, all at the same time. If they'd meant me to be labelled a drug dealer they'd have done it themselves. As it was I got the real reason straight from the Khafira police: my stories were upsetting a lot of people."

"You're very good at that, Will."

"Thanks." He took it as a compliment, the smile on his face was only half ironic.

"What else can we do?"

"Let me go back."

He could see a gleam in the tired eyes. "That'll fuck the money people; doing the job we're supposed to do!" The gleam widened to a grin, he liked the idea a lot. "How do you get back in?"

"The old way, sneak in through the next door neighbour's garden. You know me, no need for a fight, I'm not brave, I'll just go in the coward's way. It's kept me alive up until now. Anyway, Maraka is as leaky as a ninety-year-old's bladder."

"Bloody hell, Hartson, must you! What if you're caught?"

"I'll say I got lost. You know the score, you did it enough before your desk swallowed your passport."

The remark was ignored. "When can you go?"

"Next turnaround to Maraka – cargo flight if need be. There must be something in the next few hours."

Wilson went quiet for a few moments, pondering the next move. It was his career as well that was on the line. Then he spoke: "Put it off until tomorrow, Will, you and I are going for a memory lane piss-up on Fleet Street. Let's see if we can stir up a few ghosts!"

"OK boss."

May
Backtrack

Barracuda picked up his laptop and worked on it as the truck-convoy bumped along. Several times he made ridiculous spelling errors as the tyres hit a less yielding part of the sand. But finally he got his message typed out, to the Shark. "Have not sold all the goods. Returning them to the warehouse. Stand by to receive them."

He hit the send button and hoped there was enough signal on the cell phone link to take it out of that part of the desert and in to the middle of the Gulf. He breathed a heavy sigh of relief when he received a reply four minutes later. "Understood. New sales strategy, perhaps?" Very amusing Shark. He shut the laptop and looked at his watch: two hours to the inlet he figured. He might try getting some sleep – if the bumpy sands would let him.

The night's slaughter had taken its toll. Now that they were safely back in Khafira territory Barracuda found himself nodding off despite the jerking four-wheeled drive. He awoke occasionally, saw an endless orange vista of sand through the windshield, and went back to his dreams. He struggled with it because Barracuda didn't like to dream too often. Dreams were the only things in his life that scared him because he had no control and his rage was useless against them.

It was often the same dream. He'd be in the middle of a battle somewhere when hordes of dead looking people would burst over the horizon a few yards in front of him. He'd work up his fury but they'd keep coming, marching towards him, inexorable, unstoppable. Barracuda would reach for his weapons to start firing, to rub them out, to send them back to wherever he may have sent them before. But his arms wouldn't move, nor would his legs, nor would his eyelids. He could do nothing. He was defenceless. All he could do was rage and that meant nothing to them, nothing at all, they just kept coming. Then, just as they closed in on him he could see the muted fury in their dead eyes, and he would wake up shivering.

August
Fleet Street

What had they done to it! Hartson had ducked the flights back to the UK for the last ten years, he'd either stayed where he'd been posted or gone travelling to the Far East and Australia. Stories had seeped back to him about the changes in the industry but he never believed it could have come to this. Fleet Street: respectable! The adjective was not meant to go with the noun, it derided everything they had ever stood for.

It was still early evening, plenty of light, the time when early editions were starting to run and the pubs, bars and seedy drinking clubs in and around that warren of EC4 should have been filling up. By now He should have seen his first drunk staggering down the pavement or trying to hail a taxi with a rolled up copy of the Evening Standard. Cynical reporters should be regaling each other with stories of disbelief about their latest assignment. Sub editors should be in a separate corner being even more cynical just to show they were every bit as tough as the reporters. Printers should be mouthing unintelligible cockney to each other in very seedy bars indeed. But there was none of it. It was all so horribly clean!

They were in The Cartoonist, a pub Hartson had been carried from drunk and incapable, not always fully clothed, more than once in his earlier years.

"Where's it all gone, Frank?"

"It's all bankers and lawyers now, they took over the buildings when the papers moved out." Bankers and lawyers! This was not the world he signed up to those many years ago. This was a world of spreadsheets, people with unintelligible vocabularies talking about market share, a world of management speak, three-letter acronyms and procedures. This was not his world and now he had time to think he realised how Khafira made sense to him, no matter the hypocrisy or the rawness. It was all over in London, the sooner he got back to The Gulf, the quicker this horrible scene would fade. "Frank, I can't stand this. The grubbiness has gone. Can we get out of here? It's not home any more."

"It never was, it was a place we knew, that's all. No ghosts here for you then?"

"None, there's something antiseptic about it, like I've got to be on my best behaviour."

"You mean you weren't before? No one is ever on their best behaviour, everyone pretends they are." He extended his arm to the clientele in the bar, "We all have something to hide, no matter what you do or where you come from. It's what keeps you and me in a job."

"*Kept* us in a job, Frank. Not so sure now. Sorry mate, I'd love to have got pissed with you but not here."

Wilson put down the half pint remaining in his class. "All right, Will, I get it, nothing stirs for me either. It's history, isn't it!" Hartson nodded. "Go carefully, Will. If I lose you there's only me left to remember."

"Comforting thought, Frank."

They shook hands. "And send me back something to wipe a few pence off their fucking share price, at least I'll go down smiling."

He walked out of The Cartoonist, musing that it was one of the rare times he'd managed to do that, and hailed a cab to pick up some things. Randalls could send on the rest when he knew where he'd be. He checked his passport and looked again at the exit visa stamp entered only a few hours earlier at Khafira Airport. Good, it was real, he could go to another Gulf state and no questions would be asked about why he didn't have one – not that it would matter in Maraka. He punched up Ceefax on the nearest TV and checked flights to the neighbouring states. He found a flight to Maraka which wouldn't be diverted and he phoned the airline to reserve a seat - seat might be a relative term with this airline. Then he got a cab to Paddington, took the next Heathrow Express and was At Terminal Three within half an hour.

The other half

The minesweeper was following a steady course off Khafira but twenty kilometres away from the main city. Sam Jackson scanned the area with his binoculars. He stopped at a shining white vessel making quick progress from the port to the outer edges of territorial waters. He couldn't make out the name on the boat, she was too far away, but he recognised her outline; the Al Khaleej, owned by the famous Arabian Lafitte or whatever his name was.

It was warm enough to roast a pig on the foredeck without any help from a fire and Jackson looked enviously at the yacht. He could just see figures on the decks looking not particularly busy. What he would have given for an invitation to join them.

Jealousy didn't come naturally to him, but envy was another matter. He had always wanted his own yacht ever since he was a young lad taking lone adventurous strolls by the harbour at his home town. Perhaps that was why he joined the Navy. As he looked down from the bridge onto his compact, functional, sparse, grey craft he could see he still had a long way to go.

He looked up again and focused his glasses on the Al Khaleej gleaming white in the ferocious sun as if she had been sent down from heaven on loan; immaculate, beautiful, unattainable. If he became an admiral in charge of his own fleet it would never match that perfection, because it would never be his.

Her eyes blazed into furious life, she cursed the fortune that led her to rely upon this man; she did not like him, she had no faith in him and every now and then she had to screw him to keep him onside, but he was all she had. She shouted at him, she guessed she could do that from time to time if she opened her legs after she'd closed her mouth. "It is madness. All right we are safe now, but for how long! How long before the police or your embassy track us?" They had crossed back to Maraka to avoid the Khafira police, somehow they had not been seen. Perhaps Hamid had been complacent about picking them up at the embassy. Getting there early and spotting the near-siege meant they could turn around and get out before anyone was aware they weren't coming. They'd gone to a different hotel, they didn't want to raise suspicions by checking out and checking back in again within 12 hours.

The Englishman's eyes did not flicker as they looked directly back at her. That was all she needed, him having an attack of confidence. "We don't, but I had no other option except to leave you whimpering in the Range Rover. It was hardly chivalrous." There was a smile on his face which irritated her.

Chivalrous! What did he know about chivalry? He had never had to fight for his own existence before now. If he had then he would have no chivalry, it was too expensive a virtue to maintain against the threat of extinction. She knew eventually she would have to tip him from his charger. She also knew it would be easy. She throttled back on her anger and said, softly: "Where do we go now, Paul? We are both wanted, you can't sneak back to your apartment any more and pretend you know nothing."

He smiled back, good.

"What do you want me to do, turn you over to Colonel Hamid now, say you forced me to take you away at gunpoint and I only got the better of you when you fell asleep?"

Not so good. No, she did not want any of that, she wanted to be free. Free of everyone, especially him. "Something is going to happen, Jose. I just don't have an idea at the moment, that doesn't mean there won't be one."

No idea! He wouldn't know one if it unzipped his trousers and masturbated him. Why did he rush me away from that freighter officer? If she'd been aboard that ship she'd be in Mumbai now, getting hold of her money and planning her new life. She intensified the look in her dark eyes: keep him sweet, for now at least. She beckoned him seductively with her forefinger; keep him close.

"Come down here, you Englishman!" and she kissed him passionlessly. Her mind separated from her body, as it had how many hundreds of times before? It was not *HER* saying those things. *SHE* was not kissing *him*. He did not have *HER*.

The embassy

Phil Wilkinson pushed open Tom Scott Garrett's door and said: "How's the visit going."

"Good. Everything went well with Sheikh Mahmood yesterday. Apparently Sheikh Khalifa was charming, but that's not surprising, it's the only thing he's any good at. It's our turn now. We'll take him to see Samir Latif on his yacht this morning."

"I still don't know why they don't talk directly to Sheikh Issa."

Scott Garrett was tiring of being a nursemaid but he didn't let it show. "He's in London. You can do that when you have his bank account – make that his bank! He leaves it to his friends and advisers to run it all for him while he scoots off into the desert with his rifle and his falcon. Or to the racecourses of Europe."

"He always seems so tuned in."

"Oh he is, so well tuned in that he's smart enough to let the others do the work. Wouldn't you if you could?"

"No question in this climate."

"The result will be the same, the negotiations, shall we say, circumlocutory."

Wilkinson made a note to look up the word while covering his ignorance of it with a smile. Scott Garrett, perhaps sensing this, said: "So we speak to the sheikh's friends and it will get done."

"And Latif is that?"

"Childhood friends, Samir Latif and Mahmood, they used to go camel-raiding together in the Rhub Al Khali. They would raid other bands of travelling Arabs among the high dunes and steal their camels."

"What, and leave them for dead?"

Scott Garrett had never considered the moral aspects of camel raiding. He had hardly been in to the desert himself and the only camels he'd seen were at the sheikh's monthly races just outside the city. Yes, he supposed Mahmood and Latif left these Bedouins for dead, everyone did in those days, and probably still did now.

"It's a harsh world out here Phil, kill or be killed. But as I understand things camel raiding was considered more of a sport than a crime. A bit like those silly paintball games they have for little-boy executives in Europe and America."

"Anyway Latif and Mahmood are old pals and that counts for a great deal around these parts. So Issa does the dutiful thing and honours his father's friends."

The commander looked down at his tropical uniform. "Will this do?"

"It's fine. Latif's hospitality is very informal. Right, let's get to the port and board that launch!"

Scott Garrett drove the embassy limousine with Phil Wilkinson sitting in the front seat. They picked up Fielding from his hotel and drove the short journey on to the port while listening to his complaints about press harassment in the UK. It was so much easier here, apparently, even at the hotel, the local gendarmes seemed to have a much better understanding of how to protect its VIP guests. Wilkinson quietly contemplated the mutinous thought of making a Navy tender available as a press facility. It would be to see how our boys are doing at sea of course. Pretty PR pictures for the folks back home. But if they happened to stray in the direction of the minister...

But, no, he wouldn't do that, he wanted the extra ring on his sleeve to make him Captain Phil Wilkinson, and then onwards. That was as sure a way of losing it as any.

They entered the port and drove on slowly to where Latif's launch was moored up ready to take them out to the Al Khaleej.

Admiration
Sam Jackson's binoculars could make out more detail on the Al Khaleej now they were closer. The gleaming white he'd seen from twenty kilometres wasn't sullied by proximity, the vessel was kept clean and decorated to the highest standards. There wasn't a sign of rust anywhere, not even by her anchors. That was some achievement in the humid Gulf. He swung his binoculars round to port and saw a small launch approaching the yacht. He could just make out some figures on it but they were unidentifiable at that distance. One was wearing a Royal Navy uniform. A small surge of envy went through him and he took it out on the crew. "That's enough of this. We can't stand around all day watching how the other half lives."
"A lot less than a half, sir," pointed out a rating, that was all he needed, a lecture on political iniquities from a rating. It was true of course, but however small a percentage of the population the yacht represented, Jackson wasn't part of it, and he wasn't even part of the percentage who got invited to the party either.

Tom Scott Garrett sat back to enjoy the journey on the launch with the sea breeze blowing against his face. What a relief even for a short couple of hours to get away from the humid intensity of the city. He and Wilkinson made small talk with Fielding but it was more of a moaning session from him. He had grumbled about the climate from the moment they left the car in the port. He had made it plain that he didn't want to be here and he was only doing it because of the bye-election at home.
"I'm sure Samir Latif's yacht will be to your liking minister. I understand it's air-conditioned throughout."
"Thank God for that," said Fielding.
Wilkinson ran his seaman's eye over the Al Khaleej as they drew alongside. She was certainly impressive. The white glare made him shade his eyes despite his protective sunglasses. There was a metal stairladder integral to the hull on the port side. Latif was waiting at the top to greet them. Telephone bulging from a shirt pocket, his open face smiled warmly at them as they mounted the staircase to his sea palace.
"Minister Fielding," he said clasping the senior politician's hand. Scott Garrett made the other introductions including his own, although that turned out to be

unnecessary. Fielding switched from the grumpy brat in the nursery to a smooth cosmopolitan at home anywhere in the world. "So very good to meet you, Mr. Samir Latif. What a lovely yacht, I'm sure you are very proud of her." Latif expanded with the praise. Fielding knew his job, all right, Scott Garrett watched in admiration.

"Gentlemen let us have a drink to celebrate this happy meeting," said Latif. He called a waiter over. "Let us sit and talk, gentlemen," They moved to an awning where the breeze gave a welcome freshness. Even Fielding seemed to relax.

Wilkinson fell into the easy-going atmosphere. He forgot about arms deals and politicians, dead bodies and news blackouts. He wanted to know about Samir Latif the camel raider in the Empty Quarter. He had taken to the man long before being introduced.

"What have you heard about me, Commander?" said the businessman, smiling. Wilkinson smiled back. "Not very much, I would like to know more." Latif's eyes drifted off to somewhere on the horizon, sometime in the past. "I have not always had these riches commander. I started out as a poor boy working with the sheikh's family. No one was rich in those days, there was no oil. We would run camel trains across the Rhub Al Khali – the Empty Quarter. I was with our own dear Sheikh Mahmood. Camel raiding was a way of life. If we came across another train on our route we would wait until nightfall and try to get away with as many of them as possible."

Wilkinson shifted uncertainly, Scott Garrett listened and did not move. "You are surprised commander. Really it happened to us as much as we did it to anyone else."

"Didn't they try to stop you?" asked the commander.

"All the time." Latif pulled up a trouser leg and revealed a small scar in the fleshy rear of his left calf. It was ten centimetres long and glared a kind of dead mauve colour. "I got that from a rifle bullet when I was being very foolhardy one night. I was trying to prove myself."

"You have had a very colourful life, Mr. Latif," said Fielding. Latif smiled. "Perhaps I have Minister Fielding, but all that I have done in my adult life does not come near the adventures of those camel-train days."

"What happened to the people you raided?" asked Wilkinson.

"They would try to get their camels back and take ours at the same time. It was expected. It was like a desert sport, commander."

"And what about getting caught?"

"There was no shame in that. If they caught us or we caught them it was a cause for celebrations. We would slaughter a camel in honour of our guests and feed them for three days before setting them off into the desert again."

"With a camel I hope."

"Of course, but only one." Latif looked skywards almost into the sun. "Those were very different times, we cannot go back."

"Would you like to?" asked Wilkinson.

"I would dearly love to, Commander, but it is impossible. Instead of riding a ship of the desert I now ride a luxury yacht, I carry a mobile phone constantly and if I need to get somewhere in a hurry I have my own 747 jet standing by on my own airfield. I could not go back to the simple life of the desert now, it does not exist any more, there are no camel trains, and there are no boys like I was."

"How do you get your adventure now, Mr. Latif?" asked Wilkinson.

Latif paused for thought. "The thrill of business I suppose. The hunt through the commercial jungle."

"You are very good at it, Mr. Latif," offered Fielding.

"Thank you, Minister. You are very flattering."

Latif's breast pocket gave off a high-pitched sound.

Emergency call

Paul Winter waited anxiously as he held his cellphone to his ear. Samir Latif's number rang out. He was treading in areas he did not know, but he had little choice.

It rang again. Jose looked on from the bed where she had just shut him up for an hour. She was not certain of Samir Latif either, but she knew him well enough and they had done a lot of business together. She had helped to seal more than one big deal for him with her hospitality. But she was nervous, she was being sought and his protection would be essential in keeping her safe. He could intervene with Issa, or more helpfully, get her out of Khafira for good.

Latif pulled his phone from his top pocket. "Excuse me, gentlemen, this never happened when we were camel raiding." He pressed the green receive button and said: "Hello, Samir Latif...Mr. Winter, how nice to hear from you. I was hoping that you would join us yesterday." Scott Garrett gave away nothing as he listened.

"Yes of course, Mr. Winter, and bring your guest...I don't understand, you cannot go to the port...because you will be recognised?" There was a long pause, finally he responded. "Very well I shall send my launch to the Maraka Lagoon. You will know it straight away I think."

He ended the call and addressed the guests. "We will be joined by someone from my bank, gentlemen, and his guest." Latif looked around him. "He helped put together the financial package to buy this yacht. He has been very helpful in putting together the finance for many of my deals."

"How fortunate," said Fielding.

"I think you will like them both. Now let us have another drink and talk a little of what you really came here for."

Gibraltar couldn't be as bad as this, thought Sam Jackson as he turned his face into the hot breeze hoping for relief. Then he lowered his head and his brow sweated up instantly. He watched the launch leave the Al Khaleej and head towards Maraka, he picked it up again 90 minutes later as it traced back. There must be a party on board the Al Khaleej today. The minesweeper was making its own dull progress around a grid pattern. It was pointless. All they'd done was turn up bodies. There were no other minesweepers with them on the search. The whole thing was a charade. They were just keeping the Khafira government happy. A trade off: we protect you, you buy our weapons. Fine, but did it have to involve him!

He had learned a lot very quickly about the way politicians and diplomats behave. Who cares about four dead Filipino boys! What have they got to do with anything! They wouldn't be voting in any UK election, especially one in the West country. His cynicism was new but he was already wearing it like an old coat. It helped.

The launch was closer now, he focused on the passengers, only two on this trip. Then he took a deep breath and let out a sigh of appreciation. The crewmen around him looked up from their tasks expecting an explanation. He wasn't going to share it with them. His powerful binoculars had picked out a vision at the stern of the launch: dark haired, olive skinned, and with eyes he would have killed for. She was the only woman he'd seen approaching the Al

Khaleej that day. He moved his binoculars a fraction of a centimetre to see who her companion was: an anonymous man, dark haired, pinched looking, about medium height, wearing a worried expression.

Nothing could be too flamboyant for that woman, she'd outshine anything she wore. He focused as closely as he could, tried to see her eyes. Cool, pretty, exotic, knowing...and as he focused closer on her face, fearful!

"Something wrong skipper?" asked his chief petty officer. Jackson relented, it was the chief after all, he'd let him have a look.

"Nothing at all." He handed over the binoculars. "Just take a look at the stern of the launch."

The chief obeyed and smiled appreciatively. "What it is to be rich, eh!"

He handed back the binoculars and both watched the launch approach the Al Khaleej with eyes unaided.

"It would be nice to be invited to the party," said the lieutenant.

"It does look colourful over there, doesn't it," replied Jackson as he looked down again at the battleship grey of his very own minesweeper.

Maraka Airport

A beaten-up and barely serviceable 707 approached Maraka. That was the price he paid for being in a hurry. Hartson looked out of the window and saw a flame coming from an offshore burner. The beige sands of the beaches were visible on the horizon. He folded the magazine back into the storage net in the seat in front – no video on demand on this rickety old can – and prepared to land. The aircraft descended to an altitude where he could feel the warmth of the Gulf, even through the air-conditioning. He'd badly wanted a drink on the flight, he'd made it a point of principle to get as drunk as possible whenever in an aeroplane, but not this time. The cabin service, if it could be called that, was restricted to water and orange juice and if he wanted a tea or coffee he could make it himself. And usually he would have made an attempt on the hostesses – it was always worth a try, sometimes it worked – but the crew on this flight barely gave credit to the image and he wasn't about to try and pull a 50 year-old Eastern European with her teeth mostly gone and a waste measurement to rival the GDP of a small Central American country.

But, at least he would be sober for the upcoming challenges – whether that was a good thing or not was uncertain to him.

The aircraft drew nearer to the shore and he could make out the dunes beyond the limits of the city. It was so empty compared to London. The 707 landed, taxied and came to a halt. He stood with his holdall containing everything he had in the Gulf for the time being: handheld recorder, notebooks, pens, money, passport, a couple of changes of clothes, and a toothbrush. It occurred to him fleetingly that he had only eaten at a height of 35,000 feet during the past 36 hours. The cabin door finally unlocked. He'd hardly ever been to Maraka in the past, let alone through the airport. The door opened and the damp heat smacked him in the face like a hot wet towel. He slowed immediately, taking the steps one at a time and resigning himself to the growing river of sweat falling from his forehead.

He quickened his step once inside the dusty and quite grubby terminal and was almost first in the queue at Immigration; another flight from Burma was just clearing. He passed through mercifully quickly and headed straight for the coin-operated phones in the Arrivals Lounge. He knew from experience that there was virtually nothing modern computer systems couldn't do if they were used effectively and tracing a credit card call was one of the easiest, so he played safe with the phone. He could blow the whole thing on this one call but he was gambling on his judgement. He punched in a series of digits and waited for a reply. As he listened to the ringing tone he started to doubt the idea, it was crazy, he made to pull the phone away from his ear and replace it. Then it was answered. "Hello, British Embassy, how can I help?" Now was the time to stop, before he got in too deep. But, it was the only way to go forward. Make your move and pray, Will.

Sanctuary

The launch trip took fifty minutes. The sun and the breeze lulled Winter into a relaxation he hadn't expected. Nice change, there had hardly been a time in the last few days when his stomach hadn't been knotted.

He looked across at Jose and smiled reassuringly as they both got up to mount the steps. This was it, they were almost there, just a few more steps. They walked up slowly. Jose seemed to labour over every move. Samir Latif was waiting at the top, telephone lying dormant in a shirt pocket, a drink of something or other in a left hand, the right hand on a guard rail, his round welcoming face beaming a huge smile. It was going to be all right. Jose even managed a smile. They reached the top and Samir first grasped Paul's hand and shook it warmly. "Mr. Paul Winter, I am so pleased you could come."

Then his smile increased its intensity as he turned to Jose. "You look tired, Jose, you must find some rest. It is my turn to help you now." He pulled her close and enveloped her with his wide arms. She seemed to melt into them causing Winter to look away in annoyance. This was no time to be jealous, but damn it! He tried to mask his irritation, kept a tired smile on his face. He couldn't possibly match this man's enormous generosity.

He noticed there were other guests on board, he examined them superficially, until his eyes lighted on a familiar face. The tension arrowed back into his shoulders, his brow furrowed again. Tom Scott Garrett was smiling at him a few metres away. His supporter at the embassy, their way out of this hell, the bastard who'd led them into a trap.

"Good day, Mr. Winter, I hope all is well," said the diplomat. smiling.

He said nothing, he looked back to Jose who had now been released from Samir Latif's bearhug. She smiled back at him and reached out for his hand.

"I hope everything's all right," said Scott Garrett. Winter and Jose looked at each other before she whispered: "Who is he?"

"The one who tipped us off to the police."

"What is he doing here?"

"He seems to be with them," he replied, pointing to the group of politicians and diplomats he had not yet met.

"Come, let me introduce you to the rest of the party," said Latif, jovially.

He gave a brief explanation of each of them, Winter's eyes widened when he heard the name Dennis Fielding, Undersecretary of State at the MoD.

"And finally, this is Commander Philip Wilkinson of your Royal Navy."

The commander's eyes had been on Jose from the moment she boarded the Al Khaleej; everyone's eyes were straying to her.

Jose appeared not to notice, still less care. "Samir, I am very tired, I need rest badly. Is there somewhere I can go?" she said to the big man.

"Of course, I have had cabins especially prepared for you both, one of the stewards will help settle you in." He made a clicking sound with his fingers and a Filipino boy came running forward. Latif gave curt instructions and the boy led Jose away. Winter thought he should follow them but wanted to stay.

Scott Garrett appeared at his side and said quietly for only the two of them to hear: "So here you are then. So glad to see you've come to no harm. I was very worried when you didn't appear last night."

"So worried you told the Police," said Winter, bitterly, "They trace missing persons don't they. I should imagine they were very helpful."

"You seem to have misunderstood, Mr. Winter. I have been very concerned about you. We had an escape route planned and facilities laid on to take care of your companion."

"Then explain to me why your precious embassy was surrounded with police cars less than ten minutes after I called you!"

"Nothing to do with me, how could it be? I am a British diplomat. Are you suggesting that I'm in league with the Khafira police? It's a direct contradiction of my brief."

"Frankly, I don't know what to think, but I know I have passed the embassy countless times in the past at day and night time and I have never even seen one police car in the vicinity."

"This is intolerable, Winter. You have no right to accuse me of these things. I can understand that you feel fraught at the moment but it's no excuse for this kind of accusation." Winter said nothing but looked away to see Phil Wilkinson watching them both.

"You as well?" said Winter.

The commander paused and then answered: "There have been a few times in the last few days when I have genuinely believed I have been in league with the devil, Mr. Winter, but I am afraid I don't know anything about your dispute with Mr. Scott Garrett."

Winter recovered slightly and turned back to Scott Garrett. "We're here in spite of you. You can stuff the bloody Foreign Office and your embassy. This is our ticket out, we're asking Samir Latif to intercede with Sheikh Mahmood and get him to call off the dogs."

"I wish you good luck, Mr. Winter," said Tom Scott Garrett with a restored smile.

Latif's cheerful voice boomed through the tension, dispelling it almost immediately. "I am glad to see you are all getting on well here, gentlemen. You must excuse me while I continue my discussions with your minister. Please feel free, the vessel is entirely at your disposal."

"Very kind, Mr. Samir Latif," said Wilkinson.

"Oh, commander, one thought did occur to me. I wondered if the captain of your minesweeper might enjoy a couple of hours of our hospitality here."

The commander recognised an extravagant ego in Latif, one that needed feeding by making other men envious. But he covered it with a chuckle and said: "I'm sure he'd love it. By all means, Mr. Samir Latif, I can't see a problem. I think we both know there aren't many mines to be found on the bottom, don't you?"

"I think you're probably very right, commander," said Latif with a wide smile. "I will arrange for him to be contacted and brought aboard by the launch."

Diana

Hartson took a deep breath and went ahead with his quite possibly disastrous scheme. "May I speak to Miss Diana Ffrench Parsons, please?"

"May I ask who is calling?"

He paused before responding: "My name is Paul Winter from the Middle Eastern Bank."

"Thank you, Mr. Winter, please hold."

He cursed her for not being senior enough to warrant her own direct line. He'd always been able to get straight through to Tom Scott Garrett - mixed blessing that had turned out to be.

"Mr. Winter, how can I help you."

It was unmistakably the educated tones of Diana, infuriatingly sexy even from two hundred kilometres away.

"Hello, Mr. Winter."

"Hello Diana, please tell me why I've been thrown out of Khafira and what is happening in the Godforsaken place right now."

A friend in need

The cabin porthole was open, Jose was relaxing on a wide bed clearly built for two and possibly more. Latif had never done things by halves when doubles were available. She smiled as she remembered some of the more exotic times she had shared with him and his occasional guests. Latif had come once every two weeks, sometimes with friends, sometimes on his own. More often than not she and Hannah would entertain the whole party and be paid handsomely for it. Her memories of Samir Latif were only good, and his guests had nearly always behaved themselves. If not he had taken them aside for a quiet word. They had always been exhausted by the experience. Maybe, if she had stopped to think about some of the things they did she might have had doubts, but she never had.

And now the roles were reversed, Samir Latif was entertaining her. He was a friend, someone to rely on, to trust, almost, inasmuch as she trusted anyone. She cleared her throat at the thought of the idea.

There was a knock at the cabin door. "Come in," she said easily. There he was, the imposing figure of Samir Latif standing in the doorway, telephone bulging in his breast pocket.

"I hope I am not interrupting," he said.

"I am just gathering myself together," she said. "We owe you a great deal."

"It is nothing, Jose. You are a friend after all." His face opened into a big smile.

"You shall tell me all about this later. I must return to my guests now."

"Is this another of your big deals Samir Latif?"

"Possibly, you know how delicate these things can be sometimes."

"I have never asked you what you did to make your money, and you have never told me. I only know you are a man of very big influence."

"I think that is why you are here is it not."

She darkened, of course that was why they were there. "Hannah is dead."

"I know, Jose, it is terrible. I liked her a great deal. But you are alive, we must make sure that you are properly taken care of. Try to rest now."

Of course he knew; Samir Latif knew everything that happened in Khafira; every policeman, every criminal.

"We will talk later, Jose, business first." He came forward a few paces and kissed her. She offered her cheek.

He turned to walk out of the door and stopped halfway to look over his shoulder. "You are already looking better. When you came on board you looked tired, now there is life in you again. Perhaps we can enjoy some of that life together later."

There was always a price to pay. She smiled back invitingly and shifted her legs as if to show what a good idea she thought it was.

Invitation

Sam Jackson had left the minesweeper in the care of a quite put out, not to say jealous, sub lieutenant as he quickly, rather too quickly perhaps, accepted the invitation sent by radio from the Al Khaleej. He was being invited to the party after all, as a ship's captain he was being awarded the privileges of rank and he was going to make the most of them. He looked back at his ship in her diminutive grey glory. They had suspended the hunt for mines for the time being while he spent a couple of hours on "public relations" duty at Commander Wilkinson's request.

As he got closer to the Al Khaleej he saw the perfection he had witnessed from his distant binoculars remained true. She gleamed white in all the right places, and shone gold-yellow where the brass rails took up the theme. It was a magnificent sight, and he could see why. The vessel was constantly being cleaned and polished by a team of hardworking crewmembers. No doubt she was repainted every time she put into port. He marvelled at the beauty and excess that money could bring.

The launch drew alongside and he trotted up the steps to be met by his host. "Welcome aboard, lieutenant...'" – pronounced *leftenant*, as was proper in the British armed forces, "I am Samir Latif the owner of the Al Khaleej."

Latif, not Lafitte, Jackson smiled and took the hand offered to him in a warm grasp. The introductions were made with the help of Phil Wilkinson who added his own welcome. "Thought you could use a break, Sam. It's a nice tub, very welcoming."

"So I see, sir."

"Please enjoy yourself, Lieutenant, make yourself at home and have anything you want. I always insist that my guests have whatever they want, it is an Arab tradition." Latif beckoned to one of the waiters to attend to the newcomer while he returned to the politicians.

"Smart piece of kit, sir," said Sam to his superior officer.

"That's the power of money, Sam."

"Incidentally, where's the woman I saw coming on earlier."

"Keeping your mind on the job, were you Lieutenant?

"In a sense, yes!"

Wilkinson smiled a conspiratorial brotherhood-of-officers smile.

"She's a mystery. She came on with a banker, a man called Winter, then she disappeared." Jackson shrugged and accepted his drink from the waiter, took a sip and looked around in admiration. "I wouldn't mind a look over her, she is a

bit special. I always fancied myself skippering one of these."
"We can all dream, Sam, let's have a look."

Diary

There was a long pause. Hartson waited, then could wait no more. "Hello, Diana."
"Will?"
"Yes, Will-Paul Winter-'Banker-Wimp'-Hartson."
"Bloody Hell, where are you?"
"Where should I be."
"According to what I hear here you should be back in London or wherever you stay in the UK."
"Who tells you that much that you listen to them."
"There were one or two triumphant faces around here yesterday, it slipped out easily enough, especially to a callow looking female junior diplomat."
"Did you hear any more?"
"I've told you enough already, Will. I can't tell you any more. You've been sent home in the interests of Her Majesty's Government – or at least we didn't feel like stepping in on your behalf when you were told to get out."
"HM Government's survival you mean."
"Obviously, yes."
"Not so callow then."
"Hardly, Will."
No hardly at all, Diana! A warning light flashed up on the phone display screen, he pumped some more local coins. It was expensive making an international call from an airport coin booth, even if the number was only a few kilometres away.
"Anyway, Will, how's England? Nice and wet I'll bet."
The platitude angered him. "I'm not in the UK, I'm at Maraka Airport and I'm coming back in to Khafira!"
"Why?"
"Unfinished business." He was aware how absurdly macho it sounded as he said it. So was Diana. "Been watching too many Clint Eastwood films, Will."
Was that a chuckle? Bloody humiliating. Jesus, what kind of week was this in his life! Seven days before everything was normal, dull even. Then he found a

story, saw a dead whore, crossed Ali Abdul Hamid, went to bed with Diana Ffrench Parsons, got himself beaten up and abandoned in the desert, and now he'd been thrown out of the country.

"Where's Scott Garrett now, Diana?"

"Classified."

"Diana?"

"I owe you no more, Will. I gave you too much before. I told you about the bodies and the visit, you turned that in to a very hot potato around here. A lot of people were walking round with stinging hands after that. That's why you got thrown out."

Callow, indeed!

"You owe me something, Diana."

"No I don't."

May
A helping hand

The bandit convoy arrived at the inlet and Barracuda was thankful to be awake again. They were four hundred metres from the dhow and he could tell, even without his field glasses, that something was different. There was a launch tied alongside and men in olive green uniforms with M16s standing on the jetty, right next to the dhow. He instinctively reached for his AK47 and watched his driver do the same. As he got closer, 200 metres away, he saw the men still in the same position, lounging even. Their hands hadn't gone to their weapons and they didn't look as if they were there for trouble. It might be all right, thought Barracuda. A shootout in Iraq was one thing, but he couldn't risk one in Khafira without betraying the operation. It was a lot harder to cover up – why would it happen in the first place! The small convoy drew up and Barracuda saw a man with some kind of decoration on his epaulettes. He looked familiar, thought Barracuda. The convoy drew up and still the group of uniforms made no attempt to make a stand or provoke anything. What the fuck is this, thought Barracuda.

The man with the golden epaulettes came forward. He was carrying no weapon at all and his hand was outstretched. As he came close Barracuda realised where he'd seen him before, the Port Police launch a couple of days ago. He relaxed but only a little. Why was this man here?

He spoke, "I am Colonel Hassan of the Khafira Port Police," he said.

Barracuda took his hand and was surprised by the firmness of the grip and the intensity of the look in the man's eyes.

"Colonel Hassan," he said, "They call me Barracuda."

"I know said, Hassan," smiling, "With good reason I understand."

"You'd better believe it. Why are you here, Hassan?"

"You are right to be suspicious. I have been asked to keep an eye on the dhow. I believe you will need it to transfer some materials."

"And how do you know that?"

"We swim in the same waters as a man who is sometimes called the Shark."

So the guy was a fucking poet as well. Swim in the same fucking waters. Yeah. Barracuda's rage started to surge, he could feel the tautening in his arms, like he was going to throw this brassed-up cop into the same waters he swam in.

What was Shark playing at? How many other people that he swam with were in on this most secret of projects?

Hassan seemed to sense the building rage and backed off a couple of feet. He must have heard of Barracuda's reputation. But it was at this sort of time that Barracuda had learned to calm himself down. He couldn't get mad just for the sake of it. All he'd have would be a pile of bodies and an incident on his hands that he could not risk. He managed to smooth himself down mentally and said to Hassan, "Thank you for your help. You need not stay any longer, my men will be able to deal with everything from now on."

Hassan continued to smile throughout. He said, "I have been asked to give you every assistance with loading the dhow and unloading at the other end. I think you have been very busy in the last few days. Why do you not let my men do some of the work for you?"

A sudden weariness descended on Barracuda. He was tired, so were the men. He'd got them out like he always did. Sure why not let someone else do the fetching and carrying. "Thank you Colonel Hassan, a very generous offer which I am pleased to accept."

Hassan kept on smiling which made Barracuda feel uneasy, but everything made him feel uneasy. He unslung his AK47 and called to the rest of the Barracudas now standing around, "Take the load off. We're out and we've got help."

Hassan yelled out something to his men in Arabic and they fanned out among the trucks and started unloading the wooden crates from the truck and putting them back on the dhow.

"Be careful with that stuff, Hassan, don't drop it! And watch out for ten missiles without crates – we've kind of acquired them on the way."

"My men are meticulously careful," said Hassan.

That's a hell of a word to make a virtue out of a vice, thought Barracuda.

August
Unguided tour

Winter could see a vast expanse of blue leading off to mystical regions of the past: Persia, Asia Minor, the spice routes, great military marches. He hardly noticed the two navy officers approaching. He looked around when he heard their measured footfalls. They were engrossed, examining every lick of paint, every polished brass rail. The commander looked up and smiled. "It's every Navy man's dream to have his own ship, Mr. Winter."
"Mind if I tag along."
The other officer had a familiar look about him. Winter tried not to stare. Where had he seen him before?
"Not with your friend the journalist tonight, then?" said the younger man. The memory stirred in Winter's mind. A great deal had happened since then, and it was none too clear, even at the time.
"No. I know we've met, but I'm sorry, I don't remember the details."
"Too right we did," said the man with righteous indignation.
"I'm sorry I was being dragged along that night. I'm not certain what happened."
The younger man relaxed his stare. Winter fought to recognise the rank markings on his epaulettes but he knew nothing of military insignia. "Join us. We're having a look around the ship."
It was a big craft by yacht standards but not otherwise. They covered the upper decks quickly, pausing sometimes to admire a piece of Islamic artwork on the porthole windows. They found a stairway and descended into the bowels of the vessel. The exterior fastidiousness was repeated out of sight down below. The paint was more grey than white but had been meticulously applied. Somewhere in the centre of the vessel there was a door with an opened padlock. Jackson tried the handle and it gave without any resistance. Phil Wilkinson, drilled in the ways of the armed forces, asked "Do you think it's a breach of hospitality to go barging into his private areas?" Jackson kept his mouth shut and walked through. It was dark inside, He could make out nothing at all. Wilkinson slid his hand along the wall looking for a light switch. Then he heard a cry quickly stifled, it sounded like the banker.
"All right," asked the commander.

"I kicked something hard with my shin."

The digital display flashed again, he was running out of coins, he pumped in five more and hoped that would be enough. "Diana, they tried to get me sacked on a trumped up drugs allegation. Now maybe you don't think that matters, but let me tell you it does. What they're doing is wrong and they're not likely to care very much. I'm relying on you to have a conscience."
There was another silence. Finally, "I didn't know that. Who accused you?"
"Scott Garrett of course, who else! So, if your so called superiors aren't going to see fair play I was just hoping that you might have some shred of justice in you that they hadn't ripped out yet." He had to admire his own rhetoric, he might even believe it himself it was so sincere.
Another silence, she was good at those. He let the seconds pass, clocking them off on the digital display. It was up to her.
Fifteen seconds later. "What should I do?"
"Where are they now?"
"Who?" More seconds passed.
"Scott Garrett and Fielding, the real Paul Winter, the bastards who dumped me in the desert, the bastards who shipped me out yesterday." His voice was raised. He looked around, a couple of Indian porters were looking at him, but they looked at everyone.
"Don't get hysterical, Will, it's not like you."
"Just give me a clue, Diana."
"Tom's with Fielding talking to Samir Latif on his yacht out in the Gulf, that's all I can tell you, I'm not sure I should even know that myself."
"How do you know?"
"I looked at Tom's diary. I'm not supposed to but we all do it. Which rings a bell now: you did call yourself Paul Winter when you first spoke didn't you?"
"Yes."
"I saw that same name written in the diary against yesterday evening. A Colonel Hamid is written alongside it with a phone number…wasn't Winter the fool who embarrassed everyone at the café?"
"Yes, what's the number?"
She read out six figures. It was his turn to be silent now. He knew the police station number by heart, much good it had ever done him.

"Are you still there, Will?"
The bastard had sold Paul Winter and the whore to Khafira's nastiest security policeman. The idiot probably thought the embassy would help; oh no, not what they were there for – at least not what Tom Scott-Garrett was there for.

The cabin was hot. Jose awoke and lifted herself from her bed. She opened the porthole window. The vessel was obviously maintained regularly, the catch gave instantly and the round window swung out onto the upper deck with ease. She felt a breath of warm air on her face but it was a relief from the mounting heat inside. She stayed there surveying the emptiness of the sea. She could see no land from where she was but there was a quietness which was unmatched anywhere in her experience. There was a low hum from the ship's generator but it was unobtrusive and not enough to dispel the calm; she could hear nearly everything being said on the immediate upper decks.

She relaxed into the luxury. In Beirut, in Khafira, there had never been a time when noise was not present. The noise of the traffic, shouting, day to day existence. Here there was nothing except the occasional faint, disembodied call to prayer blown out on the wind from the shore.

She heard a familiar reassuring voice, it was Samir Latif talking to the other men she had met briefly. What were they, British? He sounded close, she thought of calling a greeting to him through the porthole but didn't want to disturb his dealings. That was always the rule. She went back to staring at the empty sea in front of her.

"I believe we are all men of the world here, gentlemen. This conversation goes no further than the yacht but we all know what we want, I think."

Samir Latif, she thought, still making deals and being none too discreet about it. "You want me to use my influence with Sheikh Mahmood to get him to buy your tanks and missiles. What do I get out of it?"

"You get our gratitude, Mr. Samir Latif," said an Englishman, brashly. Samir Latif laughed loudly, uproariously. She chuckled herself. Gratitude was not spent in the souk, she had learned that in her years as a professional.

"Thank you so much, Mr. Fielding but I think a little more is what I am looking for."

"Like what?"

"Let us not talk of money, that would be pointless, as you can see I have more than I need. Let us talk of how my influence can be extended in other areas." There was a pause. "I am prepared to tell Sheikh Mahmood he should buy your tanks and missiles."

"That's very generous, Samir Latif," said Fielding.

"However you will understand I have shall we say broader trading interests in the Gulf than just Khafira."

There was a silence.

"Do you mean you wish to deal with other regimes as well?" she heard the diplomat Scott Garrett questioning. She gave an uncontrolled shiver. Other regimes where?

"I am a businessman, gentlemen. Khafira has been built up on the basis of free trade. Surely I can be free to trade with whom I want."

The Englishmen, Fielding she now knew, broke in, "We have no objections to free trade, Mr. Samir, as you can imagine. The market decides where the goods will go. But there are limits. There have to be export licences and end user certificates I need hardly tell you. They can be easily traced."

"And easily forged, changed, invented, lost. I am not stupid Mr. Fielding, this is not the first time I have done this sort of thing. End user certificates mean nothing as well you know. Export licences can be granted for anything provided it is not discovered by your customs people. Do not worry, I will tell the sheikh he should pay a higher price for the weapons, that will cover the cost of manufacture from your point of view."

"Thank you, you do realise that this not a decision I can take lightly – and I can hardly refer it to my Prime Minister. You're asking us to provide extra arms for your own use. It's a dirty scheme, Samir Latif, but that's why I've been sent, I suppose," said Fielding.

Samir Latif waited a moment. Jose wondered at the commodities being dealt with here. Then he responded: "More to the point what do you lose if there is no deal? How important is this sale to you, Mr. Fielding. Can you afford to lose the sale in that constituency in England? I doubt it. I know how badly you need this. Here it is, you can have it."

The diplomats stayed silent, this was not their territory. Jose listened as the power-words fell from these men's lips.

"So we owe you a debt: a moral obligation if you like?"

"You have a strange idea of morality, Mr. Fielding. No, you owe me weapons which Khafira will pay for but will not know about."

"This is a dangerous game, quite apart from overcharging your regime for the weapons we would face international opprobrium if it ever leaked out."

"You get a bigger and better deal in your precious west country constituency, Mr. Fielding; I believe that is very important to you right now." Fielding did not falter: "Very well, but I need to be reassured that the extra weapons do not find their way into the hands of anti-British interests."

You mean you need to be reassured that no one finds out if they do, Mr. Fielding. Let us be clear, I have dealt with many regimes, some democratic, most not, none were scrupulous, why should yours be any different?"

Scott Garrett was never in doubt about his duty: it was to British interests, moral if necessary, but he was quite happy to skip that part of the democratic contract, so he listened to the exchange with equanimity. He had one more input then he'd shut up, he lowered his voice, looked at Samir and prepared to beat him into a corner where he would behave himself. He quite enjoyed threatening people like Samir Latif, he had the force of Her Majesty's Government as his authority.

"Mr. Samir Latif, I think you can rely upon our absolute discretion in keeping this to ourselves. We are well aware of what it would mean to British interests, but we must protect our friends as well and in this case that is you. If this were leak out however unfortunately it would be very bad indeed for you, but I hardly need tell you that. So we will be prepared to defend you until the end."

Samir Latif's face darkened. "Who would make that known, Mr. Scott Garrett."

"Please don't misunderstand me, we would employ 100% discretion as you might expect of us. But you know how these things get out, an accidental word to a journalist..."

There was an uproarious laugh, loud, intrusive, violent laughter. "Your history of getting journalists to believe what you say is not very good is it. We had to expel one because he refused to swallow your nonsense about a speedboat and some Filipino boys." He marvelled at Samir Latif's intelligence network, despite his discomfort. "The fact is, Mr. Scott Garrett, I have done nothing out of the ordinary by the standards of the region. And neither have you but I understand that your association with one Michel Habibi does not bear close examination."

His heart nearly stopped. His face coloured, his heart restarted and started pumping furiously, his tongue filled his mouth, his saliva ran dry. "We know you were at the scene of the crime, Colonel Hassan's men were watching you. If you threaten me you may find yourself under investigation for the torture and death of Michel Habibi."

Jose stumbled away from the porthole and fell onto the bed, stifling a scream. Hassan must have killed Michel, not this idiot British diplomat.

But much much worse: Samir Latif knew all about it.

"Diana, you have to stop them," said Hartson, almost strangling the payphone in his balled hand.

"Who."

"Scott Garrett has handed over that same mad man from the Café De Bruxelles as you call him. He's been turned over to the hardest cop in Khafira. He's in the shit."

"A friend of yours, is he? You don't have friends, only interests."

"Don't be funny, Diana, now's not the time!"

"What can I do?" He heard no contrition.

"Call Sheikh Issa."

A short silence. "Come ON, Diana."

"I can't, he's out of the country."

"Then go to the Majlis and plead with Sheikh Khalifa."

"I can't go there, they won't let me in, not properly. Anyway what difference can I make, or should I make? I'll kill my career if I do that." Of course, first things first, Diana. She was right, though. "All right, I'll get on the road and call you again, at your apartment later."

"How long will it take you?"

The money ran out. "Got to go..." The tone replaced Diana Ffrench Parsons. Bastard, Scott Garrett, Bastard.

He wasted no more time thinking about it but made straight for the nearest motor rental outfit. He gingerly handed over his passport for inspection and proof, and his credit card. Neither caused the efficient Sikh behind the counter to pause. So, no Gulfwide notifications about him; that was a good start, at least. Fifteen minutes later he had the keys to a brand new Range Rover and was adjusting the driver's seat before starting up and heading for Khafira.

May
The Inlet
 The surprise at being given help from Hassan had worn off and Barracuda was twitching. Hassan wasn't part of his plan, the Shark had thrust that on him. All right, maybe he was useful to smooth things with the regime and keep people off but Barracuda had been careful enough and this cop was just a little too close for comfort. It would be nothing at all to him to simply waste the uniformed toad and all his henchmen there and then, why would he care? But he was smart enough to know that there'd be questions, he couldn't just get rid of a Khafira Police colonel without someone wanting to know why and he couldn't afford to let anyone get close to what they'd been doing. But the guy *knew*; what the fuck was The Shark playing at! The more people who knew, the more likely there's be a leak and then some dumbfuck journalist would hear – because they always did – and it would be in a paper somewhere, then it would flash up everywhere and be playing loud and clear through the cable services in the White House, Downing Street and The Kremlin. Hassan walked past him on deck, smiling; Barracuda tightened and then eased his grip on the pistol he had with him day and night. Not right now, but sometime, maybe, when no one needed to care about all this, he would have to find a way of losing this asshole – and just maybe the Shark with him.
 Now, though, he still had 19 makeshift and useless rockets to get rid of and ten highly desirable and launchable 122 mm missiles stolen from a now dead patrol. Barracuda was still thinking straight and knew that if he dumped them here and now they ran the risk of being discovered by a coalition minesweeper, they would have to go into deep water, truly deep water, way out of sonar range; more fucking time wasting.
 Shit! The rocket he'd thrown over the side at the inlet…
 He called to Hassan, "We have to go back, we have to pick something up!"
 "What is so important?" replied the colonel. Barracuda didn't like admitting to mistakes, especially one so stupid as this. What the hell, no minesweeper would ever go into that inlet – how could it – and even if it did they'd never find it jammed up against the jetty as it was. He calculated the risk and figured that the way things were going, if it ever was found, it wouldn't be for a long time and he would be long gone with the money safely locked into his Swiss

bank.

"Maybe it doesn't matter so much. Nothing to worry about. Just keep going!"

"Of course," said Hassan.

The dhow moved out to the open seas of the Gulf leaving the inlet behind and with it a dwindling trail of dead sea life. Barracuda was so pre-occupied with Hassan and his gang of thugs that he didn't notice it. They headed out to international waters where The Shark and his yacht were waiting.

The Shark stood motionless on is yacht, looking back towards Khafira where the dhow was making speedy progress towards him. He had always liked Barracuda – if a man like the Shark could be capable of such an emotion as liking. They were two damned souls heading for Perdition and rampaging together through the wreckage of other people's lives as they found common cause. It was an alliance which had served them both well and each had been satisfied by the rage and hate in the other. They knew that while the other existed they were not alone in their ferocious despisal of anything close to normal, to morality, to ethics even.

But now that alliance must end and it would not be easy - Barracuda was formidable, he had killed more men and women than the Shark could ever know. He had maimed and tortured possibly thousands and his men were loyal. He could not say the same for Hassan and the pirates but he paid them well enough so they would do what he said.

He had a curious sense of honour about it: he must kill Barracuda and his little army, but he felt there was some kind of code he should adhere to, so he would not do it behind his back, he would look him in the eye and apologise. He was going to lose a soulmate, he would probably never find another to match his inhumanity, who else would ever understand? Only Barracuda himself, because he and The Shark swam in the same bloody waters.

He had instructed Hassan to meet them at the inlet, help reload the rockets and to bring them back to the yacht. He had told Merlin to dig deeper into his Black magic box and find some kind of poison, if not that then tranquiliser. Merlin had asked how badly they should die – a man of no emotional structure whatever. The Shark sought only to remove these men, not to make them suffer beyond that, he saw no purpose in it, his normal contempt remained dormant.

"So don't put the remains of the Mustard agent into their food then?" said Merlin. Barracuda admired the ingenuity but suggested a less agonising end for them, out of professional courtesy. So Merlin turned up a supply of Rohypnol, which made The Shark laugh out loud, how else would the utterly charmless Merlin procure sexual congress? The Rohypnol would do very well for the barracudas final journey, but the man himself would have to be conscious so that his deformed code of honour could be satisfied. And neither Barracuda nor his men could even get a sniff of suspicion, their animal instincts would tell them if something was wrong, straight away, that's how they had stayed alive and flourishing.

So Merlin injected a syringe full of Rohypnol into each of an entire case of unopened plastic water bottles. He put it right under the plastic cap seal. Then he placed the case in an ice cold fridge and kept the solution just above freezing so that when it was offered to Barracuda's company the heavy condensation as it came into contact with the 100% humidity would disguise the minute leak from the piercing hole and the seal would be undisturbed.

Merlin and The Shark knew that they would not look for a broken seal but if they saw one they would suspect something was happening. Hassan took the water from the fridge on to his launch and transferred it to a cool box, then put it in the fridge on the dhow. Then he and his men had waited. They had their instructions.

Hassan made no attempt to force the water on the targets. He said to Barracuda and his chief Lieutenant, "There is water in the refrigerator," nothing more.

Barracuda said, "Fuck the water, what about a beer!"

"I am a Muslim, I did not think to put a store of beer on board. Perhaps you can wait until we get to the yacht, I believe that the Shark has a substantial supply of alcohol."

"Jesus, Fucking Christ..." he knew the expletive and the religious reference would be offensive but there was never a time in his life when that had mattered to him and he certainly didn't care about upsetting this small town pirate cop.

Hassan looked at him impassively and said, "Perhaps you can quench your thirst with water until then?" Yeah, he could. He went to the fridge, took out the carton of water and threw the dripping bottles to his men. He felt the satisfying multiple-click as he yanked the screwcap and it broke free of the sealing ring, he took a long draught, then wiped his mouth. The plastic bottle was cold and wet in his hand, drops fell on to his skin and he wiped it against his brow as a cooling action. Then the bottle fell from his hand as he slumped to the deck.

August
Diana's dilemma

Diana did not move for five minutes, not since she put the phone down. She'd bedded a journalist; all right she fancied him, but that was all. He was supposed to owe her now, not the other way around. But instead she was running around after him, risking her career, possibly even her neck, certainly the enviable list of contacts she'd quietly and discreetly built up since she'd been in Khafira. Why should she give him any more? She'd already told him two pieces of information which would see her career shunted into managing a small town Job Centre if it became known. What more could she do? It was his mess, not hers. So what if there was injustice. What kind of world didn't have that? What could she do about it anyway? It wasn't her fault, she was only a junior diplomat, she couldn't bleat on about the unfairness of the world to her superiors, they'd laugh at her. Worse, they'd put it on her personal record: a diplomat trying to right the wrongs of the regime in which she was staying. How could any diplomat live with themselves if they cared about the places where they worked? The Soviet Union, Guatemala, Iraq, China; it wasn't the diplomat's job to care, only to deal with them. Leave the heart searching to the politicians, they made those decisions. It had gone far enough.

She still hadn't moved, a silver Parker Rollerball reflected the morning sun from a rear window, she stared at it idly. What exactly was Tom Scott Garrett playing at over this Paul Winter character? Why would he want to hand him over to Colonel Hamid? It was too much to guess, she was too low down the pecking order to know enough. She was sure it was something dark, it had to be. She thought having Hartson thrown out was a clever wheeze by the higher-ups even though it had induced a pang of regret in her. But it was dirty play, very dirty.

Finally she moved. Her hand went to a small pocket diary in her handbag. It was a document she never left in her desk, nor even in her Khafira home. It contained too many sensitive telephone numbers. There was obviously some collusion between the embassy and Khafira. She dare not upset that, but she couldn't simply do nothing at all. Dangerous thing, a conscience, most diplomats substituted it for alcohol.

She leafed through it until she found what she needed. She reached for the telephone to dial the code to get into the international network, then 44 to target the UK, London. He ought to be there, he usually was.

Cargo

"I've got it", said Sam Jackson, as he connected with a light switch about half way up the partition dividing the hold. He snapped it on and the room filled with light, his eyes cleared. "It looks like some kind of cargo hold." There was no decor, the space was bounded on six sides by four walls, a floor and a ceiling, all covered from the same grey paint pot - out of keeping with the rest of the vessel. They looked more closely at the rows of wooden crates in front of them. Jackson tried to lift one. It was immovable. "What the hell has he got in here," he asked no one in particular, "Spare bed linen judging by the guests on board at the moment," he added without thinking, then quickly glanced at the banker. Was it a smile, he hoped so.

There was an almost imperceptible swaying of the yacht. Jackson looked away from the crates for the first time and saw what Winter had bumped into when he first entered, a black plastic bucket. He gave it a kick, then saw several more close by.

Nothing unusual on a boat, they have to keep it clean. He looked down into it as he passed by and saw a kind of grey-brown powder clinging to the sides.

"So not everything is spotless, then," he said.

"The others are like it as well," said the banker as he examined them.

"It looks like mud, sandy mud." Jackson felt around the edge of a bucket, some of the powder came off on his hand.

"It's cement," he said with surprise, "...and there's some shingle here."

"What does he need cement and shingle for on this floating palace?" No one was responding. He looked up, saw some bulging paper sacks behind the crates. He moved towards them, he couldn't quite make out the symbols. No wonder, they were in Arabic. There were only three. Then he was right up close to them.

Cement bags.

To the side of them was a large reinforced metal box but its lid looked easily shiftable. No one said anything as Sam moved towards the box. The top lifted up without effort.

"It's gravel, ballast, call it what you will," said Sam, as the reality began to seep into him. He looked at the commander, recognition was in his eyes. He looked at the banker: he didn't know what was happening.

"He's been making concrete," he said, finally.

"What for?" said the banker.

Jackson let the fury flow out of him as he turned on Paul Winter, "Well it hasn't been for repointing the bloody rivet work has it, Mr. Winter?" He felt a hand grabbing him firmly by the arm. He whirled round to see it was Commander Wilkinson. There was a silence lasting thirty seconds. The commander broke it.

"I suppose we all saw the kind of boys he's using as waiters?"

Both Naval officers looked at Winter.

"What are you getting at?"

"News blackout worked better here than in the rest of the world by the looks of it," said Wilkinson.

Jackson laid it in front of the banker. "Buckets of concrete, mixed with Filipino waiters, equals four drowned bodies heaved over the side for shark food."

The banker looked bemused, Jackson turned away.

Winter couldn't make sense of it. There was a dull knocking at the door of his memory. He knew his drinking session with Hartson was something to do with this, before his life was upended. The very night it was upended in fact, when he found Hannah's body. What happened before that?

It fell slowly, laboriously, into place. He was wearing a uniform now but his face was familiar even through the drink and drama of that night. "You found those bodies, didn't you!" he said, looking directly at Jackson.

"Yes, I'm afraid I did, Mr. Winter."

He gave a long sigh, let his banker's mind take over, add up the factors, divide them by the evidence, and finally reach the awful conclusion. "So we've stumbled across who did it!"

He could see his bid for freedom disappearing over the horizon again. Now he was beaten. He'd walked straight out of the frying pan into the fire. Someone was trying to get his attention. Bugger off! I'm finished, I don't want to hear, he thought.

The commander was talking.

"What exactly are you doing here, Mr. Winter? We understand you had to dodge police at the port, I heard your row with Tom Scott Garrett, now here you are taking refuge on board this scoundrel's yacht. Why should you be trusted?"

"Do you want it from the beginning?"

He told them everything, nearly. From the time he first saw Jose in the souk, through finding Hannah, to being handed Jose by the café waiter and trying to duck the police

"How was this woman, Hannah, tortured, Mr. Winter," asked Jackson, quietly.

He told him what he could remember and tried not to gag in front of them.

"Almost exactly the same as our four Filipino boys", said Jackson.

There was another silence. Then Winter let go of the last strands of his belief in local justice. As he did so, everything became so much clearer. Oh how easy it all was when you didn't apply a moral code. Now it was straight arithmetic. It was obvious why Colonel Ali Abdul Hamid had told him to keep quiet. Samir Latif was Khafira's biggest businessman, the most influential man in the region outside of the ruling families. Of course they'd try to protect him, to blame it on someone else if they could, even an innocent banker, let alone the whore who was living in the same apartment. Who was going to care? The police didn't answer to anyone except the people who mattered. And now he'd delivered them straight into the trap.

Everybody was in hock to someone here, he could trust no one, what made him think he could. His shoulders slumped, he was impotent. Finally he shouted, "The BASTARD. He's been stringing us along all the time."

"It looks as if you've played right into his hands, Mr. Winter and I don't see quite how we can get you out of it right now - short of causing a major international incident", said the commander with his chin cupped in his hands.

Jackson was listening but he no longer felt constrained by convention, he took out a penknife and tore into the plastic covering of whatever it was being sealed there. He looked in and pulled aside some large wads of packing straw. Then he gave a loud whistle. "They're bloody weapons." Wilkinson rushed over and looked in. He saw the giveaway outlines of fins and nose cone.

"Good God, how did he get these?" But he already knew. His eyes drifted up in the direction of the politician and the diplomats on the upper deck.

"And who are they for?" added Jackson.

"That's where the money goes," whispered Winter. "He's been buying arms and running them in this boat. And who's going to stop him. Not the coast guard, not the police, no one. He's fucking bulletproof. Everyone is sewn up."

"Not quite, Mr. Winter," said Jackson, "these are Iraqi 122 millimetre rockets, look at the markings! God knows how he got them but I'm damned sure they shouldn't be here."

There was a bump against the hull, the yacht rocked slightly.

May
Farewell

He must have fallen asleep, the exertions of the last few days had taken their toll even on a constitution like his. He opened his eyes and tried to focus but could not recognise his immediate surroundings. He had been on the deck of the dhow and now he was not. He started to raise himself up but his wrists met rough resistance from chafing rope bonds expertly knotted. His ankles were also strapped up. What the fuck! He summoned his phenomenal physical and mental strength and pulled at the ropes and binding, but nothing yielded. They had been tied by proper trained seamen and would never get out of them on his own.

"They are strong, are they not, my old friend?" said the Shark looming into his view.

"What are you playing at, Man, you can't tie me up, we're partners."

"No, not any more I am afraid, and I shall miss you old friend, we had an understanding of the world which few others have shared, but now I must go alone."

"You fucking traitor, what did I do?"

"I am sorry to say that the pace of this operation made you careless. You dropped a rocket into the inlet and it killed some fish. Who would have thought such an insignificant thing would matter, but it did. Everything else seems to have met with their pleasure, but that little incident has caused some doubt. No one can ever know what you did and there are too many of you for it to be a safe secret. I am afraid this is the end."

"You wouldn't dare, my men will hunt you down."

"No, they will not, I am sorry to tell you that your men are already scouting ahead for you in Hell, Barracuda! I shall no doubt join you there in time and perhaps we will be able to laugh at this sad episode at that moment."

Barracuda looked around and it became clear that he was still on the dhow as were his men all scattered around him, still, grey, lifeless, every one with a slit throat.

"It was Rohypnol, prepared by Merlin in the water bottles," said the Shark. Hassan's men dealt with you all once you had lost consciousness."

Barracuda had a rage pulsing through like none he had never known. It was a

blood vessel bursting, impotent fury which strained at his fibres, melting his synapses and firing his arteries into such a state of agitation that he went a red so deep that it almost burned the Shark. His neck bulged, his sinews stood out like mountain relief, but still the rope bonds held. Barracuda let out a roar that was so filled with hatred it might have been the volcanic breach of Hell itself.
"MERLIN! He's mine!"
"I am sorry my old friend, Merlin was never yours, always mine. But neither of us believes in trust, it is one of the factors which has brought us together over the years." The smile never left his face but perhaps there was a hint of regret in his voice, and his eyes might have fallen a tiny fraction at the edges. He continued: "I have my instructions, but I would never be so cowardly that I would not look you in the eye while I carried out the sentence, I think our association means more than that."

Barracuda looked at him and suddenly smiled as the purple blood drained from his face, the hate slipped from his voice and he said, weakly, "Too late. I am the only man in command of my own life."

Then the decades of hard debauchery and decadence, of adrenaline and injury, of drink, drugs and smoke and of controlled fury and hate were brought together in one final outraged cry. The intensity of it was enough to close his Right Coronary Artery completely and stop his heart from working any more. The cry fell away, the breath sighed out of him and was not replaced. Barracuda died at his own hand. The hate left his face and anyone not knowing him might have thought he was at peace, but Barracuda could never be at peace.

The Shark eased his grip on the commando knife he had brought for the killing. He would not need to use it and that pleased him; normally he enjoyed killing but this would have been different. That is good, he thought, I will not have it on my conscience. Then he laughed: what conscience? Hah! But he would miss this man.

He gave another order to Hassan to continue the dhow's course into the Gulf, through the Straits of Hormuz and then far out into the Indian Ocean where the depth would be beyond any searching sonar. There, the dhow would be scuttled with the remains of the barracudas, all of them! The Shark would return with Hassan's crew and their launch in tow. He already had the ten working missiles Barracuda had brought now safely in his hold, he would think of something to do with them later. They would never be found on his yacht because no one would think to look.

He gazed out to sea as the vessels ploughed on to Barracuda's eternal resting place.

August
Strategy

The cargo hold door was still open. The hot air left them dripping. There was no breeze down below to offer the slightest relief. There was no question in Jackson's mind what the proper course of action should be. "You'll have to come off when I leave for the minesweeper. I'll take you on board and keep you there until we can get you away for good," said Sam.

"We can't do that, they're wanted by the local police, we're their guests, it will create havoc," said Phil.

"Forgive me, Sir, but that sounds like a diplomat speaking, not a naval commander."

Jackson heard the clink of steel in the reply. "Nevertheless, Lieutenant, I am the senior officer and I can't allow it. Don't forget we have a member of her Majesty's Government on board as well. How will it look if we get involved in a stand-off while he's still on board a yacht owned by a gun-running murderer! We'll have to come up with something else."

Jackson grimaced. Navy discipline prevented him voicing more dissent.

"Very well, sir, what have you in mind?"

The banker broke in. "Are you going to just let him get away with it! Leave us to our fate!"

"Do you think I want to!" the commander fired back.

Winter reeled away in frustration.

Phil Wilkinson was racked between duty and conscience. His oath to Queen and country – slightly modified by his current posting - dictated he must do all he could to protect the minister from embarrassment. But he couldn't ignore the evidence of his eyes and ears on board the Al Khaleej. Shouldn't a naval officer have honour?

He reached a decision, and with it a plan. "Look, Sam, we cannot possibly do anything while the minister is on board. He has to get off. Do you understand?"

"Yes, sir."

"You go back to the minesweeper on an inflatable. Radio the crew to send one straight away. You can tell Latif that you can't afford the time to wait for the launch. As soon as you get back aboard, prepare a boarding party from what you have."

Jackson acknowledged every word: he planned to be at the head of that boarding party.

"Bring the ship as close as you can without arousing too much suspicion. We can't fire on her while the hostages are on board. And who knows what kind of ammunition store he has next to those missiles."

"Yes, sir."

"I'll see what I can get fixed up ashore while you're waiting."

"What happens to us?" shouted Winter.

"You have a bit more to face yet, Mr. Winter, I'm afraid. Try to be calm, I'm hoping we can pull something off."

"Can't we come back with you to Khafira?"

"That makes sense," said Jackson.

"No, it doesn't," said the commander, testily, "The minister will be with us and we can't have him implicated with you, whatever this might mean. The most important thing is to know where those missiles are heading for."

"What's that got to do with us?"

A new voice entered the muggy atmosphere. The English was perfect but with a pronounced accent rooted in the Arabian peninsula. "Nothing at all, Mr. Winter, you need not worry about them again."

"Gentlemen, I believe you have someone we would like to interview," said Colonel Hassan.

The cabin was comfortable by the standards of most prison cells, it had an en-suite bathroom, even a bowl of fruit. But when Winter was thrust rudely through the cabin door he was in no doubt about where he was. As he heard the key turn in the lock he looked at Jose lying on the bed, defeat all over her face.

"It looks like I played straight into their hands. It didn't matter what I did really, we were always going to end up like this." He had done his best, risked his life, he might even be about to lose it. "You stupid bastard Englishman. You could have got me out of it back in Maraka. If you hadn't been so honorable; I would have gone with that sailor and I would be in Mumbai now, free!"

"What's done is done, Jose, don't be angry with me."

"Fuck off you silly little man. A fuck in a hotel and you think you own me...!"

What blood he had left there drained from his face. Tears formed in the sides of his eyes, he tried to hold them back. What was HAPPENING here! She couldn't talk to him like this.

"...If only I'd had the strength to take the car from you in Maraka. I had it planned, I could have left you standing by the side of the road while I drove away. I could have had a new life by now. "

He was hit by a tidal wave of fury. He raised his hand and purposefully walked the few steps to the bed. She was hysterical but he knew she meant it, every word. He'd been taken for a sucker by everyone, probably even Will Hartson. He felt like he was at school on the first day and already up for a caning for something he hadn't done. No one cared.

"Hit me if you like, it wouldn't be the first time I had taken a beating from a man. What is it about men that they like to do that? You're all cowards, everyone of you."

He stayed his hand. He wouldn't be called a coward by this whore. He was better than that. He slumped on to the bed, half a metre from her. She kicked out a shoeless leg, "Fuck off, get out of my way." He didn't fight her, what was the point. He thought he'd won her, all he'd got was the splinters from a wooden spoon. He moved away from the bed, leaned against the cabin wall, hung his head and felt worse than at any time in his life.

Tom Scott Garrett stopped speaking. He no longer felt confident to contribute to the discussions. He'd been tailed, watched and known about by Khafira's security service and that scared him; he was the one who did that sort of thing, or arranged for it to be done. He had no idea they'd been on his case. He didn't kill poor Michel, he knew that if no one else did; but Samir Latif knew who did, that was certain, so did the police otherwise how would they have known he went to the souk!

Hamid? Damn him!

At least Winter and his whore were out of the way now. They could do little to embarrass her Majesty's Government while in custody aboard the Al Khaleej. And now there was little risk of his role in their betrayal being uncovered. Something had turned out for the best then. Maybe enough to call off Hamid over this Michel business. He hoped so, he liked this posting, didn't really want to go back to Europe; or worse, somewhere like Nicaragua.

The business was over, the hospitality completed, Samir Latif stood at the rail

with the diplomatic party ready to wave them off. "Please forgive me for this embarrassment gentlemen, but you see it was necessary to lure them aboard my yacht in order for them to be arrested. They are wanted for a most appalling murder and I had to do my duty."
"Of course, Samir Latif, I can only apologise on behalf of my countrymen that a British citizen is involved," said Fielding, "I hope you won't allow it to get in the way of our future association."
"Certainly not, Mr. Fielding, you and I have become friends. I am an Arab and I never forget my friends."
"Absolutely," said Scott Garrett, glad to be getting off the boat, and none too certain about his own future.
Wilkinson said nothing.
They descended the steps into the launch. The commander looked at the police vessel tied alongside with its bow and stern bristling with machine guns. The party looked up again at Samir Latif and waved as the launch moved off and back towards Khafira.

Jackson stood uneasily on the foredeck of the Al Khaleej. It was ten minutes since he'd radioed for the inflatable, he could just make it out now, pushing off from the minesweeper. It would be another ten minutes before it arrived, and another twenty to get back. Latif approached him. "Lieutenant Jackson, Can I offer you another drink while you wait."
Jackson steeled himself and put is officer's training into effect, "Very kind, I'll have a lime juice and soda again."
"Please take a seat, enjoy the atmosphere here. I am sure it will be much hotter when you return to your minesweeper."
Hotter than you realise, he thought as he sat down and tried to relax.

The cabin had been silent for an hour. Jose heard the launch leave for Khafira. The conversational babble had reduced to almost nothing outside the porthole. She must speak to Latif, make him understand, it was all a big mistake. How could she kill Hannah, the only woman in the world she ever thought of as a friend? She lay on the bed with her back to the Englishman. She could at least be rid of him soon. She would explain to Samir that he had abducted her after she found him in the apartment. She had tried to tell the police but it was too late, no one would have believed her. Good story. She had almost trusted him, and he had not deserved it. He had let her down.

She started as the cabin door burst open. Samir Latif stood silhouetted against the glare. "Now then, Jose, you must tell me what you have been doing."

"You said you would help, Samir Latif. You said you would be a friend."

"I might still be, Jose. Tell me what has happened, what have you done. They want you for the killing of Hannah, what do you know about it?"

"I know that Colonel Hassan was the last to see her. You should not trust that man, Samir, he is evil."

"I have known him for a long time, Jose, I cannot dismiss a friendship on the word of a Lebanese whore." He turned his head slightly in the doorway. "Can I Hassan."

"No," came a harsh reply.

Latif stepped through the cabin door and up to the bed, Hassan followed him in. Jose looked at the two of them. "Why do you defend him, Samir?"

Latif smiled. "Because he is valuable. We have had many adventures together, my dear Jose. I am afraid he is much more valuable than you. Whores are easy to find, friends like Hassan are not."

"Whores are easily lost as well," added Colonel Hassan.

She sank back on the bed as the full realisation took hold. It was the end. Her benefactor, her "friend", had betrayed her. She turned towards the Englishman half expecting him to do something, he just looked back without expression. She had heard the English saying "burning your boats", now it was coming cruelly true. She was about to be roasted on this one, the Al Khaleej.

"So what now, Samir Latif. What will you do with us?" The protest had gone from her voice, only tiredness remained. Hassan and Latif smiled, laughed even, but there was no humour. Hassan detached himself and moved towards the bed.

"Perhaps you would like to watch, Mr. Winter," he growled.

"Watch what?"

"Watch what happened to poor dear Hannah, to the boys, to Michel Habibi, to I don't care how many." He laughed mirthlessly with narrowed eyes. Winter went cold. Hassan turned his gaze to Jose, then without warning raised his hand and hit her across the face.

"Whore!" he shouted, then laughed.

Winter shivered and tried to move to help her, but his legs had seized. Didn't she say she'd been beaten before? Hassan repeated the manouvre. Winter raised his eyes to Latif. "Stop him," he said weakly.

"Whatever for, Mr. Winter?"

Hassan paced slowly around the cabin, then stopped in front of Jose and snarled into her face. No words came out, only malice. Hassan's hand flicked out again, to her waist, grabbing the band of her loose thin cotton skirt. He yanked it with the strength of rage It came away with some resistance. Jose grimaced, she lay on the bed her lower half exposed. She started to shake.

"You're not human," muttered Winter.

"We are all too human, Mr. Winter", said Latif.

He said some words in Arabic to Hassan who moved away deferentially. Latif moved close behind Jose. "I would be sorry to see you go without a final reminder of our happy times together."

"No," she breathed, with almost no sound.

Latif started to remove some clothing. He was close. She could feel his hardness against her. She prepared for what she had known so well many times before, but this time with hate in her heart. She screwed up her face and clenched every part of her body to resist him.

The Majlis

Hartson took 45 minutes to get to Khafira in the hired Range Rover – a much smoother ride than the last time he'd been in that model. He drove around slowly, searching for a coin phone, they were harder to find but there were still some in the poor areas where mobiles were a rarity. It took ten minutes. He found one able to take the last few coins he'd left Khafira with the previous day.

Diana wasn't at the embassy. He called her home but got an answering machine. He saw a police car go by and turned his face away. It carried on without slowing. He walked back to the Range Rover and thought. What choice did he have? If he went straight to Sheikh Khalifa at the Majlis he might stand a chance. He was still the sheikh in residence this week, he could at least order something to happen. The trouble was getting through to him the importance of what was happening. And how did he sidestep the police to get to him? He had to risk it, there was nothing else to do. But the very word, risk, worried him. He was out of his comfort zone even contemplating it. He didn't do risk unless he absolutely had to and if anyone from Randalls was looking in his direction. Let someone else get off on the danger stuff, he preferred his slyness.

He drove to the Majlis. The day was getting longer, shadows formed. It was a gamble that anyone would be there in the late afternoon on an August day.

There were few cars when he drew up outside, but he recognised a black Mercedes from the ruling family's fleet. Khalifa was there at least. He parked, cut the engine and took the key from the ignition. He kept moving to get out but something held him back. What he was about to do weighed heavily upon him, he was effectively giving himself up after having smuggled his way back in again. He had to hope Sheikh Khalifa would see what he was driving at and apply his special dispensation. It was asking a great deal of a man who knew so little of anything.

He took a deep breath and got out of the car. He walked slowly to the entrance, nodded to the policeman on the door who didn't move. He had only left Khafira yesterday, it was quite likely news of his expulsion hadn't spread through the force. Perhaps it was never intended for them to know. He marched through the great marble archways which had been constructed to lend grandeur to the Majlis. In the end it was still just a talking shop from which decisions evolved rather than emanated. But they emerged from it nonetheless, at Gulf speed, not American or European. Urgency was a condition you left behind at the airport.

But Hartson hadn't left his urgency, that was the trouble. He needed action right now, not tomorrow or next week. He sidled up to join a small collection of people surrounding the sheikh. He tried to catch his eye. One or two turned round to see who it was, slowly the babble died down, all of them looked at him, including Sheikh Khalifa.

"Mr. Will Hartson, I am very surprised to see you here. I was led to believe you had left Khafira."

Shit, he knew! "That is correct, Your Highness, please forgive me for trespassing on your hospitality so soon after going but I have a matter of great urgency to put before you."

"What can be urgent at this time of day, Mr. Will, I have a tennis game in one hour's time. Nothing has ever been urgent enough to stop me from playing tennis."

Almost certainly true, he thought, a nuclear bomb wouldn't be urgent unless it smeared the tennis court markings.

"It concerns an Englishman and a woman with him. I believe they are in great danger." Khalifa didn't look at all interested. "Why is that, Mr. Will?" he said examining a fingernail. He opened his mouth to speak but stopped before a syllable could come out. A strong hand gripped his right arm, a harsh voice spoke in his ear. "Let us not bother his Highness Sheikh Khalifa with any more of this nonsense, Mr. Will Hartson." He knew the voice. It was over, so was he. He turned his face to see Hamid's fierce features glaring at him. Khalifa had returned all his attention to his fingernail. "Come with me!" No argument, he was pulled along roughly in much the same manner as he had been before, only this time much worse than being deported awaited him.

Outside Hamid released the grip slightly. "Why did you not listen you stupid man?" He didn't reply, he was too weary. He allowed himself to be led to Hamid's dark Mercedes. Two policemen followed close behind. All four got into the car, the two uniformed policemen in front, Hartson and Hamid in the rear.

"How did you know I would go to the Majlis, Hamid? I didn't know myself until twenty minutes ago."

"I have known exactly where you were since you arrived at Heathrow. What sort of amateur do you think I am?"

Out of the frying pan...

She couldn't hold them off. Hassan held down her arms, Latif was on her. If she resisted any more she'd be hurt. There were other ways of rejecting him. She relaxed, went limp. She would go to the very opposite extreme. Just let them do it, not respond in any way, not even move her legs apart for them.

"That is sensible Jose," said Latif. She knew he hated it, he wanted to fight her, struggle to dominate her. Just fucking her was no good. Latif always liked his power games. She stayed expressionless, unmoving, as she felt Latif forcing himself into her. It hurt anyway. Still she would not respond, no cry, no twitch of her facial muscles. She could take it. How different was it to the hundreds of other times she had done it. Only this time she was not pretending to be involved. It would infuriate him. He was pounding into her, trying to come. She stared at the cabin ceiling, Hassan's grip had eased to nothing. Latif's breath was hot on her face and surprisingly sweet.

Then he came. It wasn't the full flow she had come to know from Latif, more a weak dribble. She still did nothing. He pulled off her. Now he was silent. He stared straight at her, she continued to do nothing. He had taken her but she was not his. That was one victory for her at least.

He spoke. "You see, Mr. Winter, how easy it is."

She moved her head a little to one side to see how the banker would take it. The banker looked up with tired eyes, his voice was thin, "You have no connection with the rest of humanity, Latif. You are an outsider. You have no feelings." Jose listened to him lecturing, slowly turning her victory into defeat with every pious word.

"Do you think so, Mr. Winter. You are a supreme moralist of course, working for a bank which has been financing my exploits for decades now."

"I mean you have power and you abuse it. You take no responsibility for what you do."

"Isn't that what having power is for? Otherwise why would anyone bother?"

The banker's head dropped. Latif got his victory. Jose tilted her head back again but betrayed nothing. She didn't want to see the final humiliation on the banker's face because it was hers as well. He spoke again: "You've given us your show of strength. What now Latif?" There was something in the thin whispered voice which made Jose listen despite herself. Defiance probably, although it was no use now. The banker had courage if nothing else.

"Clearly it will be very embarrassing taking you back to Khafira, your story could easily be believed, Mr. Winter." Samir Latif developed a look of regret on his face. "I am sorry to tell you we shall be disposing of you further out in the Gulf. It will take about two hours to get there, long enough for concrete to set."

Latif laughed, Hassan echoed him. That was the only sound in the cabin for over a minute. Jose raised herself on one elbow. "Why did Michel die?"

"My colleague here was too zealous in his interrogation I'm afraid," said Latif. "When Colonel Hamid lost you in the souk Colonel Hassan here used his own initiative and went to your dear Michel's apartment. He was hoping he would tell where you were. We could not get him to speak."

Michel had only panicked, he had never betrayed her. Now, she learned, he had died for her.

"So, Colonel Hamid is in your pocket as well," said Winter.

"Not at all, Mr. Winter, I have never quite been able to work out the mind of Colonel Ali Abdul Hamid. The dispute between Michel and his friend Anwar was very loud at the Cafe De Bruxelles. I was able to deduce quite quickly what had happened. I put a call through to the police straight away." He tapped the mobile phone in his shirt pocket.

"I knew Hamid was investigating, it did not need the intervention of Hassan at that point."

"Why did Hassan kill Hannah?" said Jose mechanically.

"No my dear, he did not do it alone. I helped him, I'm afraid."

She slumped back on the bed and made no attempt to cover her nakedness, was vaguely aware of the seepage between her legs. His seed, the murderer's foul solution planted inside her. She felt nauseous, looked to Paul Winter for help. He stared straight through her. He refused to connect, what did she expect. She was completely alone, just as she had always wished. "Why?" she said, finally, weakly.

"She had been asking me a lot of irritating questions that day. You were not there at the time, I joined Hassan after you had gone. We had planned a party and had hoped you would return later.

"While we waited Hannah insisted on asking me about some Filipino boys who had gone missing. Could I help find them. Your cleaner's boys I think. Hannah knew what sometimes happens on board this yacht, just like you do. She was pushing me too hard. I lost my temper. Who cares about some Filipino boys, they are nothing. I hit her several times, then Hassan finished off what I had started. Like he probably will here." He looked up at the policeman and smiled. Jose gave in and curled herself into a tight foetal ball on the bed.

"And now I can tell you, because you can never tell anyone else, that we were not the only ones there that day. We had a special guest because you and Hannah were very special in Khafira, we thought he should be able to enjoy you. What a shame that can not happen again!"

...Into the fire

Hamid's car sped along the city roads, but Hartson couldn't see that it was going anywhere in particular. "Am I going to the airport again, Hamid, or out into the desert?" he asked, fearing a slow burning death in the sand.

"Be quiet please, I am thinking."

"What? Of how to get rid of me?" He forced the words out on a surge of adrenaline. They fell into the silence of the car. This was his last ride. The journey continued in silence. They passed a sign for the airport but didn't turn off. His heart beat faster. They weren't sending him home, then. That meant the desert again. Please! No!

Finally Hamid spoke: "You have managed to upset a great many people in a short space of time, Mr. Hartson." Not even Mr. Will now. At least Frank Wilson had stayed on first name terms when he said the same thing the day before in London. "You have exposed Khafira and Sheikh Mahmood to ridicule in the region."

"We all know Mahmood isn't in any position to care."

"But the rest of his family is. Believe me they care very much, and your role has been carefully noted by all of them."

He felt as if he'd been singled out for a special investigation by God. He was exposed. Not that it mattered now, his judgement day was about to come anyway. "Will I be tortured the same way as all the others, Hamid?" A gap of fifteen seconds elapsed before the colonel replied.

"You have a poor opinion of us in Khafira, do you not?"

"Hardly surprising is it! You cover up murders, you have people expelled. Tell me something good about you."

"I ought to have one of my men give you a hard beating."

"They've already done that."

"And still you did not listen!"

"Of course I listened. But I have a job to do."

"Honour is a fine virtue, Mr. Will, but useless if no one cares."

"So I will be tortured?" Another pause, shorter this time.

"No, you will not. If I wanted to dispose of you, Mr. Hartson, I would use some finesse." He turned his fierce gaze straight into his face, "I would take you out to the desert with your hired car. We would go deep into the dunes of the Empty Quarter, fifty kilometres from any road. Then I would leave you with no fuel and punctured tyres."

"You do like to repeat yourself, don't you!"

Hamid turned away again. "I always knew where you were when you were left in the desert. That was a lesson, that was all. You were close to a road, you were left in darkness not daylight."

He couldn't fight down the bitter irony in his voice, "Thank you very much, Hamid. Now you're going to do it properly." Hamid turned away, his face narrowing at the same time. He said nothing as the car continued to make its uncertain journey through the city. "For God's sake you owe me at least an explanation, Hamid."

Hamid turned back. "Do not blaspheme in front of my men. I have no religious convictions but they usually do." Was that a smile on his face, heartless bastard! "We live in a harsh world, Mr. Will. You probably don't realise that coming from your comfortable home in England."

"I've seen enough of it to know how nasty a place it is, Hamid."

"Not really! You have only seen it, you have never lived it, I suspect...until now." He fell silent. Why pick this moment to give him a sermon on the harshness of life? "My home was a refugee camp in Jordan. I have no roots. I have no certainty of living tomorrow. I have never had those luxuries. Nor do most people in the middle east. We have friends who become enemies, and enemies who become friends. Sometimes they are both at the same time. We live as best we can in this turmoil and try to make sense of it all."

He listened; surely the hardest cop in the Khafira wasn't looking for sympathy. "What's your point, Hamid?"

"Your interference has greatly upset what little order there is here. It is not much but there is nothing else. When you dare to impose your standards of justice and fairness you do so from ignorance. They mean nothing."

"But if they mean nothing what is there left?"

"Survival, nothing more. Every day is a test of strength against something or someone."

"And I am about to be sacrificed to that expediency, am I!" More silence. He was fighting hard not to foul his clothes. All his intellect had been boiled away, only naked fear remained. Survival: he was beginning to understand.

Hamid spoke slowly, deliberately, "No, you are not. To be frank I do not know what I shall do with you." He was joking, playing with him. "That's not funny, Hamid."

"Nothing in this sorry business has been funny, Mr. Will." He sighed, a tired sound, "I am going to explain why." The ferocity was still in his eyes, Hamid always looked menacing.

"First you believe I have taken your friend Paul Winter into custody. I have not, nor his rather unsuitable travelling companion." How did he know that?
"If Mr. Winter had just done as I told him a great deal of this would not have happened."

"But you threatened him. I saw you. I was there for..." Hamid's hard eyes looked at him reproachfully. Hartson choked back the "God's sake."

"I did threaten him. He had to be kept quiet, so did the other whore."

"For survival?" Hartson responded, surprised to find he could still be disgusted while being so scared.

"Certainly for survival, but a far greater survival than you could have known about."

Hartson looked at him doubtfully. "Surely there wasn't some sort of honour involved, Hamid."

"To a certain extent. But more to the point there was treachery, double dealing...," Hamid looked straight at him now, "...and betrayal."

"Didn't you say that was part of everyday life."

"So it is, but if you don't fight it you lose. To put it simply, Mr. Will, I needed to keep the murder quiet. It was part of a much wider investigation to prevent a coup d'état in Khafira." He was lost for a reply. A coup! Here! Not in the north? "You thought I was covering up for the police and Colonel Hassan. No, I was not. Colonel Hassan is in league with Samir Latif in a weapons dealing business. They had cloaked it in deals with Khafira but really Samir sells to anyone and has enjoyed protection from one particular member of the ruling family."

"Not Sheikh Issa, surely?"

"Most surely not." Hamid looked to the front of the car where his two uniformed police officers were sitting, then lowered his voice. "It is of course Sheikh Khalifa, the most vain, most shallow member of the family. The man most easily flattered. I cannot touch him, that can only come from his family, but they know. Samir Latif has convinced him that dealing arms to the Northern Gulf will win him influence with their president. Khalifa has been led to believe he will be installed as the ruler of Khafira if the Northern Gulf were to go to war again."

"Why didn't you pick up Latif and Hassan a lot earlier?"

"Face saving, Mr. Will. He is an old friend of the ruling family. We could not arrest him. We must wait for evidence."

"You could have arrested him for murder."

"No, I could NOT. Sheikh Khalifa was in the apartment at the same time. He is untouchable, he is a member of the ruling family."

Hartson leaned back. What a hell of a story. Would he ever get to tell it? "Why tell me all this? You know it's dynamite."

A long pause. Then: "Honour I suppose." He knew better than to smirk. Saving face was more important than ever right now.

"So how do you know so much about where I was and where Winter and the woman were?"

"Your favourite diplomat Mr. Scott Garrett told me of the latter. He was trying to garner influence, I have information which could be turned against him. I knew where you were because Sheikh Issa told me."

"But he's in England."

"They are on the telephone even there I understand."

"How did he know?"

"Your embassy here is a very leaky building, Mr. Will. A good friend of Sheikh Issa called him to let him know there was a problem."

Diana! She actually did it, she called Sheikh Issa! Maybe not everything was bad … but it certainly wasn't all good, either... although he was beginning to realise that Hamid was not going to eliminate him. He started to breathe more deeply, the fear subsided, his thoughts became clearer and moved beyond the urgent concern of survival and death. So what about Winter...and the whore, of course? Two insignificant players in this deadly desert chess.

"Where are Paul Winter and the woman if they're not with you?"

"As I understand it they have been taken to Samir Latif's yacht, the Al Khaleej, in search of sanctuary."

"What! How did that happen? From what you've just said that's the last place they should be. We must get them off."

"True, but impossible."

Hartson's eyes widened.

"I can do nothing," said the colonel. "I know where everyone is, I have spies in every corner of the Gulf, in Latif's offices, in Hassan's offices, in every emirate palace in the region. I have every piece of the puzzle, but I am powerless."

Now that simply did not make any sense at all to Hartson. "Just take a police boat and some men for ...."

"The boats are under the authority of Colonel Hassan, so are his men. They won't obey me, far from it. They are no more than well-trained pirates."

"What about your navy?"

Hamid laughed bitterly. "You know as well as me: we belong to a loose confederation of states, that is our defence pact."

"So?"

"Our vessels are in the north – helping to police the seas there – if you understand my meaning. The nearest vessel of any use is in Maraka under their command."

"Then call it up."

"Have you learned nothing in your time here? To do that would be to let Maraka know of our predicament. They would have to confront a vessel owned by a friend of the ruling family. The whole mess will emerge. Khafira will look very bad, and Maraka will crow like a shedful of cocks."

Hartson took a professional interest in the use of metaphor, a shedful of cocks; here was a man who could combine poetry and brutality.

"Saving face again?"

"Exactly."

"It seems you can lose an awful lot just to save face."

"That is easy to say coming from a Western European background. Here, saving face is more important than anything, nothing is lost in comparison."

"All right, what can happen to them aboard the Al Khaleej?"

"A great deal. Hassan has already killed another of the woman's friends at an apartment in the souk."

"Who?"

"A waiter called Michel Habibi." The waiter from the Cafe De Bruxelles, the man who had drawn him into the mess in the first place. And they'd killed him. They weren't playing with chocolate soldiers here.

"So they're likely to kill Winter and the woman as well?"

"Yes."

He had expected some qualification to soften the blow. But this was the Gulf. And there was nothing either of them could do.

"Do you care what happens to them, Hamid?"

"I cannot answer that. Their fates are not directly important to the future of Khafira. I do know I have a mounting pile of dead bodies and it must stop. I

suppose, now that I have started telling you the truth, I must continue..."
What else could add to this desperate mess?

"...your four Filipino boys were also Latif's victims."

Hartson was silenced. How could this monster be allowed to roam free and get away with these appalling acts?

"They were taken there from Maraka where they had been working at the airport. Normally Samir Latif is more careful about where he dumps his detritus, but he has been giving the impression that he is bulletproof in recent months. These were left in shallow waters – of course they would never have been found at all if not for your Royal Navy. Perhaps Latif thought that your minesweeper would dismiss them as easily as he did."

"What the..." but Hartson choked back the expletive; these people could unquestioningly stomach the murder and mutilation of the four boys and their casual disposal, but not a swearword like Fuck, that would be deeply and probably irreparably insulting. What a mad world!

Hamid broke into his thoughts: "We will add that to his list of crimes, although I believe a coup d'état outranks the disappearance of a few imported workers."

Hartson let it pass, nothing he said would make a difference, he and Hamid occupied different worlds and the only place that they appeared to meet was in the back of his Mercedes.

Hamid spoke again: "If it is of any help there is a British party of diplomats and a politician aboard at this moment. I believe they are trying to broker a deal to sell arms to Khafira."

Fielding and Scott-Garrett, so little would happen while they were on board – but what did he know.

"What's he doing talking to a man like this, why do you and Issa let him?"

"Sheikh Issa thinks a long way ahead of most others. He could easily have spoken to Fielding in England but chose to use your minister as a tool to flush out Samir Latif."

Serves the bastard right, thought Hartson. If he ever got to tell this story Fielding would be in the first par. Then he flashed back a few short days to his meeting at the Majlis with Sheikh Issa; a few little hooked worms had dangled before him by the sheikh. It became clear, he fitted each part of the jigsaw together: yes, there were arms being dealt but he would not elaborate much further. Hartson had been used as part of the flushing out process – and he might even have done it if Winter hadn't found that woman...and the Navy hadn't turned up those bodies. So he, Hartson, had become surplus while Fielding took on the unwitting role. Well played Issa, bloody well played!

The Mercedes had passed the port twice already, they were approaching for a third time. Hartson looked out of the window, he could make out the frigate at her moorings. Now that he felt less threatened he was able to muse about it being there...and who was on board. Then the germ of an idea sprouted. He let it grow for a few seconds. It wasn't impossible, they could only try, although his dealings with the Navy so far had led him to believe Britannia doesn't rule the waves any more, still less does she care about slaves, especially Filipinos.

"Hamid, it's a gamble but please try it. Drive back into the port. Go straight to the Royal Navy frigate. I'll explain on the way."

Jackson climbed on board the minesweeper and made straight for the bridge. Ever since he'd got into the inflatable to get back he'd watched the Al Khaleej weigh anchor and leave her stationary position to move deeper into The Gulf. They were moving away and he needed to keep up with them.

"Track the yacht!" he said to the helmsman, keeping his voice as calm as he could.

"She's moving off, sir."

"Stick with her, we must not lose her."

He turned to his chief petty officer, "Find every commando-trained person on the ship, round up the marines and form a boarding party of twenty, all armed."

"Sir?"

"You heard me, we've got the bastards who put those bodies in the water. Now do what I say and stand by to go on my command." He kept the discovery of the missiles to himself, that would be their justification under international law, the bodies their moral imperative.

"Yes, sir."

"Are you sure we should be doing this?" asked the sub lieutenant who had just handed back command.

"No doubt in my mind whatsoever. Keep her in sight!"

"Right!"

Commodore David Jenkins looked at the two before him with distaste. He knew of them both but had met neither. One was the journalist who had tricked Sam Jackson, the other was an unsavoury security policeman.

"So, you want me to send out a tender with some of your men to rescue two people aboard this yacht. I am a naval man gentlemen but I know something of diplomacy. I can't think of anything which would cause more harm than the active participation in an international incident."

The policeman became animated. "I fear a lot of harm is going to occur anyway, Commodore."

"I'm sorry, gentlemen, I can't allow naval resources to be used like this. We are here enjoying the hospitality of Khafira but only under sufferance, I need hardly tell either of you that. I can do nothing to afford the least offence to Sheikh Mahmood."

"I believe Sheikh Mahmood will not be at all offended, Commodore," said the policeman, "nor, perhaps as importantly, will Sheikh Issa."

"Thank you, Colonel, I am aware of the practicalities of the situation. But we are not a police force, that is your job."

The local policeman began to get angry. "I cannot do it, isn't it obvious! If I could I would not be here."

Jenkins fought back his irritation. He remembered well enough his last meeting with the Khafira police in the form of Colonel Hassan. "I remain to be convinced that you are honourable, Colonel."

Winter felt the Al Khaleej move off, he couldn't tell but he guessed they were heading away from Khafira. They were alone again in the cabin. Jose hadn't moved from the position in which she'd been left. He made no effort to cover her, why should he. He'd risked everything for her and lost. So, now she'd passed him up.

Sod her, she could die now, he didn't care. She shifted position very slightly, leaned her head in his direction, opened her mouth. She was saying something, he couldn't hear it. He turned his head away. The sight of her body, so enticing before, now left him cold.

"Please." It was just audible.

He whirled around and spat back: "Please what!"

"Please be kind to me! I am sorry."

"It's much too late to be sorry, Jose. Just shut up!" He folded his arms and turned his face away. He stared out at the sea moving past the porthole. The door opened again, Hassan stood before them. "You must be prepared, Mr. Winter. Come with us now."

Prepared for what? "Where am I going?" A sharp slap across his face forced any further inquiry back. He was led to a port side deck. "Step in here," said Hassan, pointing to a black bucket of grey brown sludge. He looked into the mess and saw in horrific reality how the boys had met their deaths. His step faltered, he resisted, refused. Two rough hands grabbed his legs and forced him into the grotesque mud. The wet concrete had only just been mixed. The roughness scoured his feet and legs as they plunged into the bucket. He fought to prevent them going in but the hands held them steady and another fist slammed against his jaw knocking the resistance right out of him.

Phil Wilkinson almost leaped from the tender to the dock and ran off to the frigate. The sweat poured from him in wide streams, soaking his uniform, attracting attention from the ratings and petty officers standing idly by the capstans. He had avoided using radio contact for fear of compromising his diplomatic role.

But now he was ashore and in a hurry. He couldn't be bothered with dignity, he had to see the Commodore. He sprang up the gangplank, gave a messy salute on the run to the petty officer at the railing, asking at the same time: "Is the Commodore aboard?"

"In his cabin, sir."

He didn't bother with a thank you as he raced along the deck to where he would find David Jenkins. He knocked on the door breathing hard, dripping with sweat, and pushed his way in. There was no time for the niceties of rank. As he entered the small cabin he saw his superior officer sitting at his table with two other men. As his eyes adjusted to the light he recognised one of them, it was the Randalls reporter – hadn't he been expelled? How had he got in on the act again so quickly? Sitting next to him was an Arab he had never met before.

"Welcome aboard, Phil. You probably know Will Hartson here from Randalls, let me also introduce Colonel Ali Abdul Hamid from the Khafira Security Police." Wilkinson took it all in and put on a none too certain diplomatic face.

He saluted the commodore and nodded at the other two.

"I've just been aboard the Al Khaleej, sir," he said directly to Jenkins. "We must intervene at once. There are two people being held prisoner..."

"Yes I've heard all this already, Commander."

The commander looked at the journalist and the policeman. They already knew, but the tender had arrived only five minutes before. Never mind, work it out later.

"...Do you also know that he has several Iraqi missiles aboard..?" Jenkins stared at the commander.

"To deal to whoever he chooses, including the President of the Northern Gulf." The Khafira policeman finished the sentence and looked directly at the Commodore. Hartson was taken aback, he'd heard nothing about the missiles, someone had forgotten to tell him – and wasn't that the point of him being used to slush out Latif?

Hamid continued: "Those could be used against your own forces at any time in the next few months, Commodore. We all know how volatile the situation is."

Jenkins leaned back in his chair and looked at all three of the guests in the room, finishing with Wilkinson. The commander didn't have time for this. He broke in: "Sam Jackson has prepared a boarding party, sir. They're only a few minutes from the yacht."

"But she's still in territorial waters. I can't possibly authorise it," said Jenkins.

"Can you check with the minesweeper where they are, sir?"

"Very well." He barked an order into his intercom and waited for the reply. Wilkinson looked at his watch. Why couldn't they hurry up!

Finally, a tinny voice scratched through the speaker on the commodore's desk. "She's three kilometres beyond the line and heading into the Gulf."

Jenkins remained silent. His eyes gave away nothing. Wilkinson nudged some more. "It may help to know it was Latif who tipped those four Filipino boys into the sea." He was so impatient he forgot the "sir".

Jenkins looked up. "How can you know that?" He explained the concrete ingredients and the buckets.

Hamid broke in: "If you are concerned about upsetting Sheikh Mahmood by embarrassing one of his friends, I think I can reassure you that your actions will not be protested!"

"He's right, Commodore," said Hartson, "If I've got this correctly you'll be doing everyone a favour – you're more likely to get a Gold Rolex on your wrist, not a slap."

"That does it," shouted Jenkins. "Let's get him. Tell Sam to go ahead, we'll follow with a party of marines." He leaped from his chair. The reporter looked surprised. "I think the stakes are a little too high to worry about a few bye-election votes. Would you like to join us gentlemen?"

The reporter was slow in getting to his feet; Hamid extended a hand to pull him up, it was taken reluctantly.

Samir Latif stood next to Paul Winter. "Do you not dislike waiting for concrete to set in your British climate, Mr. Winter. It can take such a very long time. Immensely frustrating for everyone." Winter shivered in the heat, his eyes closed. It was hot; it was always so bloody hot! "But it is very different out here in the Gulf, especially at this time of year. The heat helps it set within a very short time. So you will not have long to wait." Winter looked down into the bucket, he could still move his toes but not for much longer." He heard a familiar voice behind him. "No, Latif, you cannot do this. You must not hurt him like this." Jose had been brought. He turned round as best he could to see Hassan dragging her on to the deck. They had thrown something over her to cover her nakedness. What an evil place this was; beyond his imaginings. It can only be a nightmare, he would wake up. It will probably happen as they tip him over the side, then he would spring back to consciousness and find himself in his apartment.

No, he wouldn't. "Her too?" he murmured, quietly.

"Not yet, Mr. Winter, we have not finished with your dear loved one," said Hassan, slowly.

"What more could you do than you have already done?" Hassan took out a knife from a shirt pocket. It gleamed in the sun, he flashed it into Winter's eyes blinding him. When he recovered his sight the point looked exquisitely sharp, the edge capable of gutting a swimming fish without it ever knowing.

"There is a great deal which can still be done, Mr. Winter."

The Minesweeper was within half a kilometre of the Al Khaleej. Jackson cradled his SA80 firearm in his right elbow. He wanted to get closer before launching the inflatable with his party. The tension kept everyone quiet. He had rehearsed a speech which he now delivered.

"We all saw those bodies dragged up from the bottom, I don't need to tell you what they looked like. Now, here's our chance to have a go at the people who did it. It will be risky, they're ruthless, but that's what we're trained to do..."
"Should we wait for the shore-based marines sir?" asked a young petty officer.
No we bloody shouldn't, thought Sam. "We have a small contingent of marines here, you can see, but you're all commando-trained so let's use that!"

The sun beat down like it came straight from Perdition. Jose stood barefoot on the deck. She was forced to watch the banker struggle against the setting concrete. She tried to do what she had done all her life, shut herself off. She could always retreat to that tiny corner of her mind where no one could reach her. It had helped get through so much. But now she could not do it. The banker hadn't betrayed her, he was naive but he had tried to do his best for her. Her powerful ally Samir Latif had done no such thing, now he was going to kill them both. And he would enjoy it. The little corner of her mind shut the door before she had a chance to get in, now she was stranded outside. She had to face it. She stared hard at Latif and Hassan. They stood together, two metres away, switching their gazes from Winter to her and back again. There was no hiding the pleasure they were taking from it. Every few minutes they would give him a countdown to the time they would heave him over the side. "Fifteen minutes, Mr. Winter, not long now." Then they would laugh. The crew stayed strangely silent, they were not joining in. Perhaps it could be one of them next if they even opened their mouths. Quite likely, they all looked like low caste Indians and Filipinos. "Ten minutes, Mr. Winter." The laugh always sounded forced, always sounded dreadful.

So the terrified crew saw the inflatable with the boarding party approaching but did not say a word, to speak out of turn meant punishment; to speak at all meant punishment, so they knew to keep quiet. Hassan's men were so busy with the violence of the moment and the anticipation of what was to come that their eyes were fixed solely on Winter and Jose. Samir Latif was so certain of his dominance – his invulnerability – that he did not countenance for even a split second that anyone would dare challenge him.

Jose stared again at them. "Why do you do this, Samir Latif? He has done nothing to you. I have done nothing to you. Why should you do this to us?" She was ignored. Instead Latif said something to Hassan which she couldn't hear. Hassan moved to Winter and prodded the top of the bucket. He came back smiling. "Jose, my dear," called Latif, "we are ready. Perhaps you would like to watch while Hassan's men tip your banker over the side."

He was not her banker. But that hardly mattered now. "No."

He jumped to her side and grabbed her hair forcing her to look at the banker. "Yes!" He barked out orders to two men in port police uniform. They moved up to Winter and lifted him and the bucket to the brass rail on the port side. She had to look, she could sense everyone else was doing the same. How would he go? Would he scream and beg for mercy? Would his arms flail about in a useless attempt to keep above the surface?

She went weak with the thought. The same fate faced her - after they had finished whatever else they planned to do with her.

"Ten seconds, Mr. Winter." The two men reached down to lift the banker's legs. Jose tried to turn her head away but Latif's grip was too strong. Then she jumped in the air, her heart thumping hard, her body filled with urgency. Latif released his grip simultaneously. Two gun shots! No mistaking them, she had heard enough in Beirut. The two policemen still had Winter in their grip but they had moved no further forward.

"Put the man down." The command came from behind them, Jose turned around. A man in a British Navy uniform was carrying a rifle of some kind. Several others were to the side and behind him. They all carried small arms of one sort or another. She turned again to see Winter held in mid-air. Hassan's men had not heard or understood the command. They were staring at the man with the gun.

The deck was like a photograph, no one moved, everyone stood frozen in the position they had assumed when the naval party came on board. Jackson saw Paul Winter about to be thrown overboard and checked the temptation to put a bullet straight into Latif. He was two metres away. Instead he raised the rifle and fired into the air again. Latif barked an order in Arabic. Winter was lowered to the deck again.

"Lieutenant Jackson, back so soon. How can I help?"

"You're under arrest, Latif."

"Of course, whatever you prefer." Jackson looked straight into Latif's eyes. All the previous affability was gone. "But I shall not be coming with you."
"You haven't much choice."
Jackson was so preoccupied with stopping Winter being thrown over the side he hadn't ordered his men to fan out through the ship, he was the senior officer but the marine complement was tiny and headed by a sergeant, not enough of a rank to tell a lieutenant what to do. Hassan had slipped to one side and reappeared smiling. Jackson scanned the decks to see why he should be so pleased with himself. The boarding party was still in the same position. Then he saw why. For every one of his men, there was at least another dressed in port police uniform. Hassan had managed to have him surrounded.

The Commodore and his marine commandoes were closing on the Al Khaleej. The small SBS contingent had forced their way into the group when the Major learned there was action to be had. The tender had made good time. Hartson heard the shots. He counted them: one, two, three. He waited for more. He felt a dreadful pressure on his bowels, what the hell was he doing here among these marines all checking their weapons and looking like they mean business. This was for another kind of reporter, he didn't do this, his work was done.
"How long before we get to them?" He couldn't hide the catch in his voice.
"Patience, Mr. Hartson. Are you that eager for the action?"
No he was not, he was scared to his boots, and he had a nasty suspicion that the marines could smell his fear. He had tried to resist the pressure to come from the Commodore but Hamid had him by the balls. Sod it, he was a reporter; not a soldier, not a marine, not a policeman. The sounds of the shots had already started him shaking, a massive build up of wind in his colon blew itself out and was lost to the sea breeze before anyone could notice. His wits had always been his best weapon, not his courage. He didn't have a great deal of that. He had hoped he wouldn't be called on to use what little he did have.
"Any news on the radio?" asked the Commodore.
"No sir," replied a rating.
"He should have made contact by now. Put a spurt on, helmsman."
Hartson shook a little more.

The two men glowered at each other. Latif spoke. "You have boarded my boat illegally, Lieutenant. I am within my rights to shoot you at my pleasure."

"Be warned, Latif, there is a party of Royal Marines on its way here. You would be ill-advised to cross them."

It was a deep and powerful voice. This officer didn't sound in any way intimidated by the situation. Jose looked at him with interest. But she had seen her salvation come and go in the space of a few seconds. Latif had the upper hand; he always had the upper hand. He was rich enough to buy anyone, including her. He was ruthless enough not to care about any rules. That meant he would win every time. Hassan had returned to her side and was staring at the naval lieutenant. She looked at his smirking face, then down to his chest, saw the bulge in the open breast pocket. Then she saw her chance. She had learned the tricks of distracting a man a long time ago. Her arm reached out and touched Hassan on the opposite shoulder to the pocket. He looked around instantly but by then her other hand had the knife in its grasp and she yanked it out.

It was short, about ten centimetres, but just as deadly as the first time she had seen it. Before Hassan could recover himself enough to grab her she had the knife at his neck, the blade touching the flesh over the Carotid Artery. One nick and he would be dead, Michel had taught her that. She had the power in her hands now, but still not in her voice. "Tell them to put their weapons down," she said croakily to Hassan." He grinned back up at her, he didn't believe she could do it. She lowered the knife in order not to sever the artery and dug the point into the neck. Hassan gave a short gasp. She enjoyed hearing it. Perhaps he would believe her now.

"It is of no use Jose. I give the orders right now. I am sure Colonel Hassan would love to tell his men to disarm but they will not listen, they are mine. You may choose to hurt Hassan, that is too bad."

There was a bumping against the hull, probably the police launch still tied alongside. She kept the knife pressed hard against Hassan's neck but looked straight in to Latif's eyes, they did not flinch, he meant every word. She could kill Hassan for all he cared, it would make no difference to him, especially not now. She raged at her impotence, wave after wave of useless fury engulfed her. She could not win against people who simply did not care. She shifted her gaze around the deck, the naval officer still had a gun in his hand, his men held their weapons aloft. Latif's policemen covered them but all eyes were on her.

"I will kill him," she said, desperately.

He had seen death and violence before, sometimes up close when he hadn't been quick enough to avoid it. As far as he was concerned the best place to cover it was from a distance. Will Hartson had learned his lessons well over the years. Trying to be impartial meant being shot at by both sides,
But now he found himself unarmed just behind Colonel Ali Abdul Hamid and Commander Phil Wilkinson mounting the gangway of the Al Khaleej two steps at a time. The marines were behind him and he knew it should have been the other way around but he had been swept along on the tide of urgency as they left the tender. So there he was, moving stiffly, unwillingly and shaking at the same time. His feet dragged on the gangway, he tried to slow down the pace but the marines behind him wouldn't let him. Twice he was literally pushed up by a marine sergeant who cursed him under his breath. "Fucking reporters. Where's your clever words now, arsehole?" There was a hard shove, Hartson stumbled up another step. "Arsehole." He didn't contradict the man, he was almost certainly right. His mouth was dry with fear, the sort that makes people fumble the easiest sentences. He followed Wilkinson and Hamid as they burst onto the deck.
No one was there to confront them. He heaved a huge sigh of relief. He expected everyone to stop, take stock, plan the next move. He wanted to talk, he felt released. But the marines fanned along the deck as soon as they reached it. The commander was armed but taking his instructions from the SBS major – his junior, but an expert who was silently directing them with his. Hartson stood next to Hamid, weaponless, useless, scared. It wasn't all over by a long way.

Jackson pointed his SA80 in the air, he dare not shoot at anything. If he made a move Latif's uniformed men would react instantly. He had no doubt that in the end he would win, but at a cost. He stared hard at the woman with the knife at Hassan's throat. The bastard deserved everything he got. If he could have made it worse for him he would.
"I think I have the upper hand at this point, Lieutenant," called Latif. "What do you propose to do?"
"I could shoot you all and dump you over the side," said Latif, unsmilingly.

Jackson's party was commando-trained, there may be casualties but Latif could not possibly win against them with only himself and a bunch of police pirates. But the officer in him knew when to act and when not. "You would shoot a legitimate boarding party from the Royal Navy. You would be finished in Khafira. Who would ever do business with you again?"

"I am finished anyway, Lieutenant. This way I can at least get away to my friends in another part of the region."

"Do you seriously think they will harbour you after this!"

Latif looked skywards. "You English are so constrained. Do you really think it is a matter of morality? No Lieutenant, it is simply expediency, I will be protected, I have too much to offer."

"Like missiles?"

"Among other things."

The yacht rolled gently in the calm water. The breeze provided a light soundtrack to the drama on deck. There was the sound of a door shutting.

Her hand relaxed as she listened to Latif and the Navy man. She knew enough to know that Latif had nothing to lose and despite what the Navy man might think, that gave him the edge. She had no power at all. The man she held under the knife was nothing. A murderer, pederast, torturer, crook; maybe, but still nothing. She heard another noise and felt Hassan look sharply to his left. She pressed the knife harder.

Then she saw what Hassan saw. A marine creeping around the bridge, carrying a rifle of some kind. She knew instantly what she had to do. She must divert attention from the bridge before everyone else followed her gaze. It only took a fraction of a second, she had few qualms when she looked at the odious creature next to her. She jerked the knife hard against his neck. She felt it slice into the flesh and go through to his artery. Blood spurted out over her hand and arm. Hassan yelled and tried to reach up. She held on to the knife and dug in deeper, trying to hurt him as much as she could as he died.

"Are you enjoying it, Hassan?" she hissed in his ear. She pulled away the knife. She hadn't seen the commotion around her. When she looked up she saw mayhem. Soldiers or marines, probably British, locked in combat with Latif's men. No shots had been fired.

Hassan had slumped to the floor, the gushing blood had reduced to a trickle

now but Hassan would not live. She looked down on him and allowed herself a triumphant smirk. That was for Michel and Hannah, but there was no time for satisfaction now, and they were only partly avenged. She whirled around to look for Latif, he was no longer there. She looked at the other side of the yacht. There he was, running as fast as his fat frame would allow. He was trying to get off to one of the launches. She yelled to the Navy Lieutenant.
"He's getting away."
Then she turned back, to see a lonely figure unable to move by the side of the yacht. Paul Winter. She looked away again.

He was on his own, all the military men were in action. As far as Hartson could see they were getting on top of the situation and he was only too happy to leave them to it. Seeing Jose slice through Hassan's neck had sent a shock crackling through his whole body. This was a woman who had cringed in the passenger seat well while he was going all worldly on her only a few sort days ago. It was that more than the rest of the violence around him which made him freeze motionless. He had been unable to move while the fight went on around him. He stood at the top of the gangway where he'd been left. All he could do was watch. He could contribute nothing and he could not move to find cover.
There was shouting, he heard the woman yell once, then Lieutenant Jackson immediately after. He followed their eyes and saw why. It was Latif, his chest puffing, eyes bulging, running slowly away from the fray and towards him. Everyone else was too busy to stop him. Hartson was still and detached. He felt he was watching the whole thing from a helicopter, not involved at all, just observing. Then Latif was two metres away and looking like he wasn't going to stop for anyone. Hartson's feet became even more rooted, so much so he couldn't get out of the way. Now it was one metre, he could see the ferocity on Latif's face. In an instant he uprooted himself, was it survival, adrenaline, courage, he would ask himself later? He threw himself into the midriff of the barrelling figure. He was knocked back against the rail but Latif had been temporarily checked. He could see him reaching into a pocket. He leaped to grab the arm, yelling at the same time for help. Latif was strong and determined, he would outmatch him over a short space of time, but he held on to the arm. Latif swung his other fist and landed a crashing blow into his ribs,

but he clung on. He had no leverage to strike back, he doubted that it would do any good if he did.

"Release me, Hartson!" It was a desperate command. Latif was fighting to get away, breathing hard, speaking through gritted teeth. "Let me go or my friends will hunt you down." Another voice pierced the melee. "You have no more friends, fatty." A rifle butt crashed into the businessman's chest, Hartson saw a look of unadulterated hate directed straight at him. The rifle butt came down again, this time on the wrist by his pocket. Latif's face screwed up in pain. The rifle raised again for a third strike, Latif made no attempt to stop it, but it stayed there. "That's enough, sergeant," he heard Phil Wilkinson shout. The marine hovered over Latif but obeyed his order. He looked down at Hartson and winked at him.

Wilkinson reached down to examine Latif's now useless hand. It came from the pocket still attached to a small handgun. He looked at it and wobbled, he would have been shot without compunction. He slumped onto the deck, weak, unable to speak, this had been far too real.

"Well done, Will," said a cheery voice. He looked up to see Lieutenant Sam Jackson smiling down at him. "No hard feelings?" He nodded and smiled. "Help me up please." Two sets of hands brought him to his feet. He rose unsteadily but remained standing. He looked around the deck to see the marines and the sailors moving about purposefully. What looked like port police were being rounded up with Hamid's help and held at gunpoint. He looked away a couple of degrees, there was the woman standing alone. Three metres away from her, by the other side of the yacht, was a lone figure standing erect. It was Paul Winter. Poor bastard. He could see his legs disappearing into a bucket and took a guess at what had nearly happened. He walked towards him. Winter didn't turn, he stayed still; Hartson was in front of him, the man had a look of utter sadness upon him.

"Hello, Paul."

"Hello, Will." The voice was reedy, uncertain.

"What happened to..."

"Just get me out of this." He pointed to the bucket. "Get me of this boat, get me out of fucking Khafira." He was shaking with fear and rage. He swung round suddenly, savagely, nearly falling over in the process. "Get her away from me!" The woman didn't look round. Hartson thought he understood. "They're not worth it, Paul." Winter turned again, keeping his balance this time. "Yes, they are. That's the trouble."

Jackson inspected the deck: Hassan's figure lay with a pool of blood growing from the neck. He rushed to his side, looked up at the woman. She was doing nothing. "Were you just going to let him die?"

"Why would I want to save him? I tried to kill him in the first place. He was about to jeopardise your rescue." There was a pause. "And he killed two people very dear to me."

Jackson tried to find a pulse, there was a hint of one.

"Do not cry for him, Lieutenant, he is beyond medical help." He looked round to see a man he had not come across before. "I am Colonel Ali Abdul Hamid of the Khafira security police. Leave him here please and take this woman with you." He was so surprised he did as he was told. He grabbed the woman by the arm and pulled her away firmly. She resisted at first. He looked her straight in the eye. She looked back with an intensity which nearly unmanned him, then she relaxed and let him take her away. When he looked around again the figure lying on the deck was no longer there. The colonel was standing by the rail wiping what looked like blood from his hands. There was a short red trail leading from the side of the yacht to the spot where the man had been lying. So that was Khafira justice!

He looked round again at the woman. "Is this how things are always done out here?"

"That depends on whether you think it is a good thing or a bad thing, Lieutenant." She pronounced it Lootenant as in the American version.

"It's lef' tenant," he corrected her.

"You English must always be different." she was smiling at him. A nice smile, flirtatious. She'd just killed a man and she was giving him the come-on. Very nice too.

Hartson stood next to Hamid as he barked an order into the yacht's radio system. He struggled to take it all in. "What happens now, Hamid? You can't tip them all over the side, you know." Hamid ignored the remark. "Perhaps you will be kind enough to let me continue with my message to my office ashore, Mr. Will. Someone must receive these people from your marines."

"Be my guest. But what about Samir Latif?"

Hamid continued to speak Arabic into the microphone for several seconds. He finished and started to walk off. Hartson grabbed him by the arm. Hamid spun round and glared at him.

"I deserve an answer, Hamid."

"I doubt that the world will hear any more of him."

"You mean he'll go to prison?"

"That would be much too embarrassing for the ruling family. A long time friend of Sheikh Mahmood in prison? It would never do. There would be too much loss of face."

"What then?"

"I am afraid that will have to remain unknown to you, Mr. Will." Hartson looked away to the blood trail where Hassan had been. Hamid walked towards the Naval officers. Hartson turned his gaze and watched as two marines hacked away at the concrete on Paul Winter's feet. He was at least sitting on a deck seat. They were making jokes about taking a great weight off his mind but he wasn't laughing. He had no reason to laugh. He was staring at the woman and Sam Jackson laughing together.

They're not worth it Paul. Don't delude yourself, especially out here. Everyone is out for themselves, never forget it.

Epilogue

It was late August, eight in the evening, air-conditioned cool, sophisticated. The lighting dark, Filipina waitresses hung on their every move. Hartson sat at a table in Sheikh Issa's favourite restaurant. Favourite of all those he owned, of course. He always suspected his true favourite was one of those discreet places in Knightsbridge where it was quite likely he might not even be known.

"So you are asking me not to publish the greatest story I have ever come across? Personal drama, double-dealing, political shenanigans, duplicity, and multiple murders; and you want me to stay completely quiet? " Hamid withheld his response while he poured two generous glasses of Chateau Lafitte.

Then he replied softly, like a new friend with something to sell: "Of course, it will save a great deal of embarrassment in Britain and here."

"Hamid, you do realise what I do for a living don't you! I tell news stories and this is the biggest thing that has ever happened to me. How can you expect me to keep quiet!"

"Everyone else knows where the best course lies, Will."

It wasn't Mr. anything now, it was Will.

"How do you mean?"

"Your politicians have agreed to stay quiet..."

"Now there's a surprise."

"..and so has your navy. The embassy is hardly going to say anything."

"Quite. But why should I be silenced?"

"I am asking you a great favour, Will, on behalf of Sheikh Issa. This region is unstable, it always has been. Making this story public will only make it worse."

"Look Hamid, you're asking me not to do my job."

"Why are you journalists always so naïve? Do you think anyone in the world cares if you do your job? Everyone compromises and makes deals. That is how the world works." Hamid took a sip from his wine glass.

"Wait a minute, I thought you didn't drink, like a good Muslim."

"I have already explained that I have no religious convictions. Anyway, we have a saying here, Will; one hour for me, one hour for God. This is my hour."

Everyone compromises, does a deal, even with themselves.

"Even if I didn't publish, what about the others? Something is bound to emerge."

"I doubt it, and who will listen? They do not have access to the media like you do, no one will corroborate what they say. Poor Mr. Winter is even now preparing to travel home. He will go in style on Sheikh Issa's jet with a handsome sum in his bank account. The Royal Navy officers are under orders for security reasons; they will obey. The Lebanese whore will be paid a large amount of money. I see she has become attached to the gallant lieutenant."

"So everyone gets bought off?"

"Exactly! And now it is your turn."

He leaned back in his chair. "All right, what's the deal?"

"You stay out here in Khafira as a paid advisor to Sheikh Issa, a very well paid advisor."

"That's the deal?"

"It is a very good offer. Sheikh Issa chooses his friends carefully. He does not forget them. He has decided that you shall be one. You have benefited from his friendship before now, Will."

He flashed back to scrambling through the dunes on a hot morning.

"When was that?"

"A Miss Diana Ffrench Parsons intervened with Sheikh Issa, I hardly need remind you. Sheikh Issa does not forget." He went silent as he thought it through. Randalls wasn't the place it had once been. Here was an offer he would never get again: the chance to retire to the Gulf with wealth and never have to scratch around in the dirt looking for a story again.

So tempting.

The downside: his story would break the politicians in Britain, the bye-election would be lost, he would have the scoop to beat everything. For a week, anyway.

"What happens to Tom Scott Garrett?"

"He has been asked to leave. The ambassador agreed immediately."

"And Sheikh Khalifa?"

"He has been relieved of all official duties. He will be given an allowance and will play no further part in Khafira's affairs. I have assigned a team of men to make sure nothing similar is allowed to happen."

Hartson made a cynical sneer and made sure Hamid saw it. The punishment for treason, murder, and betrayal was a superannuated retirement fund. They had to save face, they couldn't admit a member of the ruling family had let them down so badly. They had to cover it up and let the stupid fop menace the playgrounds of the world gambling with someone else's hard-earned money. Where was the justice in that!

He didn't say a word of it. He continued questioning Hamid. "And Latif, where is he?"

Hamid simply looked at him in a way which brooked no further inquiry. He was momentarily unnerved, his bowels went watery. To befriend these people was to know great generosity, to cross them meant something quite different and it was so easy to do either.

"You have it all under control, Hamid. What about the Filipino boys, and their mother, Maria? What will you do for them?"

"A small concern, Will. She will be given a few thousand dollars and her plane ticket back to Manila. She will have a comfortable life in the Philippines with that money. She is of no great importance."

"So you're throwing her out?"

"Yes, it is the easiest way by far."

"I see."

Memories of Maria's pale silence came back to him: her desolation and helplessness. They didn't care.

"Let's eat, Hamid. I need time to make up my mind.

No he didn't. The decision was as clear as oasis water. He was already writing the story in his head as he scanned the menu. He might as well enjoy this last meal with them before being thrown out again.

The Final Analysis:
Geneva: $60milion dollars rests easy in a numbered bank account.

Geneva: a quarter of a million dollars is withdrawn from a Swiss Bank account by a Russian woman who might once have been associated with the army security police – after finding the account number in the holdall of a dead Lieutenant colonel.

Manila: Maria lives in comfort in a good house, with a maid. She now works at the university as a specialist on the social structures of the Middle East.

London: a Khafira sheikh keeps the west end casinos afloat with extravagant but unskilled gambling.

Washington: Diana Ffrench Parsons is now Cultural Attaché at the embassy.

Paris: Jose Baddradini lives in a comfortable apartment on the Rive Gauche and is studying law at the Sorbonne. Sometimes she writes to Sam Jackson.

Yorkshire: Paul Winter has a large farm and estate, a wife and occasionally teaches Mathematics at the local state schools.

Whitehall: Phil Wilkinson is now a captain soon to be made a commodore.

Westminster: Dennis Fielding will leave Parliament at the end of this term after being reshuffled to the back benches. He is worried that he will be the subject of a novel.

Bali: Sam Jackson owns a bar and holiday centre and writes once a week to Jose Badradini.

Washington: Morton is collecting together all the numbered Swiss bank accounts he's ever used...

Bangkok: Will Hartson is writing his third novel under a pseudonym, he still works for Randalls. Their expenses pay for his writing.

Made in the USA
Charleston, SC
25 May 2016